FLY *by* NIGHT

FORGE BOOKS BY ANDREA THALASINOS

An Echo Through the Snow

Traveling Light

Fly by Night

FLY *by* NIGHT

Andrea Thalasinos

FORGE®

A TOM DOHERTY ASSOCIATES BOOK

NEW YORK

FLY BY NIGHT

Copyright © 2016 by Andrea Thalasinos

Designed by Mary A. Wirth

A Forge Book
Published by Tom Doherty Associates, LLC
175 Fifth Avenue
New York, NY 10010

www.tor-forge.com

Forge® is a registered trademark of Tom Doherty Associates, LLC.

The Library of Congress Cataloging-in-Publication Data
is available upon request.

ISBN 978-0-7653-7676-3 (hardcover)
ISBN 978-1-4668-5191-7 (e-book)

Our books may be purchased in bulk for promotional,
educational, or business use. Please contact your local bookseller or
the Macmillan Corporate and Premium Sales Department at
1-800-221-7945, extension 5442, or by e-mail at
MacmillanSpecialMarkets@macmillan.com.

First Edition: March 2016

Printed in the United States of America

0 9 8 7 6 5 4 3 2 1

In memory of Gordon Haber and his book Among Wolves, *and to Friends of the Wisconsin Wolf, who are fighting for all things wild and free*

Acknowledgments

Many thanks go to Marline Stringer and the Stringer Literary Agency, for her patience and guidance, and to Kristin Sevick, editor at Forge Books, for her skillful direction and enthusiasm. To Nell Thalasinos and Karen McGovern, my faithful beta readers, for their honest feedback and support, and to Ron Kuka, my masterful writer friend, who never ceases to amaze me with his creativity and ideas.

Also, to the School of Marine and Atmospheric Sciences at Stony Brook University for letting me descend upon their department with my endless questions about marine biology. I thank them for sharing their love and wonder of all things underwater as well as their passion for science and the research that they do. They are truly inspirational. And for inviting me to tag along for seine fishing on the ocean beaches of Long Island where I saw my first and only wild sea horse, pipefish, and puffer fish. Your passion for marine life made me consider changing careers.

And to all of the numerous wild animal advocacy groups and the work they do in fighting to not only preserve the Endangered Species Act but to also have wolves relisted and protected so that we can leave an America that is wild and free for the many generations to come.

Water is the most powerful element. . . .
It can wear away rock and sweep all before it.

—F. SCOVEL SHINN

FLY *by* NIGHT

From the Start

Her father had taught her to love the sea. To love the thing that would become her livelihood. Ocean memories were alive even though he no longer was. She'd been eight when her father, who'd spent four years in the Navy as a boat mechanic as well as a lifeguard at Rockaway Beach, would swim way out past the guarded zones at the beach. Amelia was fixed to his shoulder like a remora fish.

"Are we going out to the deep water?" Amelia would ask, more as a confirmation.

"You better believe it, kiddo," he'd say.

Her chin grazed the water. She'd blow bubbles, changing her pitch as she did. Marveling as the sun made the green waves translucent, her chest open to the expanse of the horizon. Ted, her father, would swim out past the deep water channels to where he knew there to be a sandbar. His body was so sure in water, steaming ahead without hesitation, more ship-like than human.

"How do you know where the sandbar is?" she'd ask between blowing bubbles. "Don't they move around?"

"I just know."

"How?"

She felt him pause as if imagining how to explain.

"I see it in my mind and the picture pulls me."

Amelia giggled at the thought of a sandbar being in someone's mind. "The picture pulls you?"

"Close your eyes and look," he'd said.

She did for an instant, feeling the freshness of the seawater in her scalp as the sun baked down, the coolness of the air as she kicked her feet.

"Now see it?" he'd asked.

She wanted to but didn't. "No."

"Well," he said. "Don't worry, 'cause I do," he said in a way that made her giggle.

Once he'd found his footing, he'd ask, "You ready?"

She was always ready.

Pinching her nose between her fingers as he'd shown, he'd guide her down to touch the bottom with her toe. Once she felt it, she'd open her eyes underwater and look around at leathery seaweed, cloudy fragments of jellyfish, and zooplankton floating by and at the wavy contours of the sandy bottom. Her father's legs stalwart and solid, fixed to the sandy bottom that was littered with bleached seashells, standing like the pilings of an ocean pier, steady and unmovable.

When no longer able to hold her breath, she'd rocket up through the surface like a breaching whale desperate to breathe.

"I did it, I did it!" she'd squeal, water streaming through her eyelashes, her skin shining like a harbor seal.

"Of course you did," he'd say. "Did you think you wouldn't?"

"Do it again, do it again," she'd squeal. "Ple-e-ese?"

"Ready again?" he asked.

"Okee dokee," she said.

She felt him lift her higher this time before plunging her under.

Only this time her foot touched something fleshy. Opening her eyes underwater, sand flushed up in a swish as something stirred. It was as if the sea floor had come alive. Rather than being frightened, Amelia watched the fleshy mass change color quicker than a human breath. It looked at her as she looked back. It changed shape and then took off like a shot with one burst of speed.

Once Amelia began to shiver, her lips purple-blue, they'd swim back to shore with Amelia holding on to a handful of her father's meaty shoulder as she kicked her legs, riding back with the current.

1

Traffic was at a standstill and she was not happy about it.

"Great." Amelia Drakos exhaled. Exasperated, she braced her arm against the window frame and leaned. "Like this has to happen now."

The fifty-four-year-old grabbed her phone off the dashboard and checked her university e-mail for the millionth time that afternoon, searching for a grant notification from the National Science Foundation.

Instead her late father's name lit up the top of the queue.

"Wh-a-at?" she'd murmured and scrunched up her face.

A sharp beep and she looked up in the rearview mirror. The truck in front had moved up an entire car length.

"Like that's gonna get you there any faster, moron," she grumbled and then smiled at her own hypocracy as she'd done the same thing a few exits back.

Her father had been dead more than thirty-four years.

She pulled up to close the gap and then stopped.

Her green eyes, which she'd always considered freakishly large given the size of her face—like a greenfish, a creepy-looking deep-sea creature—widened and then shut for an instant. At five feet tall people often mistook Amelia for a teenager until she spoke. Yet as small as she was, it was not the type of tiny that inspired protectiveness in others.

She clicked on his name.

"*If you are the Amelia Drakos who was born in New York . . . loose ends regarding . . .*" She memorized each word and then reread it aloud just to be sure.

Amelia glanced up at the overpass, confused. "*You Suck*" was scrawled across the concrete span in bright purple letters.

Was it a new iteration of the same old Nigerian prince or unclaimed money scam that had circulated a while back?

Strange. She stared back at her father's name on the screen. *Certainly gave new meaning to Dead Letter File*—she cringed thinking it funny though at the same time unholy and a bit unloving. Maybe mention it to Bryce Youngs, her fellow research scientist, to whom she'd confess all. No matter how horrific, pathetic, or shameful, Bryce seemed to guess before she'd say a thing. But this he never would. The same went for Jennifer Hartley, another co-investigator who completed their Troika.

What loose ends could there be? Her mind ticked back to that time. She set the phone back down on the dash, remembering her father's warmth; she could feel it as if he'd breathed across her cheek. Remembering how he'd always let her row one of the oars out to where their motorboat was moored in the Long Island Sound even though it took twice as long. Seagulls would be squawking like someone getting shortchanged in a paycheck as he'd throw pieces of bread to them, hollering at them in Greek to shut up.

Wrinkling up the space between her brows, she rubbed it without realizing. Feelings gushed in like water through the breached hull of a ship.

She reached again for the phone. It rang as she touched it. The screen lit. She fumbled it, flipping it into the air like a breathless fish that's still alive but then caught it before falling into that unretrievable gap between the seats.

Bryce's name was superimposed over a photo she'd taken last summer of him giving her the finger on the bow of a research vessel in the South China Sea.

"Jesus Christ," she answered.

"I am not he," Bryce said.

"Too bad," she said. "I've got a lotta questions."

"You owe me."

There was pause.

"Really?" she said in surprise, all traces of irony gone as she paused. "It's there?"

"Um-hum."

They'd had a bet going on which would arrive first: The NSF e-mail or letter. A lobster dinner and unlimited alcohol was riding on it.

"You open it?" Her stomach was a flock of butterflies set on fire.

" 'Course not." He scolded.

But she wondered if he actually had.

"You sure?" She drew out her voice.

"Amelia," he raised his voice.

"Bryce, just open it."

"No. I'll wait."

"For what?"

"For you. For later when we're all together."

"Don't be such a putz." She snorted in frustration and tapped the steering wheel with her free hand. "Just fucking open it."

"No."

"Traffic's at a standstill—a parking lot." She looked at her diver's watch. "Plus it's rush hour to boot."

"That's okay."

Amelia rolled the window all the way down and pushed up, leaning out to spot the bottleneck. Flashing blue and red lights of police cars, fire trucks, she then waved her hand as if he could see.

"Shit. There's an accident." She sat back down, watching as a police officer directed them to merge. "You've gotta be kidding, it'll take forever 'til I'm even near the turnpike."

"I'll wait," he said.

She breathed deep. There was no coercing Bryce. Even

ordering a beer was complex. He'd think it through; employ multiple sets of proofs before making the correct choice of microbrew.

"And so uhh . . . Jen around?" she asked, trying not to sound as if fishing for an easy mark.

"Nice try, Am," he snorted. "Jen's got a thing planned."

"Define 'thing.' "

"Nothing big."

"Oh for crying out loud, Bryce," she gestured as if he could see. "A cop's setting down flares; we're down to one lane."

She heard him snort with laughter.

Amelia raked her hair with her fingers out of frustration, picturing Bryce holding the envelope like the cat that ate the canary.

Well over six feet, burly, wearing his camouflage-patterned baseball cap with clear safety glasses resting against the bill, longish brown-blond hair peeking out from beneath the cap. Often Bryce wore shorts and flip-flops all winter long—"I don't like to feel constricted"—and as husky as he was, underwater he was dolphin-like. One of the most skilled and agile divers she'd known.

"Alright," she relented, so aggravated she could kick the inside of her Jeep. "You guys suck."

"You love us," he said in a way that made her laugh.

"Right now I hate you both."

"Au contraire, darlin'. Twenty says you don't."

"You lose," she chuckled.

"You're just a buzz kill, Ammy."

She snorted, reeling from being trapped.

"So they say," she said, thinking of her father's e-mail.

"That's my Little Miss Sunshine for ya." He laughed as he said it.

"Betcha a lobster dinner back you'll never guess who e-mailed me," she said.

"Nah." His voice was thin with disinterest. "No more bets for now. We'll meet up later."

"Where?"

He paused. "Give a call when you get back."

"Who's coming?"

"Uhh—probably just us." He ended the call.

Probably? I'll kill you, Hartley. She hoped for the life of her that Jen hadn't invited Myles.

"Better be just us," Amelia muttered and set down her phone, absorbing the bumper sticker on the back of a delivery truck that said *How's My Driving? Call 1-800-FukU.*

"Aww—call him," Jen had encouraged just last week, trying to get the two of them back together. "Bet ya a dozen cherrystones at the Clam Bar the guy just got scared, he's probably embarrassed," she'd said in her puppy dog voice.

"Think so?" Amelia had countered. "Bet ya my house on Benefit Street he's just a jerk."

"Amelia, come on—" Jen had said. "Cut him some slack."

But she'd cut Myles nothing but slack up until he'd walked out of her life like a person switches off a light when leaving a room.

"I guess I'm just a hopeless romantic," Jen had said. Amelia and Bryce had shot each other side glances, both thinking of a different word. Jen gave men credit even when they didn't deserve it.

Two months had passed—the same amount of time they'd dated.

"God," she fumed as she sat, inching up behind the delivery truck, thinking of Myles, hating that each time her phone buzzed her guts roiled—that die-hard ping of hope. Wishing she could unzip her feelings and step out of them like a wet suit. This after he'd goaded her into surrendering to his declarations of how he was "so falling for her" only to have him bolt like a frightened stray once she did. *God, when would she just give up— enough humiliation for a lifetime.*

"How could I be so good at science yet suck at love," she'd asked Bryce in the aftermath of Myles.

"You don't suck at love," he'd challenged. Such words dissolved her self-indictment in seconds. His eyes had lingered as she'd felt him trying to gain an entry point to acknowledge, but she'd blocked his gaze with shade from a sweep of her eyelashes.

"I'll kill you, Jen." Amelia swore an oath to the delivery truck's bumper.

Five years ago the last grant celebration had been classic: Jen drinking too many beers, crying and getting all snotty "I love you guys so much" and Bryce passed out cold in the back of her Jeep as she drove him home. Unable to rouse him, she'd driven back to the Revolution House, threw a blanket over him in her driveway, and let him sleep it off.

Amelia checked her e-mail again. No NSF e-mail. The electronic image of her father's name was emblazoned into her mind's eye. Amelia shook her head as if ridding her ears of the echo of water.

"This is too weird."

She stopped dead in front of her mailbox slot at the marine biology department.

The box was empty.

"Damn it, Youngs." She slapped her thigh.

The department still smelled like old card catalogues despite the perpetual hum of scientific instruments.

She texted Bryce in all caps. "WHERE IS IT?"

"Taken hostage," he typed back. "Don't trust you."

"Damn right you don't." She jerked away. Her stomach was a clench of nerves, like a squid gathering the ganglion capacity to burst off with lightning speed down into the darkest midnight zone of the ocean.

"Fuck you," she texted back.

"Ahh, Amelia, my sweet . . . always promises, promises," he wrote. "But never dates, times, specifics . . ."

She could have laughed and cried at the same time, toeing the fine line of hysteria as she felt a bit of both seeping in. Her dark ponytail, beginning to tarnish with gray, swished over her shoulder like a horsetail as she rushed off to the lab, hoping to find them holed up at the deep saltwater tanks by the back door with the letter.

The narrow maple floorboards popped and squeaked as she clopped along in her quick-footed way. Everyone teased her about the bouncy adolescent walk and the excitement with which she'd show the new lab assistants how to perform even the most mundane lab work.

Bursting through the laboratory door to the familiar briny scent of salt water, she tiptoed back to the tanks, thinking she'd sneak up to snatch the envelope.

"Boo," she said around the tank but no one was there. Her messenger bag dangled from her forearm.

A few researchers and lab techs sat working.

"Your people left," one of them announced as she hurried toward her desk.

"Say where they were going?"

A few others looked up from their work but didn't answer.

"You hear yet?" the algae researcher turned to ask, a pipette in his hand. "Russell and Pam heard yesterday."

She shot him a look but then softened. He meant no harm; she was tense. She often misinterpreted when tense.

"No, not yet." She made her voice gentle.

Her fingers were still cold and clammy as she slipped off her jean jacket and bag, tossing them onto the stainless-steel specimen table beside her chair.

Sitting down at her desk, Amelia lifted the glass jar containing Tyrian purple snail shells gathered by her father from the seashore in Crete. She slowly turned the jar, watching as the shells changed configurations and clinked together, tiny grains of sand still stuck inside the glass. Studying the lavender-white ridges and spikes of their exoskeletal bodies, she remembered

the feel of being a young woman, yearning and wanting everything though not knowing what everything is.

She set the jar down and sighed. Facing the darkened
computer screen, her face was the image of her mother's. Pretty,
though tired and puffy in the same places, prominent cheekbones, hollow cheeks, and jowls ever so slightly beginning to
loosen as her mother's might have at this age.

"Screw it," she muttered and hit the keyboard, vowing to
open the NSF e-mail if it was there. Then play along with Bryce
and Jen or else fake them out by marinating her eyeballs with
saline to look as though she'd been crying.

But her stomach squeezed as the screen lit up.

"What?"

A second e-mail from her late father—her spine straightened
as if independent from the rest of her body.

She opened it. *"Sorry to trouble you again, if you'd rather phone,
I am in Wisconsin. Please call immediately . . ."*

Immediately? What was so immediate about a man dead
more than three decades? Was this a joke? A hacker parlaying
a scam off NSF e-mail addresses?

She closed the e-mail and looked away. Staring past the tanks
and out the back doors to Narragansett Bay, something felt
wrong.

"Jesus," she said, distracted from the NSF decision. She rested
her elbows on the desk, leaning her chin in her palm.

"Amelia?"

She looked up.

"You okay?" It was the krill scientist from the other side of
the bench.

"Uh—yeah."

"Your people said to tell you they're down at the AA," he
said in his soft voice.

"Thanks." She always mirrored the man's posture, hunching
over a bit like him and speaking quietly.

The Ale Asylum, or AA, was a former psychiatric hospital

circa 1920s turned brewery within walking distance of the university campus.

Just then her phone buzzed.

"Where are you?" Bryce texted.

"Where are YOU?" she shot back.

"AA. Pitchers and pizza! Waiting . . ."

"Leaving now," she typed and was about to get up when Amelia turned to face the adjacent saltwater aquarium. It didn't take long to get lost in the lush corals that undulated in the wake of the water filtration system; such beauty was always a surprise. "Geek TV" Bryce called it. The soft din of the motors was soothing. She'd bred and transported countless pairs of sea horses to the overfished areas in Indonesia, Malaysia, and many other parts of the world as well as to the New York Aquarium, Chicago's Shedd. Sea horses were the proverbial canary in the coal mine, portending the health of ocean shorelines.

She tapped on the glass. A pair of bright yellow sea horses paused in their love dance to look up. They swam to her pressed finger.

"Hi, guys." She leaned her forehead against the glass; its warmth from the aquarium lights felt safe, like she was all tucked in for the night and the world would never end. Their eyes moved independently as if deep in thought, dorsal and pectoral fins propelling them like hummingbird wings. They flitted away, resuming their intermingling and caressing of tails, once again more absorbed in courtship than fate—what it must be like to be so lost yet found.

Stuffing her phone into her pocket, she grabbed her jacket and bag and then dashed out the back doors toward the parking lot and her Jeep.

The music at the AA boomed in her chest wall. The host was about to shout a question when Amelia pointed toward the rear of the building where they always sat. The chairs were made of iron to discourage bar fights. "Had 'em made special," the owner had once told Jen. "By the time you pick up one of those suckers you're too tuckered to do any real damage."

She spotted Bryce towering against the back wall, slowly waving the NSF letter like a surrender flag to catch her attention. Jen was almost as tall and stood alongside Bryce with her glass raised.

Amelia counted heads. Thank God no Myles. Relieved yet disappointed, she shook it off, spotting a pitcher of half-drunk beer, a partially eaten pizza, and an empty chair for her.

Amelia stopped just shy of the table and swiped the letter out of Bryce's fist before he had time to react.

She held it up in victory. Jen's sequin bag sparkled in flashes under the house lights from where it sat on the table. Bryce always teased that it more resembled a Las Vegas sign than a purse.

Jen and Bryce began play fighting, trying to grab the letter back.

Nervous laughter blurted out as Amelia then stuffed it in her bra. They'd been excited to the point of being giddy since the *Ocean Explorer*'s discovery a month ago.

"Now don't make me have to go in there and get it," Bryce called over the music, hands on his hips.

"It's Bryce's turn," Jen said loudly in that big sister way she had.

"Yes, it is." Amelia turned and looked at him through soft eyes. She pulled out the envelope and handed it over, a lump forming in her throat. Every five years, they took turns opening the NSF grant notification.

Bryce then ripped open the envelope with his teeth in a hungry, pirate way, pretending to chew and swallow part of the paper flap.

"Ew—you're sick," Jen shouted over the music.

Yanking out the letter he then shot them both a goofy face before reading.

As he scanned, Amelia noticed his eyes stop. They drooped at the corners in such a way that she knew. Dive partners knew each other better than their spouses and their own dogs knew them. In emergencies they'd share dwindling air reserves with the commitment to surface together or not at all.

"No," Amelia said quietly and sat down. It was like thirty-four years ago when the embassy phone call from Greece had come in to the dorm about her parents.

Bryce closed his eyes and passed the letter as he sat.

"Thank you for your application," she read, ". . . however . . . given . . . we regret . . ." She stopped. The connecting ribs in her sternum felt like an assortment of mismatched bones that cracked as she took a breath.

She handed the letter to Jen.

"No way," Jen mouthed, shaking her head as she too sat down to read. Then she closed her eyes, hunched over, and leaned toward Amelia, resting her head in Amelia's lap like an eight-year-old.

Amelia touched the side of Jen's blond hair.

"I'm sorry," Amelia said.

The three of them sat lifeless, like a scene spliced into the wrong movie. Surrounded by gyrating crowds bursting with energy, people sang along with the deafening music.

An odd internal quiet lingered, one that often settles before the magnitude of something's about to hit. Like when a tide draws out, far out, exposing rocks, starfish, and shipwrecks as curious beachcombers stand in wonderment, sometimes following the quiet, puzzled by the ocean's strange behavior just before they spot a giant water wall blocking the horizon. As if nature's giving you the chance to rally and garner whatever strength you might need before an onslaught. Like when at nineteen years old Amelia had hung up the pay phone without speaking and chose to raise her son, Alex, alone. Just like then, there was hollowness where feelings should be. What a plucky girl she'd been—plucky yet so afraid of everything.

"I'm sorry," Amelia repeated, not knowing what else to say. "So, so sorry," she said to Bryce, smoothing Jen's hair like she had for Alex after he'd been roughed up on the middle-school bus.

In the early years she'd rehearse what to say in the event of getting turned down. Now she felt like she needed a twenty-pound dive belt just to stay seated.

"Let's get out of here," Amelia said as Jen sat up.

As they staggered out into the chilly night air, Amelia clutched her jacket around her ribs. She thought to invite them back to the Revolution House but instead had to sit. Easing down at the nearest bistro table and chair secured to the building with long cables and padlocks, she felt nothing.

Surface frost on the tabletop glittered in the parking lot lights like a crazy princess's eyes.

Bryce said. "You okay?"

" 'Course not."

The three of them were quiet before she spoke. "I just need to sit here a while, Bryce, that's all. Let's talk tomorrow—you two go on home."

She rested her face in her hands.

2

Ted Drakos Jr., or TJ, was glad his mother had died before knowing the outcome of the vote.

"I know you'll stop it, Ma'iingan Ninde," his mother, Gloria, had said earlier that morning, just hours before she'd passed.

"Feel it in my bones." She'd hugged her sides and exaggerated like an excited girl. Aside from a three-year stint in Germany as a Navy flight nurse where she'd met and married TJ's father, Gloria had lived all her life on or near the Red Cliff Ojibwe Reservation. With short gray hair and thick glasses, his mother was still a beautiful woman at eighty-six. Dimples in her cheeks had showed even when not smiling—"Laughing Eyes" they'd called her.

"Appreciate the vote of confidence, Ma," he'd said, though he knew such confidence was misplaced. Long ago she'd named him Wolf Heart, or Ma'iingan Ninde, in an Ojibwe ceremony: a heart that loves with fierce loyalty—quiet, ever watchful, but never calling attention unless required.

" 'Cause I know you will," she'd shot back.

But the sixty-one-year-old wolf biologist didn't smile, wouldn't indulge false hope. Life and death were an everyday part of his job and TJ knew full well the influence of the trophy-hunting, gun, and sporting lobbies working hand in hand with Wisconsin's new political regime to remove the protected status of the state's wolf population from the Endangered Species List.

He'd been headed down to Madison to testify before the state legislature against Act 169, the reinstatement of the wolf hunt. Despite hearing from a "friendly" senator that the bill already had enough votes to pass, heartsickness and rage compelled him to go in spite of it. He'd make them listen to his testimony so that no one could claim that *"they hadn't known. . . ."* When he was through they'd all understand the consequences of their vote. He'd expose and make public their rejection of more than thirty years' worth of scientific field data in favor of cronyism. His executive summary, as well as those of other biologists, had documented how reinstating a wolf hunt was both unjustifiable as well as potentially devastating to wolf families. With this knowledge, he thought, let them turn a deaf ear away from science and to instead embrace the bloodthirsty ways of their culture.

"You'd better leave now." Gloria had looked over at the wall clock. "Or you'll be late."

TJ had stood in his navy blue suit that was tight at the waist and already uncomfortable. Car keys jingling in his hand, he was just about to head out but something felt off.

He glanced around, feeling like he was forgetting something, and brushed back the same wisp of gray hair that never seemed to grow long enough to be rubber-banded at the nape of his neck along with the rest.

"Ma'iingan Ninde, you see with their eyes," Gloria said and smiled with an expression he couldn't read. Since he was a little boy, she'd always said that the yellow green of his eyes were the eyes of a wolf.

As young as six, TJ would sit on fallen tree trunks in the woods, quiet for hours as he waited for wolves to find him. Once they did, he'd study the micro-expressions of their muzzles and cheeks, the tilt of their eyes. By ten he'd trained his eye to spot them through the feathery cover of leaves as he'd catch their eye. Talking back using his eyes, he'd believed they'd understood. And when the prairie grasses were damp he'd catch the sweet nuttiness of their scent just moments after they'd scampered off into the forest.

Wolves had always been synonymous with his mother. Often one or two would step out, sitting just far enough away to watch her hanging laundry as TJ helped. Sometimes a yearling or two, always with an adult, would lie down in the clearing near their house to sun. On pillows of tall field grass they'd roll around on their backs, pawing at each other's mouths, teeth clicking as they'd play, baking in the sun until beginning to pant, at which time they'd jump up and saunter off into the coolness of the trees.

"You gonna be okay, Ma?" TJ raised his voice and picked up the cordless phone, setting it down next to her on the side table. "I'm calling every thirty minutes until Charlotte gets home so you better pick up."

"But you know I hate those darn salespeople—"

"Pick up anyway or I'm calling Delbert," TJ threatened. Being a nurse, his mother was funny about the 911 Tribal Emergency Ambulance showing up at their place.

Then a shade passed across his mother's face.

TJ pulled back and blinked several times, wondering if it was just dry, scratchy eyes. But he'd seen what he'd seen.

His stomach sank, arms became slack with dread. Closing his eyes for an instant he must have seen wrong. This was *his* mother.

Only once before had he seen a shade—six years earlier when Long-Tooth, or B-1, one of the oldest wolves in the Sand River Wolf Pack, had died. For fifteen years TJ had followed the pack, including Long-Tooth, collecting data and detailed field notes about the oldest pack on the Bayfield Peninsula.

At the time, TJ had been returning e-mails in his garage/

office in Red Cliff when struck with the sudden urge to stand. It was the kind of restlessness when something's about to happen.

"Huh." He'd pinched his bottom lip as he'd stood and walked to the center of the room. Turning around once, hand in his pocket, he'd wondered if maybe Charlotte, his wife, had called from the back porch.

Sliding open the door, he stepped out to listen. Just the usual woodland sounds. It was mid-September, about the same time of year, early morning and chilly.

TJ had glanced around, wondering what the hell he was doing until he'd spotted Long-Tooth standing at the edge of the woods, eyes on him. He'd then stepped out without a coat.

Turning to face the wolf, they'd watched each other's eyes. The animal's brow relaxed. A wide toothy grin greeted an old friend who'd been out of touch for some time.

The wolf was three-legged lame and limped into the tall field grass near the office and then stopped. Keeping a watchful eye on TJ, he turned in stiff, uncomfortable circles until finding the right spot. He then let out a sigh tinged with a groan before easing down onto the grass.

He hadn't seen Long-Tooth that past spring and had wondered if the old guy hadn't made it. Many of the old ones and yearlings hadn't. It was startling how much older and thinner the wolf looked. Ratty coat, tail as bald as a possum's where formerly it had been bushy and one of the most luxuriant TJ had seen when the animal would hold it high, asserting his place in the pack.

For as many springs as TJ could recall, Long-Tooth would spot him and Jimmy, his colleague, coming to perform the annual health checks. The wolf would make the pretense of running away before half jokingly turning to TJ as if to say, "Okay, go ahead, do it."

TJ would then dart him and stand by as the tranquilizer took effect, watching as the wolf relaxed onto the ground, quickly wadding up his jacket to tuck underneath and cushion the animal's head. He and Jimmy would then examine the animal's teeth and gums, the insides of his ears, test the flexibility of his joints and then draw the required tubes of blood.

Then the two men would slip a sling under the animal, lifting him to get an annual weight after which they'd sit with him until fully awake again so as to not leave him defenseless.

Sometimes Long-Tooth would spot TJ and play "catch me." The wolf would run ahead and then stop, looking back to ensure that TJ was following. Then he'd lead TJ up and down the steep ravines along Lake Superior to their den in the Chequamegon to show off his litter of four week-old pups.

This time Long-Tooth had rolled onto his side, tired from the effort it had taken to summon him. TJ sat cross-legged on the dewy grass in silence, vowing to stay with the wolf until either he got up or didn't. He was used to waiting hours, days, sometimes weeks—that was what wildlife biologists did.

Juvenile eagles had soared above, their dark brown feathers the color of tree bark, playing and chasing each other from the top of one dead white pine to another. Once the sun was fully up, Long-Tooth lay peacefully; his eyes giving a chatoyant flash of cataracts.

Gravel sounds of Gloria pulling into the driveway made them both turn. She'd just moved in after turning eighty although still volunteering at the Red Cliff Health Center to give diabetes screenings to tribal members.

TJ timed how long it would take for Gloria to get inside and then phoned.

The wolf's eyes then shifted onto Gloria as she negotiated the uneven ground toward them, a blanket bundled under each arm. Long-Tooth's face moved with small jerky turns of his head as he watched with interest.

"He called you." She said, out of breath as she reached them both, handing TJ a blanket.

"Yeah."

Gloria eased down to sit with the same stiffness as the wolf.

She wasn't one for the magic talk but then again neither was he.

"He doesn't want to be alone," she said.

TJ nodded, his head dropped.

"You've been a good friend." She touched her son's knee.

TJ choked up.

"He knows you're sad, Ma'iingan Ninde."

As she squeezed his knee TJ felt her studying his profile. His father's nose, she'd always say, only this time she hadn't. Her voice was soft, as if he was ten years old.

"But he's glad you came. They don't see death like we do."

They'd sat in silence for a while.

"He just wants company," she said.

TJ nodded.

And it was in that moment that he'd first seen a shade pass through his mind's eye, drawing down the wolf's soul as Long-Tooth's spirit grew dimmer as if clouded by a morning mist. In less than an hour the wolf had stopped breathing. TJ and his mother had stood and stepped closer, peering over to see.

"He's gone," she'd whispered. The wolf's eyes were open but not seeing, lips slack with no expression.

"Yeah, Ma. He is."

"I'm worried about you, Ma." TJ set down his keys and travel mug, crossing his arms as he stepped closer, brushing off what he'd seen.

"Waste of time," she said, tucked beneath a wool blanket though it was early September. "Worry more about your wolf brothers."

He'd squatted to eye-level, not believing her.

The suit pants cut deeper into his belly. He pulled at the

waistband to no avail as it pinched his skin. His mother always said he was built just like his father without the lean torso of her family. Charlotte had suggested the suit would give him an air of authority which only made him laugh.

"If that was the case," he'd told her, "I'd have started wearing suits a year ago." The presence of the Great Lakes Indian Fish and Wildlife Commission (GLIFWC) was pro forma. Months before the vote, the Wisconsin legislature and courts had already made up their minds to delist wolves as endangered long before they'd talked to biologists or he'd submitted his executive summary about Wisconsin wolves. It was a political, not a scientific, decision.

"You don't look good, Ma," he said and reached to touch her brow.

"I'm fine." She pulled away. "Go or you'll be late."

He was tempted to call Jimmy, tell him to go on to Madison alone. Yet they'd all agreed he gave the most professional and impassioned presentation. He was good at explaining empirical research in laymen's terms of how reinstating a wolf hunt would increase the number of wolves, not decrease it. Culling would be destructive for the future health and family structure, not to mention the genetics of existing wolf packs. There were so many other ways to prevent depredation of livestock other than slaughter. He'd seen ranchers employ fences and herding dogs, but many were lazy. More country dogs were killed each week by cars than annually by wolves. And there was generous financial compensation from the State of Wisconsin if the death of a calf or a hunting dog could be reported as a wolf depredation. TJ knew that many animals died as the result of negligent or bad animal husbandry, or due to a long, tough winter. Some hunters who trained dogs to attack bears lost their animals in the course of a hunt. But it was easier and more lucrative to blame wolves for everything.

"Ma." TJ shook her shoulder. He blinked hard several times, trying to talk himself out of having seen the shade.

"What?" Gloria brushed his hand away but then sat up and looked to the window as if a bird had collided. "You hear that?"

"Hear what?"

"That." She turned with an odd smile.

He clicked open the sliding door and stepped out onto the deck, ready to fight off anyone or anything coming for his mother. But his stomach squeezed like driving over the steep ravine on Highway K, knowing he had no such power.

Scanning around the meadow where they'd seen Long-Tooth six years earlier, he saw nothing. Just the same birch, cedar, and a few maple trees along the forest edge but no intruders, no Windigo spirits—just swallows chasing off a cooper's hawk—a leftover vendetta from earlier that spring after it had made off with one of their newly hatched chicks.

Back inside TJ shut and locked the sliding door, which he never did, and tested it several times.

"I'll call from the road."

"I know."

"Better pick up or I'm calling Delbert," he threatened again, trying to sound menacing, but she didn't take the bait.

Bending down again onto one knee, TJ scooted closer.

"Mom—." He wanted to say something but didn't know what, wanted to tell her something but it was feelings more than words.

"You've always been a good boy." Gloria touched the side of his face, which was smooth and freshly shaven. By the time he'd get back that evening, the outline of a beard would be visible once again like his father's.

Her eyes were cloudy and unfocused; he fought the memory of Long-Tooth.

Feeling shy and awkward, he leaned over and kissed her cheek. He hadn't kissed her since being small enough to fit in her lap. Her skin was cool to the touch, cooler than the air temperature.

"I'm calling Charlotte to come home," he said.

Then he hugged her. She yielded, just a skeleton in his husky frame. Her bones felt like they'd snap with the slightest pressure. When had she become so thin?

"I'll call you later," he said into her hair.

Another thing he'd never said when leaving the house.

Gloria's eyes were fixed on the window.

"Mom." He tried to get her attention. "Ma."

She didn't turn around.

"I'll call after the vote," he assured and then stood, not wanting to leave.

Then he walked toward the front door and stopped. Holding his keys and travel mug, he turned to see the back of his mother's head.

Two days later while standing graveside, TJ was dry-eyed, wearing the same wrinkled suit from the drive to Madison, feeling choked up with emotion.

Charlotte had found Gloria not long after he'd left. He'd phoned her at work after his mother hadn't answered. Unlike Long-Tooth, his mother had died alone in her chair and it ate at him. No matter how many times he'd confessed it to Charlotte, it brought no relief. He'd seen the shade, should have stayed with her, held her hand, called an ambulance; been with her as they'd sat with Long-Tooth.

"Maybe she didn't want it that way, Niinimooshe," Charlotte said. "Her way of showing how much she loved you."

He glanced at her.

"You know, maybe she knew she couldn't leave you and wanted to protect you; was afraid she'd ask you to come along," Charlotte offered. "Knew you'd never say no."

And while he didn't believe in the old ways, it felt true. The spirits of dying people often reached out to those dearest to accompany them on the journey.

What she said only partly offset the badness of his feelings, grateful that Gloria would never know the outcome of the vote.

Passage of Act 169 had set into motion the first wolf hunt since 1940, which at the time had all but eradicated the wolf population in Wisconsin. He'd spent the afternoon arguing to preserve the integrity of the Endangered Species Act of 1973, but in the end it seemed the legislature had little integrity in which to appeal. The DNR had set an arbitrary number of 201 wolves to be "harvested," as they so innocuously called it, which meant trapped and killed by permit in the coming hunting season, some to be torn apart while still alive by hunting dogs once the animal was trapped in a snare.

"Can't eat 'em," TJ had gushed with contempt in the Wisconsin State Capitol building in Madison as he hurried toward the exit after Charlotte's call. "Might as well charbroil your golden retrievers." His voice boomed against the marble walls in the legislative chamber.

Two capitol police officers, who'd been leaning against the wall anticipating protesters, moved into position.

"Shame on all of you." TJ pointed to the liberal legislators who'd gone along. "Especially you."

The one police officer touched his arm but TJ pulled away.

"Don't bother, I'm leaving." He'd shook them off, walking out on his own from the legislative session.

Charlotte had gone against his mother's insistence on a secular funeral. And while he'd trusted that his wife had her reasons, believing that Gloria's spirit would finally be at peace, he had to laugh, wondering if his mother might come back to haunt her.

TJ and his cousin Marvin had cleaned and dressed his mother's body the night before the funeral by wrapping her in strips of white birch bark taken from nearby trees. It was believed that birch trees were sacred, protecting the newly passed from harm in the spirit world.

He and his sons had carefully removed only the outer layer of the bark so as not to harm the tree. And while his mother had not been keen on the old ways, nonetheless he and Marvin had wrapped his mother's body, saying prayers before placing her in the simple wooden box for burial.

Marvin had cried but TJ couldn't. It felt too much like he'd just declared war.

Later that morning while standing graveside, 201 wolf hearts were beating in his as he watched his mother's body being lowered. They'd lived, loved, and run through deep snow in the dense woods of northern Wisconsin, unaware that bounties had been placed on their heads. Unbeknownst to them, they'd be trapped, shot, and killed by March of next year within artificial borders created and imposed by humans. All for the bragging rights of those who'd wanted nothing more than to say that they'd "bagged a wolf" and by those misguided conversationalists who'd declared that by "killing the wolves you'd save them." He'd heard the same battle cry not more than two generations before of "You have to start a war to end a war."

Snares would be set in designated off-reservation areas, where wolves would be caught by the leg, sometimes the face, howling in pain for their families to come help, with the pack coming, panicky, clawing at the trap, which drew more pain and suffering to the wolf, and finally sitting with the trapped member, bringing the wolf food and company until the end. Powerless to help them, to free them, their hearts breaking in their powerlessness—as they watch their pack mates linger for days with festering leg wounds, sometimes snared by their faces as their mates would lie alongside and suffering with them until the trapper showed, swollen with pride just to put a bullet in the wolf's scull and carry it off. TJ knew well how the dirty business of trophy hunting and trapping worked—the mythology of it often silenced critics, but he knew the specifics and true economics of it.

The 201 hunting permits were snatched up by the time he'd even reached Lake Superior the day of the ruling. And while wolf hunting was prohibited on Indian lands, it was open season in the national forests and on private lands that bordered the reservations on every side—a yearling steps foot over a reservation boundary into the Chequamegon forest, a hunter raises a scope. And TJ even knew of a few on the reservation who'd secretly bragged about wanting nothing more than to bag a wolf, to assume the power of an apex predator, the most sacred of all animals to their people.

The day before the funeral, Charlotte had sent TJ and their two grown sons, Gavin and Skye, into the woods behind their house in search of a downed birch with which to build his mother's Spirit House. Spirit Houses were placed over the gravesite and left to stand as long as the intended spirit needed them. After many winters they'd collapse and were not rebuilt. It was believed to be a sign that a person had completed the journey and were left as grave markers.

He and his sons were prepared to hike around for the better part of the morning but not far from the house TJ almost tripped over a downed birch.

"Huh." TJ stopped and set his hands on his hips. Leaning over he felt the shaggy bark as if to assure himself that he wasn't seeing things, surprised he hadn't noticed the tree before. He peeled part of the bark to feel the wood underneath. "Not sure when this one blew down," he said, looking up at the surrounding trees, puzzled.

Both his sons looked too.

"Well I'll be a son-of-a-gun, this tree's been here a while." He looked up at Gavin then at Skye, who were both dead ringers for his wife's side of the family. The tree was in plain sight of the breakfast nook where he and Charlotte had had coffee every morning for the past twenty-five years.

"Maybe you just didn't notice it," Gavin said.

"Maybe I just didn't notice it," TJ repeated, knowing that such a large tree within plain sight would have been obvious.

The three of them stood around for a few moments, looking at fall's burnished ferns surrounded by an assortment of red, orange, and yellow fallen leaves that glowed from beneath rather than being lit from above.

"So what do you think, Dad?" Skye said.

"Let's get this sucker up." His voice strained as he bent over to lift it and gauge the heaviness of the trunk. For Spirit Houses you needed a whole tree, not just part of it since it was believed that a person's spirit would embody a tree with which it had an affinity.

They bent over and lifted. TJ paused and then let go of the trunk, straightening up to rest his hands on the spot where his back met his hips.

His sons looked at him.

"Put it down."

They looked at each other.

"You okay, Dad?" Gavin asked.

"Yeah," he said and sat down on the log. "Let's just sit here a moment." Memories of Gloria, of his father rushed through him. Their story had haunted every corner of his life, like the incessant eerie hum of spring peeper frogs singing in the low-lying areas of Superior where manoomin, or wild rice, grew. Their otherworldly songs sounded as if laced with human voices, at other times with the sound of ringing bells. Such was the sadness that had enveloped TJ for the past fifty-seven years since his father had left. And just as the frogs would come out of hibernation sometime in March as soon as the coldhearted waters of Superior thawed enough for them to begin their alien and otherworldly songs, March was also the month when darkness would envelop, bundling him in a heaviness that was impossible to shake. Sometimes not until fall's first snowflakes would it lift.

March was a month for many things.

TJ rested his head in his hands as he sat on the log.

3

Amelia pulled into her driveway that evening and sat, looking up at the burgundy clapboard siding. *Better call a Realtor before the paint starts peeling.* It was anyone's guess as to how long that might be. There was probably enough in her checking account to cover next month's mortgage but that was probably it. If only she'd been better at saving money.

Her chest bones cracked back into place as she sighed. The Revolution House, as Alex had named it, could have been paid off by now. But multiple lines of credit and second mortgages to cover her son's undergraduate and master's degrees from Cornell had created a perpetual mortgage that had grown larger than the current value of the home.

The Jeep door felt heavy as Amelia pushed it open and climbed out. Grabbing her purse and bag from the back, she lugged her gear down the cobblestone path, teetering on the familiar contours as she approached the front door. The house was dark. She hated coming home to a dark house. Usually she left a light on before leaving for the lab, but had forgotten.

The streetlamp across the way reflected off the tiny square windowpanes, making the house seem darker.

On the drive home she'd called her son, Alex. His voice mail kicked in.

"It's Mom, call me." She'd always leave the same message and then chuckle to herself, like he wouldn't remember who she was.

Alex had a serious girlfriend as well a new job as a marine biologist working at the University of Vancouver. She understood the missed callbacks, lag between phone calls as evidence of his new life.

Stepping up to the front door, she fumbled the key into the dead bolt, unlocking it just as her phone rang. She looked. The snapshot of Alex sticking out his tongue at her on a dive in Narragansett Bay illuminated the screen.

Amelia sat down on the front step facing the streetlamp and leaned back against the Revolution House's two-hundred-year-old door.

She answered.

"Hi."

"Mom." His voice dropped. "Your message."

What about it?

"Your voice scared me," he said. "I didn't recognize it."

"I'm sorry, it's not good, sweetie." She wasn't aware of sounding different. "I guess that's the way the cookie crumbles." She tried to laugh but couldn't.

"It's gotta be a mistake."

The NSF didn't make mistakes, everybody knew that.

She couldn't speak.

"You're not bullshitting me this time, are you?"

"I wish." Her throat gripped in pain. A few times a year they'd play practical jokes on each other, waiting until the memory of the last had worn off. Once in April, early on in the lab's history, Amelia had begun to pack up equipment, explaining to Jen and Bryce that a different funding source had dried up and they were forced to close up. Both believed her for a few moments until "Ha-ha, April Fools," Amelia had said with her shit-eating grin. Jen had gotten so furious that she'd chased Amelia around the bench in a fury, swatting at her with lab goggles until Bryce calmed her down. They were ten years younger then and were legendary for joking and betting. Often they'd switch labels on each other's solutions that were used in routine experiments.

"I'm telling you, Mom, they made a mistake," Alex repeated.

If only. "Doubt it."

"I'll call Anna, my principal investigator," he said. "She's sat on the U.S. Appropriations Committee before. Maybe she can make a few calls tomorrow."

"Tomorrow's Saturday, sweetie."

"I-I'll fly out," Alex offered. "Take time off."

"No," she said. "Let's save it for Christmas." It was an expensive flight.

The NSF denial wasn't personal—political but not personal. The field was trending in a different direction. And while she'd written the new grant differently, trying to catch the current fascination with male pregnancy in sea horses by focusing on the brain chemistry of paternal gestation, she'd missed it. It was as simple as that.

"Don't give up, Mom," he urged.

What did that even mean?

"I'm okay, sweetie, really." Of course she wasn't.

Yet somewhere along the line she'd lost heart. She'd felt it. Said nothing to anyone, went through the motions—worked day and night to prepare the grant application while feeling like something was different—different from all the other renewal cycles. Those had left her sleepless and terrified. This was quiet. Even after the excitement from the ship-to-shore call from the *Ocean Explorer* that vindicated her theory of a deep-water sea horse migration in winter, the news hadn't been enough to counter that sinking feeling.

For years Amelia had found it curious that sea horses along the northeast coastline disappeared by the end of August. And while other marine biologists postulated a migration south to warmer waters, Amelia didn't buy it.

Sea horses were not proficient swimmers. Their tiny hummingbird-like dorsal fins were better at quick maneuvers than long-distance travel. So rather than journeying hundreds of miles into tropical waters, Amelia theorized about a migration down into the cold quiet depths of the North Atlantic reefs for shelter. Safe from getting smashed against rocky shoals during violent nor'easters or being separated from their lifelong mates, which for sea horses, Amelia had observed, was a fate from which many never recovered. And this had been the basis of her research for the past five years. She, Bryce, and Jen along with her volunteer dive team, had tagged hundreds of sea horses from southern Nova Scotia all the way down through coastal Virginia to determine where they went after the waters cooled and the first few snowflakes fell.

So far there'd been no sign of the creatures anywhere, until two weeks earlier, before the NSF grant notification when Amelia had received a ship-to-shore call. Their ROV camera had spotted dozens of Amelia's tagged sea horses lounging about on deep-water reefs in the canyons of the north Atlantic off the coast of Maine.

At the time Bryce and Jen had danced in the aisles of the lab thinking that such a windfall discovery was a slam dunk. But Amelia had smiled quietly to herself, harboring the knowledge that one had little or nothing to do with the other.

"Ahem," Amelia had said at the time, folding her arms and giving them a "get-a-grip" look. "I hate to be the wet blanket here."

"So don't be," Bryce had said. But Amelia knew well the ways of soft money and so did they. Hard workers with discoveries new to science got the boot just as quickly as lazy asses that did nothing but read newspapers and stink up the lab with their farts and French fried takeouts. No matter how special you thought your work, your mission, your self, no one was immune. One swipe of the Appropriations Committee pen landed many a researcher rinsing out test tubes in some backwater laboratory.

"Mom." Alex's voice demanded her attention. "Listen to me; it's going to be okay."

She smiled, picturing him nodding in that overly encouraging way he had of bolstering up the flagging confidence of rookie interns on a first dive.

They still had funding for summer—the Andaman Islands— from Sea Life Conservation and Ocean Watch. The Andamans were some of the more unexplored islands where they'd previously discovered several new species of sea horses. Just a few days ago she'd been combing through diver applications, on the verge of making contact.

"Bryce. Jen—" She struggled to finish her thought. "Our stipends . . . end in a month."

Alex was quiet.

"And after that—"

Amelia could have kicked herself for getting sucked up into the frenzy at the AA, for not being more cautious.

She was tired. Maybe find a soft place to fall—pull up a chair at a lab bench somewhere, coast for the rest of her working life.

Amelia stood and turned, lifting the wrought-iron handle to open the door. It creaked with the same yawning sound it had probably made since the early eighteenth century when the house was built. She stepped inside as light from the streetlamp cast her shadow long on the floor.

Just then her phone beeped with a low-battery warning. Amelia dropped her gear bag and purse on the threshold where she stood, hoping it wouldn't die.

"I'll—" she started to say, but tears of humiliation, shame rushed at once. She was embarrassed, not wanting him to worry or pity her or to see the soft underbelly of fear that she'd always kept hidden lest he be frightened as a little boy. ". . . figure something out."

"Ma, go ahead and cry, I'm crying."

"I'm sorry," she whispered.

"Don't be, Ma, you're the best. Everyone knows it," he said. "It's not fair." He said it like a little boy.

Yes, my little Einstein, what is fair? If somebody wins, another loses. Her breath was jagged as she wiped her nose on the cuff of her jacket.

"Ma, fuck the NSF—something better's on the way. Maybe it's time to move on."

"To what?"

"Uh . . . don't know," he said. "Maybe it's time to find out. Know what I mean?"

"No, but keep talking." She liked the sound of hope.

"We've got the entire summer in the Andamans." She knew how excited he was to be on his first dive as her colleague. "It's gonna be great."

"It will be." She mustered up enthusiasm.

"Well the offer's good," he said. "One call, I'm there. Word."

"I know you mean it. You're the best kid a mother could have."

"And you're the best mom a kid could have, I mean it." She loved when he'd still say it after all these years. He was her prize. When so many people had tense or distant relationships with their children, she cherished theirs.

"Love you."

She hung up thinking of the e-mail from his dead grandfather and felt the same panic she'd feel when silt from the ocean floor stirs up, blinding one to all sense of direction. Years ago she'd disciplined herself to remain calm, breathe, and follow the stream of bubbles to the surface. She clung to the feeling of safety from Alex's voice.

She shut the front door. No matter how hard you'd slam it, nothing shuddered. Amelia had always attributed the Rev

House's soundness to the New England shipbuilders who'd built the entire block for their families.

When people would ask who Alex's father was, she'd often answer Poseidon, the Greek God of the Sea. When Alex was twelve she'd told him the story, although there hadn't been much to tell. A young, vulnerable girl who'd just lost her parents in a car crash on Crete and an older professor who knew how to play it.

Amelia set her phone on the floor alongside her gear bag and stood, at a loss for what to do next.

The darkened living room reminded her of all she didn't have. Stepping into a trapezoid of light from the street, she switched on a lamp by the couch.

The Revolution House had its own cave-like atmosphere—damp and cool even in summer. Aside from added electricity, heating, indoor bathrooms, and a kitchen from several families ago, the living room's gas insert fireplace was her only break with authenticity. The walls were made from horsehair and wet straw to form plaster that bowed throughout the oldest parts of the house. The heavily wooden-beamed ceilings and doorways were low. As Alex grew taller he'd had to duck but for her the height was perfect. Many of the windows had the original tiny squares of wavy glass panes like the bottoms of vintage Coke bottles. Underwater mortgage. She'd be lucky if she could sell it and walk away with a pair of underwear and a bra.

For a single mother, living on five-year soft money grants, buying the Revolution House had been a gutsy move. She'd swung it with a small but dwindling inheritance from her parents, never worrying about the lack of a permanent faculty position. She'd so believed in the mission of her tiny Sea Horse and Shoreline Ecology Lab that she and Bryce had cobbled together an assortment of funding to keep it afloat.

This coupled with a discovery by two Long Island fishermen

ten years ago when they'd snagged a pair of sea horses in their seine nets, the first ever recorded presence that far north. After that Amelia believed the discovery had put her work "on the map."

At the time, the New York Department of Fish and Wildlife had called her down to confirm the presence of *Hippocampus erectus*. She'd caught the next cross-sound ferry and within two hours was standing on that very same dock, watching the sea horse pair cling to strands of seaweed floating in a white plastic bucket like monkeys from a jungle tree branch. La-de-da-ing without a care in the world, the pair intertwined their tails as they performed love dances, not giving a care as to who was watching.

"Yep," Amelia had confirmed all the *holy shits*, and *no freaking ways* from the department authorities. Later that year she'd gone on to discover permanent colonies as far north as Nova Scotia. Grant money poured in like crazy from private organizations like the Sea Life Conservation, Ocean Watch, and others tasked with investigating the health of the world's busiest coastal waterways—New York, New Jersey, and New England. A lesson in science: what one doesn't seek, one won't find, and the lab had provided a good, long run as her own protective reef, sheltering her and Alex for the better part of their lives.

Still in her coat, Amelia sunk into the leather couch. It was scuffed and well-worn like an old bomber jacket from a generation of Alex's friends horsing around. They'd beaten the crap out of it with their late-night video games and sleepovers, with their floppy boat-sized sneakers. She'd loved every minute of the happy chaos. Even the throw pillows still smelled of her son's hair. Friends would sink into the crack couch as they'd called it, making jokes about never being seen or heard from again.

She grabbed the gas fireplace remote from where she'd dropped it last night. One click and flames pulsed in a whoosh.

She loved the sound. It was a kind of power, albeit man-made. Picking up her laptop, she logged into her university e-mail. She looked at the Ted Drakos e-mails. Her mother always said that bad luck comes in threes. Where would the third come from?

"Thanks, Penelope," she mumbled a memory. *Quit while you're behind* another of her aphorisms. "You always knew how to make a bad situation seem worse."

Her stomach rumbled. Eating meant she'd have to get up. Right now it felt like she'd been hit by a couch. There was plenty of ketchup and mayonnaise but no ice cream. Instead she tugged at the corner of the down comforter draped on the back of the couch. With little effort it slid and landed on her in a heap.

She clicked on Ted Drakos's e-mail again. *"If you are the Amelia Drakos . . ."* At the bottom of the e-mail was an electronic signature: Ted Drakos, Fish and Wildlife Manager, Great Lakes Indian Fish and Wildlife Commission, Bayfield, Wisconsin. *"If you are not that Amelia Drakos, please disregard this e-mail and I will not bother you again. Thank you for your time."*

She stared at the name. There was no cousin Ted. Immigrant families knew everyone. She hit reply and sent: *"I'm not sure who you are but I have no relatives up in Wisconsin and can be of no help. Good luck in your search."*

Her mind started racing. She could rent out a couple of bedrooms to grad students to help make the mortgage.

She rearranged the throw pillow under her head. Amelia began to relax until she heard the screen door open, the pinging sound of the rusty springs reverberating.

A knock on the door. She sat up and looked at her watch. It was after eleven.

"Nothing good comes from late-night visitors," more words of wisdom from Penelope.

"Shit."

Bryce? No. He would've yelled her name as he did his comic knock of tap tap tap tap tap in rhythmic succession, waiting for her two knocks back to complete the sequence. Jen did the same thing. It was their "High Sign," as they called it, used in some of the more obscure if not dangerous parts of the world.

A second knock.

Motionless, her eyes darted to the front windows. Damn, she'd forgotten to flip up the shutters. Someone could see right in.

She sighed with exasperation and let her head drop. "Damn it, Jen," she whispered. Maybe she'd phoned Myles, giving him the news and encouraging him to stop by.

Amelia rolled off the couch and onto the floor like a ninja, only her foot snagged the electric cord of a Tiffany-style lamp, dragging it with her as it toppled over, the shade bonking her in the head just as she caught it before hitting the slate floor in the foyer.

"Fuck," she whispered in relief.

She set the lamp upright, as gently as one would place a live fish back into the water after accidentally being caught in a net.

Crawling over toward the window-seat ledge in the darkness, her elbow then bumped a potted Christmas cactus plant, knocking it over. But as she went to catch the pot she knocked it farther, hearing the clunk of the clay pot as it broke apart on the oval braided Colonial rug.

"Oh shit." She'd forgotten about having moved the plant earlier that morning to get more sun. Amelia tried to scoop the clump of damp soil with her hand from the braided Colonial rug. It smelled like the backyard in spring. Why not use a piece of the broken pot, but then she stopped, annoyed at feeling like a fugitive in her own home.

Then a type of slap-happy giddiness set in, the type that's as uncontrollable as it is scary, a one-way ticket on the crazy train. She was bowled over with hysterical laughter, unable to stop or catch her breath until it had run its course. She sighed and looked at the dirt.

"Jeez." She looked around, wondering what she'd wreck next and snorted a short laugh.

Stepping back to the window, she looked for signs of Myles's car but there was nothing. His Lexus was too long to park behind her Jeep so typically he'd park on the street.

As she sat down on the window ledge a burst of freedom warmed through her. Unbidden in its lightness, she was buoyant as if just having dived off the starboard side of a ship when in an instant the heavy dive gear becomes weightless, once the forces of gravity are suspended, leaving one's body to be as light as a chiffon scarf.

"Wow." She stretched her legs. How had a kernel of excitement worked its way in on the heels of such despair?

"Thank you, Alex." She looked toward her phone. Had the battery not died she'd have called him back and thanked him. Maybe she didn't need to know what came next.

Amelia then sat down on the rug and rolled over onto her side. Her cheek rested on the woolen braid, recalling the immortal lives of jellyfish. *Turritopsis dohrnii* in particular, when threatened, begins to age in reverse, cycling away from death and back to the moment of its birth. Though brainless with only sensory organs, the creature knew enough to begin the process of repair until refreshed and ready to take on the ocean anew.

The smell of wool, dirty adolescent feet, and soggy ranch-flavored Doritos mashed into the spaces between the rug's braids—strange how she'd never been this close yet had vacuumed the rug more than a thousand times if she'd done it once. Gazing into the space under the sofa there were paper clips, white plastic caps from soda bottles, a misplaced sock, and all the little indistinguishable objects that had gone missing over the years.

She eyed her dead cell phone on the floor next to her bag in the foyer, wishing she'd kept her landline despite Alex's reasoning.

The screen door's old rusted springs pinged again, indicating someone was still there.

Amelia sat up and crawled over. Resting her ear against the inside of the door, she listened. Someone was shuffling. Myles's shoes made a certain clicking sound on hard surfaces. She wasn't sure. Sometimes there are no second chances.

The screen door then banged shut. Her skull absorbed the bang. She scrambled up and over to the window to catch anyone walking away but saw nothing.

He'd given up after two knocks. She frowned. That was Myles, alright. Persistence was not his strong suit. What a disappointment yet a relief at the same time.

"Jerk," she mumbled, rubbing the side of her head. *You can't fire me, I quit.* "Shoulda dumped your ass first."

But it wasn't true. It hurt to say it, hurt even more to feel the bitterness of it all and she wished her heart would calcify like an exoskeleton, impervious to the whims of love.

Tiptoeing to the front window, she then flipped the louvers shut and settled back into the crack couch.

The brightness of the fireplace's flames helped dim her thoughts. Kicking off her clogs, she tucked her feet under the down comforter and began to drift.

Once asleep, she dreamed of her father, carrying the red-and-gold-plaid aluminum beach cooler by the handle into the darkened Jones Beach tunnel at Field 4. Loaded with ice chips and drinks they marched out to the ocean beaches on Long Island. She was eight. The silhouette of her father's shoulders was outlined in the darkened tunnel by light from the other side. She glimpsed his long strides as he moved toward the water.

Suddenly she was falling backward off a tall pier at the Captree State Dock at the tip of Jones Beach, backward into the water.

Amelia bolted up; catching herself with such a start she could have vomited. Covering her mouth she thought to run to the kitchen sink as she tried to catch her breath. Her head pounded in time with her heartbeat.

"Shit." She breathed through her nose, trying to calm down; maybe the fireplace was too warm.

But even as she settled, in her mind's eye was the shadow outline of her father's form, remembering the feel of cool, damp sand under bare feet on the tunnel's cement walkway as she followed him, advancing toward the water.

"Dad," she said into her hand and started to cry.

4

The tree wasn't nearly as heavy as they'd first thought and between the three of them the shaggy-bark birch was easily loaded into the back of TJ's dusty black truck.

They'd headed off to old man Whitedeer's sawmill just on the other side of Red Cliff. The sound of truck tires on the old man's gravel driveway brought Whitedeer shuffling out in his bed slippers to see who was there.

"Whatcha boys got there?" Whitedeer called out before they'd come to a complete stop. "That for Gloria's Spirit House?"

TJ didn't answer. His sons were equally as quiet as they unloaded the tree, TJ still uneasy about going against Gloria's wishes for a simple burial without all the hocus pocus, as she used to call it.

"Nice Wiigwaasi-mitig you got there." Whitedeer ran his hand along the birch tree's bark. "Where'd it find you?" The old man eyed TJ.

"Laying not fifty feet from the woods near my breakfast nook," TJ gestured toward the direction of his house as if seeing the back windows.

"You put tobacco down?"

TJ didn't answer.

The old man rolled his eyes and shook his head as he said. In a teasing voice he said, "Of course not. Ma'iingan Ninde, why would I think you'd do the right thing. You of all people, the protector."

The old man laughed as he watched TJ fidget. "Way to teach your boys to give thanks, whatcha think lads?" The old man opened his arms wide and turned toward them. Neither spoke.

TJ had no comeback either. He was no protector. He'd been powerless against the courts, the special interests, he hadn't even stayed with his mother as she was dying. He shook his head slowly and shrugged. Little did the old man know that he was right for completely different reasons.

TJ glanced over to Skye and Gavin and each shrugged and turned, chuckling to see their father humbled and busted by an elder for tobacco blessings, where years ago it had been one of them.

"I'll give you tobacco," the old man said to him. "Do it when you get back."

"I will."

"You're full of shit," Whitedeer mumbled under his breath and turned to Gavin and Skye. "Do it for your stubborn-ass Nindede." The old man threw up his hands in mock disgust. He then began to examine the birch trunk. "Been down at least six months or so, I'll bet," the old man said, his eye still on TJ. "Given the underside rot."

Old Whitedeer smiled in a knowing way.

"Your mom's spirit tree." The old man looked at TJ as he touched the shaggy bark. "Laughing Eyes was special alright. Didn't believe a word of the old ones but I'm old enough to re-member back to the time when she did." He held TJ's eye. "But it don't matter what a person believes." He grinned in a secre-tive way. "What is is what is." He waved for them to follow him into his shop.

TJ and his sons carried the trunk, following the old man along to his sawmill, his slippers making scuff marks in the dirt without so much as lifting his feet.

"Bring 'er in." Whitedeer kept motioning with his hand as he held open the door, waving them in as if they were backing up a trailer. He then held up a hand to stop. His long white ponytail was snaked up around the nape of his neck. He reached and flipped on the overhead fluorescent lights of the shop.

He motioned for them to pivot the birch trunk as he studied it.

"Hmm," Whitedeer said, seeing things in the wood. His callused hands made swishing noises over the shaggy bark. "You limbed it clean. Most don't bother. Lay 'er down there."

Whitedeer pulled his hands back and clapped with a decisiveness that spoke of a plan. "Alright." He motioned with one clawlike finger that was more clawlike than human.

They set it down exactly where he'd indicated on the table near the saw blade.

"Now go wait by the door, all of yas." The old man waved them away. "I'll call if I need you or when I'm done," he said. "Go, get outta here." He shooed the three of them out like a black fly swarm. "I ain't responsible for no lost fingers and parts," old man Whitedeer muttered.

His whole operation was rickety; the saw blade looked precarious if not lethal, the old wooden bed was wobbly. There'd been talk in the community of shutting him down before he hurt himself, like adult children take car keys away from elderly parents. But no one dared since they marveled at how the old man still had a full set of digits. Yet with each job, people held their breath, not wanting it to be their project that broke the old man's lucky streak.

As the birch made several passes through Whitedeer's hands to debark and be flattened on all four sides, the sweet minty scent of wintergreen infused the air; the three of them inhaled the pungent fragrance of birch. After several more passes, the tree was cut into more than enough boards to build Gloria's Spirit House.

Whitedeer stopped cutting and shouted to TJ over the noise. "Asphalt or shake roof?"

"Uh—shake."

"For Laughing Eyes," the old man said, and then worked the boards into smaller and finer pieces.

Whitedeer switched off the power and said, "For the one who'd lost faith though we'd all believed in her."

The shop was disturbingly quiet. The silence was like another person in the room. Gavin and Skye were somber. The old man had stacked the wood into two piles, motioning TJ over.

The old man searched TJ's face as if wanting to ask something but then forgot.

TJ reached for his wallet from his back pocket.

The old man held up both hands, powdered with sawdust. "No charge for Spirit Houses. Especially this one."

The rough-cut boards had been trimmed to the exact length. All TJ needed to do was assemble.

"This stack is her house. I'm numbering 'em all." The old man touched the pile of freshly cut wood, winking at Gavin and Skye in such a way that made them smile. "You kids call it idiot-proof."

Then he turned to TJ. "The other is leftover." He touched it with the toe of his slipper. "It's important to take this pile out first before anything else. Leave Laughing Eyes's wood in your truck. Bring the extra to the exact spot where you found the tree. You following me?" he asked, waiting for TJ to nod. "It's important," the old man said. "Clear all around it, put down tobacco, and then burn it like we do—ask Charlotte. She knows the prayers." His eyes stayed on TJ until he nodded and then he turned to Gavin and Skye. "Help Laughing Eyes make the journey. Her spirit came to you in this tree," he said as he touched the stack of wood. The old man seemed to choke up. "Now she needs release. Sprinkle tobacco around where you found it to give thanks. You, her only blood, can do it."

Later that afternoon Charlotte had joined to witness the burning, pulling the sides of her sweater close around her ribs in the chilly September air before the fire caught. Once it did, the wood had been so dry it was ablaze, the heat so intense that the four of them stepped back as if pushed. Charlotte, slipping her arm through both her sons', watched as the smoke rose up through the trees, up into the blue sky that Gloria had so loved that she'd painted all the walls of her house the same color.

It didn't take long before the stack was reduced to white ash. The words *purification* and *free* drifted through TJ's mind.

They'd worked late into the night in the garage, assembling and nailing together Gloria's Spirit House. By midnight it was finished and they'd all stood watching, imagining it in place over his mother's final resting place.

Gloria's funeral was held on Tuesday, on one of those September days when the sky is so blue it doesn't look real and its reflection on Lake Superior even less so.

Golden birches flourished the tops of the red rock cliffs for which the reservation was named. They cast images onto a lake so glassy calm that you'd have blinked and strained your eyes, thinking it a mirage. Hard to believe in only a month angry Superior would be tossing up boulders the size of small cars.

Someone had tied tobacco pouches of blue and green in tree branches toward the eastern doorway. Giving thanks for his mother's long life. She'd helped and touched so many as a nurse, as a friend, and all stood facing the east where spirits begin to journey—the east, which breathes life and then takes our last exhale to complete the circle.

As TJ stood graveside his brow furrowed, watching how upset the others were. He hoped no one would notice he wasn't. Gavin and Skye huddled next to him, solemn as they watched their Nokomis's body being lowered into the shallow grave in the quiet cemetery tucked away on Blueberry Road.

"She lived a long and good life," Charlotte whispered into the collar of TJ's shirt.

He grunted back. "It wasn't a good life." He resented the stab at revisionist history. There'd been enough of that around for centuries.

"It was her life, her way, her fate," Charlotte said. "It was what happened."

He didn't answer.

Some had come out in their finery; others from an interrupted workday, the health-care workers in uniform from the Tribal Health Clinic that Gloria had helped establish.

Even fleets of fish tugboats had taken a momentary pause during high gill net fishing season as captains and multigenerational fisherman had shown up, having had Gloria treat them for simple wounds, removing fishhooks from delicate areas over the years.

TJ had even heard that Petersen Foods, the reservation grocery store, had locked its doors for an hour so that staff could attend and the Spirit gas station a block away had stuck a note on the door, *Be back in an hour.*

Tears finally stung his eyes. For the life his mother almost had but didn't and for both of their fires that may have burned brighter had his father kept his promise. Sadness radiated down into his fingertips—a woman with a broken heart who by proxy had broken his for the better part of his life. And he'd been powerless to unbreak it though there'd been nothing more that he'd wanted to do—an unbreakable love that had broken her.

Gloria had carried her sadness quietly for the rest of her life, hoping that no one would notice. Wrapped around her like a blanket for all of her eighty-six years, wanting neither pity nor remembrance, but TJ knew. He could see it by the turn of her head or in the motion of her hand to brush away a wisp of hair from her eyes.

After the funeral he'd said to Charlotte, "I feel cleansed, at peace—like after a downdraft blows the ground clean."

"You mean the downdraft that comes right before the storm?" Charlotte had laughed in a menacing way.

A flare of anger had clutched at his chest—a little boy's undefended heart—as they'd driven out of the cemetery. A surge of dread followed in the form of a whisper, saying that all he'd been hiding would soon be exposed. *She whom his father had preferred.* And before getting out of the truck at home, he was a seven-year-old boy again. Running after his father's car in the red cloud of road dust, yelling for him to come back.

"Don't leave it to the attorneys," Charlotte had said, staring at him as he glanced away. "You know what you have to do. Find her. Do it or I will." His wife climbed out of the truck and closed the door. "I'm sick of living with ghosts."

TJ sat for a few moments longer.

Just then a gust of noodin, or wind, blew through the needles of a white pine, making clacking noises like chattering disembodied voices. Another breeze blew through the drying leaves of an oak tree, tricking him to look for the sound of rushing water.

TJ looked up. It was only the tree. He'd lived there all his to know there was no running water. His mother's spirit breathed into the wind and was gone.

"Bye, Mom." He mouthed the English words; there were no words for good-bye in Ojibwe.

5

Her nose was always in a book. Amelia would sort through the different species of dolphins and squid, and riffle through the piles of library books that littered her childhood bedroom floor as she contemplated the composition of seawater vs. brackish water. Thick glasses from second grade on had made two semipermanent dents on either side of her nose. Well into adulthood she would smile through closed lips, concealing teeth that were slightly bucked, noticeable enough to elicit "Uhh, what's up, doc?" Braces had been out of reach.

And while Amelia hated the mall, she'd beg to be taken back to the New York Aquarium in Brooklyn.

"Can we go again, please, Mom?" she'd bargain. "I'll even clean the toilet."

"Tell your father to take you on his day off." Pen would push back her bangs as Amelia sensed her mother's patience was shot after a long day.

Then a teacher of Amelia's called one day after school.

"Is this Mrs. Drakos? Amelia's mom?"

"What'd she do?" Pen put the dishrag down and sat at the kitchen table primed for a good story.

"Nothing—I mean everything's fine," the teacher reassured. "I want to talk about Amelia."

Pen paused. "So what about her?" she asked, hoping to hear

some juicy story about Amelia getting caught smoking in the girls' bathroom or with makeup, anything to peg her daughter as normal.

"Amelia has a very keen mind."

"Yeah, so?"

The teacher was quiet.

"With your permission, I'd like to put her in the school science club with some of the older children."

"How much older?"

"Seventh graders. Two years older."

Pen imagined her underdeveloped daughter, always on the low end of the pediatrician's growth charts, surrounded by older children. Amelia was vulnerable, yet impenetrable. How could a child be both?

"Umm . . . will there be boys?"

"It's all boys."

There was a long pause. It might not be bad, depending on the type of boys who would be in a science club.

"I'll have to talk to my husband about it," Pen said.

"But she'll be able to learn more," the teacher advocated. "Plus the New York Aquarium is running their annual contest for students to win a spot in their four-week summer camp."

"I said I'll talk to my husband," Penny said.

"Alright, Mrs. Drakos," the teacher said. "Can I speak to Amelia about it?"

"I told you I'll talk with my husband first."

"Alright then."

Each of Amelia's childhood friends was just like her. Amelia's mother would sigh and shake her head, at a loss as to how to spice up the life of a child who found her own birthday embarrassing. Who would marry such a girl?

"Jesus, she's that smart?" Ted asked later that night after Amelia had gone to bed. "Sure she's mine?"

Pen punched him hard in the arm as he feigned having the wind knocked out him.

"Let her do the science club for Christ's sake, Pen."

"But don't you think it'll make her—weirder?"

He chuckled. "Hey—Amelia's Amelia. She's not you." He got up and reached for her, pinching Penny's buttocks on the chair until she squirmed, playfully slapping away his hand, acting disgusted yet still delighted after all these years.

"You were probably sexy even at that age." Ted moved to pinch her inner thigh.

"Oh, stop already." She slapped his arm again, this time with a different meaning.

At eighteen years old Amelia was awarded a full scholarship to State University of New York at Stony Brook's prestigious School of Atmospheric and Marine Sciences. To her parents' delight they could instead spend their savings for her education on a trip to Greece.

"We're taking our second honeymoon," Penelope announced while driving Amelia to the freshman dorm that fall. In reality they'd never taken a first. The couple had gotten married on the fly with Amelia well on the way—her mother's growing abdomen camouflaged by creative fabric draping on the bodice of her wedding gown.

Amelia's father, Ted, had worked as a pressman, running building-sized machines that spun rolls of newsprint into daily newspapers. Penelope, or Pen as they called her, worked as a product assistant in a pillow factory in Long Island City typing, filing, and placing orders for fabric.

Amelia was quiet like her father, an anomaly to an ebullient mother who frequently exploded into tears, laughter, or fighting words. Often, her mother wouldn't even know if her daughter was home.

"Am?" Her mother would pause, calling after hearing a few indiscriminate noises. "That you?"

"Yeah, Ma, it's me."

Amelia did everything she was told without complaint, though often her mother would try to provoke a reaction, just to check that her daughter was human.

"What can I say?" her mother would remark to Ted, throwing up her hands in response to a daughter who coveted the *Encyclopedia of Marine Life* more than experimenting with makeup or getting her ears pierced. "All this kid does is read," she whispered.

"So what, Pen?" Ted would say over the top of the *Long Island Press* newspaper. "It's not heroin."

"I know I couldn't ask for a better daughter," Pen would qualify, murmuring just loud enough for him to hear. "Dear God, help me raise this strange child."

"Hey—we're all different." Ted would raise his voice. "You wanna believe the stork fucked up, then go ahead and believe it."

Before her parents' trip to Greece in November, they'd let Amelia use the car while they were gone, providing she came home to drive them to JFK Airport. What luck to take other students along to the more obscure saltwater tributaries along the easternmost sections of Long Island's South Shore to look for puffer fish.

Amelia had never seen her mother as happy as the day she dropped them off at Kennedy Airport. The day before they'd left, Penny had come in and sat down on Amelia's bed, smiling eagerly as she nodded. "You want a gold bracelet from Greece? A necklace?"

Instead Amelia had handed over a detailed list complete with descriptions and drawings of seashells from the Aegean Islands where they were headed.

"Look for this one." Amelia pointed to one drawing as her father listened in the doorway.

Her mother had already lost interest and stood to leave.

"This is the important one."

"What's so important about it?" he asked, replacing Penny in the spot on her bed.

She began to read. " 'The Tyrian purple snail has long been prized for its dye dating all the way back to the Phoenicians and Hebrews.' " She'd looked up. "Dad. You listening?"

"Uh-huh," he hummed.

" 'Long prized for its purple color that does not fade,' " she looked up again, " '. . . but rather becomes brighter with sun exposure.' "

"Okay," her father said. "So where do I find them?"

"Low tide. Near caves."

"Can't promise, but I'll look."

"The Mediterranean only has a two-foot tidal flow," she went on. "Not like the ocean. It's kinda landlocked, the only opening's at the Strait of Gibraltar."

He stared at her.

"Dad, what?" she asked.

"Nothing." Ted shook his head. His gray curls wiggled.

"Dad. Why are you looking at me like that?" She chuckled, not sure if she'd gotten some of her facts wrong.

"Nothing, Am." Her father continued to stare, unnerved by both the depth of knowledge and the authoritative tone in which it was delivered. "You just learn that in college or something?"

"Sixth grade report."

Yet from sixth grade she remembered it in detail, her mind still seeing the illustrations of the shells she'd painstakingly drawn from the encyclopedia.

Ted looked like someone had cracked him over the head.

"Dad. What?" Amelia blinked several times and grabbed his arms, shaking him. "Why do you keep looking at me like that?"

"Because you're my beautiful daughter and I love you." He reached to grab and kiss her but she pulled away.

"Get outta here." She began laughing along with him.

A week into her parent's trip there was a knock on the dorm room door at 3:20 a.m. She and her roommate, Kate, had been up until 2 a.m. working to finish a final chemistry project due the next morning. The resident advisor of the dorm opened the dorm door with the master key.

"Amelia." The RA had shaken the mattress to rouse her. "Phone call."

"What?" She looked up. The hall light stung her eyes.

Amelia slid her legs over the side of the bed and stood. Shuffling over to the black receiver she lifted it, placing it against her ear.

"Hello?"

"Amelia Drakos?"

"Yes."

"I'm Douglas Donnelly from the State Department. Sorry to wake you at this hour and with bad news. There's been a terrible car accident involving your parents in Greece."

She'd stood with her uncle from Boston on the JFK tarmac watching her parents' coffins being off-loaded along with their luggage. They signed all the appropriate papers from the State Department to claim the bodies and belongings. The rest of the family had come down from Boston for the funeral that week. Her aunts had stayed with her in the house.

The funeral had deteriorated into a circus. Her aunt Sophie pulled at the lapels of her father's suit, trying to drag the body from the casket. It had become freakier than death itself. Amelia backed away, slipping into the narthex of the church. By the doors, she tucked herself near the icons and flickering candles.

Later, after the graveside burial service and the Makaria, the traditional Greek Orthodox fish dinner with wine, everyone returned to Amelia's house. People would often show up at these events even if they'd never known the deceased, calling around to locate the closest Makaria.

Her aunts and uncles were passed out, snoring in various configuations in bedrooms or on couches in food comas.

Amelia crept around the living room, squatting in front of her parents' suitcases. Unzipping the big one, she felt the silkiness of Penelope's dresses, the smell of her Avon Cotillion cologne, flat cottony weave of her father's shirts—smell of Old Spice. She leaned her head on the suitcase and closed her eyes. Then her finger hit a plastic case. She pulled it partway out. Her father's shaving case. She unzipped it about an inch and felt white toilet tissue. Wads of white toilet paper wound mummy-style around an object. Parting the tissue, she spotted the spiny edge of a Tyrian purple snail shell. She slipped in her hand and counted five, each having been safely insulated so as not to bump against the other. Precious treasures all cushioned and protected, tucked away in her father's shaving case.

She pulled out the shaving case the rest of the way, peering around at the sleeping relatives to avoid their questions and dodge another encounter. Slipping into the bathroom, Amelia locked the door and turned on the fan. It rattled like it was filled with street gravel. Sitting down cross-legged on the cold pink tile floor, Amelia unzipped the case to study the five carefully wrapped bundles.

"Dad." She broke down before she could get the word out. Joy mixed with sorrow opened into an interior room she'd call The Place of No Comfort. There were no salves, no words, no ocean layers complex enough, no car fast enough to outrun it. She'd learned to sit there until the Place would fade, like the ocean's phosphorescence does at sunrise.

She smiled, guessing he'd snuck the shells into his shaving case before Pen had the chance to complain about getting sand in her clothes. Amelia pressed the grains into her index finger, lifting them to study—possibly from a beach in Crete, possibly their last day before the drive, possibly the last thing her father had touched. And he'd touched them. Little treasures he'd gathered for her.

Amelia zipped up the shaving case, shut off the bathroom fan, opened the door, and searched out her duffel bag in the pile of her relatives' suitcases. Slipping her father's shaving case in with her jeans and socks, she said nothing.

6

"You're stalling," Charlotte announced in that gentle way she had of dropping bombs.

He looked at her. "With what?" And while he knew better than to play dumb with her, he thought he'd give it a try since like with gambling, sometimes you win.

He'd bundled all of Gloria's papers, including her will, into a paper grocery bag and set it against the stone fireplace wall with a yellow Post-it Note that said *Mom*.

"That." She'd gestured to the brown bag with her chin, and an expression that said she wasn't born yesterday, and then eyed him from where she stood behind the stove browning venison meat with onions in a skillet to add to her spaghetti sauce.

He looked up at her over his brown reading glasses.

"We're a little busy right now, Charlotte,"—he gestured to the papers covering the dining room table.

She glared back.

"Mom's already dead." TJ then pointed to the paper grocery bag before holding up a legal brief. "These two hundred and one wolves are not."

It sounded harsh but it was too late. That's how he felt. Too stressed out to manufacture a softer tone.

He felt Charlotte back away from the stove as if to put a safer distance between them.

"That wasn't necessary, TJ." Charlotte stood holding the dripping spatula in her hand as she glared back.

Court documents were strewn across the kitchen table. TJ was compiling them into an executive summary before meeting with the GLIFWC attorneys to finalize an injunction to block the wolf hunt. The tribes had tried buying up all the wolf hunting permits to stop the hunt but the DNR had gotten wise to the blockade and quickly restricted the number of permits issued to tribal members. Next a discrimination lawsuit was filed against the DNR since no other group of people had been singled out for restriction.

TJ was planning a last-minute trip to Madison to persuade state judges to uphold the Endangered Species Act of 1973 and file the injunction. The hunt was to begin in November, less than two months away. TJ's emotions were so riled he could hardly think. His edginess spilled into everything and he found himself resenting sounds of the wind, crows calling to each other—everything was irritating and seemed to break his concentration.

Earlier that morning he'd been pacing the living room until Charlotte finally said, "That's it—take out the dogs, walk to Minnesota if you have to. I'm ready to rip out my hair; you're driving me crazy, pacing like some Frankenstein man tromping around in a bus station or something." The hanging decorative plates on the wall were rattling with each footstep that seemed to get heavier than the last.

"A Frankenstein man," he repeated. "That's a new one." That was the only thing that had given him some relief, his mouth agape in a frozen smile.

"Just go." She turned away, disgusted. And he'd already walked for almost an hour but it hadn't helped.

"Gloria's attorney called," Charlotte continued. "He found her e-mail and address."

He didn't look up. "I'm busy."

"Everyone's busy." Charlotte glared back over the stove. "It takes a minute to write an e-mail."

He took a deep breath as if just remembering it was a necessary body function.

"When *will* you have time?"

He turned to face her, wondering if he should say something or not. He could have a rough tongue and would often fight to soften it.

"What's the rush?" He raised his hands about to stand in aggravation. "Mom's house isn't going anywhere—it'll be there in November. Don't you traditionals always wait a year before executing a will?" His voice was sarcastic. "So what's with lighting a fire under my ass right now?"

She'd laughed as he'd said it and TJ snorted in an ironic way, not wanting to sound snide. He thought back to the Spirit House they'd just placed over his mother's grave. There'd been tension between them regarding his mother's wedding photo.

The walls of the Spirit House were two feet tall; it had a slanted roof for snow to slide off, and openings on either side for Gloria's spirit to come and go until prepared to make the final journey. There was a small internal shelf where Charlotte had placed her mother-in-law's favorite coffee cup, quilt, and photos of the boys. But then TJ had spotted his wife slipping in the framed wedding photo of his father and mother from Gloria's fireplace mantel. He'd stepped in to intercept the photo but Charlotte faced him down. Their eyes locked. He backed off. She'd won that one. Hands clasped behind his back he'd walked away, noting the surging green grass that would always sprout with the abundant autumn rainfall and cooler temperatures. He was no match for her.

"Not everyone waits a full year and you know it, Niinimooshe." She called him sweetheart to defuse the situation, and snickered at being caught at her own game. She tilted her head, watching him as she stirred the meat.

He loved it when she mixed this term of endearment with a twinge of sarcasm. It was their long-standing joke.

Their eyes smiled into each other's as if calling a draw.

The smell of cooking venison was intoxicating. TJ stood and scurried over to grab a spoon from the dish drain. Barging in front of her he reached under Charlotte's arm to steal a scoop of meat as she tried to block him. They both started to laugh as he managed to fill his spoon.

It was almost an apology, a sign of affection as he tangled with her at the stove. Blowing on the spoon, he gulped it down and went in for another.

"Stop it." She play-slapped his hand away with the spatula that splat on his arm. "There won't be enough for the sauce, you know how Elton hates it when you gobble up all the meat—he likes a meaty sauce."

His uncle Elton was coming over for dinner. They hadn't seen him since Gloria's funeral and TJ was going to pick up the old man who no longer drove at age ninety-one.

He stood holding the empty spoon, the salty taste of meat on his lips.

"Attorney says she's in Rhode Island." She looked at him.

He controlled his face.

"Oh." He knew.

"At the university there."

"Really." He knew that too.

"I have her e-mail address," she said.

"I told you, after the injunction is filed."

"Why not now?"

"Charlotte." He was no longer playful.

"Charlotte, what?" She glared back. "It would take you a minute."

"No, it won't."

She sighed with exasperation.

"That," he tossed the spoon in the sink with aggravation, "can also wait a coupla' weeks."

"Stop playing this game with me." She blocked the doorway with the spatula in her hand. He could tell she was losing patience.

"You know what's at stake." He squeezed past her and rustled up the reports and affadavits from the table, quashing them against his chest as he hurried off to his garage/office with an abruptness that made Charlotte turn.

He'd considered leaving it to the attorney. Have him contact her, get Amelia to sign off on the sale of the house, property, and then split the proceeds. Why Gloria hadn't rewritten the will he'd never know and hadn't asked. The property, house, and all its contents had been left to the descendants of Ted Drakos Sr., which included him and Amelia, providing no one else stepped forward.

TJ hurried through the living room and out the back as the screen door slammed on its own momentum. He'd apologize later.

He'd been grateful for Charlotte's patience for the past few weeks while the wolf hunt was pending before the state legislature. He'd walk the floors like a departed soul looking for absolution or an entry point into the next life. For weeks there was a cool empty spot beside her in bed as testament to his restlessness. The lives of animals he'd known better than family members were in peril and he was powerless, there was nothing anyone could say or do to make it not be so.

But what Charlotte hadn't known was that thirty years ago in graduate school, TJ had found Amelia. He'd never told anyone. It felt a bit pervy and voyeuristic but he'd kept it secret nonetheless.

There'd not been much to know aside from her address

and phone number, but once the Internet had exploded he'd discovered Amelia's Sea Horse and Shoreline Ecology Web site and would visit several times a month, careful to do so only when alone. Following their travels and findings, TJ uploaded videos from their site and knew Bryce and Jen's credentials by heart. He was current on all of their latest publications and fancied himself an armchair expert on their work.

Charlotte knew nothing. It felt like cheating and the longer it went on the more difficult it became to divulge. A few times he'd been on the verge of coming out with it but chickened out at the last second.

"What?" she'd ask, smiling as he'd start the one sentence he could never finish. "Out with it."

"Nothing," he'd say.

"What?"

"It's just that I can't believe how incredibly lucky I am," he'd say and then stop.

"You're so full of shit." Her eyes would glint with a mixture of worry and whimsy and they both knew a secret kept them separate.

Even when hiking through forests searching out wolf scat and evidence of a new den, he'd imagine Amelia at her work. Diving, swimming along in endangered coral reefs somewhere in places he'd never get to see, reflecting on how odd it was that their livelihoods had shared similar purposes—the love and stewardship of nature and the passionate desire to protect.

And then seven Octobers ago while in Boston attending a National Wildlife and Natural Resources Management Conference, TJ had gone so far as to rent a car and drive to the University of Rhode Island. He'd sat outside the marine biology building for the better part of an hour, watching the comings and goings of students changing classes, researchers and staff leaving work, hoping to catch a glimpse of her.

He'd wondered how one goes about meeting a sibling and not have it become TV talk-show crazy? As soon as he'd drummed up the courage to park and go inside, a campus security vehicle had pulled alongside, "Hey buddy, you in the fire lane." That was all the encouragement he'd needed to get the hell out of there and drive back to Boston.

Months before, after Gloria had first taken ill, he'd phoned the Sea Horse and Shoreline Ecology number on their Web site, letting it ring long enough to hear Amelia's voice.

"Hi, this is Amelia Drakos. You've reached the Sea Horse and Shoreline Ecology Lab. Please leave a message: for Bryce press 1, for Jen press 2, for me, Amelia, press 3."

It was disappointing. He'd expected her voice to trigger some sort of genetic memory or recognition, but it hadn't and he'd felt stupid for even expecting such a thing. It was just some East Coast stranger-woman's clipped accent. It had bothered him just how ordinary she sounded. He hadn't called back.

As a boy, during his father's summer visits he'd always count heads in the approaching car, hoping for a second, shorter one in the backseat, primed for a surprise. But the surprise never came. The closest he'd come were new photos of Amelia and he'd been too shy to ask why his father never brought a camera to take photos of him.

"Does she know what I look like?" TJ'd once asked in a very quiet voice, not sure his father had heard, even less sure he'd wanted the man to hear.

He had a collection of Amelia's photos up until her high school graduation, all safely hidden in the garage office, tucked under files. Birthday photos of Amelia, one of her smiling with a space between her front teeth after she'd mastered riding a bike.

TJ lived with the feeling that Amelia had been the grand prize. The girl who lived near the place of Great Salt Waters had prevailed.

The Sea Horse and Shoreline Ecology Web site filled his laptop screen. He hadn't checked it in months, since their last summer dive project offshore of Phuket, Thailand, in the Andaman Sea.

TJ was so wrapped up in the updates to Amelia's Web site that he didn't hear Charlotte's footsteps.

Chin resting in his hands, TJ leaned on the desk studying the updated photo of Amelia in a Zodiac, with wet hair, in a wet suit. Her eyes looked different. Maybe it was just getting older but there was something of her father there. Signs of age crept into that perennially young face that he'd only known in two-dimensional form. Gray threads wove into her hair, gentle wrinkles around her eyes and bracketing her mouth, a softening around her cheeks, no longer as angular as they'd once been. Amelia's sea-green eyes were the same color as his.

Older images had shown an intensity and drive about them— excitement while holding a sea horse in her hand, or on a Zodiac with her face mask set up on her forehead, talking into the video recorder, explaining the new species they'd found just offshore.

But this latest expression he couldn't read. Fatigue or loss of heart; her face looked tired or resigned. Something had changed. Maybe he was reading too much into it in the week since Gloria's death and the pending wolf hunt. Many years' worth of images had shown her flashing a smile with large white teeth with a slight gap in between the front two, there'd been an unself-conscious happiness and ease about her. This smile was more measured and circumspect, as if her mind was many other places rather than focused on the camera. Even those teeth in her infectious smile were concealed by lips that gave only a hint that wasn't reflected in her eyes.

"She looks sad." Charlotte's voice startled him. Her mouth

was so close to his ear, it might as well have been a bull-horn.

He jumped into the air.

He turned to face her.

They stared at each other.

He was caught. He'd never betrayed her before. TJ couldn't speak, couldn't move, he felt flushed, ashamed.

Charlotte moved the pile of papers and articles off the adjacent chair and sat down beside him, sliding her arm around his upper back and neck.

"So that's her," Charlotte said with finality as she scooted the chair closer. "Uh-huh. You two look a lot alike."

He still couldn't speak. "I-I . . ."

"Niinimooshe," she said, smoothing the back of her hand against his cheek as she sighed deeply. "You're up at bat now. Nothing stands between you and her."

It had been as much a refuge as it had been a torment.

He said nothing but hung his head.

"I'm sorry."

"So *this* is your secret."

"I'm sorry," he said again, looking at the floor.

"It's okay, Niinimooshe. Look at me." This time she said it without sarcasm.

She held his gaze and smiled in relief, nodding slightly as if this was the final puzzle piece she'd been expecting.

He rested his head on her shoulder, about to cry. Losing his mother, he let the broken heart of a boy wash through him.

She held him with the relief of a best friend's forgiveness.

TJ sat up, watching as she looked with interest at the Web site.

"So, that's her, eh?" Charlotte said quietly, studying the familial contours of the woman's face.

He nodded.

"Same color eyes, shape lips." Charlotte then began reading the text under the photos.

"And she's a marine biologist."

"Yes, she is," he said.

"So, why don't you start by telling me all about her?"

7

It was morning. Amelia opened the front door in the middle of Bryce's sequence of knocks, her cavernous yawn being a replacement for the last taps back.

She squinted and lifted a hand to shield her face. The bright sunshine felt like bees stinging her eyes.

"Going somewhere?" Bryce tugged at the sleeve of her jacket that she'd slept in.

She snorted a laugh mid-yawn and was about to tell him to shut up but then remembered the NSF. The sick feeling in her stomach returned.

"Nice to see you too," Bryce said.

"God, what time is it?" Amelia stepped aside to let him pass.

"Almost eight."

"You're kidding." She hadn't slept that late since having the flu.

Her neck was kinked, her body so stiff it felt like she'd pulled a muscle.

"I called last night," Bryce said.

"My phone died." She looked to where it lay after talking with Alex.

"Stopped by, knocked."

Her eyes widened. "Really."

"Really," he repeated. "How come you didn't answer?"

"How come you didn't do the knock?" How stupid to have thought it was Myles.

"Did you see my truck?"

"No."

He always did the knock. "You didn't do the knock," she said.

"Nothing like the sound of tautology first thing in the morning," Bryce said.

Not knowing what else to say, Amelia headed toward the kitchen to make coffee.

"Coffee?" she asked in the middle of another yawn.

"Sure."

Grabbing the kettle, she filled it and set it on the burner.

"You gonna—" he said.

"Gonna what?" She looked up.

"Helps if you turn it on, darlin'," Bryce reached across her and turned on the burner.

"Oh." She rubbed her face. "Sorry," she said in a yawn and then stood hypnotized by the blue flames tickling up around the circumference of the kettle.

"Jen thought you might be with Myles."

She snorted in a disparaging way and stepped to retrieve the phone and plug it in by the toaster.

"Your front shutters were open; I'm surprised you didn't see my truck." Bryce sat down to face her at the breakfast bar.

Her face felt hot, she hoped he hadn't seen her crawling under the windowsill, spying out for Myles. Then she squelched a laugh. Ordinarily something like that would have been the first thing out of her mouth, describing in detail to Bryce how idiotic she'd been.

"Yeah, well." She rubbed her eyes. Water in the kettle began to pop. "The laws of thermodynamics are our friends," she said in a snide way.

She heard him smile. His breath always changed when he did.

Slipping off her jacket, she tossed it onto the couch. "Talk to Jen yet?"

"Nope. Probably still up from last night."

They were quiet as the kettle became noisier.

"So tell me why you didn't answer the door?"

"Tell me why you didn't do the knock." She threw up her hands and then leaned on the breakfast bar, chin in hand, staring back.

"We're having a staring contest?" he said.

She turned away.

"You lose," he said.

"In more ways than one," she mumbled, reaching up for two of the largest coffee mugs in the cabinet. Setting them onto the counter, she began to spoon out double heaps of instant coffee.

Springing her barrette, Amelia re-combed her hair using her fingers, raking out knots as she watched him patrol the living room and then re-clipped the barrette. Leaning on the kitchen counter, she traced a crack with her fingernail.

"I was worried when you didn't answer," Bryce said. "Jen thought of calling the cops."

"The cops." Amelia looked up and nodded, placing her hands on her hips. "Really." She nodded. "And Jen wanted to call Myles too."

She imagined a squad car with lights ablaze in front of her house.

" 'Dr. Drakos,' " she began in an official voice. " 'You're under arrest for hubris and the crime of never believing the NSF would turn you down.' "

She'd almost succeeded in comedy until she choked up in a spastic, embarrassing way. Her throat pinched. She covered her face.

"I'm so sorry, Bryce," she said through her hands. Her lower lip quivered. Looking up at Bryce her face clenched. "I let you both down."

He rushed to her. Her head didn't even reach his shoulder as she buried her face into his fleece. He squeezed so hard she couldn't breathe for a moment.

The kettle's screaming whistle broke them apart.

She poured water over the instant coffee crystals and handed him a cup.

"We've got a month to vacate the lab space," he said.

Amelia looked at him, stirring her coffee as she thought. People switched careers over less. Losing a grant of this size often shook the foundation of a person's life. A few dark grinds floated to the surface as she picked them out.

For years her backup plan had been to teach high school science. For the past ten summers Amelia had created and ran her Teen Summers at the Sea program for adjudicated youth as part of the NSF community outreach. She'd always figured that if need be she could parlay it into a job. Now she wasn't so sure.

For more than twenty-five years she and Bryce had sat elbow to elbow at the same lab bench, five as co-researchers in a larger lab, twenty years running their own gig. She'd known Bryce longer than she'd lived in the Revolution House. Bryce was the only other living human who'd watched Alex grow up. He was like an uncle or a de facto father. He'd played broom ball on the floor of the lab with Alex when school was out or he was home sick. He'd taught Alex to scuba dive, helped him earn his certification through the more difficult scientific and professional licensing. And Alex's foray into marine biology was inspired by watching the two of them work together all those years. After school he'd come help run experiments under Bryce's supervision, prepare Petri dishes, rinse out specimen tubs, and help to rearrange coral and transfer sea horses—an endless array of tasks that by the end of tenth grade had turned Alex into a bona fide laboratory assistant.

"—there'll be another grant, Ammy," Bryce said, his voice soft.

She looked up at him, guessing he hadn't slept much either. His eyes were red and watery, the rims inflamed, making the blue irises look more vivid, like the horizon of the Indian Ocean.

"Something'll turn up."

"It'll be different." She made a face.

He looked at her as if deciding something.

"What's wrong with different?" Bryce bent to eye level.

"Maybe nothing depending on what different is."

"Grant money dries up, new funds flow," he said. "Life goes on."

"Yeah, but Jen's and my stipends end in a month."

"We'll get new funds."

"That could take a year."

It would leave her and Jen with no income until summer. Bryce had a cushion of family money. She and Jen lived hand to mouth. Amelia still paused before buying paper towels in the grocery store, thinking of them as a luxury item.

"Last night we tallied a spreadsheet," he said. "Later today we can go over it at the lab."

Over the years she'd sat with scientists in this very situation, listening as they'd read in the most bureaucratic of terms that "your career has been canceled." In some cases trying to offer comfort, encouragement while secretly harboring the unspoken belief that somehow the scientist had screwed up. Now she smiled at herself, reeling at how her own judgment had come full circle, after having been so self-assured that it would never be her in that position.

Amelia sighed deeply and looked down at her toes, guessing that as kindhearted as the scientists in the lab might act, they were probably thinking the same thing.

They turned as her phone beeped—having charged enough to have a voice.

"Probably fifty messages from me," Bryce said.

"No doubt," she said. "Yep. Five thousand and one to be exact," she said. "One from Diane," she said and jerked up to check the clock on the stove.

"Oh shit, shit, shit," Amelia yelled. Diane was director of the Biomes Marine Biology Educational Center where Amelia maintained the aquaria as a condition of one of her smaller grants.

"Holy shit." She looked at Bryce as she punched Diane's number. "I'm supposed to be at the Biomes now. Right fucking now—oh my God, I totally forgot."

Amelia sighed and dipped her face into her hand, waiting for Diane to pick up.

"Oh my God, Diane, I'm so, so sorry." She looked at the clock on the stove again, running her hand through her hair as the digit flipped to one minute later.

"Don't worry, Amelia. Take your time, there's no rush."

She'd never been late to the Biomes before.

"I'm leaving right now." She hurried into the living room, dropping to her hands and knees to hunt down her socks and shoes. Pulling on one sock and then the other, she mouthed to Bryce that she'd call him later.

He strode over and bent down and kissed the top of her head in such a gentle way that it made her stop.

She looked up at him; such an odd kiss. Their eyes searched one another. His with a sad expression she'd never seen; was it a good-bye kiss or perhaps a hello?

He waved good-bye and mouthed "Later" and then left as the heavy front door yawned before shutting in that satisfactory way it sounded as it closed.

She watched out the front window as he circled around her Jeep and climbed into his truck. Something felt unsettling, like she wanted to run out and stop him, talk to him some more. She wanted to get Diane off the phone so she could call him.

"First off, I'm so, so, sorry about the NSF, Amelia," Diane said.

She turned away from the window, already in flight mode she hurried into the back room where she stored her dive gear, sorting through damp wetsuits to determine which was drier and then tossed a pair of fins into a gear bag hoisting up her tank and regulator and setting it all by the front door.

The Biomes was an hour drive from Providence, and she cal-
culated just how badly she'd have to break the law to shave off
maybe fifteen minutes. The place opened to schoolchildren and
Diane always like to have the business of underwater maintenance done before the buses arrived.

Rushing to the bathroom, she grabbed her toothbrush, furiously brushing while trying to mask the sound of doing so.

"Uh-huh, Diane, so you said it's the reef that looks like it's
in decline," she said after rising out her mouth and spitting into
the sink.

"When you get here I've got a couple of ideas," Diane said.

"About the reef?" The toothbrush dropped onto the side of
the old porcelain sink with the double spigots as she tucked the
phone under her chin while securing her hair.

"No, about you," Diane said. "About Bryce and Jen too."

She dashed to the kitchen and grabbed an apple on the
way out

"Oh?" Amelia asked. "What about us?"

"Well—just drive safe," Diane said. "We'll talk when you get
here."

8

Amelia texted Diane as she pulled the parking brake. She then tore across the lot toward the Biomes facility, feeling as if her shoulder would separate as she lugged the heavy gear.

Fumbling with her security card, the Biomes metal door beeped and unlocked. She grabbed the handle and pulled it open as a caffeine depravation headache set in with a dull ache. Hurrying into the women's locker room she yanked off her top, a few threads popping as she did, and kicked off her jeans. Wriggling into a bathing suit she pulled up the wet suit.

Grabbing her BCD vest, she attached one air tank, grabbed her dive fins and belt, and headed out toward the marine exhibit area to wait for Diane.

Climbing up onto the deck of the marine tank, Amelia set the air tank into the water and then stepped down the ladder into the salt water. The whoosh of the water felt like heaven, fresh, cool as she visualized the coral reef. Sometimes reefs did decline in large aquaria but it wasn't often.

Swimming into the BCD vest, she clipped it on, slipped on her fins, and hooked one arm through the bottom rung of the ladder, treading water as she waited for Diane.

Amelia closed her eyes and lay back, floating in the cool water as it cradled her head, giving into weightlessness, trying to slow her mind as it was still speeding on the highway.

She pulled the face mask down over her nose and eyes and wiggled it into place so that it wouldn't leak and moved her fins ever so slightly to stay buoyant, imagining a jellyfish in reverse evolution.

Tears slipped out, down the sides of her head as she floated. So often she was alone except for Bryce and Jen. And now Alex seemed to have settled so far away. Alone except for when face-to-face with a bottle-nosed dolphin or when a wild sea horse wound its tail around her finger and she was one again claimed by the sea.

Her face mask quickly fogged. She flipped over and pulled it away ever so slightly to dip it in water and then set it back on her face. She looked at the time, wondering what was keeping Diane.

A stingray swam just beneath the surface and she watched its billowing form.

The scraping sound made by the metal security door made her tip upright. In came the singsong greeting from Diane.

"Hi, Amelia." Diane's cheery voice laughed as it always did when entering the marine tank area. About the same height as Amelia, Diane wore thick glasses, had cropped gray hair, and was always more professionally dressed as if in meetings all day long. "You're such a doll for coming in given what's happened."

She didn't think of herself as a doll. She could fast-talk her way onto any research vessel in the world, or out of trespassing violations in international waters when local authorities would threaten to arrest her team and take command of their ship.

"I'm so, so sorry," Diane said.

"Yeah, well," Amelia looked into the clear water. "What are you gonna do when you live in a shoe?" Amelia snorted, something she'd always say when in a jam. This was her last funded dive in the facility. The Biomes had just lost a grant that helped pay for Amelia to maintain and preserve their reefs and aquaria, though she'd promised to come work for free.

"I mean it, Diane," she said in that nasally way through the dive mask. "This keeps me sane."

Diane tried to catch her eye to smile.

Holding on to the ladder's bottom rung, Amelia watched as a puffer fish swam by, inflated as perfectly round as the planet Venus except for the two eyes, a beak for a mouth, and spikes that hurt like hell.

For a moment neither spoke.

Diane broke the silence. "I mentioned that Felice thinks the big reef's in decline."

"Yep, I'll go take a look, let you know what I find."

Amelia gave the OK sign, bit into the regulator, and slid beneath the gleam of the waterline. Her head rushed with the roar of her first breath, the feel of her lungs—she was one of them— an Aqua-Lung.

Water flooded the roots of Amelia's hair as long strands whooshed with the current, blending into the reef—heaven for a woman whose heart pumped seawater.

The two e-mails with her father's name came to mind. Why think of them now? It made her shiver, recalling the Arctic folktale of Sedna, the Inuit sea goddess whose father had thrown her overboard to appease the raven spirit he'd enraged. Sedna's hair was hundreds of fathoms long and was believed to get tangled up in the nets and propellers of Arctic fishermen even to this day. Ever since eighth grade the folktale had both fascinated and horrified her. As Sedna had grasped the side of her father's kayak, he'd axed off her fingers and shoved her under with his oar. Each of the young woman's severed digits was believed to have turned into all of the lobsters, crabs, sea urchins, and other marine animals that make up the ocean floor. Instead of perishing, Sedna had become goddess of the underwater Arctic.

Gliding toward the reef, Amelia tucked the tips of her

fingers into her dive belt, imagining Sedna as she thought of her father's e-mail. Her dive fins and the gentle movements of her hips guided her forward. Silence blotted out time and urgency. She imagined it was quiet under the Arctic Ocean.

Stingrays and sea turtles billowed past as Amelia watched for unusual behavior. As she swam through their water currents, she spotted the reef in question. Like glittering jewels, clusters of green cabbage coral, honeycomb, and fuchsia clumps of mushroom corals had all grown together in gardens. Tiny colonies of marine invertebrates with saclike bodies swayed in the wake of her fins. Their calcified cone skeletons grew outside of their bodies, like residents in high-rise apartment buildings, thriving on only food, sunlight, and good water flow.

Amelia touched the leathery edge of a cabbage coral and lowered to get a better look. Instead of in decline it was a new colony of coral reef polyps—evidence of health and new life.

Then a pair of orange sea horses flitted toward her. She offered a finger. The female, the bolder of the two, wrapped its tail around her index finger. Turning its head sideways, it studied her with a black shiny bowling ball eye. Her mate's belly was swollen with a clutch of babies, looking as if he was about to give birth.

A sea horse's metamorphosis made them impossible to spot in the wild. Twenty-two years ago Amelia had spent an entire year swimming past coral reefs, seeing nothing until her eye had finally learned to spot them. The little buggers could mimic the exact details of coral reefs and underwater grasses, making them virtually indistinguishable.

This particular pair of orange sea horses had been bred in her tiny lab at the University of Rhode Island, Narragansett Bay. The female held on to her finger with her prehensile, monkey-like tail, not letting go.

Gently unwinding the sea horse's tail, she placed the female back on a fan coral next to her mate. The two turned to face each other, undulating in the current of a disgruntled sea bass as it swam by.

Amelia then approached one of the largest natural clam shells growing in an American aquarium, one she'd secured out of harm's way by a proposed oil rig in the east Indian Ocean. She touched the outside of its shell. Bubbles escaped from its fanning lips as it sensed her presence as a disturbance in the current.

Approaching the surface, she saw Diane's face, distorted through the water's own fun-house mirror, looking like a worried Miss Piggy, scouring the tank for her. Bubbles careened up in time with each convulsive laugh into the regulator as Amelia chuckled, feeling bad that she found it so funny—but it was.

"The reef's fine, Diane," Amelia called out after removing the regulator from her mouth, squelching a laugh, not sure the woman would find it as funny. Tucking the face mask under her chin, Amelia grabbed the ladder and stepped up. Amelia's chin dripped water as she pulled off her face mask and tossed it on top of the gear pile.

"Just a new colony—nothing to worry about," Amelia said. Sliding off her lime-green dive fins, she set them up on the deck and slipped out of the buoyancy compensator vest. Rolling the air tank up onto the deck, water rushed down. As she climbed up the ladder, torrents of salt water streamed past her ankles. "Probably have to move some of the sponge coral, transplant the polyps."

Amelia sniffled and wiped her nose on the sleeve of her wet suit. She squeezed water out of the long strands of her hair as if it was a wet towel.

"How 'bout you get changed and meet me in my office." Diane crossed her arms and tilted her head to one side as the two women looked at each other.

. . .

Amelia pushed open the locker room door, hurrying to pile her fins and dive equipment into the gear bag. She grasped the zipper pull along the back of her wet suit and guided it down to the base of her spine. Wrestling out her arms, she pushed the neoprene form past her hips, pulling out one leg and then the other. Standing in her bathing suit on the cement floor, she held the wet suit as her hair dripped.

"Good enough." She jammed the wet suit on top rather than artfully arranging it as she usually did and forced the zipper closed, the plastic teeth straining and pulling apart.

"Shit." She left it.

She quickly rinsed off in the shower and then rushed to the hand dryers, hitting the metal button and leaning over as she fluffed her hair to make it dry faster.

Her jeans felt grubby as she wriggled them up over damp thighs, jumping to yank them up so she could button the top.

Since 1980 Amelia wore only blue jeans, black T-shirts or turtlenecks, fleeces, black one-piece bathing suits, clogs, or else just dive gear. Blending into the topside world was her adaptive niche.

Jen would encourage her to live large, coercing her into buying colorful T-shirts and sweaters though Amelia counted herself lucky if she could find two matching socks without holes. "Never buy anything that's for sale" was Amelia's policy as she raided the lost and found box, looking for items that had been in the lab for more than sixty days.

"Bet ya a new face mask you'd get more dates if you wore pink."

"Bet ya there's a greater chance of a catastrophic asteroid collision with earth than there is of me finding a man even in pink," Amelia shot back and made a sour face.

"Keep making that face and it's gonna stick," Jen warned with her pointer finger.

Neither had she any jewelry nor did she want any. What could match the beauty of marine life? She'd seen an octopus disappear against a rocky cliff wall and watched sea horses change color faster than a human breath. Some grew filament tendrils like bridal veils to mimic the surrounding reef corals and grasses. Had she not seen all of this Amelia would have chalked it up to someone's fish tale.

She'd played tag as Galapagos dolphins chased her Zodiac under the blackest new-moon night as sea water phosphoresced a milky greenish blue that only single-cell plankton give off when disturbed—nature's burglar alarm. The grooves and arcs of the mammals' necks and tails were illuminated as they sliced through in hot pursuit.

On research vessels, sitting down in the darkness of marine labs, Amelia, Bryce, and Jen would be watching live feed from deep-water ROV submarine cameras. Seeing a creature new to science, a species with bioluminescence—animals that manu-factured their own light in the midnight zone of the ocean—close to cracks in the earth's mantle where not one photon of light was anywhere to be found. With crazy, neon colors, oscil-lating in patterns in the blackness like some far-fetched sci-fi alien movie, but it was all real, all in their oceans that few would get to see. For Amelia, there was nothing more spectac-ular than this.

She buttoned the top of her jeans and then sat down on the wooden locker-room bench, plunging her arms into the sleeves of her black fleece jacket and zipping it up to her chin. She shoved her waterlogged hands into her pockets and thought of her father. He'd always say, *"the older you get the more like your-self you become."*

"If you are the Amelia Drakos Greek-American who grew up on Long Island . . . your father . . ."

"Dad," she said and closed her eyes. It sounded unprac-ticed, strange. She'd not said it since 1978. She'd think of him especially if she'd smelled someone smoking Pall Mall king-size cigarettes.

"My father." Her own voice sounded strange even saying it. Who would she tell? Why would she tell? There was no e-mail the year her father died. Too bad the dead couldn't drop a line now and then, check in, and catch up.

She buried her face in her fleece jacket as she sat on the wooden bench. Calm settled like a narcotic. It always did after a dive. She hunched over and let it wash through and claim her—a decompression necessary to gain her emotional sea legs.

After about a minute, she sat up and pulled out a metal barrette from her jeans pocket. Harnessing her damp hair into a ponytail, she could still feel the warmth from the hair dryer along her spine.

Tugging up her wool socks, she thought back to March just after the Java Conference. She'd warned Bryce and Jen that it might be a rough ride—researchers with more institutional clout than her worried about the fate of their labs. And while neither Bryce nor Jen believed her, she couldn't shake the uneasy pall that had accompanied her return from the conference.

After Java, Bryce had teased, even though ordinarily cautious and prudent to a fault.

"Amelia's like Chicken Little. This is her." He'd blown up a latex glove and somehow managed to attach it to his head while dashing through the aisles of the lab calling out in a scratchy chicken voice, "The sky is falling, the sky is falling." Everybody laughed, including her.

"Funny, Bryce." Amelia said without a laugh. "But things are different."

"You know, Amelia," Jen had affirmed, nodding in her big sister way. "You do say that every time—sorta like the Boy Who Cried Wolf." Her Orange County golden hair shook like a mane. Tall and runway thin as Amelia used to call her, Jen's heavily made-up eyes had locked with Amelia's in trying to get her to concede the point—eyes that remained, to Amelia's amazement, always lined with makeup, even when out on dive projects.

She knocked on Diane's office door though it was open.

The woman motioned to come in and have a seat though she was on the phone, having a discussion about an invoice.

Amelia sat, pretending not to listen as her eyes drifted up to an image of a giant eyeball on a poster immediately above the woman's head. WHO AM I? asked the huge eyeball of the giant squid.

Amelia stared back at the eye, returning its intensity. *"No one knows the mind of a squid,"* her father used to say.

Underneath were the words, I AM GENUS *ARCHITEUTHIS,* with a long explanation comparing it with others of the same genus. I AM A CEPHALOPOD. . . . Off to the side of the desk were piles of colorful educational folders and brochures for the children's programs at the Biomes.

Amelia turned as Diane ended the call.

"Okay, Amelia, sorry to keep you waiting." She jotted down a few notes and then looked up. "You look tired, dear," Diane's face softened in a motherly way as she cleared stacks of papers off the middle of her desk and then leaned on both elbows, resting her chin on each palm.

Understatement of the year. Amelia nodded.

"I made a couple of calls last night," Diane said. "You know how bad news always travels faster than good." She looked straight on at Amelia. "So I did some checking."

She waited. " This was a very political decision." Diane's eyes narrowed.

Amelia furrowed her brows. *Aren't they all?*

"Someone who worked in your lab . . ." Diane waited for Amelia to guess. ". . . took your theory of the winter sea horse migration in the northeast, added some other lines of inquiry to hide the intellectual theft, and submitted the grant as her own."

Amelia sat thinking and then turned to her, almost laughing at the preposterousness of who it might be.

Amelia wrinkled her forehead and sat up. "Juney?"

Gauging by Diane's reaction she'd guessed right.

"You gotta be kidding me." It felt like she'd smacked her head on the hull of a ship in the sudden wake of a storm. She laughed, shaking her head in disbelief.

"It certainly didn't hurt that a close personal relative with the same last name was on the funding committee." Diane pursed her lips and rolled her eyes.

"But I hired her." Amelia stood up and began to pace. "My God, Diane, I gave her a post-doc three years ago when no one else would take her seriously." Juney Lowell had worked with them for two years until the post-doc ran out and Amelia hadn't renewed it.

And while she and Juney Lowell had never warmed up to each other, Amelia attributed it to both Juney and Bryce being from Rhode Island's old moneyed families. She could measure Juney's resentment at taking direction from her and Jen by her terse little movements around the lab as if considering them more fit to be running a string of nail salons rather than being principal investigators with the authority to call the shots.

Early on Juney and Bryce had also begun sleeping together for a short period of time until Amelia and Jen had arrived at the lab one morning to discover Bryce's clothing and toothbrush strewn on the laboratory floor along with a Fuck You note. Jen had commented, "Well, she looked like a rough ticket from the start. Guess she threw him out with all his shit." It had made for some tense times in the lab, even more so seaside where they'd worked for weeks at a time out on the ocean.

The crew didn't have much use for Juney either. She was never around when the dive grips on the ROV needed to be replaced or when it was her turn to clean the latrines. She'd put Bryce up to it.

"Where's Juney?" the captain had asked.

"Probably cramps again," Jen answered deadpan, hating how Bryce was "under her spell," attributing it all to "the power of pussy."

After Juney's uncle had been nominated for the Nobel Prize in physics she was insufferable, declaring that ". . . the roots of inquiry have always run deep in my family."

Needless to say when awarded to a different scientist, Amelia and Jen were clinking glasses down at the AA and cackling up a storm.

"So." Diane pushed a printed copy of Juney's grant application across the table followed by a memo listing names on the Appropriations Committee. "Remember . . ." Diane looked at her. "You never saw this." Diane pointed but didn't speak as if there were people in the corners listening.

Amelia picked up the documents.

"Anything look redundant?" Diane asked.

She read Juney's abstract and then bowed her head. The sting made it difficult to speak.

"Diane." Amelia looked up. "I took that girl on dives, shared all our information, and included her in everything. I taught her how to dive, how to use scuba equipment. She knew nothing, had no equipment, not even a face mask. I took her to the store, advised her what to buy."

"Now look at the names of the award committee." Diane pointed on the paper.

The name Lowell: Nobel Prize loser.

"See how it's been written as to make you redundant yet not be in violation."

Amelia looked up and frowned, shaking her head and opening her hands, asking why.

"Because she could," Diane said in a sad way as she sighed and raised her eyebrows into high arches.

Amelia closed her eyes, reeling with a tangle of thoughts and emotion.

"You brought something new to science; she maximized

your discovery, your hard work, and used it against you. The grant was well written."

Amelia laughed out loud. "By someone else. Not Juney, that's for sure. Juney can't write worth a shit," she almost yelled. "I've corrected Juney's writing."

The two women sat thinking. Amelia resolved to never tell Bryce or Jen.

"Shit." Amelia covered her face with her hands, feeling bitter. "Too bad the *Ocean Explorer*'s phone call hadn't come in January."

Diane leaned over and touched Amelia's hand.

Amelia looked up.

"Amelia, don't get stuck here."

Alex had said as much on the phone last night.

"Sometimes we need to get shook loose to get free," Diane said.

Amelia looked down at her waterlogged hands, the skin on her fingers still prune-like.

"Don't know that I have that kind of resilience, Di."

"Maybe not now, not today." She looked at Amelia in such a way as to hold strength for her. "But you've raised your wonderful son, built a research lab from nothing and kept it going more than twenty-five years, discovered all sorts of new things. How many people have done that?"

"But I'm so tired, Diane." She rubbed her face, trying not to cry.

"You're tired now."

They sat for a few moments as Diane's phone rang but she let it go to voice mail.

"You've got funding for summer?"

She nodded.

"From whom?"

"Ocean Watch, Sea Life Conservation, a small grant from the Shedd, and a few others."

"Thought so." Diane pointed a finger at her, opened the top

desk drawer, and pulled out a brochure. "Now, before you say no, hear me out."

Amelia crossed her arms, sat back in the chair, and watched Diane set a brochure down on the desk.

"There's an opening for a director and animal care curator at Sea Life Aquarium in Minneapolis," Diane said.

Amelia recrossed her legs, not ready to listen.

"I'm personal friends with the director who's retiring. They're the largest retail franchise of the Sea Life Conservation Foundation in North America."

"Sounds like Burger King."

Diane raised her brows again as if to cut off the smart-ass comments and squelched a laugh. "They've funded your summer dives for the last several years."

Amelia nodded in contrition, correcting her tone. "Yes, you're right, they have."

"She mentioned a few others retiring along with her," Diane said and tipped her head sideways, holding both hands up in conclusion. "I know you three musketeers are close."

"Minneapolis?"

"Nothing wrong with Minneapolis, Amelia," the woman said. "It's in the Mall of America to be exact."

"A shopping mall." Amelia leaned forward in the chair.

"Biggest one in North America."

All sorts of thoughts rushed at once.

"We'd have to relocate."

"Won't kill you."

Amelia looked at her.

"You'd be responsible for all the marine life," Diane said. "You'd oversee the creation of new exhibits, some work with donors, and be in charge of the children's education programs. It's everything we do at Biomes but on a much larger scale. You'd also have a staff and interns to manage; but you're good with people."

"Oh yeah, like Juney." The words scorched as they came out.

Diane reached over and pressed her hand. "Be angry for a few days but don't get stuck, Amelia."

Easy for you to say.

And while it was true that the Sea Life Conservation Fund was a major contributor to her work, Amelia had relied on their Habitat Action Grants and those of Ocean Watch to support many of their dives throughout the world and her breeding of sea horses in the lab.

Diane motioned to stacks of material on the floor.

"You're so good with those kids in your Teen Summers by the Sea program. It's a serious position, Amelia," Diane said, shaking her head. "Hell, you could be my boss for Christ's sake." Diane looked around as if it were obvious to everyone including the squid eyeball just above her head.

She could have laughed. Then her stomach rumbled.

"Did you know the NSF thing was coming?" Amelia asked.

Diane smiled in a sad way and paused as if carefully choosing her words.

"Let's say, Alfred heard things," Diane said. "I'd kept hoping he'd heard wrong."

It made her stomach flip yet there'd been nothing Diane could have done. Nothing anyone could have done.

"Think about Minneapolis," Diane said and pushed the brochure toward Amelia. "Here." She then pulled it back, grabbed a pen and jotted down a number on a yellow Post-it Note and pressed it to the brochure cover.

"It's a great city. Met Alfred there." The woman smiled. Amelia felt her reading her reluctance.

"That's her number." The woman moved it farther toward her. " I mentioned you to her this morning," Diane said.

Amelia smiled. "Thanks."

"I know you," Diane said. "Before you say 'no,' hop on their Web site, give it a look," Diane said. "I told her you might call."

Amelia's chest burned. *Don't get stuck.* Maybe it was too late. She felt mired.

Diane tilted her head to catch Amelia's eye.

"There is life after this, Amelia, I promise you."

Diane came out from behind the desk, motioning for Amelia to stand up for a hug.

She stood and leaned in as Diane hugged her. Amelia rested her head on the woman's shoulder. Tears rolled out with no effort.

"Thanks, Di," she said into the fabric of Diane's sweater. "You're a good friend." She tried to imagine standing before a hiring committee after thirty years. Whatever would she wear? She had no understanding of clothing.

How she wished for the super powers of a cephalopod or octopus that through complete command of its central nervous system could change from purple to orange when afraid or stressed. If only she had the power to reconfigure the National Science Foundation's decision that had been meted out in black laser marks on the white skin of paper. But no one had those powers in topside life.

Yet maybe Diane was right.

Walking out to her Jeep in the parking lot, the cold air felt clean. Maybe this was the sharp knife needed to slice through the moorings that had kept her feeling bogged down for months, even years. In a strange way it was a relief.

Popping open the Jeep's back gate, she set her gear down and shut the door and then climbed in to start the engine.

"Come on." She pressed the gas pedal, racing it to warm up faster as her fingers felt the air vents.

Her breath formed an icy skin inside the windshield; evidence of Rhode Island's advancing autumn. The defroster was fighting a losing battle. Her breath frosted up the inside windows and she wiped it with the side of her hand, hearing Alex's words scolding her, *"Don't, Mom, you only make it worse."* *Ah yes, little Einstein.*

Resting her forehead on the steering wheel she imagined her father. She was a good ten years older now than he was when he'd died, yet she still thought of him as having been an old man.

While driving away from the Biomes she heard her mother's voice, *"Any job's better than no job."* Penelope's words churned in her stomach like a bad meal though she'd eaten nothing.

9

The next morning while sitting at his desk at GLIFWC's office in Bad River, TJ anguished while composing an e-mail before he lost the nerve. He'd erased to a blank screen several times. The first draft he'd explained what had happened during his childhood and that he had known about her but she not about him and then thought it creepy and deleted the whole thing.

The second version was much shorter but he lost his nerve before hitting the send key.

By the third time, his cell phone began ringing from one of the field biologists—a call that he needed to take, but such distraction had given him the strength to hit the send button without a second thought. He'd later sent a second with his personal phone number.

He'd waited a few days before telling Charlotte, but then after they'd gotten into bed one night, his arms slipping around her in the familiar way they had for more than thirty years, he'd said, "I did it."

She turned to him. The sheets made swishing noises.

"Really?"

She turned to face him, searching his eyes in the darkness. "Did you hear back?"

"She says she has no idea what I'm talking about."

"Of course not, call her."

"No."

"Why not?" Charlotte kissed his neck and slipped beside him in the space that was hers.

"I don't want to sound like some creep."

"But you are a creep," she said as he laughed. "But you're her brother too."

He pushed her back and looked at her as if she was nuts.

"Uh—at best I'm nobody to her."

"E-mail her again." Charlotte ignored the comment. "Maybe you didn't explain it well."

Of course he hadn't. Who just up and writes a letter like that after a lifetime to someone?

"TJ . . ."

He didn't answer. It was his characteristic "I'll think about it." Not a "no" but not a "yes" either. And while Amelia had blown him off, there was something exciting about returning the volley. The smart thing was to let the attorney contact her, but he'd wanted to. Yet the intensity of his desire to do so worried him. He'd hidden such eagerness from Charlotte, feeling in part that it was unnatural. Maybe nothing good would come of it and yet when flipping the situation to imagine what he'd have done, TJ knew he'd have jumped at the chance, jumped at being found, reached back to whomever was reaching toward him. But he wasn't her. He was desperate, maybe she wasn't. He hadn't a clue as to what Amelia's personal life had been like, which was why he'd hang up halfway through her recorded message before the beep. Pressing *69 to hide his number, hide his existence just as his father had kept him hidden until now. He was so keen on her knowing about him yet so chicken about taking the first step. Just like all those years ago when as a child he'd pretend and imagine that he knew her from the photos his father would bring. Sometimes setting one up on his desk and talking to it when Gloria was working the late shift at the hospital, and he missed his father, wishing he could reach through the printed images and have her know of him just as he knew of her. As a child walking to school, pretending she was walking beside him.

There were so many things he couldn't tell his wife, so many feelings, confusions, and compulsions that weighed so heavily.

As he turned back to hold her he felt Charlotte's eyes on him even though the room was dark.

10

A month had passed since Amelia was last underwater, the longest stretch of topside life since the weeks following Alex's birth.

It had also been a month since the closing of the lab and as Amelia came home from the grocery store she stepped up onto the stoop. Balancing the bag on her hip, she grabbed the mail and bit into the two letters, holding them as she fumbled for the house key in her purse.

"Where the hell?" She finally felt the outline of her key and fished it out of her purse.

She paused to look at the letters, a perfect mold of her bite impression in half-moon shape.

On top was a letter from the mortgage company. She gulped down a breath. *No.* A foreclosure notice after only one missed payment? The second payment bordered on being late though she'd spoken with a rep and pending approval they'd worked out a repayment schedule. *If you're losing money, then do it as slowly as possible.*

The other envelope bulged with folded papers, sporting a return address from Wisconsin and Ted Drakos Jr.

"Uck." She leaned over the stoop's railing where the garbage can stood and let go of the letter.

Then she closed her eyes and took several breaths to stave off hyperventilation.

"Maybe it's okay." Maybe just the repayment schedule they'd discussed.

Pushing open the front door, it yawned, her house smelled like coffee and leather.

What if it wasn't? The thought made her seize up. All the positive self-talk Jen practiced wasn't working.

Shit. They were coming for the Revolution House.

She staggered to the breakfast bar and set down the grocery bag and the mortgage company's letter. Stepping out of her clogs, Amelia ambled over to the couch and sat up straight on the edge of the cushion. How she wished Jen was home. Her friend had moved in earlier that week. Jen's pay from a part-time job in a doggie day care was not enough to make rent.

"I don't know what to do." Jen had called, explaining the situation in high-register sounds that Amelia identified with being close to tears. Her mobile phone was cut off; she'd missed two rent cycles, sounds of barking dogs in the background.

"For crying out loud, just move into Alex's bedroom," Amelia said, thinking of Jen's junky rusted-out Toyota that refused to start when the woman was running late, and burning through a cushion of overdraft protection just about the time she'd managed to pay it off. But Amelia wasn't much better. The barking set Amelia on end. She'd always been afraid of dogs since getting bitten as a child. Bryce and Jen found it amusing since she'd faced down many a shark and moray eel, but dogs made her nervous.

"Thank you, thank you." Jen began to cry.

"Aw, don't cry, Jen." It always made Amelia sad. "I'll have dinner ready. Nothing great," Amelia said. "Give you a key. I still have cable."

"Thanks."

"Everything's gonna be okay," Amelia said, though she was a fine one to talk.

"I don't know when I can pay."

"Oh stop it—your money's no good here," Amelia said as if talking to her son.

Massaging her scalp, Amelia tried to disperse the dull beginnings of a headache. Would her shoulders ever relax? Would she ever get a full night's sleep again or spend a full day awake?

No more bad news, things taken, people leaving. She flashed on Bryce's eyes as he'd opened the NSF envelope.

Grabbing her cheapie reading glasses from the coffee table, she mustered the courage to walk over and open the letter.

Money for October's house payment had been spent on re-locating pair-bonded sea horses to facilities throughout the country that had promised to keep the lifelong mates together. Tossing and turning for nights, Amelia had walked the floors like the ghost of Revolution House past. She'd never missed a house payment. And while there were nightly news reports of people walking away from homes, she promised the Revolution House, "This will not be your fate."

Perching the glasses on the end of her nose, Amelia eased down onto the bar stool. Thumb in the flap, she snagged it open and read. Ninety days to become current or the account would be transferred to a foreclosure agency.

Panic-stricken at the sight of those words, she thought of Diane, of Christmas shopping at the Mall of America. Maybe the job was still open. Earlier that month she'd mentioned Diane's tip about the job openings to both Jen and Bryce, who'd just stared back deadpan, like "Really."

Then, she looked around for her laptop.

"Where the hell is it?" her voice grinded out as she got up, spotting it by the fireplace.

Carrying it into the kitchen, she plugged it into the wall by the toaster and searched. Sea Life Minnesota came up in an instant.

"Now where'd I put . . ." She looked around at the paper clutter on the counter. Where was the brochure and phone number Diane had given her? Maybe she could fast-track her way into the place.

"Damn." Amelia riffled through receipts and letters from aquariums acknowledging the lab's "Gift" of the animals, cursing herself for not having put the Sea Life brochure in a safe place. She looked at her watch. Diane was out of town visiting her husband's mother.

You're on your own. Amelia turned back to the screen.

Sitting up straight, she focused on the Web page—blond child models oohing and ahhing as they ran through a ferny jungle trail walled in by fish tanks, turtles, and sea horses as tall as a man. It seemed there were more Sea Life Aquariums in Europe and in over thirty countries and only five in the U.S. She had no idea that such an extensive shopping mall–based network of aquariums existed. More than eight million visitors a year in the Minneapolis site alone, like having the entire population of New York City trickling through each year. In Sea Life's Minneapolis location they housed over ten thousand marine animals.

"A bad job's better than no job." Thanks, Penelope.

She clicked on their employment opportunities. The animal care curator and two associate positions were still listed.

"Oh, thank God, thank God." She bowed in relief. They had time. The deadline was the end of next week.

Minnesota: mosquitoes, freshwater-lake ecosystems, and Garrison Keillor. Too bad it wasn't closer.

Amelia skipped over the job description, nodding in furious agreement, anything to save the Revolution House.

"Whatever." She hit the *To Apply* link. "I can play Dolphin Girl," she muttered a quid pro quo.

After typing in her first name, Amelia read it over a few times. The spelling suddenly looked strange; cursor blinking at the end of the last letter.

She picked up her phone and texted Bryce and Jen, pasting

the link. "Filling out application for Sea Life Minnesota. All three jobs still open!!! DO IT." She hit send.

Leaning on her elbows, her mind raced as she thought ahead.

Rent the Revolution House, work in Minnesota until new grants came through. If Jen and Bryce came along maybe it would feel more like being on location for an extended period of time than being landlocked on the prairies. The Revolution House would rent in seconds being so close to campus. How crazy to move fourteen hundred miles to save it, but hell, she'd done crazier things.

Clarity arose out of a burst of energy fueled by terror. Enough to compose a personal statement, cover letter, look up references, and complete the online form. Amelia imagined herself like some aging Mary Tyler Moore in a snowy Minneapolis apartment.

"I can do this," she affirmed against her better judgment, looking around at the kitchen cabinets for support. Funny how cavalier it felt: just apply for a job, rent the house, and move to Minnesota like it was no big deal. And maybe it wasn't. Or maybe it was but would hit much later in the middle of a deep sleep in the form of bolting upright in a panic when after, as she and Bryce used to say, "The drugs wore off." Or maybe the job had already been filled, she was off the hook and could bemoan about "having tri-i-ied."

She hit the send key, the screen blackened.

"No!" she yelled. Had it gone through? The battery on her laptop had dislodged. One of the tabs to secure it was broken and when juggled in the slightest would dislodge. She'd repeatedly proofed her statement and cover letter, rooting out sounds of desperation. "Everyone's desperate," Bryce would say. "Some of us just hide it better."

She shoved the battery in and rebooted. Getting back onto their main Web site, again she hit the *To Apply* link. Nothing happened. She checked her e-mail, there was no confirmation of her application.

"Damn it," she yelled.

Slumping over in defeat, Amelia rested her head on the edge of the breakfast bar.

"Shit, shit, shit." She wanted to cry but couldn't. *Maybe it was a sign. Of what?*

Peeking over at the stove clock she counted down on her fingers—11 a.m. in Minneapolis. Saturday at the mall, people were working.

"Okay." She spotted the Web site's *For More Information Call* and dialed. A recording answered.

Then she dialed the number for *Party and Event Reservations,* thinking a live person might answer. *Everyone wants money.*

"Hello, Sea Life." A youngish woman's voice. "Planning a party? I'm Marissa. How may I help you?"

"Hi." Amelia explained the situation. "I'm having trouble getting the HR link to work—I think it lost my application." She began to explain but then stopped, realizing how crazy she sounded.

"Oh," the youngish woman chuckled. "Some of those positions are already filled maybe that's why."

Shit. "Do you know if the director and curator position is filled?" As the words sailed out Amelia knew she was asking the wrong person. But the mix of adrenaline, the beauty of the sun shining through the 230-year-old windowpanes of her house made her want that job more than anything.

"Let me put you on hold," the young woman said.

"But—" Michael Jackson's "Free Willy" was playing. Strange choice. Amelia closed her eyes and chewed on her knuckles.

"Hi." The person was back. "Sorry to keep you waiting. Try it again. Someone said the system's been down."

"Thanks," Amelia said, hoping that was the case and not her laptop shutting down before transmission. "If I it doesn't work can I call you back?"

"Sure." The young woman chuckled with no conviction. A child was crying in the background. "Well, good luck," the woman said. "You scared of the shark, honey? It can't bite you." Her voice trailed off as the call ended.

Going back to the *To Apply* link, Amelia clicked again. Her application came up under *saved.*

"Oh thank God, thank God." She hit the send key before her computer quit, pressing it down long after her application was gone.

A window popped up. *Thank you for your application. Someone will contact you shortly.*

Amelia then rested her head on her forearms to stop from shaking. It felt like the fatigue that came after she'd been swimming a reef for hours. More panic set in as she realized what she'd done and paced the creaky floorboards of the Revolution House, wandering like a disembodied spirit, waiting for Jen to come home.

Closing the lab had kept the three of them busy for weeks. She and Jen had ferried across to Long Island to deliver the rest of the sea horses to their new exhibit in the New York Aquarium that had been rebuilt after Hurricane Sandy. But busy as they were, Amelia fought blind panic as she avoided the issue of work, income, and what came next. She focused on "one foot in front of the other," like a scientist does when following step-by-step methodological research protocol for an experiment. This way of thinking had saved her years ago when she was nineteen and pregnant with Alex.

On the lab's final day, Amelia had felt like a cop being stripped of gun and badge as she'd surrendered all of their plastic university key cards and ID badges at the security office. She'd watched as the clerk checked off each card on the computer screen, for Bryce, for Jen. They'd been parts of each other's bodies for years, her cards still warm from having just been on the cord around her neck.

Walking down the hallway in the marine biology building

toward the exit, Amelia wanted to run just as much as she'd wanted to walk as slowly as possible. Though it was no longer her place, it would always be. Eleven a.m. and she had no idea what to do. Too early to go home and go to bed, too late to start a new life, what on earth would make the hours pass?

She'd touched her phone with the impulse to call but Jen was at the doggie daycare job and Bryce was attending his grandfather's funeral.

Just outside of the building Amelia stood dazed as the rush of changing classes engulfed her. Students whizzed by, backpacks grazed her; others glanced and then rushed off.

The fountain had just been winterized and covered with an aluminum shell for the season. Swollen charcoal clouds hung low over the bay. Sugar maples and birches had begun littering gold and yellow leaves.

A set of surrounding benches were empty. They'd been there as long as Amelia yet never once had she taken the time to sit by the fountain.

Touching the edge of a bench, she sat down.

Dried-up brown fall leaves blew in circles as birds chased each other, carried by the wind currents that moved like dust devils between the buildings.

Inertia kept her there until a damp wind off Narragansett Bay made her stand. She crossed her arms and headed toward where she'd parked the Jeep.

They'd always likened themselves to being the Three Little Pigs. Bryce was born into the house of brick and mortar, Jen into that of mud and straw, and Amelia into that of sticks. Each had lived at the mercy of "I'll huff and I'll puff and blow your house down" with Bryce having gotten the better advantage of the three deals.

Jen had grown up in the South Boston projects as well as intermittently in motel rooms that her mother would rent. Unlike Amelia, Jen's early home life had been unstable, sometimes being in foster care when her mother would get picked up for soliciting. But like Amelia, school was the one constant. Jen would often joke about having spent more time in the grade-school nurse's office than anywhere else. The school nurse would sneak in peanut butter and jelly sandwiches since Jen's mother had been out all night, forgetting to leave Jen lunch money.

Being smart had landed Jen a National Merit Scholarship. Graduate fellowships had taken her through and into Amelia's lab. The three of them had forged bonds like family for the ten years that Jen had worked there.

For Bryce, after a brief eighteen-month drug-themed stint after boarding school, that included following the Grateful Dead around after high school (just to shock his prominent Rhode Island financier father who drank scotch while sailing high-end racing boats for fun), Bryce had gotten serious. He'd breezed through his academic career and then emerged from graduate school as one of the more promising marine biologists. He and Amelia had met working in a lab at Cornell before stepping out to start their own gig at the University of Rhode Island, where they'd become co-investigators.

Money for Bryce was not a fungible concept. He lived like he had none, spent nothing on himself, gave much of it away to marine/environmental causes, and let the rest pile up. She and Jen would tease him about wearing the same running shoes for years at a time with the same exact hole in the fabric positioned right over his left big toe. The soles were worn so thin they'd speculate as to how much pressure it would take for a spiny sea urchin to puncture the rubber. Much of the food in his house was long past expiration dates, and he'd eat leftovers that both Amelia and Jen swore would kill the average man. Bryce's apartment was graduate-school threadbare except for his giant saltwater aquariums that spanned the entire living area except for the small space that housed his drive-in movie–sized plasma TV. On several occasions the brightness of the aquarium lights had prompted night visits from the Providence police popping in to "check that it hadn't turned into a decoy for an urban marijuana farm."

Jen had called down the stairs in what she thought was a Fargo accent, "Betcha a night with a hotty lumberjack it might be fun, Am." She'd just submitted her applicaton to Sea Life late that night after doggie daycare.

"Betcha a pint of mint chocolate chip ice cream they don't talk like that," Amelia yelled back up.

"Oooh." Jen had come running down the stairs and pulled open the freezer. "Do you really have some?"

It was Sunday morning and Amelia was well into her second cup of coffee; Jen was passed out upstairs in Alex's old bedroom when the phone rang. She'd been debating whether it was too chilly to sit out on the patio and then looked at her phone.

Minnesota number.

"Hello?" she answered before the first ring was over.

"Dr. Amelia Drakos?"

"Yes." Her answer was short and clipped.

"Kyle Sanborne, here. HR manager, Sea Life Minnesota." His voice had that ex-college-jock-cum-marketing-major quality to it, more like a sports announcer.

"Hope I'm not disturbing your Sunday morning—"

"Please." Her laugh was tense. "Disturb away."

He chuckled back.

"Just received your application for aquarium curator and . . ." He said it like a greeting. "It's been brought to our attention that

you've worked with us over the past several years with summer funding through our Sea Life Conservation Foundation."

"Yes, that's correct."

"And it looks like you're funded for this summer in the
Andamans as well."

"Unless you tell me otherwise," she said, immediately sorry
she'd said it. Too dark, Jen would say.

"Well, congratulations!" He sounded like one of those calls
about winning a free Caribbean cruise. "You've been selected
for the first round of phone interviews for director and senior
animal-care curator."

"Thank you."

"First of all, are you still available?"

Amelia stifled a laugh. *Oh, brother, am I.* "Yes, I am."

"Awesome," Kyle said. "We're scheduling phone interviews
starting tomorrow and want to work you in ASAP."

"Uh—how many applicants?" She stepped out onto the
patio and brushed orange leaves off the chair, wrapping her
cardigan around her like an Ace bandage. The ground was a
jigsaw of red and yellow maple leaves, their edges crinkled with
frost. The sun's strength was fading.

"Eight in the pool." The man chuckled as if expecting her to
laugh. "Bad pun, sorry."

She was too tense to laugh and wondered who. Most people
in the field knew each other or at least knew of each other. Asking would be the height of unprofessional etiquette.

"Tomorrow, Monday, kicks off the first round."

"Okay."

"Mind if I put you on hold?"

"Of course not."

More of "Free Willy" as she waited. She hoped he wasn't
changing his mind. The three of them had discussed the possibility of only one or two of them getting chosen.

Maple leaves made scratching noises on the redbrick patio
as they tumbled in a wind gust off Narragansett Bay.

Her life felt as loosely knit as the weave of her house sweater. The elbows blew out first before the rest of it disintegrated after a season or two of constant wear. Looking like a vagrant came effortlessly. No wonder Myles had bailed. His new girl-friend was probably more polished, more sophisticated. The hand-printed kimono and lingerie Amelia had bought in a flurry of excited hope were now stuffed into the bottom dresser drawer. She'd only lounged in them when Myles stayed over, pretending she wore such beautiful things all the time. They'd still smelled of him. She'd neither the heart to wash them or go the St. Vinny's drop-box route.

Clouds from the bay shifted into the layered steel-colored shapes of fall. Canada geese honked as they flew in V forma-tions from the bay right over her house.

She moved her feet up onto the rungs of the wrought-iron table as she listened to Sea Life's announcements of upcoming exhibits.

A yellow leaf sailed back and forth in the air current before drifting down to land on her thigh. With her finger she traced the veins throughout its leathery skin. Picking it up to exam-ine the stem where it had detached from the woody branch—still supple, moist. Years ago she'd explained to Alex from this very spot how declining sunlight and cooler temperatures had caused leaves to change color. The five-year-old had been amazed as she'd explained how the red, yellow, and orange col-ors were present in leaves all summer long but were masked by green chlorophyll. Once the fall sun began to fade and the chlorophyll receded, only then were the hidden colors of autumn revealed. The boy had looked up, scouring the sur-rounding oaks, maples, and birches for telltale signs of color. He'd believed this was their secret knowledge that only the two of them shared.

"Sorry about the wait," Kyle said as he picked up after the long hold. "We're having Web site problems—having trouble accessing the scheduling. You know what they say—when the technology works it's great."

She nodded again, thinking he sounded Alex's age.

"Interviews for the position begin tomorrow through Wednesday," he said. "Is there one day that's better?"

"Um . . ." Get it over with. "Why not tomorrow?"

"You okay with that?" he asked.

Do it before you chicken out.

"Yes."

"Okay . . . tomorrow at ten a.m., eleven a.m. your time."

"That's fine."

"You'll be the first," he said. She heard him hesitate.

Just get it over with.

"I'm e-mailing you a PDF about the aquarium, its policies, plus a map." Then he began reading what sounded like a script. "Successful candidates will be invited to Minnesota for a final round of interviews where they will be given a full tour of the facilities. Final interviews begin the last week of October."

"You mean next week?" She hard swallowed a gulp of coffee.

"We need someone in place November tenth, before Thanksgiving."

Holy shit. Two weeks away. "I see."

"Is that a problem?"

Everything was a problem. "Oh no," she said with too much enthusiasm, examining the bubbling paint on the back clapboards of the house.

"Awesome," he said. "Got a question for ya."

"Okay."

"Without violating confidentiality . . ." He paused. "I've got an applicant for one of the associate's positions who's listed the same contact number—"

"Oh, no problem, I'll get her."

"Uh—okay." He seemed flustered.

Amelia set down the phone and bolted inside, bounding up

two stairs at a time to Alex's old bedroom. Barging through the bedroom door, she jumped on the bed like it was a seventh-grade slumber party.

Jen jumped up, startled, her eyes glassy. "What? What?" she yelled, looking around, her eyes not focused.

"Get up," Amelia yelled. "Sea Life's on the phone. You're getting an interview."

Bryce's phone was ringing after Jen had scheduled an interview. Amelia walked back outside and brushed more leaves off her thigh just as he answered.

"You owe me," he answered. They'd made a bet as to who would get called first.

"Uh—not so fast, buster," she said. "What time?"

"Just now," he said.

"Jen beat you. Was a doubleheader at the Rev House since she listed my number."

"That's sorta cheating, Am." He acted incensed.

"There were no conditions placed." Amelia leaned both elbows on the iron table. She started laughing and couldn't stop.

"God, I hate when you do this," he said, which made her laugh even harder. "Amelia?"

"Sorry," she said, wiping her eyes. "It's just funny. The whole thing is funny."

Sounds of running water and Bryce clanking dishes were in the background.

"When's your interview?"

"Friday," he said.

"Ah ha," Amelia said. "Mine's on Monday, Jen's is on Thursday. Still got you beat."

He was quiet for a few moments. "Well, I'm bringing the whole aquarium, Amelia," he said. "Coral, sea horses, everything. Nothing gets left behind." He sounded vaguely hurt, not quite defensive, like a little boy insisting that he bring all his toys.

"Whoa, whoa, cowboy, slow down," Amelia's voice softened. He was upset. "No one's got a job yet," she reasoned, curious by his sudden emotion. It was the first time since the NSF denial that she'd heard Bryce so upset.

11

She knocked on the passenger side window to get the cab-driver's attention at the Minneapolis airport.

The man looked up from his phone and rolled down the window. Amelia waited for him to speak.

"You on duty?"

His long gray/blond hair was matted past his shoulders. Amelia hadn't seen muttonchop sideburns and a Fu Manchu mustache like that since 1970.

He said nothing.

"Is the mall far?"

"Nope." He turned back to scrolling through phone messages.

"Uhh . . . think I could get a ride?" She suggested, half laughing as she held both sides of her unbuttoned coat together. Armed with a new dressy wool coat and interview suit, Amelia was already uncomfortable in clothes that felt like somebody else's, begging for a new life from people she didn't know in a place she'd never been.

"Metro's faster," the driver said without committing. "Cheaper too."

"Appreciate the advice but I'm running late for a job interview."

She couldn't recall ever asking permission for a cab ride anywhere in the world, from Bangkok to New York. The mall's Web site had mentioned "easy access from the light rail," but she didn't want to waste more time, since a bird strike in a connecting flight from Philadelphia had caused her to be running late.

Her two-inch heels sank into snow like augers.

The driver made a face. "It'll run ya forty-five; cash up front."

"Done." Amelia fished out enough cash from her wallet; her eyebrows rose in sync with the cash. The warmth of an impish smile spread through her cheekbones. It surprised her how light she felt.

The taxi doors clicked to unlock. The driver didn't budge as Amelia struggled with her bag.

As she opened the back door her toe slipped on a patch of ice and she tumbled faceup onto the backseat, her purse and roller bag banging between her legs like an eager lover attempting to mount. It set her off into a slap-happy laugh that she struggled to squelch.

Amelia fought to sit up as the driver peeled away from the curb.

She pulled off the coat and blazer, flapping her elbows. The back of the beautiful ivory silk blouse she'd selected with so much care was plastered to her sweaty back. The lace collar and embroidered appliqué reminded her of some of the more delicate coral reefs she'd seen in parts of the South China Sea. Though the hair clip still held the bulk of her hair in a French knot, it felt looser than earlier in Providence.

In less than ten minutes the Mall of America's red, white, and blue sign was visible. They queued up in a long line of cars, trolling toward the building.

She looked at her diver's watch. Twenty minutes until the interview. Unbuckling the band, she tucked the watch into her purse like Jen had advised—too clunky with the outfit.

"Is there some kind of special event going on?" she asked.

"Other than the holidays?" He snickered in a way that made her feel foolish.

"Which way's Human Resources?"

The driver motioned over the mall to the other side.

"You're kidding."

His white-blue eyes in the rearview mirror said he wasn't.

"Think I could walk faster?"

He shrugged.

"Think I'll get out now." She handed a tip through the space and slipped both arms through the sleeves of her blazer and coat.

Everything was covered with snow. Earlier, as the aircraft had passed Lake Michigan, Amelia noted fields and treetops looking as though they'd been dusted with a powder puff.

The cold air made her gasp. Her ankles and feet shriveled in the thin stockings that now felt baggy. The new "interview" pumps felt large and sloppy.

The roller bag immediately flipped over.

Entering the mall, she tried to imagine where the HR office might be. Often when searching for a reef, she'd close her eyes and imagine, gliding through the water only to open her eyes and find it right in front of her. It was a trick she'd learned from her father that she told no one lest they think she was a kook.

Pulling out the folded map and directions from Kyle, she tried to make sense of it. Crowds of families scooted past; some looked somewhat annoyed at her being in the way. She dialed Kyle and left a message about running late.

The momentum of the crowd sucked her inside and spit her out like an undertow. Groups of teenagers sped past, like schools of blue jack fish syncopated with knifelike precision to dart this way and that to avoid bumping into her roller bag. She hurried past battalions of strollers the size of grocery carts.

Looking up, she counted four levels of stores and restaurants. The ground courtyard was jammed with roller coasters, rides with swinging arms, and families with crying children holding balloons. The ceiling was glass, supported by steel girders. It was a living, breathing centipede, writhing and undulating. Sunlight streamed in to brighten gardens of pink, red, and white flowers.

"Excuse me?" she asked a woman pushing a stroller. "Do you know where Nordstrom is?" Which was the landmark Kyle had given her. *"Take the escalator to the fourth floor by Nordstrom."* The woman shrugged.

A roller coaster zoomed by close enough that Amelia felt the breeze on her cheek. A full-sized Ferris wheel began turning. The swinging metal arms of a ride with a sign reading SHELL SHOCK began swooping just above people's heads. Riders were strapped to seats, shrieking. Amelia was the only one who flinched as she raced past stunned, bewildered-looking parents. She'd wanting nothing more than to sit and gather her wits but there wasn't time.

Passing twin towers of SpongeBob and Dora the Explorer that reached the ceiling, she looked for a security guard, an employee, someone to ask directions.

Lines of children wound back and forth, like airport security lines at Boston's Logan Airport. "Huh, look, Dora," some little kid gushed. The voice was so sweet she smiled, reminding her of Alex at that age.

Full-sized fir trees were interspersed in the courtyard and crowds filled the available floor space. The merry-go-round, the din of voices, and noise made her head swim.

Spotting a mall security guard, she made a beeline, cutting through a crowd of people waiting on line for pizza.

"Excuse me," she called. "Am I going the right way for Human Resources?"

"Which HR?" he asked.

"Shit." She could have cried. "There's more than one?"

He nodded. "Facilities? Janitorial? Management."

She held up the folded paper.

"My interview's in a few minutes." Her voice was getting louder. "Please help me?"

"You want Nordstrom."

"I know," Amelia said. "Can you show me?"

"I can't leave my post." The guard scanned the area as if it was a test or some sort of entrapment.

She surprised herself by choking up. "Look, I walk fast, I swear. No one'll know you're gone."

He glanced around, conflicted, and then waved for her to follow.

"Thank you, thank you," she called after him, keeping sight of his tall-drink-of-water frame slicing through the crowds, crisp white shirt and black security cop–looking hat with the gold-braided trim.

At one point she lost sight of him but then spotted the Nordstrom sign. He then pointed to an elevator and even pushed the up button for her. "Fourth floor, turn to the right," he said and then hurried off.

"Thank you," she called after him, out of breath. She'd tip off Jen and Bryce.

Elevator doors opened to the executive suite. Dark and quiet, it was another world. Her ears still hummed with noise. The walls were paneled in cherry wood. A tufted leather couch looked more impressive than comfortable. Glass tables with arcs of yellow orchids flanked it. She touched one just to see if it was real. Celtic harp music played above. The moment Amelia sat down, the door of a conference room opened and a woman stepped out with hair as white as her skin.

"Amelia?" The woman's voice was almost a whisper as if she didn't want to awaken anyone.

"Yes." She stood.

"Hi, I'm Grace." The woman extended her hand. "We spoke in the phone interview. Nice to meet you in person."

"Yes, you too." Her hands felt airport grimy but she reached to shake anyway. "Sorry I'm late."

"Almost everyone is."

Amelia's mouth was dry and sticky, her hairline damp, and the French knot had half fallen, tugging a bit with each step. It wasn't clear if the clip would hold through the presentation but it was too late to redo it. She guessed her eye makeup had either rubbed off or else was smeared beneath her eyes.

"Would you like to take a few minutes to prepare?"

"I'm fine." She just wanted to get it over with. Afraid that if she paused for even a moment to fix her hair or check her eye makeup in the ladies' room she'd lose the nerve.

She quickly unzipped the front pocket of her suitcase and grabbed notes along with the flash drive for her presentation.

The woman turned and walked toward the double doors, indicating she should follow.

People sat making notes as she walked in. All eight looked up at once. A few smiled. All stood and reached to shake hands across the table.

Sweat had dampened the armpits of her new blouse. She left the blazer on.

A sudden pang hit after plugging in the thumb drive—waiting for her presentation to load. She could have cried right there, but nevertheless turned to smile at the table of judges.

12

❧

TJ decided to call after a few weeks of not hearing back from Amelia after mailing the transfer of property documents as well as a cover letter he'd composed, explaining the circumstances of their family.

He'd e-mailed again, inquiring if she'd received the documents but it had bounced back. TJ checked and the address had been correct.

"Huh." He was puzzled.

"Call her lab," Charlotte suggested. This time the number automatically switched to the marine biology department, instructing to call back during regular hours.

TJ hung up the phone and looked at Charlotte.

"Maybe it's after hours," he said and looked at the clock. Something felt wrong. It was 6 p.m. Rhode Island time. But he'd called before on Sundays, Saturdays, late at night, early morning and Amelia's voice mail had always picked up.

His stomach lurched. He touched his lip with his hand as he sat thinking. What if something had happened and he couldn't find her?

"You'll find her, Niinimooshe," Charlotte said, reading him as she always did.

He felt despondent and blinked back tears. Tears surprised him. There were several calls to return—reports of wolf hunters planning to poach on the more remote reservation lands.

For as long as he'd been following Amelia, the phone number had been the same. He looked out the office window. It had begun snowing. He turned to search the online Whitepages but found a Providence address but no phone number. The Sea Horse Laboratory Web page was still up but the phone number had been deleted.

It was a restless sleep that night. Between Amelia and the opening of hunting season on wolves about to begin Thanksgiving weekend, he'd thrashed about, trying to rid his mind of these worries.

After giving up on sleep, TJ kissed Charlotte and got up. All of their five dogs stood from their beds and shook off hours of sleep, following him into the kitchen.

"Hey, Penny." He petted the fifteen-year-old who was still excited to see him every morning. The others were mostly strays or pups no one had wanted. The dogs stood at the counter waiting to be fed.

He looked at the clock.

"We're two hours early." He smiled. They all listened to him, sitting like good dogs, their tails wagging on the kitchen floor like windshield wipers, dispersing dog fur and other debris of the house.

"What the hell." He opened the cabinet, taking out all their bowls. He began to fix a bowl for each, containing the various concoctions of foods, pills, and whatnot that each required.

"Okay now," he said. "Places." At the word, they all scattered to their designated spots that were distributed in the kitchen and breakfast nook and then turned and stood, waiting and watching as he placed down a bowl for each, beginning with the oldest first.

Then TJ sat down at the kitchen table trying not to clock watch, though he knew it was three more hours before the marine biology department's office hours in Rhode Island. He considered calling and leaving a message, but decided against it. What if they didn't check messages or it took a day for someone to call back?

He glanced over the reports of invasive species such as fireweed on the L'Coutere Reservation area; the surge in manoomin that year where the harvest of wild rice had reached record proportions. He glanced at the kitchen clock.

He kept reading the same sentences and not making sense of them.

After the dogs had finished and drank their fair share of water, he then walked over to the coatrack, grabbed his down parka, and slipped on his boots.

"You guys ready?" He opened the front door quietly as the dogs rushed out, their tags jingling as they raced each other to the trail that skirted along the lake. TJ slipped out and shut the door behind him gently, as if not wanting to wake a baby. He first smelled the wind. It was an easterly wind. A chill from the cloud base made him turn.

"Huh." Wind from that direction always brought a storm, though he'd just checked the radar moments before. He tucked his watch into the inside pocket of his coat and followed the dogs.

It was an inky kind of darkness, so black he almost couldn't see the trail had it not been for the stars. They served as guiding landmarks, shadowing the outline of the cliff's edge into the huge negative space that was Lake Superior. The place his people had been directed to more than a thousand years ago by a holy man who'd instructed them to leave the Place of the Large Salt Waters, or the Waabanakiing, and follow a trail of the miigis shells and to stop at the place where food grows on water. Gloria had chosen the lake or the Stopping Place over his father. His father had chosen the Waabanakiing, along with other things. He'd wondered about choosing place over person, which it seemed that both of his parents had done.

Nervousness fueled his pace. Walking faster than usual his

breath frosted up his glasses in the chilly November predawn, though even Penny, the old one, kept up with him. Hands in pockets, his thoughts meandered.

He fought the urge to pull out his watch but did it anyway and pressed the light button. Only fifteen minutes had passed. TJ could have sworn it was at least forty-five and looked forward to the sunrise that would break in a few hours.

Rhode Island was one hour ahead. He'd walk toward the Pow Wow grounds, go past a ways, and then turn around and come back. That would eat up an hour or so.

He whistled. "This way, guys," he signaled and veered onto the other trail. The dogs paused and then turned, excited at the break with their normal routine; the younger ones sped up to pass him.

"I'm sorry but Dr. Drakos is no longer here."

He glanced at Charlotte as she sat beside him, her hands quietly clasped together, still in the sweatpants and T-shirt that she slept in.

"Really. Since when?" TJ hadn't expected that.

"Ooh . . ." The secretary seemed to be thinking. "A little over a month ago."

"What happened to her lab?"

"The operation closed down."

He didn't know what to say.

"Do you know where she went?"

"With whom am I speaking?" the woman asked.

"I'm a wildlife biologist and would like to speak with Dr. Drakos," he said.

"Are you a prospective employer?" the secretary asked. The woman sounded nervous and he bet it was about breaking protocol.

He didn't say no. He'd thought to say "family" but then family would know that she'd left.

"Do you have a contact number?" he said without answering her question.

"In that case, yes." The woman's voice relaxed. "She'll be happy to hear from you. You can reach her at Sea Life in Minneapolis. I don't have a forwarding address as of yet—"

"Sea Life?" he said. "Mall of America, Sea Life?"

Charlotte made a funny face and then clapped her hands together.

"We're in Providence, Rhode Island, sir," the woman said. "So I'm not familiar with Minnesota—I just know she's moved to Minneapolis."

"Would you happen to have a number?"

"I can't give out her personal number, but I have a general number for Sea Life information."

"That'll do, thank you."

TJ wrote down the number and sat mesmerized. She was only three and a half hours away by car.

"In Minneapolis?" Charlotte asked.

He nodded, not sure what to make of it.

"At the mall?" she asked, filling the teapot under the faucet to make another pot of coffee. "The place we took the boys all those years ago?"

He nodded and looked back at the number he'd scratched down on the side of some of his papers.

"You've got that conference down there next week," Charlotte said.

He nodded and slowly looked up at her.

13

It had been September of Amelia's sophomore year in college, months shy of the one-year anniversary of her parents' death, when she met Christopher Ryan. Amelia had been selected for participation in the Semester by the Sea program, usually reserved for seniors.

Ryan, a visiting professor of marine biology from California, was prematurely gray, wore rumpled clothing, sported a reckless attitude along with a beat-up Jeep with a canvas roof and no doors. His skin was deeply tanned from being outside, didn't give a shit about convention, and had quickly become everybody's favorite. Amelia's command of marine biology came under his notice and she was asked to become one of his ad hoc helpers.

After the first two weeks he and Christina Kingsley, the other professor, invited her along with them after class to Nathan's for hot dogs. The three of them had sat at the counter as Amelia listened in awe about their dives and explorations of deep ocean trenches where volcanic activity had prompted the growth of strange wormlike creatures living near the heat vents deep in the ocean floor.

"You know, Amelia," Kingsley began. She and Ryan could have been siblings. No makeup, hair pulled straight back into a ponytail, tiny button earrings, windburned face with no regard to appearance. "Stick with your studies and you'll be doing work like this."

Chris Ryan nodded as he tipped back a Heineken.

A week later at the end of the day, Professor Ryan asked if Amelia could stay behind to help with docking the boats and preparing slides for tomorrow's lab class.

Amelia lit up. She worked alongside the grad students and Dr. Ryan as they pulled in the rest of the booms and buoys and shored up the equipment until the next day.

He started walking to his Jeep, keys jingling as he stopped.

"You gonna go eat?" he asked.

She looked at her watch and shrugged. "Nah, looks like I missed dinner again."

"Well how 'bout dinner at Nathan's again? My treat for helping." He placed both hands on his chest and bowed in apology.

"Professor Kingsley coming too?"

He took a few steps, craned his neck to look toward the parking lot. "Car's gone; looks like you're stuck with me."

Amelia looked at the empty space.

"That is, if you can stand me." He'd said it in such a disparaging way that she felt at ease.

She hoped there would be enough to talk about and felt odd at being singled out. The man had a shiny gold wedding ring that made her feel safe and she chided herself for being skittish. After all, he was old enough to be her father.

She looked around to possibly drag someone else along but the other students were gone.

"I'm fine," she lied, chalking up her reticence to the fear of long silences with a professor.

During the twenty-minute drive, conversation was easy and they'd chatted about one of the boat engines that kept conking out. Laughing about how fifteen of them had been stranded in the sound until one of the grad students came out in a Zodiac to help restart the engine.

Amelia rattled around in the Jeep since it didn't have seat belts, a canvas top, or doors, so she held on to the dashboard as they hit bumps to keep from being thrown. The vehicle looked like it belonged somewhere out in the field. Huge tires, racks welded in places that held all sorts of marine tubing and equipment.

They sat at the counter, each picked up a menu.

"Order whatever you want, it's on me."

"Wow, thanks." She ordered franks and fries.

"No fish sticks for you tonight, young lady." He looked over the top of his menu and smiled. "Bring me a Heineken," he said to the waitress. "Getting enough time to get your work done or are you fighting off boyfriends right and left?"

"Right," she snickered. "A few students go out to the Hamptons afterward, but most of us stay behind and catch up."

"So I take it you're serious, not one of these girls who wants to grow up to be a dolphin trainer at SeaWorld."

His eyes narrowed. It surprised her. He'd been so encouraging to students no matter how many mistakes they made; she wondered if it was all just an act.

"I don't see anything wrong with being that if a person wants to," she said.

He smiled with closed lips at her comment, looking amused and pissed off at the same time.

"I-I want to do work like you and Dr. Kingsley, be a professor somewhere." She felt foolish as she took a sip of the Coke that the waitress had just set down along with the food.

"Boy, I bet your folks are darn proud of you." He turned on the stool to study her, finishing off his Heineken and motioned to the waitress to bring another.

"Uhh." She looked down at her hands. "My parents died last year." Everyone in the program knew. Dr. Kingsley had known.

They'd even briefly discussed the idea of putting off the Semester by the Sea until next fall if she wasn't feeling up to it just yet. The one-year anniversary of their death was coming up. At the time Amelia had insisted on going ahead with it, since this is what helped her feel better.

"Oh . . . I'm so sorry."

She stopped eating and withdrew her hands, placing them in her lap.

"I didn't know." He covered her hand with his. It was warm. He reached for the other and held them both. She didn't pull away.

"Excuse me." She pulled away and hurried to the ladies' room, embarrassed at crying. Confused at how much she liked the feel of his hand. Why did he want to know about her parents? She was doing well in the program; it wasn't interfering with her progress or work.

She soaked bunches of toilet paper under the cold water and pressed it against her eyes, holding it there a few moments to cool them. Then she looked at herself in the mirror and redid her ponytail, brushing back some stray hairs that kept falling in her face.

Walking back to the booth, she sat down. He'd stopped eating after she'd left.

"I'm really sorry, Amelia, I didn't mean to upset you," he said.

Her hands were in her lap. She then tucked each one under a thigh to warm her fingers.

"Please eat." He pushed the plate toward her in a way that felt fatherly.

She shook her head. "Thanks but I'm kinda full."

"Dessert then?"

She shook her head.

"They've got those great ice cream sundaes here," he offered to lighten the moment, cajoling her to smile but she didn't.

It was an awkward silence as they waited for the check.

. . .

As she climbed into the Jeep he reached across the gear shift to hug her.

"I'm so, so, sorry," he said.

Her body was rigid until he touched the top of her hair with his hand.

"I miss them so much." She relaxed. His skin smelled of dried saltwater and sun.

"It's okay." He sighed deeply as he started to rock.

They sat there, rocking, with him cradling her until she calmed enough for him to kiss her on the lips and then he nuzzled into the crook of her neck as he kissed her.

He'd dropped her back at the dorm two hours late. The front door was locked so she had to ring the bell for the RA to come let her in.

Amelia bounded up the one flight to her floor, holding her sides as she jogged down the hall to her room. The odd fluttering in her chest mixed with shame made her feel sick.

"Hi." Her roommate for the summer sat on the floor with two other students. "Wanna play hearts? We need a fourth person, Amelia."

"I thought you said she always wins," one of the other students muttered.

"No, thanks," Amelia said. She hid her eyes, not wanting to make eye contact. "I don't feel good; think I'll shower and crash."

"You okay?" the roommate asked.

"Getting a cold."

"Ooh, summer colds are the worst." Her roommate collected all the cards, the bowl of popcorn, and stood. "Let's go down to the lobby, maybe we can find a fourth person there."

"Hope you feel better," they all chimed in.

She didn't answer as she grabbed her towel and hurried down the hallway toward the showers, hoping they were empty. She quickened her pace as she neared the doors. It seemed the only safe place on land. She then stood under the scalding water, face toward the spigot, wondering what she'd done.

Over the next six weeks, for the duration of the Semester by the Sea, they met several more times. Dinner, then make-out session in his car; sex couldn't come too soon as her breasts ached to be touched and her hips arched to take in the sweet dampness of it all. Then during the day when taking water samples he'd act like he barely knew her. And while Amelia was relieved that no one could tell, it hurt that he could be so aloof. She'd lie in bed confused, longing yet ashamed. It hurt to look at him with such desire on the boat as they waited to collect samples. Amelia's face would blush scarlet knowing where his fingers had probed only hours earlier while he demonstrated how to preserve sea grass samples. Grateful she was at the back of the group instead of the front where she'd usually stood. Withdrawing, she folded her arms and averted her eyes, avoiding making contact with any of the students.

But she was hooked on Chris Ryan. She'd clasp his back and feel about to burst. In his car, he'd reach over to kiss her and she'd kiss back. The fluttering in her chest became almost unbearable and before she knew it they'd made love in his summer cottage that had been closed for the season.

"I'm assuming you're safe," he whispered into her hair as she clutched his chest with her legs.

"Safe?"

"On the pill."

"Oh."

The expression on his face changed. He pulled out so abruptly it hurt and he sat up on the edge of the bed, his feet on the floor.

"Oh yes, yes, of course I am," she lied. Immediately feeling flushed. It was their second time and she'd figured he'd know what to do.

"Maybe this is not such a good idea after all," he said, as he bent over, reaching for his clothes.

"What are you saying?" She felt panicky, trying to soften her voice. "Come back." She reached out her arms.

He looked at her and paused. She could feel whatever resolve he'd mustered, dissolve.

"My God, you're so beautiful," he said.

Kneeling down on the bed, encircling him in her arms, in seconds he was deep inside. She felt him about to explode.

By the last week in November the Semester by the Sea was winding down. The program ended two weeks earlier than the regular semester and students usually took that time to finalize papers, research projects in the lab.

They all hugged good-bye, they'd become as close as a tribe, except for Amelia who'd stood apart from her classmates in a way she'd never done. Silent, sullen, and off to the side. And while everyone knew it was coming up to the one-year anniversary of her parents' death, they'd said nothing. But it came on the eve of her second missed period.

14

🦢

"Dr. Drakos! I *thought* I knew you," the intern exclaimed as Amelia was being introduced during her first day on the job.

Amelia bristled at the young woman's tone. Her scalp tightened. Vaguely familiar, Amelia couldn't quite put her finger on it, although Juney came to mind.

It was the first day of work at Sea Life. Amelia, Jen, and Bryce were each being given separate tours by the staff.

"It's me, Meagan Hanson." The intern extended her hand to shake, all smiles.

"Amelia Drakos." She reached back.

"I kn-o-ow," the young woman said, nodding in a way reminiscent of Eddie Haskell in *Leave It to Beaver.* "A year ago this past summer? I was on that dive in the Solomon Islands? University of New Hampshire's program?"

Bits of vague recollection surfaced and Amelia recalled a controversy surrounding this intern.

"Two weeks ago I recognized you. And I saw Bryce and Jen later that week during the job interviews." It unnerved her that the intern had presumed first-name informality with Bryce and Jen.

"You mean Drs. Youngs and Hartley," she added.

She noticed as Meagan glanced at the seven other interns as they nodded in unison, seemingly under her power.

She was terrible at remembering people and even worse at

navigating the spats and cliques that often formed between dive interns on the months-long summer projects. But there'd been something about this young woman that she recalled had ended badly. It made her wonder why Meagan wasn't hiding in a broom closet rather than offering herself up in such a glad-handing way.

Amelia's answer to what she'd called the "stupid bullshit" of personal pettiness was to put them all to work. "Suit up, dive portside," she'd instruct. "And don't come back unless someone's hurt, low on air, or you find the first sea horse—whichever comes first," much like during her Teen Summers by the Sea.

Jen was better at catching squabbles and dissolving coalitions before they'd form. "We're all working together," she'd say. "It's like boot camp. Lose your identity as an individual and become one with the dive team. The person you least like may be the one who saves your life. We're only as strong as our weakest link, and that may be you!"

On the other hand, Bryce was more heavy-handed. He'd turn; hold up his thumb and index finger like a handgun. "You—shut the fuck up." If he was feeling charitable, "Knock it off." But his ultimate threat was "Do it again and your ass'll be on the next Malaysian fishing vessel that crosses our path." Bryce could be a legendary bastard and everyone knew it. His size alone held authority, combined with a booming voice and reputation as a world-class diver, which elicited crushes from many of their female summer interns. The combination quashed all pettiness. One look from Bryce and it was over.

"I'm interning here both semesters!" Meagan covered her mouth with her hands and did a little excited skip.

Amelia stopped herself from making a face that she knew would be taken the wrong or, actually, the right way.

"Good to see you again, Meagan." She extended her hand to shake and could have gagged at the phoniness in her own voice but didn't want to get off to a bad start. Her eyes darted about for Bryce or Jen to save her, make some funny crack to put them all at ease given the irony of the moment. But she'd seen them moving along faster on the orientation and they'd already entered the off-exhibit area behind the double metal doors.

"God, she was chief marine biologist on that project," Meagan gushed to her gaggle of interns. "She gave the most *amazing* talks on the restoration of sea horses." With that they began scrutinizing Amelia and looking her over, searching for what was so special.

The adulation made Amelia uneasy, it sounded more mocking than sincere, reminding her of one particular wise-ass girl in her Teen Summers by the Sea program.

At almost a foot shorter, Amelia's hair was pulled straight back into a ponytail, wearing the same regulation Sea Life aqua-colored polo shirt as the interns. She had a son older than all of them, had wrestled an adult black-tipped shark into submission, and if needs be could out-swim every one of them.

"Looking forward to working with *all* of you." Amelia swallowed hard and stepped to shake hands with all seven to underscore that she was their boss, not Meagan. Most looked sincere and ready to work, others already beaten, and one or two along for the ride.

"Well," Amelia said. "Gotta move along on the orientation." She pointed toward the double metal doors and felt them watching as she moved on.

She quickly spotted Bryce and Jen leaning on the black laboratory benches as they listened to a man in "dressy casual" giving a talk.

Amelia joined them and leaned over to Jen, whispering.

"Do you remember a Meagan Hanson?" she asked, her thumb like a hitchhiker's motioning to the door.

"Holy mother of God," Jen turned and covered her face with a hand, muffling a whisper. "The one that had a mouth on her like an exit wound."

"That'd be her."

"She's the one who tried to cozy up in Bryce's lap and told

everyone they were sleeping together. Christ—he'll go apeshit."
Jen's blue eyes widened with amusement.

Their whispering prompted a cold stare from Bryce as the
fund-raising director (who'd funded their summer dives to the
Pacific and Indian Oceans) was giving detailed background information on the organization's funding structure and the
new habitat campaigns they were getting ready to announce.

Meagan was yesterday's news. At the time Amelia and Jen had
dragged Bryce into the galley after sending all the dive interns
off to explore the reefs surrounding a World War II shipwreck
not far from where they were anchored.

Jen had cornered him by the sink.

"Okay, did you fuck her or not?"

"No," Bryce said. He looked to Amelia for help but she gave
him none.

They'd stared at him long enough to make him angry.

"God damn it. Nothing worse than being accused of sleeping with someone you didn't." He'd fumed and stormed off
down to the specimen laboratory.

Jen raised her eyebrow and looked at Amelia.

"He's telling the truth."

Jen nodded.

Later that afternoon Jen had taken the young woman apart,
"South Boston style." Not only did she get Meagan to confess
to making up the story, but to clear the air Jen required that the
young woman stand up at dinner and apologize to the entire
crew and to Bryce for fabricating such a lie. And if she'd refused,
Jen had arranged for her to be sent packing on a Zodiac toward
the harbor.

After the donor's presentation, Bryce walked up smiling until
he saw their faces.

"What?"

"You tell him." Amelia stood with her arms folded.

"No, you."

"Tell me what?" He began to chuckle, anticipating something funny.

"Meagan Hanson," Amelia said.

The smile left his face and he walked away.

Jen turned to her. "Does she seem sufficiently humbled?"

Amelia crossed her arms and looked hard at her. A sinking feeling nagged at her. "You'll have to see for yourself."

The three of them had driven westward from Rhode Island like some historic New England wagon train. None of them had ever "crossed the plains" as Bryce had put it, always waxing poetic on the new and mundane. The night before leaving Amelia couldn't sleep. It was 2 a.m., they were leaving at six. She'd called Bryce.

He'd answered on the second ring.

"What's up?"

She could hear him turning over in bed.

"Kinda freaked."

"Not surprising."

A long silence enveloped them.

"It's going to be okay, Am.

"A bit like dressing up mutton to taste like lamb."

"It'll be fine. We'll make it fine."

"You always say this." She rubbed her forehead and then ran her fingers through her scalp.

" 'Cause it always is," Bryce insisted. "We'll all be together. Remember what you said?"

"No." She chuckled and then blew her nose, not remembering a word. "I'm sure it was pure bullshit."

" You said it was a time-out, a safe place where we can work to get new grants," he said. "Keep faith in our work, Am, in our science. Jen and I are. Something will come of it. Besides, it'll be fun. Hell, where else can you ride a fucking roller coaster on your lunch break?"

"Or a Ferris wheel."

"There you go, that's my girl."

She breathed. They made each other laugh at everything; even the terribly bad things became funny around Jen and Bryce.

"Thanks, Bry."

"Feeling better?"

"No."

"Well, go to sleep anyway." He yawned. "Jen's gonna be knocking in a few hours. Gotta pick up the U-Haul."

Early, before they left, Bryce had stood with her in the living room of the Revolution House before meeting up with Jen. Two carloads to Goodwill in the intervening weeks had thinned out the house for the renters. For the first time she'd heard the echo of footsteps.

"How you doing?" he asked.

She'd turned to him. "Shitty." Walking toward the front door, she opened it. The door made the same yawning sound it always had.

"Anything I can do?" Bryce had asked in a voice that sounded more like he was trying to determine why the live feed on a dive camera of an ROV wasn't working than offering comfort.

She looked at him and then smiled and nodded.

"You're already doing it, Bry."

The Revolution House was safe for now. Odd that she'd had to walk away to keep it. Give it away to get it. *Blah, blah, blah,* she thought—all that New Age Buddhist shit people spouted.

"Bye for now," she'd said to the horsehair-and-plaster walls.

Amelia had sat in the driveway a few moments longer after Bryce had left for the U-Haul place. Keys in the ignition, head hanging, afraid the uprooted feeling of shock might never leave along with the corresponding anguish of a heart that was divided not to mention scattered in several places. Hard to believe she wouldn't be home that night but another family would be. Setting their things around the fireplace mantel, her kitchen counters. She might never be home again and she thought of Alex. Maybe she should have taken him up on his offer to come help with the drive out to Minnesota. But he'd had plans to spend Thanksgiving with his new girlfriend's family in California. He'd been nervous and excited for months; she hadn't wanted him to cancel.

The reality of letting Alex go had snuck up on her the day she'd driven him to the dorm at Cornell his freshman year. Until Christmas break she'd slept under a down comforter on top of his twin bed with his familiar scent. She'd then straightened up the sheets and covers so as not to look as pathetic as she felt.

And from that time on she fought her instincts in order to safeguard his independence, suddenly knowing why dolphins, whales, and most marine mammals live in family pods for life. Leaving was unnatural, against the grain of not just their biology but all that was sacred to them. Death was the only separation and even that might set off a grieving process that lasted for decades if not a lifetime. Had those human instincts become nonexistent or had we stifled them? She'd squelched hers the day she'd helped Alex carry his things up to the dorm's second floor. "Leading their own lives" is what people said of their offspring. Can't get attached to a house, a town, or a set of friends. "Gotta go where the opportunity is, where the career lands them," instead of staying near home in some dead-end job, some dead-end life, sacrificing to be near loved ones, yet what did that really mean? Some researchers in the lab had lost their children to Europe, Australia, Thailand; she'd lost hers to Vancouver—at least it was in the same hemisphere.

Heading out of Providence that day opened memories of other leavings and losses. Like being eighteen again, that phone call from the U.S. embassy, or leaving Stony Brook after the charming Chris Ryan. A few times she'd called his office but hung up as soon as he'd answered. In a gutsy move after finding out she was pregnant, she'd driven to his house using her late parents' car and parked down the street, watching as a car pulled into his driveway. Presumably his wife climbed out, carrying grocery bags toward the door. The front door swung open and a blond daughter much taller though not much younger than Amelia came running out to help unload groceries. Amelia watched with the type of shock that wises you up and makes some things as clear as a bell yet so many others not clear at all. She sometimes wondered what their lives would have been like had Alex known his father.

Amelia remembered thinking it was good that her parents had died. They hadn't lived to see what a mess she'd made of her life, what a disappointment she'd become.

As she'd sat driving to Minnesota, it now seemed like a harsh judgment to pronounce on herself at nineteen. And Lord knows, she'd spent the better part of her life atoning for if not trying to prove it wrong. Memories dogged her, bumpety bumping along as if someone had tied rusted cans to the chassis of her Jeep. The Place of No Comfort—clattering and clunking against the asphalt as reminders that sorrow had pulled up a chair again; demanding to be heard until, for some reason, crossing into Ohio. Maybe it *was* possible to run away from yourself if you crossed enough state lines.

The job at Sea Life would be different. No lab to run off to at 3 a.m. when she'd thought of something or needed to run away from something else. But now there'd be no open seas in which to dive and extinguish her soul's burn.

Like Jen had once said, science is easy, life is hard. To enter a stream of focus to the exclusion of all else was heaven's reward for scientists. Once the overdrive of concentration kicked in nothing could penetrate, not memories, nor the question of what it would be like to love without doubt. Work had helped tamp down the unraveling corners before they'd land her in the Place of No Comfort.

That first night they'd piled into a Red Roof Inn on the outskirts of Cleveland, all of them collapsing dead asleep within moments of settling in with bags of microwave popcorn from the vending machine.

But then Amelia bolted up awake as adrenaline blasted through her like someone had fired off a shotgun. She struggled to modulate her breathing to calm down.

"Hey." Jen looked over from the other side of the bed. "You okay?"

"Think I'm gonna take a walk, maybe get some fresh air."

"Want me to come?"

"I'll be okay," she said. But it was 3 a.m.; a tangle of interstate highways bordered the hotel on both sides and the rushing of cars and trucks offered no relief. She went back inside and walked down the hall toward the vending machine and studied the offerings. Nothing looked good except for Good 'N Plenty, her favorite, and that selection was sold out. She sighed and went back to the room, lying awake until it was time to leave.

Climbing into the Jeep for the last day's drive to Minneapolis, she felt excited, the kind that happens when one makes a new best friend. She followed behind Jen's rickety Toyota Corolla, leapfrogging through traffic, calling each other on their phones, since Amelia had added Jen to her phone plan, reminiscing about stupid things that had happened, captains that Jen had slept with, including one who was a polygamist and wanted to take her back to the Sudan to be his third wife, as they wove between interstate truckers when things got boring.

Bryce followed with his van loaded with all the aquarium

gear, buckets carrying sea horses, anemones, and coral along with other aquatic plants and oxygenation machines pumping in air through hoses so that all of it would stay alive until they reached the "Gopher" state. Stopping frequently at the interstate waysides across Wisconsin, they checked on the marine life and made adjustments to the buckets. So far there'd been no casualties as the three of them stood discussing each animal as they feasted on vending machine Kit Kats and tiny bags of chips.

Sight unseen they'd rented a two-bedroom apartment online just a short bus ride from the mall. They'd spent years sleeping berth to berth in close quarters on research vessels, not to mention 24/7 summer dives where they'd often slept burrowed together on boat docks on several continents. They'd worked through having nothing to say, along with the embarrassment of unseemly body smells and noises.

Jen and Amelia would share a room; Bryce would pay more for having his own. There was enough living room floor space for him to set up his fifteen-hundred-pound saltwater aquarium and they prayed the floor joists were sound enough so as not to be awakened by the sound of it crashing through to the apartment below. The aquarium filled the living room and they had to scoot sideways to get near the couch to watch TV.

While the apartment listing described it as "convenient to Minneapolis/Twin Cities airports," it was really code for being on a flight path. The walls rattled and conversation was silenced in regular intervals to wait for jetliners to pass.

The apartment's only saving grace was the fireplace. Each would come home exhausted after a twelve-hour shift. Amelia came home first, since she was the early bird and had volunteered to get the 5 a.m. shift. She'd hit the fireplace ignition and then collapse in her down coat onto Bryce's couch, too tired to crack open the prepared salad she'd brought home. Dozing off, the sound of keys in the lock and then Bryce's footsteps were comforting. She'd hear him uncapping a beer bottle.

"You gonna eat this?" Bryce asked. It was after 11 p.m., the crush sound of his down jacket as he'd plop down in the opposite chair, her unopened salad in his lap, his clothes smelling of singed french fry fat.

"It's yours," she'd say into the throw pillow. "There's a new bottle of ranch on the counter too."

"Already got it." He'd said as she heard the peeling off of the plastic wrap around the top.

"Jen home yet?"

"Went out with some musician/mall guy she just met," he said.

"What's a musician/mall guy?"

The roar of a jetliner shook the walls and he paused. "Uch— this place is such a shit hole."

Likewise, the three of them shared a cramped office at Sea Life, not much larger than the lab space they'd had in Rhode Island, only now Amelia was their supervisor. A manager she was not, so they'd work as they always had back in Rhode Island, as partners. The first three weeks were spent mostly underwater, getting to know the marine animals, assess their health, behavior, and overall habitat.

Amelia noted how the staff glanced at watches to mark time, clocking each other's breaks. Elements of it felt more like an after-school job.

During the first week they'd gotten lost in the main floor of the mall together during a lunch break, coming back late and joking about it with the staff. Amelia kept getting lost during lunchtime, a few times calling Jen's phone for directions back.

"Jesus, Mary, Joseph. Amelia, twice this week." Jen's muffled voice, Amelia could hear she was busy.

"Sorry, Jen." Amelia turned in circles, disoriented as she held the phone to her ear. "But it all looks the same." She'd walked around a good ten minutes with no sense of direction.

She'd heard Jen's exasperation. "You navigate the world's waterways but can't handle a fucking shopping mall."

"Alright—I said I'm sorry." She whirled around, half laughing as she looked for landmarks.

"Okay," Jen said. "Look for SpongeBob."

She spun around until she spotted him.

"Got him."

"Okay," Jen continued. "Turn left like I've explained before." Amelia could hear the studied patience in Jen's voice as an intern was asking questions. "Walk past the *Death Star*, back past Build-A-Bear, and you'll see the orange-and-blue Sea Life sign and the down escalators."

"Sure you guys didn't move all this crap around just to mess with me?" she joked but Jen had already hung up.

Lunch breaks had become too anxiety-provoking so instead Amelia brought sandwiches from the corner store near the apartment and tucked them behind tissue samples in the laboratory's specimen refrigerator.

Sea Life's hallways and ceilings were clear Plexiglas and circumnavigated the entire exhibit, the Ocean Tunnel. Visitors were surrounded by marine life in what appeared to be seamless divisions of salt water and freshwater tanks. People paused to watch stingrays, green moray eels, horseshoe crabs, and puffer fish. Others pulled out phones to capture images of sand and tiger sharks, sea turtles, sawfish, a restless arapaima, an alligator gar, and an antediluvian sturgeon.

The aquarium offered overnight birthday parties as well as special underwater "experiences" to hand-feed fish. Amelia, Bryce, or Jen were required to supervise these parties with two interns at a time, teaching children to snorkel in groups of twelve at a time. Plus there were "Package Experiences" that the franchise would tailor to any group. Overnight sleepover parties, wedding receptions, and experiential learning for elderly adults were promoted aggressively.

Over the first few weeks Amelia took groups of younger children snorkeling in the freshwater tanks with some of the sturgeon, stingrays, and alligator gar, taking older children with scuba experience into the saltwater marine tanks. This was the more enjoyable part of the job so far, reminding her of the many years she'd spent running the Teen Summers by the Sea for the Department of Corrections of Rhode Island.

Twenty-two years ago during her first grant renewal cycle, Amelia had created her Teen Summers by the Sea program as a type of community outreach and science boot camp for adjudicated youth, funded through a blend of Rhode Island's Department of Juvenile Corrections and a section of the NSF grant earmarked for "Community Awareness."

It had taken a summer before Amelia had figured out how to play them. On day one, she'd wade through installments of "fuck you" and "I hate this shit," until someone broke down to ask the first question: "How come the north shore beaches are so rocky when the south shore is as smooth as powder?"

This prompted a hush—everyone listened while pretending not to—that would not be cool.

Amelia then would explain how "the Late Wisconsin glacier had stopped and melted mid-island, ten thousand years ago, dumping enough rock and debris from as far away as the Arctic Circle to fill up the entire New York State several times over."

"Wow. Man. That's just fucked up." One of them shook his head as others concurred.

"At its thickest point the glacier had carried thirty-three hundred feet of packed ice and debris," Amelia had gone on to explain. "Almost three Empire State Buildings' tall."

No one spoke. She could hear their minds clicking away as

they stacked one Empire State Building on top of another and another.

"But why? What made it melt?" another asked without the slightest trace of irony.

Amelia glanced down to hide her smile. She had them and she knew it.

She explained what makes a rock a rock, why seashells only wash ashore in halves, what causes ocean waves, and how the moon's cycles temporarily elongate the earth's crust with high and low tides.

"Holy shit, that's too fucked up." Someone else squealed, others were silent as their imaginations pictured the earth's travail—torn between an indifferent silver moon and its own molten core. Their adolescent faces, some sprouting crops of whiskers like itinerant weeds, were rapt with the first burn of curiosity.

She'd taught them to swim and snorkel as undergrads with lifeguard certification. They'd look through their face masks, eyes stripped away to baby innocence in the water's silence, asking her permission with a slight tilt of a head if they could lay a finger on the fleshy skin of a starfish, or the shell of a sleepy, half-buried horseshoe crab. She'd wanted to shelter them, take them back to the singularity of her lab in Rhode Island rather than return to families who so often were the authors of their strife. But life doesn't work that way. No one's safe for long. And last year's state budget cuts as well as the end of the NSF grant had spelled the end of the Teen Summers by the Sea.

By comparison, the kids at Sea Life were tame. With most of them having grown up landlocked, with the exception of lakes, the underwater forays were uneventful. Most were scared to death they'd drown if they didn't follow her instructions carefully and Amelia did little to dissuade that type of thinking. She appreciated that level of cautiousness—especially as it was making for easy crowd control.

. . .

The day after Thanksgiving was open season. Holiday shoppers flooded into the mall in record numbers since Chanukah
and Christmas coincided that year. Lines at Sea Life's front admission counter would snake all the way to the bottom step of
the escalator. Even the interns were working twelve-hour shifts,
after Bryce had said during a staff meeting, "All hands on deck,
nobody ask for time off, the answer's 'no' already," to which
some laughed, others gave him a dirty look. But customers
began lining up with young children by 7:30 a.m., an hour before the doors opened.

College students (mostly with an interest in marine biology)
staffed the front entrance, clamping wrist bands as customers
coughed up the $20-per-person entrance fee. A crowd-control
strategy for incoming visitors was to get families to pay another
$10 for family photos, grouping together in front of backdrops
of their favorite fish.

Amelia arrived by 5 a.m. along with Meagan and a second
intern (she'd become Amelia's charge since Jen and Bryce
would have nothing to do with, in their words, the feckless
intern), the three of them carrying a change of fresh T-shirts
and caps for the day's shift. Normally it was a job for just one
intern, but as Jen had pointed out about Meagan, "Bet ya a
hunj that if we could buy her for what she's worth as an intern
and then sell her for what she think's she's worth we'd make a
killing."

Amelia swiped her card to enter the treatment rooms. Suit-
ing up alongside Meagan and the other intern, every day they
dove the tanks before the aquarium opened, searching for
animals that didn't look right, were sick, injured, or deceased.
Amelia called it "Death Patrol."

"Don't want to have some little kid spot a sick or dead animal
first thing in the morning," Amelia said in a cheery voice, under-
playing how early and how cold the tanks were. "Sort of casts

a pall on the day." Any such animals were removed or cordoned off into the off-exhibit area for further examination, or to perform a necropsy to find out cause of death and test for other more menacing conditions.

"Come on, ladies, chop, chop," Amelia said as she climbed the ladder up to the saltwater tank. "Time's a-wasting." And as she looked back, catching their grim faces, it was all she could do not to laugh.

15

It was the first week of December when Amelia went to check on a juvenile sea turtle that had been laying on the bottom of the saltwater tank. Bryce had told her that it had been listless.

Amelia suited up in scuba gear, sealed her face mask, and slipped on her fins. The official policy was to check on animals either before or after hours but she was more concerned about the turtle than the rules. The display staff watched as she geared up.

"Bet ya a latte the thing's dead in the water," Meagan said. Her eyes ignited seeing Bryce climb up onto the deck to help.

Amelia eyed her.

"Interns don't get to bet, Meagan," Amelia said.

"I thought they liked it on the bottom," the intern said as Bryce brushed past her. Meagan had this crotchety way of swallowing her words into back-throat vocal-fry noises. Amelia noted several of the others had begun to sound just like her.

Amelia climbed down the ladder and slipped underwater.

Visitors gathered in the Ocean Tunnel to watch her glide toward the turtle and she smiled and waved, grumbling to herself. The turtle offered no resistance where ordinarily a healthy one would have swam away. She tucked his bony body under her arm and glided toward the ladder where Bryce was waiting on deck with another staffer to help haul the turtle out to be examined.

Amelia then circled around the rest of the tank, studying the movements and demeanor of stingrays and other saltwater species, checking for signs of lethargy.

Later she entered the examination room, her feet squishing on the cement floor as she squatted to watch the sea turtle as it lay still in the holding tank.

"So what do you think?" she asked.

Bryce stood with his hands on hips watching it. "Well." He turned. "He's still alive." It wasn't encouraging. She'd seen this before in the Biomes with one of their turtles when there'd been a problem with the oxygen levels. Sea turtles were particularly sensitive.

"Could be failure to thrive," Bryce said. "He is quite young."

"Wonder where he came from."

He shrugged. "Haven't the foggiest." Bryce flipped the turtle over as if looking for a manufacturing label. "That's the problem. We still know so little about any of these guys." Bryce turned the turtle back over and set him in the shallow water.

In the lab in Rhode Island as well as in the Biomes and surrounding aquariums, she and Bryce knew everything about the filtration systems; they'd torn the system apart multiple times, rebuilt some of it, and knew where all the marine animals came from. Here it was anyone's guess. And while the water quality was tested several times a day, they were told not to monkey with the equipment because they had a crew from the University of Minnesota contracted for maintenance.

Amelia stayed after her shift was over and by late afternoon the turtle had skipped the last two feedings. Closing the door to the holding area, she walked down the corridor to the Ocean Tunnel, pulling on her bottom lip, worried. She leaned against the Plexiglas wall, observing the two other turtles.

A sudden disturbance in the Ocean Tunnel startled her. Loud voices, a crowd of kids were laughing and chasing each other. Reflexively, Amelia darted and grabbed an elbow to pull out one of the boys.

"Whoa." As she pulled him aside, the others stopped. "What's going on?" she demanded before seeing a volunteer guide clapping to encourage the commotion.

"It's after-school fun," the guide said but stopped laughing once she saw Amelia's expression.

"Really," Amelia said. "Why don't you stop by my office after the tour and we'll talk."

The group stopped and huddled together with somber faces as they watched the showdown between Amelia and the guide.

The woman turned her face away and didn't answer, instead motioning for the group to follow. A few of the children slowly backed away from Amelia, one turned to glare at her like *"meanie."*

She believed aquariums were meant to be quiet, introspective places full of wonder where people took in marine life and not venues for playing tag or climbing on benches and squawking like they were on jungle gyms.

There was a memo on her chair early the next morning, asking that she meet the management team upstairs by 11 a.m. It was the same office where she'd had her initial interview. As she entered the conference room, the furniture had been changed. Three managers sat in armchairs in a U formation, close together like an alliance, with one empty one facing them that she presumed was meant for her.

"Have a seat, Amelia, please," offered Grace, the head of HR. "Can I get you anything? Fizzy water, coffee?"

"No, thanks." *Just get it over with.*

"We've had a few reports from parents as well as from one

of our staff volunteers who, by the way, is the wife of one of our platinum donors, as to how you're handling conflict," the woman said and folded her hands.

She thought to the incident. The guide hadn't come to her office for a discussion.

"You mean complaints?"

"More like areas for improvement."

The three of them looked on gravely. Her surge of anger was surprising.

"It's important that we stay in the good graces of our visitors," the woman went on to explain. Grace's manicured nails and sparkly rings shone as she gestured with a pen toward a paper file with handwritten notes sitting in her lap. Her power skirt hiked as she crossed her legs and smiled at Amelia. "Children are our wealth," the woman said, lowering her voice and shaking her head as if Amelia knew nothing about raising children. "Everyone's here to have fun as they learn. It's our mission."

"I have some safety concerns," Amelia said, feeling her anger flare. She tried to tamp it down. "About supervision. About running through exhibits. Our classes are not daycare."

"They're just children," the woman said in a soothing voice, nodding slowly as she explained. "It's up to you to redirect. Maybe they're bored. Maybe you need to think about how to engage them better."

The three managers focused on her.

She had the feeling they were about to get to the point.

"A few parents complained about your new curriculum— they said it's like sitting through a university lecture, not a children's program."

Another manager spoke up. "Court the parents; encourage them to donate and remember. . . ." The man paused, smiling in a measured way as if about to drop a gem of wisdom. "Once you have a child's interest, you have that child."

All three managers nodded in agreement and sentenced her

to watching an online series about conflict resolution and reading a book called *Getting to Yes* as a requirement of further employment and placed her on probation.

"Perhaps in your work situations in the past," Grace had gone on, "with crew and colleagues things were different, and you all had a certain work rhythm. Here we're meeting with the public."

Apparently they'd believed she was unschooled in the protocol of how to ask "nicely" and HR sought to "expand her repertoire of appropriate responses in hypothetical situations," just shy of requiring she take a class where she'd have to role-play a series of scenarios with other employees. She'd quit before that.

She was used to working with professionals who took instruction, direction without getting hurt feelings. Likewise she couldn't ever remember feeling wounded because someone hadn't said "please" when ordering her belowdecks to check if a bilge pump was working. Now she'd been put on notice to second-guess and think twice before asking anyone to do anything.

Amelia hurried down four flights of stairs to the main floor, racing past the Ferris wheel, the SpongeBob tower, and toward the down escalators and Sea Life. Narragansett Bay was in her mind's eye, the feel of the sun on her skin and the salty residue of the water on her shoulders. The ocean skies of many moods, the sound of water lapping against stones. Why had she come here? She missed her juvies and how she'd taught them to love the sea. They'd made no pretense about who they were, what they'd done to land in her custody for the summer but would fall in love with the underwater world, for some of them on the very beaches where they'd gotten busted.

Maybe this whole thing was a mistake; maybe she'd panicked and should have waited it out for a different job. She'd dragged Bryce and Jen into it, encouraged them to dissolve their lives, the dutiful friends that they were. That much she hoped they still were.

16

It was standard practice for the Sea Life staff to pull nine water samples a day to test for water quality in all the various tanks—pH and oxygen levels, bacteria. Amelia was just finishing a special tour for Sea Life's top brass who were visiting from California when one of them asked to see how the water was maintained.

She used her security badge to open the heavy metal door. The entire room was humming.

"Here's our filtration system." She propped open the door. "It's for salt and fresh water and consists of sand filters, ozone, and protein skimmers, it fills the entire room, closed off to the public."

She looked around as people studied the pipes, some snapped photos with their phones.

"Daily maintenance consists of backwashing the tank water by removing particles normally found in marine waters so it can look completely clear for the public. People like to see fish swimming in a glass of water as clean as if it was from the kitchen tap."

The visitors chuckled at her analogy.

"Natural freshwater and seawater bodies are never clear," she went on to explain. "But in public aquariums if the water is cloudy people think it's dirty. So the system filters out many of the naturally occurring nutrients that in fact are beneficial to the marine life."

"Does it hurt the sea creatures?" an older man asked.

Amelia thought for a moment before answering. These donors directly funded their summer dive in the Andamans.

"Ah." Amelia smiled at him. "Great question." The man folded his arms and nodded once, pleased at being complimented. "It doesn't directly hurt them because we add special nutrients that don't cloud the water in order to make up for the absence of what nature adds in the wild in perfect balance."

An hour later in the off-exhibit area, Amelia had been trying to coax a shark to eat when she heard someone enter the secure area. Standing on the platform above the tank with a pair of long tongs in her hand, she made clicking noises with a device to cue the shark to eat.

"Now don't fall in there."

She turned to look. The lighting was dim.

Heat passed her through as she missed a breath, seeing the outline of his form against the open door.

"Myles?"

He bowed slightly. "I am he," he said in a voice that joked but didn't mock. His face was shadowed.

"What are you doing here?" Krill was smeared in her hair and under her fingernails.

"Attending a conference in St. Paul. Heard you'd moved here, thought I'd drop by."

A crush of emotion silenced her.

"You didn't call first because . . ."

"I did."

True. Her personal phone was in her office.

"Your voice mail picked up."

She stood on the platform, reluctant to move. The Sea Life

cell phone was clipped to her dive belt, she'd been waiting for a call from her friend in the New York Aquarium about the shark. There were crates of juveniles that had just arrived from a Sea Life in Kansas City that needed to be examined and acclimated before being added to the exhibit.

"Who let you in?"

"Bryce."

Damn him.

"Just a moment," Amelia said.

She stepped down from the platform in her wet suit as Myles approached.

As they sized each other up, Myles had the unfair advantage as she stood there in the form-fitting neoprene wet suit; he in a long woolen coat, sweater, and trousers. She'd never known a man to change clothes so many times in a given day and have more outfits than any woman she'd known.

"You look good."

She said nothing back.

"Heard what happened in Rhode Island," he said. "It's great you picked up something so quickly."

She still said nothing.

"Hey." He paused. "Thought maybe we could have dinner."

She didn't answer.

"I feel badly about how we left things."

"We?"

"Okay, me," he said.

She was silent.

"Is this not a good time?" He gestured in a joking way, looking around the empty rooms.

There was no good time.

"How about tonight. Dinner?" Myles asked. His voice was as seamless as ever.

She didn't know what to say.

"I'm staying in the Grand Hotel." She remembered their first dinner together in Providence. As he'd unfolded and smoothed the cloth dinner napkin across his lap, she'd felt like a condemned woman, seeing as he was from a much better family than she was.

"Gorgeous place," he said in a polished way. "Have you been?"

Of course she hadn't.

"They have a wonderful world-class chef there," he said. Her stomach tightened, remembering how all his inflections bordered on affectations.

"Great." Her voice was flat. She looked at her hands. Grime under her fingernails, reminding her of her father's and how he'd sometimes come home from work after working a double shift with printer's ink embedded into the calluses of his hands, making them look like swirling designs.

One side of her watchband was split in half. She ached with what she hoped to be one of her last cycles of menstrual cramps.

"Maybe tomorrow you can give our group a tour of Sea Life," he said as if giving instructions to someone working in a car wash on how to better wipe the dashboard.

And maybe you could just go fuck yourself too.

"Dinner then?"

She hesitated, ticking down the possibilities.

"Okay."

"So tell me where you live so I can—"

"I'll meet you in the hotel lobby at eight thirty."

"I'd love to come pick you up." His voice was as polished and lilting as ever. She remembered how his hands were so smooth, manicured fingernails, the dark hair that grew along the topsides always so neatly trimmed, pressed dress shirts from the cleaners, his gold watch. She also remembered how sheltered he'd made her feel. As if he'd unbuttoned his long cashmere topcoat and wrapped her in it, blanketing and protecting her from the outside world. She'd never felt like that before but remembered how good it felt.

Acid from lunchtime's turkey sandwich crept up into her esophagus.

"I'll see you later," Myles said and took two steps back, then turned and left.

"Fucking Bryce," she swore under her breath.

She waited, listening for the sound of Myles's shoes clicking down the long cement hallway and out the corridor, waiting for the thud of the door to ensure he was gone.

Setting down the shark tongs, she stormed toward the laboratory where she'd find Bryce. Sliding her security card, she pushed open the door and spotted him hunched over a shallow tank where newly arrived starfish were under observation for a type of sea star wasting syndrome that was devastating populations all along the northwest coast. He'd been making slides and running tests to determine if this group was infected before releasing them into any of Sea Life's other exhibits.

Bryce looked more frightened than startled as the door flew open and in she stepped. She leaned against the black lab bench. Folding her arms, she glared at him.

"Let's go somewhere and talk."

He looked up from the microscope.

"Shall we?" She could tell he knew he was in trouble.

"Sure," he said slowly.

She smiled and waved to the other techs working at the lab benches. A few looked up.

"Just a sec," he said as she watched him transfer a specimen to a slide for examination. Her chest tightened.

He stopped focusing through the microscope lenses and turned, looking at her through his safety goggles.

Amelia thumbed like a hitchhiker.

"In our office," she said and left, marching down the hall as her feet squeaked, still wet with water from the tank.

Bryce stepped in. Amelia closed the door and leaned against it.

"How could you do that to me?" She raised her voice.

"I didn't *do* anything to you—"

"Letting Myles in like that without asking, asshole."

He looked at her for a moment and then dropped down into his chair, crossed his leg, ankle on knee, and leaned his chin on his hand.

"You're right," he said. "I apologize."

She was taken aback, not expecting him to concede so quickly, furious at the concession.

"Imagine what that felt like." She raised her voice as her hand hit the counter, shouting to make him feel it, though he already seemed contrite.

"I'm sorry."

"But why? Why would you do such a mean thing?"

He only shrugged and shook his head as if it was all a mystery in which he'd found absolution.

"Sometimes I just don't *get* you."

She flung open the door and left, her damp feet squishing along as she headed toward the women's locker room to change.

Something about Bryce bothered her. He'd never done anything like that before. Maybe he was angry for letting her talk him into moving to Minnesota. And for that matter, maybe Jen was too.

She had nothing to wear.

Pushing open the mall's exit doors, the freshness of arctic air made her eyes tear as she headed toward the bus stop. The sun was low, the sky a sluggish orange and gray since the days were some of the shortest of the year. She hurried along the sidewalk around to the bus stop, lamenting how reciprocity in love was such a tough thing to find. She'd dragged half-conscious men through enough quasi-relationships to know better. But the reverse was no better either—trying to fall in love with a man who began talking about finding a larger house together after only a few dates. She'd awaken each morning, hopeful that some cosmic love switch had flipped on so that she could say "I love you" and mean it, but instead their hands felt more like chemical irritants on her skin. And for six years she'd given up, taken herself out of the game until meeting Myles. And maybe it was precisely that state of deprivation that had made her an easy mark for such a polished man.

Hustling toward the bus stop, she spotted the long line. People stood motionless, thumbing through messages on their phones. Amelia slowed with relief, taking her place at the back of the line and burrowed behind the taller bodies for warmth. Each in their own thoughts, phones, although she was starting to recognize people on the same shifts.

Fast-food workers, store clerks, some uniforms barely concealed beneath coats—layers of plastic IDs and security cards dangled round their necks in glassine holders, some from rhinestone cords. The air felt good after the suffocating warmth of the mall's microclimate. Unzipping her coat, Amelia held on to both sides and fanned it.

Overly made-up salesclerks teetered on heels. Some had downgraded to sneakers, which looked odd given their lace-patterned hose and skirts. Eye makeup had melted into splotches beneath their eyes after standing nine hours greeting customers.

From walking around the mall, Amelia could spot some of the same women flagging down customers in Nordstrom, offering makeovers or cotton balls soaked in fragrance. If only they gave do-overs—nothing that the right product couldn't cure except for maybe low wages and no social supports. Here and there stray clumps of finely dyed hair indicated that their coiffures were giving out too.

She noticed the furrowed brows and clenched faces of the young "Mallers," as Bryce called them all, and it brought her back to when she'd discovered she was pregnant.

. . .

At the time Amelia had been three and a half months along, just after finals during winter break when she'd worked up the gumption to tell the dean she was quitting school. Amelia had sat on a chair in the reception area, waiting.

"Welcome, Amelia." Dean Williams had stepped out of her office after the last appointment. "Please." She'd graciously ushered Amelia into the office. "Have a seat."

As Amelia sat, so did the dean. The woman had been so helpful in the months following her parents' deaths; Amelia cringed at having to deliver the news.

She'd looked down at her fingers. Taking a ragged breath, she toyed with telling the truth but then decided against it.

"Good to see you, Amelia." The dean beamed a smile.

She looked away.

"So tell me," the woman asked. "How're things going?"

"Um," she faltered, forcing the words out. "I have to withdraw."

The dean looked at her as if not understanding.

"Withdraw," the woman repeated.

Amelia nodded.

"From school?"

She nodded again.

The dean looked from one corner of the ceiling to the other and blinked several times. Amelia could feel the woman's years of experience zooming in on her, waiting for an explanation.

"The end of the semester is tough on everyone, Amelia." The woman tried to defuse. "Let's face it, it's been a hard one," the dean qualified. "How were finals?"

"Fine. Still have a four-point."

"Well then. The holidays, the New Year—they're tough with your parents being gone a year—"

"Yes, I know, thanks." She'd cut the woman off, knowing how skillful the dean was in talking people out of things. "I just think it's better if I withdraw for now."

Hearing her sigh, Amelia watched as the dean clasped her hands and focused on her.

"Students feel overwhelmed; even in the best of circumstances, they want out. Hell—the faculty want out." The dean chuckled airily and leaned back in her chair, rearranging her dark curly bangs.

"Uhh—it's more than that," Amelia said.

The dean stared at her, trying to divine the reason.

"Well, how long are we talking about?"

"At least a year."

"A year?" Dean Williams lurched forward.

"Maybe more. I'll have to see."

"See what, dear?" The woman leaned both elbows on the desk, trying to engender enough confidence for her to share.

"I'd rather not say." While she felt the dean deserved an explanation, she couldn't say it.

The woman sat back and looked at her with suspicion. "Gifted students don't just withdraw willy-nilly; won't the semester break be enough?"

She shook her head.

The dean was quiet. Her expression then changed to official business.

"You're forfeiting your scholarship."

"I'm aware of that." Amelia looked down at her hands, feeling the beginnings of a protruding abdomen.

"And you're willing to give up."

"I'm not giving up; I just can't do it now."

"Are you in some sort of trouble?" The dean's eyebrows rose as she said it and she stepped out from behind her desk.

Amelia smiled. She'd never been in trouble in her life.

"No."

They stood in silence, absorbing the gravity of the moment and of decisions made.

She moved toward Amelia to hug her, but instead Amelia waved and slipped out of the door.

"Call if you change your mind," the woman called after her.

Another thing about adult life she hadn't known—how to get birth control, how to sell a house, how to open a checking account, how to sell her parents' furniture. Funny how she knew in depth about the fertility cycles of marine animals, but hadn't thought about her own. And neither had Penelope mentioned it, possibly thinking it might be centuries before her daughter would even think such things, much less have the opportunity.

After the meeting with the dean, Amelia had gone to a pay phone in the lobby of the administration building, plugged in a quarter, and called Chris Ryan's office. This time he answered.

"Chris Ryan speaking, how may I help you?"

Silence. She listened for a few seconds and then quietly placed the receiver back in its cradle and stood there, intent on never speaking to him again.

After her conversation with Dean Williams she needed to think. Leaving her parents' car in the dorm parking lot, since the needle was brushing the empty line, she buttoned up her black peacoat, wrapped a red plaid scarf around her neck, and took off walking until she reached the university entrance sign on North Country Road. She stood for a few moments. Turning left she tucked her hands into her pockets and headed east along the shoulder of the highway toward the Port Jefferson harbor. The faster she walked the less nauseous and panicky she felt. Her breath puffed in streams. January's raw, damp maritime wind left a bone-penetrating chill for which the only cure was nothing short of a hot shower.

While the road was clear, snow lined the sides. Passing cars kicked up the slush mixed with sand from the last storm. Some sprayed her. She'd reared back to shield her face.

As she approached the town, snow piled up deeper off in the woods; tiny square Cape Cod summer cottages set back in the trees looked snowed-in. An occasional passing car honked.

From up on a ridge on the outskirts of town, the masts of tall ships were visible from down in the harbor. She inhaled the comforting smell of salt water and seaweed.

The road then began a steep, winding descent into sidewalks like switchbacks down to sea level.

One long blast of the Bridgeport–Port Jefferson Ferry startled her, announcing its departure, carrying cars bound for Connecticut.

The street was lined with wrought-iron, Victorian-looking streetlamps; across was a massive parking lot at the ferry entrance.

Port Jefferson was a historic whaling town dating from the mid-1600s. In eighth grade Amelia's class had taken a field trip when they were studying the earliest settlements in colonial America. Named after Thomas Jefferson, who'd invested funds to help shore-up and stop the town from its perpetual flooding, Port Jeff, as it was called, had been known for its whaling and fishing. The town retained the flavor of colonial-American roots by city ordinance as all of the buildings in the historic district were required to reflect that heritage.

Amelia stopped to watch as the ferry pulled away from the dock, hands in pockets. A loud squeaking made her look up. Overhead was the gold-leaf painted form of a swordfish, that said FRESH FISH MARKET in painted gold letters. The fish swung in the gusty winds off the harbor.

The storefront faced the harbor with nothing to block the wind. Another gust hit and knocked her off balance but not before she'd spotted the HELP WANTED sign tucked in the bottom corner of the front window. Spray from the waves hit the dock and made a thud as it landed on the hoods of cars waiting to load onto the next ferry.

Amelia ducked into the alley alongside the market for shelter and then noticed two men unloading wooden crates from the back of a truck. She hurried toward them and spoke up.

"That's some nice-looking black sea bass you got there."

Both men glanced over like, *beat it.*

"I see you got some swordfish there too." She'd pointed to another wooden crate packed with headless fish and ice chips. "Looks freshly caught."

"Can I help you?" said an older man, sounding more like, *get lost.* With wavy gray hair and a mustache, he placed both hands on his hips and walked toward her, wearing a rubber apron, gloves, and waders.

She was so tiny there'd been nothing about her that merited such an aggressive stance. She remembered wanting to start giggling.

"Yeah." She'd put her hands on both hips too and faced him up. "I need a job."

The other younger man, about her age, stopped unloading to stare at her too. They had the same shaped mustache. She imagined he might be a son.

"What are you, like twelve?" the younger one quipped. Both raised their gloved hands and began laughing in a way that might have chased off someone else.

"Nineteen," she called back; her voice pealed through their laughter, clear and firm. "Twenty next month."

They were quieted.

"I can show you my driver's license if you don't believe me."

They studied her—long dark glossy ponytail almost to her waist, black woolen peacoat, plaid scarf, and jeans. She looked more like an adolescent, but stood like she'd take on either men, if needed.

"You know fish?" the older man asked.

"Boy do I know fish," she said, nodding as she smiled.

And for many years Amelia would remember the feel of that smile.

"Hey—nothing personal," the younger of the two said. "We don't hire girls. They're bad luck and bring trouble," he said with the kind of hesitation borne of knowing you should keep your mouth shut.

"You don't hire girls," Amelia repeated, nodding, looking into the inert eye of a sea bass that lay under chips of ice, only its face exposed. "You're kidding me, right?"

He shrugged a response.

The back screen door was rickety and the son held it open for Amelia. Piles of crates to be hosed out sat under a sign that ordered: WASH.

Amelia heard shuffling around in a tiny office the size of a bathroom stall—a desk touched both walls on either end and it was piled with papers, envelopes, an adding machine, a dog-eared Rolodex, and a wheeled desk chair.

"Hey, Mom?" the son called as he walked down a short hall-way that led behind the counter.

"Hay is for horses," she heard a woman's voice grumble. "I'm in here."

"This person's looking for a job."

Mrs. D'Agostino looked up with a curious and hopeful ex-pression that soured once she saw Amelia.

"Uch. No more girls, no more girls, no more girls." The woman launched into a diatribe half in Italian with enough En-glish peppered in for Amelia to catch the gist of it. The woman stood, untied her apron, and threw it on the desk. Storming out of the front door without a coat, the bell at the top of the door jingled to announce her departure.

It was too cold to be out without a coat. Amelia looked from father to son, wondering who wore the pants in the family.

Both shrugged an apology.

Just then the shop door burst open, ringing the bell again as

Mrs. D'Agostino popped in to holler a final warning in English. "You mark my words, that girl's gonna be trouble."

The woman glared at Amelia just long enough to elicit an adrenaline jolt at the truth of the woman's words. And she wondered how long she could hide it.

Then the woman stormed back to her office and slammed the door.

Both son and husband turned to Amelia.

"Well," the father said, and then threw Amelia a rubber apron and a pair of gloves, motioning for her to follow out back to finish unloading.

After each day of work Amelia trudged back along North Country Road to the tiny one-room cottage she'd managed to rent.

The bungalow was originally built as a summer rental and not suitable for year-round occupancy. Its insulation was nil, not to mention the roof's viability. In the corner was a wood-burning stove that when fully torqued made the place suffocating and a window or two had to be cracked in order not to break a sweat.

On the plus side, a huge woodpile had been stacked to cover the entire side of the collapsing wall of gray weathered shingles so that she never had to worry about running out of wood even if she kept a fire burning 24/7. The landlord, who lived in Smithtown and had inherited the place from his family, was almost slap-happy at receiving a rent check before Memorial Day and even more grateful that Amelia was so young and ignorant as to not report him for the shoddy, code-violating conditions of the house.

She'd stand gutting and cleaning fish in the back room, elbow to elbow with the D'Agostino men, shoveling fresh ice chips into the cases before rearranging the fish. Propping up filets of Atlantic salmon and white bass, she'd garnish each with parsley and kale to separate from the cooked lobsters, fresh steamers, cherrystones, and littlenecks, working behind the scenes until a customer had a question.

"Amelia?" One of the D'Agostino men would call her out.

"How's the best way to cook this?"

She'd explain in detail whether or not to wrap in foil, bake, broil, pan fry, steam.

"Now this one . . ." She'd hold up a bluefish fillet as if it were the guilty party as she'd begin to tell the story of at what ocean depth the species lived. "These guys have nasty bites." She laughed, remembering having been bitten by one and showed the sickle-shaped scar on her right hand as evidence. "They reproduce in spring, can live up to nine years," she said as the customer's eyes widened. "Found from Cape Cod to North Carolina but also in the Mediterranean." Customers would listen as Amelia would create an entire undersea eco-world so vivid that even young children would listen. "They mature as females but then change into males during winter."

During her first few weeks at the Fish Market, Amelia began a tradition of drawing and posting pictures of the catch of the day just inside the glass of the front door. The practice prompted a surge in sales and within weeks the catch of the day began selling out by noon. Freehand on butcher-block paper she'd draw the likenesses of various fish in their habitats, sometimes surrounded by coral reefs, others in eel grass. The images were so beautiful and detailed that many customers would offer to purchase them along with the fish.

"How such a tiny thing could inject such new life into this store," Mrs. D'Agostino had marveled after only a month and gave her a dime-an-hour raise. "My God, I eat my words in spades about girls," the woman swore and guilt tortured Amelia in direct proportion with the swell of her pregnant stomach. "Ammy," Mrs. D'Agostino went on, "you're our lucky charm." The woman bent down and leaned her dyed-red curly head on

Amelia's shoulder as a sign of forgiveness. "God brought you to us for a reason." The woman beamed as Amelia's chest tightened in a heartsick way, feeling like a scamp. She was on a collision course with the truth but banished such thoughts just as quickly as they'd bob to the surface.

Before Alex was born she'd stay after-hours, wiping down the entire place as if it was a laboratory at the New York Aquarium to comply with New York State health regulations. Making sure the lobster tanks were clean, the composition of salt water and oxygen were in the right balance along with temperature.

Luckily it was winter.

She'd managed to hide her increasing girth by wearing a man's down vest beneath a barn jacket, all covered up by a rubber apron. And since it was cold, the D'Agostinos never saw her without being all bundled up. During the course of the workday she was outside, unloading fish, packing ice, and unloading ice chips, everything that required that she be covered up and bundled in many layers.

One afternoon she'd felt Alex's foot pushing out against her abdomen wall. She'd paused and smiled, pressing back with her fingers at the tiny foot through the many layers of clothing.

Amelia looked up to see Mrs. D'Agostino watching. The woman's eyes narrowed as she dragged Amelia into the fish cooler and shut the door.

"You lied to me," Mrs. D'Agostino said.

Amelia had no response.

"You made me the fool!" She raised her voice, more hurt than angry.

"No. You gave me a break." She smiled with sadness.

"Why didn't you tell me?"

"Because you wouldn't have hired me."

"You got that right, I wouldn't have," Mrs. D'Agostino hollered.

Amelia raised her hands and eyebrows like, *see?*

They sat in silence on two boxes of frozen shrimp, looking at anything but each other.

"So what now?" Amelia asked, relieved that the secret was out and yet curiously not worried at all about getting fired.

"I can't believe you wouldn't tell me," Mrs. D said, shaking her head, looking wounded. "That you wouldn't have enough faith in me to have mentioned it."

"Ha!" Amelia laughed out loud and grabbed her stomach like Santa Claus. "You weren't going to hire me, remember? You just said it."

"That's right, but I didn't know you then." The woman rushed back in her defense.

"And you never would have, 'cause you wouldn't have hired me."

"True." The woman sat looking at Amelia as if wondering if she'd been tricked in more ways than one.

"I needed a job," Amelia said. "You needed an employee."

"So what the hell were you planning on doing?" The woman slapped her thighs as she turned and hollered at Amelia. "Opening your legs to give birth behind the counter?"

At that Amelia was laughing so hard, she tried to hide it, feeling relieved as Mrs. D fought to stay angry.

"I didn't have a plan."

The two of them stood. Mrs. D touched Amelia's shoulder.

"Does the father know?" she asked in a soft voice.

Amelia looked down at her steel-toe boots, her feet so small they looked like stubs.

"He doesn't, does he?"

Amelia didn't answer.

"Any reason why not?"

She maintained her silence.

"Who's gonna help you, Am?"

Amelia looked at the woman.

"Who are your people?"

She didn't have any, and was more ashamed of that than afraid of what lay ahead.

After Alex was born Amelia worked part-time until two years later when she graduated from the marine biology department down the road at Stony Brook. She'd lined up an off-the-books babysitter who smoked incessantly and did tarot card readings out of her home. It was close enough for Amelia to either bike the six blocks or walk with the stroller to pick up Alex.

Between medical assistance and student loans to cover tuition, daycare bills, plus her cheapo off-season summer bungalow, she was able to make it to graduation. Mrs. D would show up with grocery bags filled with baby and toddler clothes from the people in their church and with bundles of fish.

Once Alex had turned two years old, Amelia had walked across the stage at Stony Brook to receive her undergraduate degree with high honors. She'd been accepted into the graduate program in marine biology at Cornell where she was awarded a fellowship that included a stipend to pay for family housing on campus.

Amelia had always suspected that the family had kept the fish market going for an additional two years longer than they'd planned so she could graduate. At her graduation, Mrs. D'Agostino limped along with her new artificial knee, the whole family attending the ceremony, bringing Alex along so he could yell "Yay Mommy," the minute he spotted her in cap and gown crossing the stage.

The D'Agostinos had been the closest thing to grandparents Alex would ever know. After moving to Cornell, Alex would ask for them. They'd sold the fish market soon after and had retired down to Florida along with their son and his family—the promised land for the elderly first-generation northeastern immigrants. Neither had lived much long after.

•   •   •

Standing at the Mall of America bus stop, Amelia spotted her bus. She wondered if any of these young mothers were lucky enough to have a Mrs. D'Agostino showing up with grocery bags and hand-me-down baby and toddler clothes. She remembered with crushing humility, wondering if she'd ever have made it without them.

She watched and listened as the young Maller women checked their phones and made calls to babysitters. How well she knew the torque and strain of such responsibility that never lets one fully relax. Perpetual worry, always on the brink of getting a major utility disconnection or having a grocery store checker load milk on top of bread to squash it all because you'd paid with food stamps.

The crowd looked up as a line of buses rushed in to snuggle up to the curb. Nearby a garbage truck's engine whined as it struggled to get free from a fortresslike snow pile that surrounded a set of Dumpsters.

Christmas music was piped outside, though the Mallers had stopped hearing it weeks ago. "Silent Night" and "The Little Drummer Boy" were lost on most, though a few silently mouthed the words as they stood curbside.

The bus pulled up. Amelia's heart pierced. So grateful for all those years, so hard, yet in some ways they'd seemed like they were where the real living had taken place.

17

She paced the living room. It was too early to leave to meet Myles. Having rearranged the coffeemaker and toaster, and emptied the crumb trap that she didn't know existed, Amelia then tackled the refrigerator with a bottle of Clorox, wiping it down like some laboratory protocol. She still had a few minutes.

Emptying her clothes from the stackable dryer into the white vinyl laundry basket, she carried it over and sat down alongside it on the coffee table next to where Bryce was laying, watching reruns of *Deadliest Catch* after his shift.

She glanced at her watch. Not enough time to start anything, too much to be milling about and she certainly wouldn't show up fifteen minutes early. It was too cold to sit in the Jeep.

"You hate me," he said.

"If only."

He glanced at her. Beer bottle in one hand, an open bag of convenience-store popcorn lay on his chest with stray kernels that had missed his mouth littering the collar of the Sea Life polo shirt he'd neglected to change.

"I told you he'd show up," he said.

"So what you did was right."

He turned and gave her a look. "That's not what I said."

"What are you saying?" she said.

"Nothing. You're still pissed."

He resumed watching as the crew of the *Northwestern* pulled another empty crab pot over the ship's starboard side from the Bering Sea. "Damn," he said for them.

"I think you're the one who's pissed," she said and began to pick out socks from the laundry basket and drape them over her thigh, looking for the mate.

"And how do you figure that?"

"Why don't you tell me?" She looked at him.

He met her eyes and then looked back to the crew pulling another empty crab pot over the side of the ship.

"Letting Myles in like that was an act of aggression." She felt as angry as when she'd punched a captain of a trawler who, through drunken negligence, had collided into their ship.

"Oh please . . ." He shifted on the couch. "Enough with the Greek drama."

"Fuck you."

He turned and looked at her hair. "Ni-ice," he said.

She got up and entered the bedroom, carrying folded jeans just to cool down. Why were they fighting? She thought to explain that she would have washed her hair anyway, but that was so defensive, and why did she have to explain anything?

"What do you want me to say, Amelia?" she heard him call to the bedroom.

She stepped back into the living room.

"This from the guy who hasn't been on a date in a year—"

"Hasn't gotten laid in a year," Bryce corrected as he raised his beer, toasting like that was some sort of accomplishment.

She wondered who he'd been out with.

The TV got their attention. Another empty steel crab pot was being hauled from the Bering Sea. "God, poor bastards, it looks colder than fuck," he mumbled just as a monster wave hit the side of the *Northwestern,* coating the railings in another layer of ice.

He raised his eyebrows. "Things could be worse. We could be there."

But rather than fight any more with Bryce, she riffled through the laundry basket, pulling out more socks and bundling the matching pairs together.

"You're still pissed," he said after tipping up the beer bottle and swallowing.

She didn't answer.

She watched him feel around on the floor for the remote before he gave up.

"I already said I'm sorry."

"Forget it." She pulled out the remote from under her thigh and handed it over.

"You know, since Captain Phil died," he went on, "I just can't get into this show."

Amelia looked at the screen.

"Yeah, I know."

The room was too small to get enough distance to see the whole picture without getting a distortion headache.

She felt the sudden urge to cry.

"Think something's wrong with me, Bryce?" She almost couldn't get out the words, her throat was too constricted.

She tossed the last ball of socks into the basket and rested her hands on her thighs.

"No."

"I mean I'm gonna be fifty-five and—"

"No."

Her scalp relaxed at the speed and certainty of his response. She looked up.

"You're not with the right guy."

Just then a forty-foot wave hit the *Northwestern*. They both looked. Her heart was on deck with the crew. She longed to see open water, to be tossed about like nothing by something so grand that it could kill you as a matter of course and not have it be personal.

He sat up. "Holy shit, that motherfucker just pitched up the whole bow." The ship breeched like a whale and then slammed down. "That's enough to knock out your teeth." Ocean spray knocked the sorting table loose from where it was locked.

"Look at that thing go," Bryce said. They both watched it roll like a speeding vehicle across the deck, prompting a string of bleeped expletives from the crew.

Her stomach jumped, re-experiencing being seaside in a storm.

She wanted to revisit the man thing.

"You think it's just about meeting the right guy?" She expected a complicated missive about demographics and women her age—Bryce was ever the statistician and scientist.

"Yes." The answer came quicker than she'd imagined. "You need more of a lunatic."

"A lunatic."

She felt him look over.

"Like you?"

He didn't answer.

She needed to hear it again and again, but knew there'd be a tiny window of opportunity of information from Bryce.

"So you think it's that simple," she affirmed.

He gave her a brusque look. "Quit second-guessing yourself, okay?"

"Have *you* ever met the right person?"

He sharply tipped back the beer bottle and swallowed quickly. "Yeah, but I fucked up."

Amelia figured Juney. She'd never say what she'd learned from Diane.

They sat in silence, watching the Bering Sea waves washing over the deck of the ship.

He exhaled and pursed his lips with disgust.

Another crab pot was raised up, teeming with moving claws as the crew swung it onto the deck. "Yeah, baby, now that's what I'm talking about," the men started clamoring. Cigarettes dangled from the mouths of the deck crew.

"Would you date Juney again?"

"Nope." He emphasized the *p*.

"Even if she dumps that guy?"

"Never." He tipped back the bottle.

Amelia wondered what he'd think if he knew how Juney had worked against them with the NSF grant.

"Think we get a second chance if we blow the first?" she asked.

He turned to look at her.

"Sure hope so." He said it in a way that suggested he did and pushed up onto one elbow.

She wondered if she'd gotten a first. Maybe chances had passed by unnoticed. She thought back to the men she'd dated. Even the few who'd practically lived in her house, the "week-enders," as she'd call them. But even after a great weekend she'd be left with the feeling that she was reaching for something that wasn't hers. And so far no one had felt that she could "unpack her suitcase" as Penelope, of all people, would say. Men had felt forced or sketchy. Scared would be okay, but sketchy, no. Maybe you had to work for *right*. Friends who were happily together advised that *right* was effortless and immediate, albeit scary, but then as easy as an autumn breeze that you hope blows on forever and if you're smart and maybe lucky, it does.

She looked at her watch. Time to leave and meet Myles at his downtown hotel. Bryce reached over to pat her arm before she stood.

"Thanks, Bry," she said. The gesture made her want to cry.

Tonight she felt more like a prehistoric sturgeon, old and bony-plated with grandma hands.

Just then the late Captain Phil let loose with a string of profanities that bleeped out a full ten seconds of airtime. They both laughed. The Captain looked into the camera and said "A boat's not like a woman. Here you can close the door and walk away for six weeks."

"Whoa, I loved that guy," Bryce said, blinking sadly as he raised his beer.

She recalled sprucing up the Revolution House like a madwoman with fresh flowers, new bath towels, bath mats, and shower curtains, hitting Pier 1 commando style in search of new throw pillows for the couch, a trip to Macy's for new underwear and bras for a shot at a new life. But just as the rusty gates of her heart began to creak open, Myles had bolted. No reason, no explanation given, just no. Not now, not ever.

"Think I'll ever be excited about someone again?" she asked, slipping into her coat.

Bryce set his beer down on the coffee table and turned to study her.

"Yes."

"Thanks, Bry. 'Cause fat or bald, I'm not picky."

She reached out and squeezed his meaty forearm, brushing off popcorn kernels from his chest and onto the floor. For some reason tears lined her eyes.

She looked at her watch. "Oops." She smoothed down her jeans and grabbed her messenger bag from where she'd tossed it earlier.

"Who's paying?"

She gave him a look to stop but then laughed.

Light from the aquarium silhouetted the shape of Bryce's head, his camo cap sitting on the back of the sofa. She ached to lean over, rest her head on his shoulder, but didn't. The smell of his shaving cream, the tea tree scent from his hair shampoo that she always called his hippy shampoo, was home to her. She stood with her hand on the doorknob, her chest aching. She missed him though she hadn't left. Tears stung her eyes. Amelia turned to watch the aquarium; coral polyps swayed in the current caused by the oxygen bubbles.

• • •

There was street parking a few blocks away from the Grand Hotel and Amelia opted to walk rather than use valet parking just in case.

It had begun to snow as she walked and flipped up her hood. Her chest felt tight as she slipped her hands into her pockets. Fine grains of snow accumulated on the sidewalk. Not enough to be shoveled, but enough to leave footprints.

Reaching the hotel, a doorman opened the tall doors as a dressy couple entered. A woman teetering in very high heels on the fine layer of snow made Amelia smile.

As soon as she entered the paneled lobby, a concierge approached.

"Amelia Drakos?"

She was surprised.

"Yes."

"Please come this way."

Her stomach was jumpy. She followed the concierge down a long hallway through a set of double wooden doors to a private dining area with only three tables. A roaring stone fireplace covered an entire wall. On top of a small platform was a grand piano and 1940s slow jazz made everything feel smooth.

Myles stood. "Amelia," he said, looking at her in that emotional way he used to just before he'd bend over to kiss her.

She didn't know what to feel.

"I can take your coat." The concierge touched her collar.

"Thanks, but I think I'll hold on to it." Amelia smiled in a gracious way.

The woman nodded and then quickly left, closing the doors.

"So good to see you," Myles said and moved into position to pull out her chair and help her be seated. "You look so lovely." He then reached down to kiss her on both cheeks, holding still and turning his head in the slightest way as if waiting for her to reach back to kiss his lips, but she didn't.

"My God, I've forgotten what a beautiful woman you are," he said as if flustered.

She hadn't known Myles to get flustered. Still in an expensive-looking navy-blue suit, minus the tie, he sat down and fabricated a look of wonder as if drinking her in.

"You got new glasses," she said, more as an observation. His eyes kept trying to catch hers in this way they had of softening into hers.

Myles leaned on the table as he gestured toward the musician as if at a loss for what to say. "That's Doby Manogoian," he said. "Young guy, very talented pianist, mostly jazz and blues." Myles filled her in on the times he'd heard him play in Boston, talking like almost five months hadn't passed since they'd last talked.

Something about the musician looked familiar. They kept glancing at each other as if trying to figure it out.

"I've been meaning to get some of his CDs," Myles said. "How lucky to have such a world-class musician here in Minneapolis; I'm surprised you haven't heard of him, Amelia."

It was more of a scolding than a chiding. She didn't answer.

The musician looked about Jen's age. As the man moved to readjust the seat and twist the microphone closer, he stared at Amelia. She looked away. Where did she know him from? Was it from Sea Life with baby mamas and hordes of children? She turned to look at the young man; he looked back with the same puzzlement.

"So tell me how you are." Myles unfolded the dinner napkin in his supreme ritual. In the past she'd have quickly copied him, wanting to be part of the club, but now she left it folded on the charger plate.

"Quite busy. Jen's here too," she said.

"Are you happy with the position?" He clasped his hands together and leaned forward, consciously giving his full and undivided attention. She felt his eyes searching her face like a space probe scanning the surface of Mars.

Her eyes narrowed. She smiled, realizing what was differ-ent. She didn't like him anymore. She wondered if she ever had.

Amelia re-crossed her legs under the table, remembering the rush as his car pulled into her driveway. Expensive cologne that she could smell into the next day in the Revolution House, tai-lored clothes—now he just seemed like some guy who changed his clothes more often than most.

She had to stifle a snicker, watching him labor to carry a con-versation where in the past it would be her doing so.

"The position's fine for now."

The pianist paused to take a sip of water and then peered at Amelia.

"And your son?"

"Assistant professor at the University of Vancouver, diving away, just back from Bimini."

"You've done so well with Alex given your history."

"My history?"

"You know." He made circling motions with his hand. "All you've been through."

What kind of backhanded compliment was that? She couldn't think of a comeback.

"Sorry, please don't take that the wrong way." He held up both hands and turned his head in a cute *forgive-me* gesture.

"Which was what . . . ?" she said and watched him struggle, not at all moved to help him out. So different from how they'd fall into conversation in the warm Providence evenings that past summer. Sitting on her outdoor sofa on the back patio, leaning against each other as they drank coffee on a clear night under the stars at the Revolution House, chatting, never run-ning out of things to say until right before dawn as the sun was about to rise when one or the other of them would fall asleep.

In the weeks after he'd dumped her, Amelia had snooped around in secret on the Facebook page that his daughter had set up for him. She told no one, ashamed and nervous each time she'd logged on. There had been photos of someone named Tina. Tina was tagged on his arm, in his car, at official functions with his investment firm. Tall, strapless dress, nails, hair, diamonds by the yard, she was it.

"I have to apologize for what happened," Myles began, hanging his head, reminding her of the ten-year-old boy she'd scolded in the education room that day after he'd written "Fuck" in Magic Marker on the hem of the girl's coat sitting in front of him.

Earthquakes happen. Tornadoes happen.

She looked back at him with no expression.

"About how I left."

Amelia's eyebrow rose as she folded her hands, leaned her elbows on the edge of the table, and listened.

"I didn't tell you this at the time but Shelly, my ex, found a lump. The kids were devastated and I had to be there for them, for her. I had to focus on her and couldn't have you clinging," he said, looking down into his hands.

"Clinging?" Amelia blinked and tilted her head.

"I had to be there every step of the way, helping to make every medical and surgical decision, being there together as a family."

"I'm so sorry," Amelia said. "And what type of breast cancer did she have?"

He looked vacantly.

"I mean, there are many different kinds, Myles," she said. "I'm a scientist, remember? Did she have a lumpectomy? Radiation?"

It was an innocent enough question.

"Uhh." He looked around the room, embarrassed.

"Did she opt for chemo instead?"

He sat dumbfounded and then shifted in his seat, looking for a comfortable position.

"Surely you'd have known since you were so involved in your ex's medical decisions," she said.

His phone pinged on the table. The face lit up. She read TINA upside down, a skill that all research divers perfect when having to read the registration numbers on the hulls of ships while underwater. He quickly pocketed the phone in his suit jacket.

"Sorry," he said. "You were asking what type of . . ."

"Bye, Myles." She slipped both arms into her coat sleeves and pushed out her own chair. Standing, she turned to him.

"And by the way?" She moved closer to his face. "Your world-class pianist is working mall security." She nodded at the pianist who then nodded back in recognition as if just having placed her too. Amelia then hurried through the double doors before the waitstaff had the chance to let her out.

She was home in twenty minutes, found a parking spot right in front of the building, which was no small miracle, and bounded up the stairs to their apartment.

Bryce turned from where he'd been wrestling with a pre-packaged dinner and a steak knife, trying to saw through the plastic wrapper. That someone so adroit with delicate, sensitive scientific instruments and microcellular organisms could be defeated by molded plastic.

He looked up and dropped both knife and plastic package. "Now that was the fastest dinner in recorded history."

She smiled in relief and leaned against the closed apartment door, feeling like she'd just gotten home after a long trip.

"Figured you'd be out with Jen getting some food."

"She's meeting the mall cop after his piano bar gig."

Amelia stood with her hands on hips, smiling. "I just heard her new beau playing."

He raised his eyebrows in surprise. "Any good?"

"You know me," she looked at him. "I don't know music." The wind and waves were music. The ambient background noise of blue whales emitting a series of clicks as they listened for the time it took for the echo to return was her language.

Heavy rains, lightning; undersea landslides all created underwater sound. Even something as tiny as shrimp communicating
with one another as to where they'd found food was distin-
guishable. The occasional rumble of an underwater earthquake
plus the comforting chatter of dolphins and porpoises reminded
her that she was not alone.

She walked over and seized the steak knife.

"Give me that thing before you hurt yourself."

He threw the frozen dinner in the sink.

"I'm still hungry. You?"

He turned and snorted. "As a matter of fact I am."

The apartment air was chilly. Saltwater scent from his aquarium made her ache with the feeling of home. She closed her
eyes for a moment.

"Got this sudden hankering fo-o-r . . . Chinese?"

"You're on." He nodded and smiled.

"Hong Kong Café?"

"Let's get outta here."

Amelia grabbed his jacket from the coatrack, tossed it.

"Nice catch," she said. "Knew there was a reason I liked you."

"God, I'm starving," he said.

"Bet ya I'm hungrier than you."

Bryce shook his head. "Nope. No way to baseline that kind
of bet."

"Fair enough. Just sayin'."

The place was a three-minute walk.

18

"Call Sea Life. Arrange to see her when you're in Minneapolis at the conference." Charlotte picked up the phone and held it toward him.

TJ didn't move.

"I bet they're open now." She looked up at the kitchen clock.

"I'll do it later." His voice came out with too much force.

She glanced at him, puzzled.

They were eating breakfast after the Rhode Island call yielded Amelia's whereabouts in the Minneapolis mall. She hung the phone back up.

"Why not set it up now?"

"Because I told you I'll call next week."

"Okay . . ." She said it like an open-ended sentence.

TJ crossed his arms as if to protect his torso from someone's punch.

She looked at him.

"TJ, I'm not trying to give you a hard time, honestly," she began. "I'm suggesting this because it might be good to call first, explain who you are before showing up to ambush her," Charlotte said in an exaggerated way.

He smiled and then laughed like a kid who'd just gotten caught.

"Oh so that was your plan," she guessed, laughing along with him. "How come I knew that?" she said. He hated talking on the phone, was more of an *uh-huh, yeah* guy.

Instead he shifted his gaze, examining where the tops of the walls met the ceiling.

"Jesus," she said. "You're stubborn as an ox. If you call now, you can arrange to meet somewhere in Minneapolis, explain the situation, and see what happens."

He shifted in the chair as if his back hurt and he couldn't find a comfortable position. Though the TV was too loud, he didn't want to turn it down either, hoping Charlotte would get absorbed in a news story and forget the whole thing so that he could gather his papers and slink off to his office.

"So what do you think about what I just said?"

"Sure." TJ then stood up from the table as if his half of the conversation was over.

"Sure what?"

He sauntered over and sat in one of the stuffed chairs near the fireplace and resumed working on the latest draft of a paper to be presented at the Minneapolis conference. He'd spread out his papers on the coffee table. Since Gloria's death he'd felt restless, unable to focus. He wiggled his foot in a nervous way. Maybe call and get feedback from one of his colleagues on the joint paper.

Charlotte stood. "I hate it when you walk away like that." Her voice rose. "It's insulting."

"I'm listening," he said.

She made a disgusted noise and shook her head. "How about 'Sorry'?"

"I heard every word you said, that I should call and talk to her, break the ice, set something up when I'm in Minneapolis," he repeated.

She glared at him. That he'd heard angered her even more.

"I didn't say 'break the ice,' but it was a nice touch," she said, though still irked.

"I'll call." He picked up his notes and then logged in to his laptop. "If I have time."

Charlotte took the remote and turned off the TV.

"Make time."

"I told you." He turned to her. "With more states proposing wolf hunts the conference is going to be a bloodbath."

"This is bullshit and you know it." She continued glaring. "What does one thing have to do with the other?"

"I'd rather wait."

"For what?" Charlotte held up her hands, looking around the room in an exaggerated way.

He had no answer other than he couldn't and looked at the words on the printed copy of his paper and then at the e-mail notes from his colleague.

"Sometimes you have to hold your nose and jump—"

He looked away.

"Take a chance on being happy for once, Niinimooshe," she said, getting up to see if the coffee was ready.

As she poured coffee, she noticed something she'd not seen before and set down the glass pot.

"You're scared," she said in quiet surprise.

He looked away.

She walked over and set his cup down, studying him. He didn't answer the charge, refute it, or look at her.

Blowing on his coffee, he took a sip.

"You are," she said again, her voice quiet as she sat down on the opposite chair.

"I just think it's better if Gary handles it." He turned to face her.

"Oh really. So. Now you're going from reading Amelia's publications, her Web site," she said with sarcasm as her eyes narrowed, "to suddenly letting the lawyer handle it." She laughed in a way he found irritating.

He looked at her and frowned. "Lawyers are better at handling sensitive situations," he said, avoiding her eyes.

"Really?" She paused. "Like you don't handle sensitive and difficult situations?"

He pulled a file of notes from the bottom of the pile and opened the folder.

"Okay," she muttered and stood up. "Rewind thirty years. For starters, standing on the boat dock at Lac du Flambeau when you and the others decided to exercise our tribal fishing rights for the first time ever in the history of the state of Wisconsin," she said in an exaggerated way. "Angry white fishermen spitting, cursing. But you don't remember that."

He frowned and looked away.

"Shoving you, threatening your life, you must have forgotten that too."

"Oh come on—"

"Oh come on what?" Her words were like bullets as she stared him down. "You stood them off. You, Elton, and the others. You faced them down time and time again, every season you showed up with absolute calm until the court upheld the treaty rights."

"I wasn't calm." He laughed in a disparaging way.

"I knew that, but they didn't." She held his gaze for an instant. "The times they followed you home, tried to run you off the road, spray painted 'fucking redskin' on our trucks, the side of our house, punched you, and you still went back to spearfish day after day. All of you did." She raised her voice. "Contacting your sister is nothing by comparison."

"That was different."

"How different?" Charlotte folded her arms and took a step toward him.

"This is personal."

"It's been personal for more than four hundred years. 'Spear a pregnant squaw, save two walleye.' Remember?" She almost spat.

They didn't speak for a few moments.

"Now they're killing our wolves, our brothers, and you tell me that's not personal?" she almost shouted. "Afraid of facing your sister who might in fact be very interested to discover she's got a family?"

For some reason saying that made Charlotte cry.

He looked down at the pile of papers. The tips of his ears were burning. His gut pulsed with remembrance of those days down on the boat docks. Maybe he'd been another man back then.

"Don't forget she lost two parents back then too," she said. "We don't know what her life's been like. The woman's lost her sea horse laboratory, her livelihood; think about it," she shouted. "She's working in a goddamned shopping mall, for Christ's sake, TJ."

He was silent. No rebuttal, no argument.

"What's got you so spooked anyway?" Charlotte sat down next to him on the arm of the chair.

"She never responded to the probate documents that Gary and I sent from his office—they explained the situation." He leaned over, riffling through copies of his notes.

"Maybe she didn't get them," Charlotte said. "Maybe they got lost in the move to the Twin Cities—"

"Or maybe we should just let Gary handle it, mail them to Sea Life, have her sign off, sell the place; send her a check for half."

Charlotte looked at him for a long while.

"Is that what you really want?"

Her eyes sat heavy on him. He didn't know what he wanted.

From out of nowhere his throat constricted into a painful knot and he battled to find a place of calm. He was a little boy again, chasing after his father, trying to get the man to see him, to change his mind.

Charlotte sighed as if reaching the end of her patience quota.

"Here." She got up, wrote down the Sea Life number onto a piece of paper, and tore it off, setting it on the side table next to his coffee cup. "Do what you want. I bet they're open, it's after nine."

He shook his head. "She wanted nothing to do with me. Said so in her September reply to my e-mail. Thought I was a lunatic."

"You are a lunatic," Charlotte said under her breath in a way that made him laugh. "Maybe if you'd explained who you were in that e-mail we might not be having this discussion."

"You just don't call someone up and tell them, 'Oh hi, I'm your long-lost brother,' " he said with a laugh in his voice.

"Why not?"

He sat shaking his head.

"It happens all the time, the world hasn't ended," Charlotte said in a quiet voice. "What's the worst that can happen; she calls the National Guard?"

He began to snicker at the preposterousness of it all.

"Don't worry, Niinimooshe." Charlotte patted him on the shoulder from where she stood. "I'll come visit you in Guantanamo, love."

He gave an amused smile.

Then she leaned against his shoulder, trying to get him to push back as their mutual sign of affection but he didn't. Instead he crossed his arms.

"Here's a thought." Charlotte smiled with what he called her "predatory grin" when she'd think of something no one else had. "Just what if she gets excited and wants to drive up, become part of your life?"

She watched him squirm.

"Oh, so I see," Charlotte said as she watched.

He looked revolted and angry, as if he hadn't thought of that.

She paused and stood up again, smiling. "So you'd play hard to get," she said sarcastically. "Didn't know you were the type. Who would have thought after all these years . . ."

TJ squirmed; his eyes darted from side to side.

"So if she's open to you then you can ignore her and punish her for something she's never done."

"You don't know what you're talking about." He crossed his leg away from her, irritated.

"You think it's so simple." His voice was getting angrier. "Like it's no big deal." He imitated Charlotte's intonation and started to move his torso about in a comical way like she would. " 'Just walk up to her, TJ,' " he went on mimicking her. " 'Explain it and you'll both hug it all out.' "

A laugh burst out of her.

"She's not a complete stranger, TJ, she's your sister—"

"She *is* a complete stranger; that's my point." His voice rose as he turned to face her and then stood up. They locked eyes. "That's my point exactly."

Neither spoke.

"So what? Grow up; it's gotta be done." She turned and began to walk out of the room. "Do it for yourself, love. Hate yourself a little less, love yourself a little more. I'm sick and tired of it."

19

Amelia called security. A group of teens was incrementally raising their voices. What had begun in horseplay was now bordering on a fight.

"Oh, great, the fake cop's here," one of them sniped.

"Get lost or I'll sic the real cops on you," the security guard said and herded them out until they dispersed up the escalators.

The guard paused to look at her. He took a few steps closer.

Her hair was semi-damp from having been in the water all morning.

"Hey," he said. "Weren't you in the Grand Hotel this past Friday with some dude old enough to be your father?"

Amelia laughed as he said it for reasons that made it funnier. The uniform cap said MALL SECURITY, but she recognized the sideburns, the black curls spilling out from the hatband. She smiled.

"You're Jen's friend." He looked different under the fluorescent mall lighting, a lot less impressive.

"Tell me that guy wasn't your your husband." He frowned as he said it with more of a dash of pity than anything else.

She stared at him in an incredulous way.

"Uhh—then a Match-dot-com date?"

She snickered and looked at him. "Bet you a quarter you're an idiot."

"None of my business, but the guy looked like a real jerk."

"I call off the bet. I like you better now."

"Hey, I'm Doby." He held out a hand to shake.

"Yeah, I know," she said. "Looking for Jen?"

"If she's not too busy," he said. She detected a Boston accent. "You got a name, Little Mermaid?" He chuckled.

She gave him the finger and he laughed.

"I like your spunk," he said as he read her name tag.

"Oh right, you're Amelia, Jen talks about you all the time," he said. "Amelia as in Earhart?"

She frowned. "Right, that's why there's an X on the roof of our apartment complex."

"Oh, ho, ho, ho, sorry Little Mermaid. Sounds like you guys got suckered in by one of those 'convenient to the airport' places?"

"Yeah, yeah, whatever." Amelia motioned for him to follow.

He seemed in a totally different class of men than the usual ones Jen picked, the ones who'd phone early on a Sunday morning looking for her to make bail.

Jen stood explaining to the volunteers how it was important to warn visitors not to step on the intake hoses as she said, "Ask yourself why there's always time to do it over again and fix it but never enough to do it right." Her eyes softened when she saw Doby.

"Hey, Jen." Amelia motioned for her to come over. "I'll take over, you guys go on ahead."

"So who's the cop?" Bryce asked Jen late that night after they'd all gotten home and he'd set out an entire takeout order of Italian food on the coffee table in Styrofoam cups that they picked at with the accompanying plastic utensils.

"Well, Dad, I met him a few weeks ago while getting coffee." Jen stood up to get plates that Bryce and Amelia refused: "Less to wash," they both maintained.

Jen shook her head from side to side. "He's a world-class blues musician working tons of jobs to save money."

"A world-class musician working in a shopping mall?" Bryce started his mocking laugh, but Amelia punched his arm and gave him a look to shut up.

"Okay, so I'm an asshole."

"You are," Jen said.

In the past whenever one of them had a secret, the other two would zero in.

The side of Jen's cheek had turned red.

Bryce immediately sat up. He studied her as he forked a meatball from a Styrofoam cup.

"She likes the cop," he said as if Jen wasn't in the room.

Jen looked down at her hands, emotional all at once.

"Shit. I think she loves the cop," Bryce whispered in a voice loud enough for the sea horse in his tank to hear.

Jen started laughing and crying. She swatted at Bryce to shut up.

"Dad's never seen you love someone like this before," Bryce said and scrambled over to put his arm around her.

Jen wiped the corners of her eyes. "Thanks, Bry. But he's moving this spring, opening a restaurant/music venue with a few investors on the Duluth lakefront." She grabbed the Styrofoam cup off the coffee table and forked out the rest of the meatballs before Bryce had the chance to polish them off.

Amelia and Bryce shot glances at one another.

"Impressive," Bryce said. "Congrats, sis, many standard deviations away from the usual lot, pilfering change out of vending-machine coin returns."

Jen laughed as she punched him.

"It kills me to think about him leaving." Jen almost couldn't finish the sentence.

"And so you're . . . not . . . going with . . . him because . . ." Amelia began, and looked long and steadily at her friend. They looked at each other in surprise.

"I think I love him," she said and kept wiping tears.

"Then go," Amelia said, on the verge of tears herself.

Jen looked at her. "It's not until June."

"Maybe you're up at bat this time, puppy," Amelia said.

Jen hopped over onto the couch and buried her face into Amelia's shoulder.

Early the next morning when Amelia showed up for work, someone had placed a paper memo on her office chair.

Amelia bent over, reading it before putting down her bags. The memo asked if she would please call the HR office to schedule a time to come in for a meeting.

"Fuck." She dropped her bags onto the floor. What now? She thought back to what she could have done.

The day before she'd instructed one of the volunteer tour guides not to dive in the saltwater tank without permission since it wasn't a personal swimming pool. Later the woman who works with the Amazon poison dart frog exhibits pulled Amelia aside, warning her that the woman was the daughter of one of the "head honcho HR dudes" (in her words) and that Amelia should be careful.

Picking up the memo, Amelia moved it off to the side.

She needed to go get a coffee—nothing like a strong cup of coffee to settle her nerves.

"I'm going to get some coffee," she announced, having opened the prep kitchen door. "Anyone want anything?"

A collective sigh of thanks, they all shook their heads.

Riding up the escalator, Amelia weaved through the tangle of roller coasters toward the coffee bar. They knew her by name and upon sight would begin filling a large cup of coffee before she'd even ask.

In the flow of crowd traffic walking toward her, a man slowed down to a stop. His face followed her as she headed toward the coffee bar. He looked dazed, as if someone had hit him over the head hard enough to get startled but not enough to knock him out.

Amelia slowed at his reaction. Something about him was familiar. He'd moved off to the side, out of the flow of the crowd and faced her. He looked about to speak. She racked her brain. Where did she know him? Was it from a dive project? From the U of M water-quality program?

Then a family with a double-wide stroller cut between them and paused, blocking the walkway. Giving instructions to their children as to how far to wander, Amelia glanced around the negotiating family but the man was gone.

Once the stroller and family passed, Amelia stepped toward where the man had been standing, but there was only a miniature Christmas tree and a clump of flowers where he'd stood. Searching for him, she then backtracked, trying to spot him but he was gone.

After a few moments she gave up and headed back to the Sea Life escalator, forgetting why she'd gone up to the mall level in the first place.

20

It was almost noon and Amelia still hadn't responded to the memo. It was the Friday before Christmas and Alex was due in that Wednesday. Amelia and Bryce stood in a shallow pool in the off-exhibit area, suited up in wet suits, trying to secure a new tiger shark to check for pregnancy.

The memo from HR filled her with a sense of doom.

"Jeeze, I probably should have called by now," she said.

"So call after they're gone for the day, which is what? Two p.m. at the latest," Bryce said as she laughed. "Leave a voice mail."

She liked his strategy and chuckled, looking up at the top of his sandy-colored head. A lot more gray had come in since she'd last seen him without his cap.

They'd struggled for twenty minutes along with the interns to catch the shark and then hauled it in a sling into the back room. Once into the shallow pool, Bryce and Amelia had finally restrained it so that Amelia could safely measure its belly.

"Amelia?" One of the interns called over toward the tank.

"Yes, Amber?"

"Someone's here to see you."

"Oh shit," Amelia murmured to Bryce as he held the shark's front end before they could measure it. "It's that woman, Grace." She softly started singing a rendition of "They're coming to take me away ho ho, he he, ha ha . . ."

"No, it's not," Bryce said. "They never come down here."

"Do you know who it is, Amber?" she called up.

"I don't know," the young woman said.

"Can you tell if it's a manager?" she asked Amber, her eyes on Bryce.

"It's some older guy," Amber said. "He asked for you by name."

"Shit."

"A hunj says you're fired," Bryce said in a low voice.

She frowned and shot him a snide glance. "Shut up, that's not even a bet."

"Think you could take a message or a number, Amber?" she called out. "I'm super busy right now." She looked at Bryce who rolled his eyes.

"He says it's really important." The intern was beginning to sound distressed.

Amelia looked up at her. The young woman's face was burning red. She knew Amber to be on the autism spectrum and today was her day to practice greeting visitors, not get stuck between head-butting adults.

"Can you tell him I'm in a tank with a shark at the moment," she said.

"Why do women always say that about me," Bryce murmured so only she could hear.

Amelia tried not to laugh and lose her grip on the shark.

"I'll try," the young woman said.

Both heard distress in Amber's voice.

"Hey, Amber?" Amelia called up to her.

Bryce looked at Amelia.

"Forget it. I'll be right there."

Bryce let go of the front end and threw up his hands. The shark immediately thrashed free as she let go of its tail.

"Fuck," she whispered, climbing out of the tank.

"Thanks, Amber," she said, her feet back on the cement lab floor. "You did the right thing by coming to get me." She patted the young woman's shoulder.

Amber gave a doubtful smile. Amelia didn't bother to change out of the wet suit as they walked up to the admissions entrance, slapping a trail of wet footprints behind her. She braced for the next "talking to," maybe even "judgment day," as Bryce alleged. The three of them had never had bosses before.

"God, we're just the world's shittiest employees, aren't we?" Jen had observed after a few weeks, as none of them seemed to be able to take anything seriously, excepting animal care.

At the front entrance, a man turned to look.

It was the same man from two hours ago on the mall level.

"This is Amelia, our animal-care curator," Amber introduced.

"Hello," Amelia said. "How can I help you? I'd shake but my hand is sort of slimy." Amelia held up her hands as if it was a holdup.

"Amelia Drakos?" He held his breath.

"Uh . . . yeah." She hesitated. It felt like she was about to be read her rights. In the background there was frantic beeping of credit card machines as college interns swiped people's cards.

"Sorry to just show up like this but I e-mailed a couple of times, sent a copy of some papers explaining the situation."

He paused as she stared.

"I'm Ted Drakos Jr."

"Oh." *Shit.* She looked down at her bare feet and then crossed her arms, flustered and frightened by the vague family resemblance.

Backing away toward the Ocean Tunnel she said, "Look, I e-mailed you back. We're not related and I'm *really* super busy right now." She wondered how he'd tracked her down.

"There's something I need to discuss," he said.

She kept stepping backward. "I-I told you I can't help."

"It's about your father, Ted Drakos."

"My father's dead." She stopped and shifted her weight onto one foot.

"Born in Boston, lived in Baldwin, New York," he said,

watching her face to detect the slightest response. "Worked as a union printer."

That was her father. It was his voice too. She folded her arms. He had her attention.

"He's been dead over thirty years."

"I know."

How would he know? They looked at each other. She couldn't believe his face, her mind kept scanning his features as they came together and then broke apart. It was a mix of many confusing things. There was no privacy in the Ocean Tunnel, the slightest sounds echoed against the Plexiglas.

"Is there some place where we can talk?" he asked.

"I'm working."

"My late mother's will involves you."

Nothing he was saying made sense.

Her face scrunched into a question mark.

"I'll explain everything and we can be done with this business."

"What *business*?" She suddenly felt afraid, cornered.

"Please, can we go somewhere private?" He followed her as she backed away toward the Ocean Tunnel. "Or if you could take a few moments."

There was a sudden lull at the admission desk.

Neither said a thing for a few moments.

"Twelve thirty. Pizza Leanings. It's upstairs to the left." Amelia pointed to the escalators.

He looked at his watch. "In an hour?"

She nodded, turned, and hurried away. Back toward where she'd left Bryce.

The heavy metal door of the off-exhibit labs shut behind her as Bryce began to gear up to catch the shark again.

"You get canned?" Bryce called up to her.

"No. Weirder." She climbed back down into the tank, trembling as she tried to shake it off.

"What?" He looked closely at her.

She told him about the e-mails back in Rhode Island, the letter she'd tossed without opening.

"How come you didn't tell me?" Bryce asked.

She flashed him a look. "Uhh, like there wasn't enough shit happening at the time."

"What's he want?"

She sighed deeply as her stomach jumped.

"I don't know; just grab the head before the goddamned thing bites me."

Christmas and Chanukah coincided that year and the Mallers who'd worked there a while kept remarking on how unusually packed the place was. You had to wade, not walk down the pathways. And while Bryce had wanted to accompany her to Pizza Leanings, Amelia insisted on going alone.

"There's tens of thousands of people milling about," she said laughingly through the locker room door as she changed into street clothes. "You think the guy's gonna jump me across the table?"

"It's not so much that—"

"I'm more worried about Minneapolis Fire Department's occupancy codes," she said. The center courtyard was so packed she worried that if someone fainted there'd be no room to collapse. They had to suspend the line at Sea Life, despite angry parents of cranky children waiting for visitors to cycle through.

"Amelia?" Jen knocked on the door, folding her arms in concern as Bryce let her in. "Bryce just told me."

Amelia emerged in jeans and a Sea Life polo.

"You should let us come with you."

Amelia harrumphed as she looked from one to the other. "Only if you both put on the Neptune and mermaid costumes from the interpretative theme room and come along."

"Stop it, Amelia, we love you, you're making it sound stupid." Jen raised her voice.

"Fine." Bryce touched Jen's arm. Together they walked away. "Leave her."

"I'm sorry," Amelia called after them as they both walked away, realizing she was angry and nervous at the same time. "That was really bitchy."

Amelia kept checking her watch. She was more nervous than she'd thought about meeting Ted Drakos Jr.

She'd managed to salvage fifteen minutes to Google Ted Drakos Jr. at her desk. Up came his work Web site, Great Lakes Indian Fish and Wildlife Commission, a photo of him standing alongside eight other wildlife and fish biologists. She'd picked him out in an instant, the constellation of her father's eyes, chin, and forehead. Her stomach leaped. Sitting on her desk was the last photo taken of her parents, probably snapped by a tour guide, standing on the steps of the Parthenon days before the accident. She'd kept the photo next to the glass beaker of shells on her desk because she'd never seen her parents look so happy and there was a type of memento mori sentiment about the photo, to keep as a reminder of the transience of life.

She climbed the stairs near Pizza Leanings and saw Ted Drakos Jr. Taller and broader than her father but with more of an ashen complexion, she studied him watching for her. She noticed a gray ponytail wound and tied neatly at the nape of his neck. He wore an unzipped navy-blue winter parka, button-down blue oxford shirt, with a pair of jeans. Up close he was a larger facsimile of her father. Her neck and shoulders tensed, her emotions were wobbly.

"Ted?"

He turned.

"Hi." He reached to shake. "TJ, please. Everybody calls me that. Thanks for meeting with me," he said. She motioned for them to sit at the only empty table in Pizza Leanings. A young high school–aged worker had just wiped off crumbs with a damp rag.

"This good?" she asked. It felt like an awkward first date.

He nodded and sat.

She felt him taking stock and studying her face as carefully as she was studying his.

"You hungry?" he asked.

"Not really," she said as she sat down. "But please go ahead."

"Think I'm gonna grab something." He touched the button on the front of his shirt and then gestured to her. "You sure? Slice of pizza, Coke?"

"Thanks but no." It felt paternal. Her stomach was clenched.

She watched him up at the counter. The set of his shoulders was so familiar. He turned to look for her. She ducked to check her watch, hoping he hadn't seen.

He returned and sat, placing the cardboard cutout of a Leaning Tower of Pisa in the center of the table, showing the embossed number.

"I have an hour." Her watch beeped, indicating she'd set a timer. "So, who are you?"

He looked at her but didn't smile. His face was sad, as if about to share bad news. Her mind jumped from her parents who were already dead, to Alex, who'd just texted to ask if he should bring a sleeping bag in case they didn't have a couch, to Jen and Bryce who were down at work.

Green flecks glittered in his eyes. His large hands were clean as he sat with them folded on the table. She guessed maybe five, six years older, though hard to tell.

She watched him hesitate, carefully picking and formulating words. Then he took a deliberate breath before giving up and just saying it.

"I'm a relative," he said and looked down at his hands.

He looked conflicted.

"Your half brother."

"My half brother," she repeated and frowned. She rubbed her brow without realizing. "And how's that possible?"

"Your father married my mother when they were in the Navy, both stationed in Germany, six years before he met yours," he explained.

He placed a thick white envelope on the table and then was quiet. She recognized it from Rhode Island.

"Okay." She stared at the back flap of the letter. "So . . . then they got divorced like everyone else in America," she said to put an end to the mystery and both of their discomfort.

"No," he said. "They stayed married."

"They stayed married—what does that mean?" She leaned back, folding her arms and tucking her fingers into her elbows.

"It means they never got divorced."

She stared back.

He didn't answer, didn't blink either. He only looked sad.

"TJ?" He turned toward his name and stepped toward the counter.

A woman wearing a hat with a 3-D leaning tower of pizza handed him a tray.

He set it down on the table and Amelia watched as he sat back down.

She felt nothing for this person who didn't fit into her understanding of anything.

"Greek men don't have two wives." She could smell his shaving cream. It was odd enough to learn of her father having had another family that neither of her parents had ever mentioned.

"He was trained as a mechanic in the Navy, my mother a flight nurse. That's where they met. Married in Germany, moved back here. He couldn't find work."

TJ looked down at his hands. She could tell there was more to it. He moved the envelope toward her.

"What's this?" She gestured with her chin to the letter.

The food sat untouched.

"My mother just died." He touched the envelope.

She looked at him.

"The will leaves the property to both of us, Dad's descendants."

The word "Dad" cycled through her confusion. She reared back a bit.

"There's a house and fifty-four acres," he continued.

The silence between them felt permanent.

"No one's lived there for years," he said. "Utilities were cut off since my mother moved in with us. Their will stipulates for the property to pass to us both."

Amelia said nothing; her chin leaned on her hand, pressing so hard into her palm that her elbow hurt against the table.

"I'm the executor," he said.

A feeling of cumulative jealousy hit for having shared her father—for her mother, for herself as a daughter. Had this man diverted what had been rightly hers or had it been the other way around? The thought pierced her and she looked at him— such sad eyes.

Might this have been her father's preoccupation while driving on the road in Crete? A momentary lapse in attention where he'd failed to notice an oncoming truck crashing through the median divider? Or heaven forbid a chance for a hasty exit without scandal.

They stared at each other. He looked away first. She started to tremble and couldn't stop. She felt she was going to be sick.

"When are you off for the day?" he asked.

Never. They sat until Amelia blinked and sat up with a start, having been shaken out of her thoughts.

"I have to go," she said in a hushed voice, out of breath as she stood.

"Amelia." He reached to touch her arm as she stood.

His sad eyes were her father's.

Grabbing her wallet, she rushed off, leaving the envelope. Practically knocking over an elderly couple as she dashed toward the flight of stairs down two levels, her feet moved like Fred Flintstone pedaling a Stone Age vehicle that with one misstep would send her tumbling down the travertine steps to the main level. Glancing back, she checked to make sure he wasn't following. She elbowed her way through the crowds in the main courtyard, looking to the safety of the Sea Life sign and escalators. *Oh, thank God.* She struggled through the people, to get away from him. She cut ahead of customers standing in a line near the down escalator.

"Excuse me, sorry, excuse me." She contorted to slip through. "Pardon me, sorry." She squeezed by, hurrying down the collapsing metal steps past the entrance sign and rushed into the facility.

"Hey, Amelia," a few of the interns greeted her but she rushed through the family photo station, not saying hi and high-fiving as she normally would.

She needed to be underwater. Had to grab her gear, feel the water on her face, in her hair.

"How'd it go?" Bryce turned with a starfish in his hand; he and Jen had been ribbing the interns about something. "Amelia?" He set down the starfish and followed her into the back office.

"What happened?" The latex gloves were still on his hands. Amelia paced as she pulled her lower lip. "Talk to me."

Jen hovered behind Bryce on tiptoes, straining to see over his shoulder.

Amelia slid out her gear bag from under the desk and rushed toward the changing room. She shut the door and locked it.

"Amelia? What the fuck? Talk to me," he said, knocking on the door. "Am," he called. "What happened?" He began knocking on the door with open hands. "Are you okay?" There was panic in his voice like she'd never heard but she couldn't reassure him of anything.

Stripping off her clothes, she heard something tear. Kicking off her pants, clogs, she pulled down her underwear, pushed down each sock with the other foot. Wriggling up her bathing suit in a blind frenzy, both shoulder straps not quite in place; she wrestled into the wet suit and grabbed her snorkel and fins out of the bag. Opening the door, she rushed past Bryce as he followed.

"Hey, hey, slow down." He grabbed her elbow.

"Let go." She yanked free. Her voice convulsed as she held up both hands to ward him off. Angry at Bryce too, angry at everyone, everything in her path. Missing the Revolution House, Narraganset Bay, the tank with sea horses.

Grabbing her fins, she pulled open the heavy examination room door like it was nothing and rushed down the corridor toward the ladder into the saltwater tank. Pulling on her face mask, she sealed it around her eyes and bit into the snorkel's mouthpiece. Climbing up to the deck, she slipped into her fins and slid into the water like a sharpened knife. The coolness of the water barely registered on her face and scalp as she sank.

People paused in the Ocean Tunnel, watching in wonder as they snapped images of her with their phones as she swam by. Her long hair pulsed behind with each advancing movement like the dangling tentacles of a jellyfish.

How she longed to be in the limitless ocean, to be able to swim without boundaries, borders, walls, just as the captive fish and mammals she fed and cared for each day must feel.

Once out of public view, Amelia headed for the larger saltwater tank for marine animals. Surfacing to fill her lungs, she drew a deep breath before grabbing on to her knees, tucking into a cannonball position, and drifting down to settle on the bottom of the tank. Crabs scampered past. A sand shark brushed her shoulder as she dipped her head, staring off into nothing as her hair floated up around her in dark swishes.

21

"Char." TJ had phoned just as he turned onto the ramp for I-35 on the way back up to Bayfield.

The divisions and passions at the conference had risen to such a flashpoint that it had felt like one spark might make the whole place go up. Some in the pro-wolf hunting groups had spat at the biologists at GLIFWC, heckled his presentation, and hurled epithets at the tribal position on wolf hunting. And if that wasn't enough, his meeting with Amelia had clinched his decision to pack it in and head home a day early. He'd finished his two-day presentation and had claimed that pressing business was calling him back to Red Cliff. He was tired, shaken up, and needed to see the lake, the North Woods, and his wife's beautiful smile.

"How's the conference going?" Charlotte asked.

"Oh, pretty stormy and intense just like we'd figured. I'll tell you more when I get there. Reminds me of so many things I can't even begin," he said, thinking of the other day when Charlotte had reminded him of spearfishing and the violence on the boat landings, and of other more recent conflicts with lodge owners over easements that had erupted with such virulence it left him wondering where such anger had been hiding all those friendly years.

"Where are you?" Charlotte asked, hearing sounds of traffic, his blinker, and the familiar music he played when he drove.

"I-35."

"You coming home?"

"Yep."

"What about the rest of the conference?"

"Bagged it. Tomorrow's just brunch and the awards. I'm beat."

"You sound tired."

He couldn't even begin to say what he was.

"So . . . uh . . ." she began.

"Yes, I did." He answered before she even asked.

"You did."

"Yep."

For a moment neither spoke.

"Tell me you didn't just show up, TJ."

He didn't answer.

"Oh, TJ." She felt his discomfort. "What am I going to do with you?!"

"Anything you want," he said, rubbing his face as he exhaled, wishing he could quit everything for a day. Putting on his blinker, he merged onto the interstate heading northeast.

"Oh, sweetie." She laughed in comforting tones.

Neither spoke.

"So—uh—you met her?" Charlotte didn't know what to ask first.

"Yep. Met for lunch, though she didn't eat, didn't even drink water." He sighed so deeply she could feel it.

"And . . ." She could tell it didn't go well.

"I probably should have called."

"And . . ." she repeated.

"I showed up."

"You said that."

"Yep."

The line was quiet.

"So what happened?" She wanted to ask ten things at once.

"Well." He chortled as he began to explain. "Thought I'd do a little reconnaissance."

He'd gone to the mall after his second presentation was over and the conference schedule had broken for lunch. He'd thought to get away from the tension, the vitriol by heading to the mall to check out Sea Life, get a feel for the place; see if he could spot her.

"Hadn't counted on running into her," he said.

But then he'd felt emboldened.

"I figured what the heck, she's just a person."

"And . . . ?" Charlotte could see it coming.

But just as he turned to walk back toward the parking ramp and leave he'd spotted her. Walking along in a blue Sea Life polo shirt, plastic ID tags dangling around her neck, she'd looked just like her online photos only annoyed and thoroughly human, approachable, but then he lost track of her in the crowds.

"Sorta rattled me," he said, remembering his racing heart, his adrenaline spiking to the point that his hands were shaking. "Had to sit down, got a cup of coffee to regroup."

"Nice." Charlotte chuckled. "That's my guy—living in reverse, coffee to calm down."

"Once I did, I decided to go to the aquarium."

And then as he'd stood in the entranceway waiting for Amelia, a sinking feeling made him second-guess. He'd wanted to leave though the front desk had already called her up and he'd given them his card. But then he'd spotted her walking up front in a wet suit, felt her zero in on the outline of his form. He'd wanted to shrink, have her unsee him, recede back into being a stranger once again, someone she'd blown off through e-mail several months before, but it was too late. However misguided and clumsy, he'd reached out, tried to follow his wife's example. Like the day he'd shown Charlotte all his old photographs of Amelia and she'd rushed out, bought frames, and intermingled them with those of their combined families on the dining room wall above the sideboard; the "family wall," as they'd called it.

"You were right," he confessed. "I should have called."

"What's done is done," Charlotte dismissed.

"Yes, but she could have absorbed it in private," he said.

"You don't know that, she might have told you to get lost and hung up."

He could tell she was trying to soften it.

"Then she took off running—" He took a gulp from a 7UP can he'd bought while gassing up the car for the drive back, thinking it might settle his stomach.

"Running, Char," he said. "People turned, looked at me like I was some kind of child molester or something."

"Wow." Charlotte quieted as if feeling into the moment. "That's shock, alright."

"Ya think?" He laughed bitterly but was glad she only listened.

"Well," Charlotte started. "You took the first step, Niini-mooshe. Maybe we can call her tonight or tomorrow, apologize for springing it on her like that."

He let her talk. He'd vowed not to call, not after that. He'd have Gary send a copy of the probate papers and be done with it.

"How's that sound?" Charlotte asked.

"Sure," he lied, not wanting to argue with his wife. He'd acknowledge and ignore, not wanting to argue with anyone for a while.

The four-hour drive couldn't go fast enough. He needed to feel Charlotte close, to feel her warmth, and once again be back in the safety of his home.

22

Later that night after work Bryce and Jen listened without interruption as Amelia recounted the meeting with TJ.

An order of Chinese takeout sat untouched on the coffee table in two brown bags. Bryce took off his camo baseball cap as he listened, as if it would sharpen his insight. Jen was curled up into a ball, motionless as she took in each detail of the story.

"Think he's telling the truth?" Jen asked.

Amelia looked at them. "Let me show you a picture of my father and you tell me if he's telling the truth. I found his photo on the GLIFWC Web site." She clicked on the link and raised the photo of TJ and the staff. "Now wait." Amelia held up a finger as she hurried into the bedroom, rummaging for an old family Christmas photo taken at her aunt's home in Boston. An overhead aircraft rattled the walls. When they'd first moved in, each would raise their voice instead of conceding to the racket.

As she sat down with the photo they all scrunched together on Bryce's couch, all three asses like segments of a caterpillar as they did a side-by-side comparison of photo and Web site.

Bryce broke from the lineup in a matter of seconds.

"I'd say there's a lot of genetics going on there," Bryce said. "I hope you're not pissed at the guy."

"At TJ or my father?"

She felt Bryce watching her facial movements.

"TJ."

Her answer came quick. "Why would I be?"

He nodded. "It's no more his fault than yours," Bryce said.

Amelia turned to face him. "Orphans of the same father?"

"Yeah, something like that." Their eyes met, and then she turned to watch as two sea horses flitted about. A few more were suspended on coral branches, watching.

"I still say hire a private investigator," Jen continued after the airplane passed.

Amelia and Bryce looked at her.

"Shit. You never know," Jen cautioned and held up her hands. "My mom hired a P.I." She stood up in a huff and began unpacking the tubs of Chinese food and utensils. "You wouldn't *believe* all the shit that turned up on her ex-fiancé."

"Yeah, but it's just too fucking weird not to be true," Bryce said. " Just look at them, Jen." Their eyes darted from one photo to the other. "And it's not like the guy's asking for money or credit card numbers, it's quite the opposite."

They nodded in agreement.

"You scared the shit out of us, though, Amelia," Jen scolded. "Man, I hate it when you freak like that."

"Sorry," Amelia said. "I should have asked him questions—I just tore out of Pizza Leaning like a crazy woman." Amelia turned to look at her.

"I'd tear out of Pizza Leanings too," Bryce said and pressed his chest as if to underscore heartburn. "But hey, I'm sure it wasn't easy for him either."

"Way to make her feel better, jerk-wad." Jen glared at him over Amelia's shoulder. She took every opportunity to gang up on Bryce.

It made Amelia laugh. "No, no, he's right," she said.

"I mean, think about it," Bryce said. "He probably just found out too," he said as Amelia nodded. "Your mom dies. You read the will. Surprise! It takes one incredible pair of balls to show up like that, gotta give the man that. Could've left the dirty work to lawyers."

"He's reaching out, Am," Jen said and made a face at Bryce.

"Yeah." Amelia nodded, remembering the e-mails she'd deleted, the unopened letter she'd tossed in Providence.

"It was rhetorical, Jen," he said as if explaining rhetoric to a fifth grader.

"Shut up, Bryce," Jen said.

"God. Stop fighting, kids," Amelia said. She sighed, thinking of TJ sitting quietly, taking whatever bombs she'd thrown. No anger, no resistance.

"Well, you know what they say," Bryce started. "We hurt the ones we love the most."

"You're such an asshole," Jen scolded yet giggled at the same time.

Bryce pushed against Amelia's thigh with his foot.

She didn't react.

"Too soon for jokes?" he asked.

There was a pause.

"Nah." Amelia pushed back with her foot. "It was funny, Bryce, it was. Just wait till I drop the bomb on Alex next week at Christmas. 'So what's new, Mom?' 'Well, kiddo, for starters you've got a new uncle, I've picked up a long-lost brother since moving here, and guess what? Your late grandfather was a bigamist.' "

"Why wait?" Bryce chuckled as he looked at her.

"Yah," Jen agreed in what she still thought passed for a Fargo accent and stood up. "Kids are tough these days, they're used ta all kindsa shit." She reached for the container of cashew chicken and a pair of chopsticks wrapped in paper. "They can take it."

Amelia smirked. Alex was hardly a kid yet they all still thought of him as being one.

"Okay if I start eating?" Jen said more as statement than a question, holding out her arms like: *Give me a break.* "Bloodsugar drop, I'm about to faint." Jen broke apart her chopsticks and popped off the plastic lid.

"I freaked out worse than that time out in the South China Sea," she said to Bryce. "The time you fucked up the ROV camera because you were so hungover."

"Excuse me." Jen coughed up a cashew and pointed at Bryce with her chopstick. "For that you deserved to be drowned."

Amelia nodded. "I'd considered it."

"Too bad," Jen mumbled, reaching into the container with chopsticks to pick out the rest of the cashews.

Bryce gathered up the white plastic forks and stood. Walking into the kitchen, he stepped on the pedal of the garbage can and dropped them in like they were biohazards.

"These utensils suck." He then retrieved two metal forks from the dish drain and walked back, handing one to Amelia.

"Eat, Amelia," Bryce commanded. "Or we'll be forced to tube feed you like the baby sea turtle."

"I'll do damage control with the interns tomorrow," Jen said as she chewed.

"Oh shit." Amelia covered her face, thinking of the scene she'd made.

"Got ya covered," Bryce said as he picked up the tub of Mongolian lamb, exhaling as he settled back onto the sofa. "Said you'd just told Myles you were pregnant."

She smacked his shoulder as hard as she could as they all laughed.

"You're such a piece of shit, Bryce," Jen replied.

"Yeah, you really are," Amelia agreed.

The three of them were quiet as they began to eat.

"It's really kinda cool, though." Jen looked at Amelia and smiled. "I mean, think about it," Jen said with a mouthful of food. She stopped chewing as she studied Amelia's face while she was thinking. "A new brother. Sort of like . . . discovering that Santa's real."

She looked at Jen and smiled.

"Maybe," she said and they looked at each other as if imagining the same thing. A sublime type of peace, something

Amelia hadn't known in topside life for many years settled on her like a dollop of grace. A new connection to her father that was prematurely severed and now reanimated. Curiosity and warmth filled her as she pictured TJ being held by the same arms. The same man who'd reached to scoop each one up just moments after birth, had walked the floor many nights to comfort the many earaches, colds, new teeth erupting through inflamed gum tissue. The same man had held them both, had watched as they'd taken their first steps and taught both how to ride a bicycle. And the same man had left each long before his time.

"Just think," Jen went on. "Hearing about your dad will be like meeting him for the first time."

Despite the rush that comes with a newfound sense of kin, Amelia reached for more sobering emotions. Not wanting to romanticize it yet equally as riled up about fast-forwarding to do a crash course on her father's early life and TJ's family. Shared information that only the two of them might know—*A o nia minimi*—the Greek Byzantine chant of eternal memory—the only other person who'd known her father in such a way. Feeling a bond with him already, she wondered if he'd felt it back.

"Yeah." Amelia's voice was lighter. "It could be kinda cool."

Bryce sat back and picked his teeth after polishing off the tub of Mongolian lamb and glanced at his watch.

"Well, maybe give Mr. TJ a call tomorrow," Bryce suggested. "To be continued," he said, standing as he stretched and yawned.

Amelia nodded and looked at her watch. It was almost midnight. Too late to call even though she wanted to. Instead she fired up her laptop and e-mailed an apology, asking if tomorrow there'd be a good time to call.

Amelia's head began to pound from the emotional exhaustion after Bryce and Jen had gone to bed.

She sat up watching the soft leathery toadstool coral under the pink fluorescent lights. Part of its white bony branch was visible beneath its fleshy leaves that were dotted with dozens of tiny green polyps. Each was covered in slime to catch floating vegetable and animal matter as they would dissolve zooplankton and send the nutrients to its body. The whole fleshy mass would inflate to catch food and then deflate in an instant, almost unrecognizable with the least bit of turbulence in the water. Reaching in a hand would do it. Bright green and red anemones had flowered, spreading along a rock that Bryce had placed in the sand. A few sea horses were coiled around a coral branch, perfectly still as if asleep.

Then Amelia settled back into the couch and began searching for Ted Drakos Jr. Her search yielded pages of information and articles. She sat reading for hours about his work with wolves in the Great Lakes region, in Montana, Alaska, and with GLIFWC. She found the International Wolf Foundation in Ely, Minnesota, and clicked on it, listening to TJ's testimony and then onto Wisconsin Eye, to listen to his presentation before the Wisconsin legislature and the DNR against reinstituting a wolf hunt and how it would negatively affect the population. He moved like her father. He sounded like him too; she could close her eyes and hear him.

Bryce walked out of his room about 3 a.m. and stopped on his way to the bathroom.

"Whoa, cowgirl, what the hell are you still doing up?" He yawned out the question as the bathroom door shut.

"Can't sleep," she called back.

"Can't or won't?" he called through the bathroom door and the sound of peeing.

Jen was snoring in her bedroom.

He walked over and stood behind where she sat on the couch and began to read along about TJ.

Then he plopped down, shoulder to shoulder next to her and continued to read.

"Done?" she asked before scrolling down to the next page.

"Yeah. Wow," Bryce said. "What a cool dude. Who would've thought you'd have a brother almost as cool as you."

She turned to look at Bryce and smiled, feeling her eyes getting moist. He kissed her on the forehead.

23

Amelia phoned TJ that day after work. He hadn't returned her e-mail but she couldn't wait. She was nervous and excited, feeling like a teenager.

"Sorry if I startled you," he said after they'd gotten past the usual rounds of hellos.

"Like I wrote in my e-mail last night, sorry I took off like that." She laughed as if all was forgiven. "This whole thing must have been a shock for you too." Her laugh was uncertain, hoping he'd taken that into account and excused her behavior.

"And thanks for being brave enough to show up like that," she said, feeling giddy, like she should stop blabbing and give him a chance to speak.

He didn't answer.

"I want to get to know you," she went on, uncomfortable with his silence. "To know your family, have you know Alex, my son, and Bryce and Jen who are my best friends and fellow scientists." She felt herself gushing, emotion spilling over with all the unbridled foolishness of a child but couldn't stop short of sliding into kook territory. "I mean it's kind of amazing. I couldn't wait to call today, apologize for running off like that."

He didn't respond. She felt embarrassed.

"I mean I was just blown away a bit yesterday, weren't you?" she offered a chance for him to interject. "Why didn't you tell me in those e-mails that you were my *brother*?"

"*Half* brother," he corrected.

"Oh." It felt like a kick. She wondered if she'd offended him more than she'd thought.

"Okay, *half* brother," she conceded, emphasizing the word. Maybe her gushiness was off-putting and she felt like a kid sister who's always wrong.

"I wrote your e-mail off as a scam."

"A scam," he repeated.

"Yeah. You know, unclaimed money scams? You pay a grand to find ten dollars somewhere in a defunct grandma's savings account?"

Apparently he didn't. The line was silent.

"Hello?" She looked at her phone.

"Yeah I'm here," he said. "And the legal papers about the property?"

His voice was stern, as if giving correction. She was tempted to lie for a moment, claiming to have never received them but forced herself to tell the truth.

"Um . . . I—uh, tossed 'em in Providence." She chuckled with embarrassment, hoping that confession would help them move forward. "Sorry."

"A public place probably wasn't the best idea," TJ admitted. "Charlotte, my wife, suggested I call last week."

"Well," Amelia joked. "Nobody died, your strategy worked."

Both were quiet. Neither knew what to say. Amelia felt that sudden awkwardness when the eagerness for a relationship outpaces shared history.

"So you must have just learned about me too."

The line was quiet and she checked for the connection.

"TJ?"

She heard the hesitation.

"Why didn't our father tell us?"

There was a pause.

"I can't answer that," he said.

"Or at least tell my mother?"

"What makes you think he didn't?" he said, with a bitter laugh as if the joke was on her.

Amelia didn't know what to say. His words were unsettling, his laughter stung. It was a breezy chuckle that sported an edge she couldn't interpret. As if something was her fault. Maybe this was a bad idea. She couldn't imagine Penelope knowing and not screaming bloody murder all day long within a fifty-mile radius of the New York area.

"Thank God he's out of my hair for a week to see his mother," Amelia remembered Penelope blabbing on the phone to her friends during her father's regular, if not mysterious, trips to Boston. *"May the old lady live to be two hundred."* Amelia could hear her mother cackling and swearing in Greek from all the way back in her bedroom.

The house was too still whenever her father would go, like he'd packed up the house's breathable air into his suitcase and taken it with him to Boston. It would become Penelope's domain. Amelia would retreat into her bedroom, staying clear. All evidence of low-impact-Ted was stashed into magazine racks, hall closets, and of course, the garage. Amelia had never understood why her father wouldn't take her along. Her mother would be out the nights he was gone, unboxing a turkey pot pie, setting the timer, and telling Amelia to finish her home-work before she'd gone out.

"Did he visit?" she asked TJ.

She heard him pause, sounds of a calculating response being formed.

"A few times a year. Until his death."

Amelia looked down at the floor and smiled in a knowing way. It now made sense. All those trips to Boston were lies. His trip to visit old 102-year-old Aunt Athena in New Hampshire was probably bullshit too. The woman had probably been dead and buried for years. The only thing not bullshit was that their father was killed on Crete and that he'd produced two descendants.

"So—uh—did you know about me?" She felt timid about asking again.

"Yes." The answer came fast. His voice changed but she couldn't put her finger on how. "Told me when you were born that I had a sister."

A sister not a half sister. What a foreign object. And to have the word attributed to her, that he knew of her since she was born but she not of him. What had he done with that knowledge, what had it meant for him. Knowing but not being known, like some child of a lesser god, a second-class citizen who sits in the cheap seats. The hair on her body bristled.

"So how come I didn't know about you?" Her voice was quiet, wrapped in tenderness as the picture began to unfold.

The pause was too long. She checked the bars on her phone again.

"I can't say."

"How come?"

"Uhh—maybe that's a conversation for another time."

Privileged information that she guessed might be given up later, after time had passed, maybe through more exposure, several more conversations, maybe trust, she wasn't sure.

"Why not now?" She pushed against her better judgment.

She'd grown up with a father, he hadn't.

She waited but felt bricked out.

"Well, I think it's cool our livelihoods, our purposes are similar," she said to break the silence. "But with different species."

"I suppose," he said and sighed with what sounded like disinterest. The distance became harder to negotiate. It left her wondering why she kept trying. TJ turning away, her pursuing, maybe just end the call. Maybe she'd blown it at Pizza Leanings or maybe there'd been nothing to blow. Or maybe it was payback for when Penelope would say, *"Help me here, Amelia, it's like talking to the wall."*

"Sounds like maybe I caught you at a bad time," she said. "It *is* late." Sounds of her defensiveness and insecurity bothered her. She felt a hole open up inside, the Place of No Comfort.

"Not really."

"You sound busy or preoccupied or something." She'd give him an out. "Is there another time that's better?"

"No, this is fine."

Really. "The other day you mentioned something about your mom and our father meeting in the Navy in Germany," Amelia said.

"Yes, they met, got married. Got out of the service, moved back up here."

"Why did he leave?"

TJ was quiet.

"I guess you could say, uh, it didn't work out."

Then more quiet.

"How so?" she pushed.

"Things happen," he said. "Nothing's unbreakable."

"Unbreakable," she repeated, thinking of the family pods of marine mammals.

He then sighed as if tired and the conversation was making him even more so.

"You'd know it if you'd had one."

She guessed that she hadn't except with Alex, Bryce, and Jen. "I suppose," she said. Heaviness settled on her that felt permanent.

Maybe Bryce had it with Juney. Jen was still young enough for there to be hope, maybe with Doby, but for Amelia, she'd along ago figured that the love ship had sailed. She'd said *I love you* back to a few men, even when it felt like a lie. And lately she'd come to believe that the ones who'd told her first probably had known as little about love as she. The biochemical science of pair-bonding was a mystery, in marine animals as well as humans.

"So why marry my mother?"

He didn't say. She was losing patience with Mr. Tight Lipped.

"Well you know, it's too late for me to ask *her*."

"Sorry but I can't answer that for you either."

He didn't sound sorry at all. Her chest tensed with that same bad feeling when things don't add up because someone's withholding.

"So why not get divorced like everybody else in the world?"

"Don't know." His voice was deeper but sounded so much like her father's.

"So why leave property to both of us and not just you?"

"Because it's stipulated in the will."

"And your mother didn't change it because . . ."

"I don't know."

That she believed.

"Last month our attorney tracked you down," he said.

That's what had prompted his e-mails.

"It wasn't hard." The way he said it made her feel foolish.

"So what?" she snapped. "It's not like I'm in a witness protection program."

He didn't laugh.

"So why didn't your lawyer contact me?"

"Because I wanted to," he said.

"Really." How surprising.

"It's in the will; you're part of this family."

She was taken aback by the sudden inclusion—strange mix of heart and ice. Her eyes narrowed, noticing a crack in the bedroom wall. She didn't know what to say.

An uneasy silence began to imprison them. She wanted to ask more, scramble to create a rapport, fast-track it to closeness, but the conversation wasn't heading there, if it was a conversation at all.

"Look," he began. "As soon as you sign off on the document I'll put the place up for sale, split it down the middle." He sounded resolved. "No one's lived there for years. Been paying property taxes ever since Mom moved in with us. The land's more valuable than the house."

"Oh." She was surprised at the barrage of information.

"Property taxes are due next month; your half is around twelve hundred dollars—I'll let you know the exact figure."

"Okay." How odd, getting a present and a bill for it at the same time, like getting a kiss on the cheek and a slap in the face. In her mind's eye she tried to imagine her father, a consummate urban dweller and ocean lover living in a place so far away from both.

"Hey look, Amelia," he said in a voice that sounded like he was leveling with her. "The attorney'll send you another set of papers to close out the estate. Just sign off and then you never have to see me again."

What made him think that?

Her heart hurt after he ended the call.

"Take care."

24

It was not quite 6 a.m. on Monday, the morning after her phone call to TJ. Both Amelia and Bryce had the day off. Across the hall she heard him stirring in his room.

She stepped through his partially open doorway, already in her down parka. With her hand she nudged the door open a bit more.

"Hey, Bry?" His breathing sounded like he was awake. "You awake?"

The sheets swished. He looked at the doorway.

"Am now," she heard him say.

"Up for a drive?"

The sheets rustled as he scratched his nose.

"Where?"

"Lake Superior, to the property."

He sat up and looked at her as if she were crazy.

"Oh come on," she said. "It's not that far."

"Jesus, what time is it?" He looked at the window and then around for his phone until finding it on the night table where he'd left it.

"Almost six," she said.

"Christ. It's so dark," he said, rubbing his eyes. "When?"

"Now." She chuckled.

"Now?" He spotted her down coat. "Holy Christ, you're not kidding, are you?"

"Nope."

"Isn't there a winter storm warning? I heard my phone app go off about an hour ago." He picked up the phone, examining the radar and then turned it toward her, the bright blue bands of snow swirling to cover the screen.

"Eh, alarmist," she dismissed with a hand. "We'll be back before it hits."

"Uhh—don't think so, Am." His expression was one of disbelief as he held up the screen.

They'd done all sorts of crazy things before: gone out in rickety boats, flipping off all manner of small-craft warnings. In looking back she was sometimes amazed that Alex hadn't been orphaned before he'd been of legal age. And that they'd never once gotten arrested or jailed on foreign soil, always making it back to the host families who'd cared for Alex when he was too young to come along and crew.

"For Pete's sake, it's only a three-and-a-half-hour drive," she said, which was nothing considering how they'd bomb up and down the coast of Maine in search of remote marshy backwaters, crashing overnight in the back of her Jeep with young Alex in a sleeping bag on the backseat, she and Bryce cramped in the back or else on a beach.

Bryce rubbed his eyes again, yawning as he said, "I don't know, Am."

"What's not to know—said I'd drive," she offered, leaning in his doorway. "Egg McMuffins on me."

He swung over his legs, touched the floor, and stood.

"God, I hate it when you use food," he said and remained noncommittal as he ambled past her into the kitchen, opened the refrigerator door, and then burped.

"Jesus—you're the only person I know who burps the second they wake up."

"It was more than a second," he said. "God, it sucks there's never anything to eat." Bryce shut the refrigerator door, and looked at her as if it was her fault.

She raised her hands. "Do I look like a grocery store to you?"

He sighed in disgust and turned.

"Come to Lake Superior and I'll feed you," she said in what she thought was her hypnotic voice.

"Jen coming too?" he asked mid-yawn, looking for signs of their roommate as he scratched his side. He'd slept in his Sea Life polo shirt after the late-night shift.

"Stayed with the cop last night."

"Girl's in love."

"Yes, me thinks," Amelia agreed.

"So were you hatching this little plan in lieu of sleeping?" He walked toward the leather couch and collapsed.

"Actually, no," she said in a sober voice. "I sort of woke up with this wild hair up my ass."

Bryce made a contemplative face and nodded thoughtfully. "I appreciate wild hairs." He rubbed his chin and turned toward her with a certain regard.

"Offer on Mickey D's still good?" His face relaxed into what she called his sleepy-time smile.

"Canadian bacon," she confirmed in a singsong voice. "Only the best, Brycie."

He held out a hand to shake. Instead she chuckled.

"God, you really know how to hurt a guy," he said, shuffling back to his bedroom.

She dragged one of the kitchen chairs over to the aquarium, positioned it. She then retrieved the food from the fridge, climbed up in her coat, and lined it up along the edge. A few frozen chunks of brine shrimp, plankton, dropping in the pieces as they floated by like melting icebergs. Then she sprinkled in flakes of vegetable matter. The leather toadstool coral pulsed; reaching its fingers toward what it had just sensed was food.

Earlier she'd considered slipping out alone but couldn't imagine not having Bryce along for the adventure. It was like taking Alex in that Bryce was never judgmental and was most importantly, funny.

He emerged wearing a gray rag-wool sweater half pulled down over his stomach, still with plaid pajama bottoms on. The blue Sea Life collar poked up beneath the crew neckline. His sandy-colored hair stuck up straight like in silent movies when an actor has a fright. Stepping into his snow boots, he grabbed his hooded down coat, phone, and slapped on his camo cap.

"Mind if I don't brush my teeth?" he asked.

"Is it that much of an effort?" she said, making a face.

He walked toward the front door, looking at the weather radar on his phone. "It's coming toward us, Am."

"No, it's not. 'If you can't look to the west and predict the weather for twenty-four hours you've got no right to be in a boat.' Remember saying that, Brycie?"

He turned the screen toward her, frowing, but she looked away, dropping more vegetable flakes into the aquarium.

"We're not in a boat, Brunhilda, we're in a car."

"So what, we'll outrun it." She smirked in a way that let him know that she knew.

"You call your bro?"

"Too early," she said, figuring she'd crash the party, see his reaction. The old "better to beg forgiveness than ask permission"—the operating principle of crossing into international waters without authorization. "I'll call around eight. Already texted Jen we'll be back around dinnertime."

She brushed her hands together over the aquarium, knocking off the remaining fish flakes and frozen bits of food before climbing down.

"Can I drive?" Bryce asked and stepped into the hallway that always smelled like a chlorine swimming pool despite there not being one in the building.

"I told you I would." She pulled out keys from her coat pocket. "You just eat, sleep, and navigate—though not all at once."

"Whoever reaches the Jeep first, drives," he said.

She grabbed her messenger bag. The two of them raced toward the stairwell and down the stairs toward the street. They ran until they began to laugh but Bryce touched first.

"So okay, you won," she said. "Your legs are longer."

"Always making excuses," he said as he brushed off a layer of snow.

"I do want to drive." She looked up at him. "You mind?"

" 'Course not."

Amelia climbed in to warm the engine and plugged the GPS into the cigarette lighter and entered the property's legal address that TJ had let slip into the phone conversation.

After McDonald's, they headed toward the interstate on-ramp exchange to I-35 W, heading north. As soon as she turned to follow the signs to Bayfield/Superior, Wisconsin, her stomach jumped.

"I know this is weird, but . . ." she turned to him. "I have butterflies in my stomach." She pressed through her coat. Bryce looked at her for a while and smiled.

"Butterflies?" He stopped chewing the hash brown patty and offered it to her.

"No thanks. Like I'm going to see my father after having been away for a long time," she said. "I'm burning with curiosity but feel like I'm snooping."

"I feel it for you, Am," he said, stretching and looking out at the scenery. "Does feel good to get the hell out of Dodge though. Was getting some serious cabin."

"It's a creepy feeling," she said. "Like I'll bump into my father there, like he's lived a secret life all the while I've been thinking he's dead."

They looked at each other. His face was serious as she shrugged.

"I hope TJ'll meet us there," she said, thinking he might be one of those people who were better in person than on the phone. "I know it's short notice."

"That would be cool," he said. "Did he say he would?"

"Haven't asked; will when I call."

"Thought you arranged it last night on the phone?"

She felt her face get hot. "No."

"Meet your *brother.*"

"*Half* brother," she said, holding up her index finger to remind Bryce how she'd been corrected.

"Eh—that's just bullshit."

"It's biology."

They were quiet, watching as the shorter trees turned into forests.

"Why did TJ know about me all these years?"

He looked at her and rested his arm on the top of her seat around her shoulder.

For some reason it made her eyes tear.

"Don't know, Ammy."

"Strange, eh?" She smiled.

"Not really," he said. "It's strange because it's your father."

She wiped the corners of her eyes with one of her thumbs tucked into the cuff of her parka sleeve. "I want to smell the air, look at the land, and figure out what drew him, why he left that woman and abandoned his son."

Bryce shrugged. "Hey, some of us *wished* our fathers would have abandoned us."

It made her laugh.

"But seriously?" Her voice became soft. "I just hope TJ doesn't hate me."

Bryce turned to face her full-on.

She turned and shrugged as if it might be true.

"No one hates you, Am, no one."

She raised her eyebrows as a challenge. "I'd hate me if I was him."

She felt him look at her. They sat in silence for a few moments as if he was trying to decide whether to speak.

"He dumped them for Penelope and me." She felt her throat constrict.

"He didn't say that," Bryce said.

"Didn't need to."

"Venturing down the road of conjecture is dangerous territory, you know that, Amelia."

"Talk about a shitty thing to do," she said, not hearing him. "Really shitty. I mean, think about it, Bryce."

"You don't know what happened."

They sat quietly for a while.

"All I know is that TJ grew up without a father and I didn't."

"I just don't want to see you get disappointed."

"I'm already disappointed." She pushed back stray hairs that had slipped out of the hairclip.

"I mean disappointed that you won't find answers."

"I mean it was my dad, Bryce." She turned to look at him. "Abandons his son—"

"If that's what he did," Bryce qualified. "Maybe the woman kicked his ass and all his shit out."

He made her laugh.

"Marries two women." She glanced at him, nodding. "That part's true. Granted, the man was distant, sort of elsewhere all the time."

"Wasn't that everyone's father?"

She hadn't once thought she wouldn't find answers but now she wondered. In marine science there are always answers. Unanswered questions are answers in science. Mysteries like bioluminescence, biofluorescence, or the discovery of previously unknown creatures inhabiting the strange underground river-like flows beneath the ice in Antarctica were yet to be understood, loaded with unanswered questions that would someday be known.

Not so with the human heart. It remained a minefield of secrets and fears that if one trickle of truth escapes it might cause a flood in which everyone drowns. Or that life is so fragile it can only continue on through lies of omission. Like her father going out to make phone calls with nobody noticing but her.

"Don't think there's much danger of us turning into the Waltons," she said.

She felt him look away.

"You never know," Bryce said. "There've been stranger things."

They sat without talking until the falling snow became heavy enough to break the spell of private thoughts.

"Just flurries." She held up her hand, waving like it was no big deal.

"You're so full of shit," Bryce said as Amelia smirked. He was checking the radar again and he made a face as he turned the phone's radar toward her. She looked away.

As luck would have it, the winter storm warning had expanded to include the entire northern Minnesota/Wisconsin area up to Lake Superior.

"Driving back might be a bitch."

Bryce looked back. "You've gotta be kidding."

It was finally 8 a.m. and Amelia called TJ, hoping he'd pick up but got his voice mail instead.

"Hi, TJ, it's uh, Amelia. Today's Monday. Bryce and I thought we'd get an early start and take a drive up on our day off. I know it's sort of a spur of the moment thing but I'm hoping we can connect. Maybe meet at the land and have lunch or something after. I've got the GPS address from our conversation last night and we're about an hour away from Duluth. Give me a call when you get this message, looking forward to seeing you soon."

He didn't call back. As traffic slowed down and they were delayed, Amelia gave another call.

Two hours later she tried again. "Hi, TJ, it's Amelia again. We're sort of slogging along in the storm, it's taking us far longer than we thought but I was hoping to hear from you. Maybe we can connect later today. Give me a call, and let me know if that's going to work."

All she had to do was to sign off on the papers and never have to see him again. Maybe he'd meant it. Maybe that's what he wanted. She hoped not.

Snowflakes swirled across the road in patterns that played tricks on her eyes. The sky darkened to navy blue. Can't make somebody want to know you, can't make somebody want to love you either.

25

Snow was falling in white sheets as Bryce dozed with a full McDonald's belly. Amelia slowed down as road conditions worsened and he woke up with the change in speed.

"Everything okay?" He sat up, rubbing his eyes and blinking as he looked around. "Holy cow, how'd all of this happen?" Neither had ever seen such accumulation before.

"So what do you think?" she admitted defeat with a gentle voice, still unsettled by her own emotions. "Turn around, go back before we get stranded?"

"Nah. Point of no return, Am, point of no return." He tapped the screen of the GPS with his finger. His voice was light. "Once we get to Duluth it's a hop, skip, and a jump to Bayfield."

She wasn't so sure. Amelia had seen lake-effect snow once before while visiting a friend up in Buffalo, but this was different.

"Bet ya dinner it's falling three inches an hour," she said.

"Oh, so now you're Ms. Caution, are you?"

She tapped his arm and laughed in a conciliatory way.

"Hear from the bro yet?" Bryce asked.

She glanced at her phone on the dashboard, wondering about reception in the storm.

"Maybe he's out of town." *Or maybe he wants nothing to do with me.* TJ hadn't mentioned being away; maybe he was out in the field.

The sky closed around them like a dome. Everything darkened and though it was early morning, it looked like dusk. Snow clouds hushed down in steel-gray puffs, enveloping the tops of trees almost midway toward the bottom of their trunks. The road narrowed to one lane, closed in by walls of white.

Amelia was glued to the red taillights of the car ahead; her shoulders cement as she gripped the wheel. They slowed to 30 mph, then 25. It seemed they were the only two cars on the road.

"You okay driving?" Bryce asked.

She glanced at her watch but didn't answer. It was taking far longer than the three hours, seventeen minutes the GPS had indicated.

The wheels were floating and it felt like the Jeep was bucking to slide into the oncoming lane without notice. There was no center guardrail to block such movement.

The car she'd been following put on its blinker and exited.

"Shit," she murmured. Whether at its destination or giving up, it left them on the road alone. Snowflakes had knitted together a tunnel, accentuating the narrowing of the road.

Amelia looked at her watch again.

"I can take it from Duluth," he suggested.

"I won't fight you," she said, and rolled her shoulders to try and relax.

The windshield began to fog. Ice inched up on the outside, invading her line of sight despite the defroster working at full bore.

"Pull over and I'll scrape," Bryce suggested.

She wanted to but ahead she spotted a new line of dim taillights following what appeared to be a snowplow.

"I don't want to lose sight of them." She gestured, fearing whiteout conditions. There was no place to pull over. They'd already passed stranded vehicles.

"Damn," she said. "You're right about having planned this better," she admitted.

"Hey—what's life without a little excitement," he said and play-punched her shoulder. "Can you reach the scraper?"

She felt his eyes on her.

"Thanks."

Amelia reached under the seat and felt the familiar plastic handle and handed it over.

"Allow me." Bryce rolled down the window, hoisted himself out, and scraped as far as he could reach. Snowflakes covered the sides of his hair and the top of the camo cap as he sat back down.

"Your turn." He handed it over and took the wheel; his foot nudged hers off the gas pedal.

Amelia rolled down the window, stood and did the same, feeling the wheels sliding.

The streetlights had clicked on like it was night just as they reached the Duluth city limits before noon.

"Pull in there." Bryce pointed to the first gas station/convenience store.

Once parked, the Jeep's doors wouldn't open.

She shouldered the door.

"We're frozen in," Bryce said and then laughed. "This is like that drive through New Brunswick."

It took several more shoulder butts before Bryce's side gave. Amelia then climbed over the gearshift and out. Then he opened the driver's side. The entire exterior was iced over, with clumps of frozen snow jammed up into the wheel wells and under the wipers.

Amelia stood and stretched.

"That was rather harrowing," Bryce admitted and again scraped off the windows. He grabbed the last bottle of pink de-icer from a wooden pallet and headed inside the store.

The store's warmth felt good. Amelia dug her fingers into her neck muscles.

"Hi." She walked up to the attendant.

"You guys in from the Cities?"

"Yep, on thirty-five." Bryce set the pink jug of de-icer on the counter.

"Some storm, eh? Coupla fellas just came in. Whiteout conditions going west," the young man said, looking out the window at the Jeep. "Lucky you—got the last gallon of that, probably walk outta here and sell it for a cool fifty." The attendant chuckled. "More's comin' tomorrow. Any gas?" The clerk held his fingers just above the register keys.

"Just this and two coffees," Bryce said.

"We're headed for Bayfield," Amelia said. "Know anything about the roads?"

The attendant pointed at the TV monitor in the upper corner of the ceiling, indicating a large and expanding splash of royal blue fingers moving northeast.

"Worst is on your tail," the attendant said. "But them little coastal towns along the lake'll get hammered in no time." He looked up at a clock embedded into a neon Point Beer sign and leaned on the counter as if telling her in confidence. "Storm just closed down the Cities. Airport, buses, MOA."

"MOA?" she asked.

"Mall of America."

"Ha." Amelia laughed, thinking of Jen and turned to Bryce as he approached the register. Her cheeks glowed with warmth. Something about the closure was deeply satisfying.

"Storm closed down the mall." Amelia grabbed his arm and shook it. "No buses, airport's closed."

His eyes widened. "Really." They both smiled a secret, greedy smile and looked at each other. "Would've made for a quiet day at home."

"Think Jen's stranded?"

He shrugged. "Bet she will be if the cop is."

"If she's lucky they'll get stuck in Macy's," she said. "Just imagine the two of them snuggled up in those poufy, cozy-looking Ralph Lauren down comforter display beds they have in the front window."

They both chuckled, imagining Jen. "Bet she'd be like the princess and the pea, though," Bryce said. "That girl's happiest sleeping out on a rickety boat dock somewhere in the South Pacific."

Blaring beeps from the TV station's weather alert made them all turn. Radar flashed as the image recalibrated, now showing dozens of blue and white fingers stretching east toward Lake Superior to gobble up the entire Bayfield Peninsula. Red-banded warnings crawled across the TV screen about blizzards, wind-chill, whiteout conditions.

"Well?" Amelia looked up at Bryce.

"Well what?"

"Keep on going?" she asked in a soft voice.

"Well, hell yeah, Am." Bryce turned on her as if she'd lost her mind. "You're not getting soft on me now—no way we're turning back; we'd be driving back into the worst of it."

"He's right, you know." The attendant nodded somberly as he caught Amelia's eye and then looked out the storefront window up at the sky. "Hittin' the city limits just about now. Better leave if you're headed east—roadworker guy left right before you got here." He pointed toward the door like a hitchhiker. "Plows'r already out."

As the three of them studied the TV weather storm coverage, Amelia's stomach jumped. She looked at her phone, nothing from TJ.

"Is there cell phone reception in Bayfield?" she asked the attendant.

"Ooo—can be pretty spotty up there even when the sun's shining. Lotsa hills, that old Iron Range is up there, you step twenty feet, your bars disappear and you're in a dead zone."

It made her feel better to think that maybe that's why TJ hadn't called.

Just then a white Jeep Grand Cherokee with Wisconsin plates whipped into the parking lot just shy of bumping into the storefront's plate-glass window. Amelia noticed the same rust pattern along the bottom edge of both doors like a Rorschach inkblot.

"Here's Darlene." The attendant motioned to the window and then stepped out from behind the register, past the roll of Lottery Quick Picks and 5-hour Energy drink displays. "She'll update ya 'bout the roads."

A dream catcher dangled from the woman's rearview mirror. A youngish woman hopped down, cigarette dangling from her lips, an unzipped camo-patterned sweatshirt with hood hanging off her shoulders, a Packers T-shirt underneath. She had long dark hair strewn as if not having had a comb-through in days, not a stitch of makeup as she trudged toward the door. The woman took one long pull from the cigarette, yanked open the door, and ditched the butt into a snowbank without breaking stride. Amelia nudged Bryce.

"BFW." She whispered as the woman entered.

"Too young," Bryce said, his eyebrows rising slightly as he checked the woman out. They played this game: BFW meant Bryce's Future Wife. And then there was AFH, which for some reason was always funnier.

The woman stomped snow off on the rubber mats by the front door.

"Hey, Darlene."

"Hey, Kev." She rushed toward the soft drinks, slowing ever so slightly past Bryce before opening the refrigerator door and grabbing a couple of Red Bulls.

"These folk're heading out to Bayfield."

The woman approached the register, the cans tucked under one arm.

"If you ain't leaving now better get a room." She croaked out a smoker's laugh. "Picking up Grandma before all hell breaks loose."

Bryce stood up straighter, looked at Amelia, and raised his eyebrows, his head tipped toward the door.

The woman's face was deeply lined with that leathery look that comes with hard living, too much sun, bad luck, and bouts of heavy drinking to make it all feel better.

Amelia strolled up to the storefront window. To the west the clouds had already changed. Thicker, lower, and an even darker navy blue. Everything was still. No birds flying, even cars looked quiet.

"Looks freaky," Amelia said to Bryce as they headed toward the door for the last leg of the drive.

"You wanna see freaky, stick around," the woman called after them, croaking out a laugh.

It was different from a New England sky—rawer, like the atmosphere of another planet or unexplored region of Earth. The clouds had traded celestial citizenship for earthly residence as they continued to lower to encase houses on the steep hills. The fear in her gut was exhilarating. It always was when diving in a part of the world she'd never been; where the angle of sun, soil, and water color are so unlike anything she'd seen that it's never really clear if they're friend or foe. Her eye could never take in enough differences, always teased by thoughts that these might be the last scenes she'd see.

The edge of the storm pushed up against Duluth. Snow had begun to fall unbroken by the slightest breeze; silent, gentle, and seemingly harmless all the while portending that something else was on its way. Nature's early-warning system for all who knew to listen: fly home to roost in the thickest of fir branches, burrow into the deepest dens or under the bushiest of evergreens. Cars parked along the street were already heaped like frosted cupcakes from a day-old storm. Some buried mid-door by the efforts of snowplows to clear the street, looking as if their liberation depended on nothing short of heavy equipment or the arrival of an early spring.

"Let's hit it, Am," Bryce said as he brushed flakes from the front and back windows and then finished filling the wiper fluid.

Highway 13 to Bayfield narrowed to one lane. The surface was snow covered, making it difficult to determine the lanes. Bryce slowed to 30 mph.

"How you doing?" Bryce asked.

"Excited, nervous." She glanced at him. "A bit freaked out."

"Me too."

Private thoughts and feelings began to seep through. Luckily Bryce was one to respect long silences. It was code on dive projects. Chatty nonstop talkers were never hired back or else sustained a direct "talking to." The mournful solace of a sunset, the call of a baby seal waiting for its mother to come back with food did not require comment as the limitless ocean caused them to sink into the deepest recesses of beautiful loneliness. Lost in thought, crews would go hours sitting side by side on deck without speaking. The wonder and tragedy of seaside life demanded silence.

Bryce glanced into the rearview mirror.

"Look."

Amelia turned. A low-hanging storm front was roaring toward them, as thick as a shelf, it tailgated like it knew where they were headed.

Twinges of adrenaline and longing made her want to park the Jeep and scramble down into one of the steeper ravines. Hunker down, let the storm catch them as they were tucked and sheltered under a bevy of pine boughs, to be in the storm but not of it. To smell the white ozone of its arctic heart all the while hiding with one cheek against the rotting fecundity of autumn's burnished grasses and fallen leaves, burrowed in alongside white-tailed deer curled up on the safety of the forest floor.

The houses along the highway looked cozy. Their dim interior lighting and smoke fires evoked sadness and yearning that reminded her of the little cottage in Port Jefferson with its wood-burning stove where she'd holed up with Alex as a toddler. Weathering a few hurricanes and nor'easters, they'd hide under a pile of covers from the sounds of rattling rafters. Back then, all of their belongings smelled of wood smoke. Even after they'd moved up to Cornell for graduate school, she'd pull out something that had been boxed up and the smell of smoke set off a longing that she never knew what to do with—a bottomless hollow for which there seemed to be no antitoxin as one might have for the sting of an Australian box jellyfish. Now life felt so slipshod, so pasted together, so fly-by-night.

The coastal sections of Highway 13 on Lake Superior were windswept with sculpted snowdrifts with smooth-edged grooves and curves resembling the shoulders of angels. Some reached the Jeep's wheel wells.

Bryce shifted into lower gear and powered through. "Gets worse we might have to get out and dig."

She tried to phone TJ again but there was no service.

As the road curved, Amelia held up her phone and saw two bars. She spoke in double time while they held out. "Hi, TJ, we're getting closer to Bayfield, was hoping to hear from you. Gosh, it's beautiful up here; I had no idea how beautiful. Sorry to keep calling, was hoping to connect. Do you guys have moose, bears—" She continued talking as if to him.

"Or polar bears," Bryce called into the phone. "Wish we'd brought a dogsled, looks like we might need one."

She laughed.

"On our way up to the property, was hoping to meet you up there. Jeeze, I feel like a stalker calling so many times, but if you're in town and can make it there, though it looks like a storm is coming, would love to see you. Even if you can't, give me a call and maybe we can make it another time. My, it's breathtaking up here! Roads are sort of rough, so I understand if you don't want to come out, but maybe we could come see you at your place."

They crawled through each tiny coastal town without witnessing a soul, the dim interior glow of house lights the only evidence it wasn't a ghost town. An eerie stillness marked each town. The uneasiness was thrilling. As the intermittent scent of birch fires filled the car, she imagined her father. So often her father would remark how the aroma of a wood fire was so comforting, though they'd never had a fireplace.

Amelia touched the window with the back of her hand to gauge the outside chill.

Who was this woman her father had married? Why hide such an important part of what proved to be a short life? Had he lived longer would he have come clean? Or else lived to be a hundred without saying a word until that e-mail from TJ?

She glanced into the snowy woods through her father's eyes, searching them: an ocean-loving city boy trying to become a woodsman in the far north. Maybe that's what the Navy and Cold War antics had done to him, made him want to become someone else. Perhaps such identity fraud had caught up with him once he'd realized that swapping one life for another doesn't work.

Amelia remembered him stepping out on Thanksgiving, Christmas, thinking it didn't make sense. He'd claim there was a mechanical breakdown in the presses that required his attention, only he'd leave home and return sooner than it would have taken to drive to the plant, much less make repairs. At eight years old she'd noticed. If Penelope had, she didn't say.

"Where's Daddy going?" she'd ask as her mother wrestled to baste a turkey on Thanksgiving.

"I don't know, Amelia," she'd snap back. "But stop being a pain in the ass and go set the table."

"I already did!"

"Then go find something else to do or I'll find something for you."

Remembering back, there was a melancholy and restlessness about him on holidays.

"I'll be back, Pen," he'd say to his wife on Christmas Eve. "They called me to do a press-check, on the way home I'll call the Boston crowd," which was his Boston family that he'd call from pay phones, claiming it was cheaper.

"Can I come?" Amelia asked.

He'd looked at her in an odd way. Not angry, not even annoyed by the question. She'd sense him mulling it over.

"Not this time," he'd say. "A broken press might take a while to fix," he'd say.

"I'll bring my book," she'd said. "I'll be so quiet you won't even know I'm there and this way I can say 'Hi' to Aunt Athena."

Then he'd bend down, engulf her in his arms, and squeeze like he'd never see her again or else was counting on her being the anchor that would allow him to drift only so far in the current.

"Dad." She'd laugh. "I can't breathe." She'd fake being crushed. He'd let go, laughing. "Please let me come?" she'd ask, always feeling unsettled when he'd go off alone.

"I'll be good," she'd say, clasping her hands together in that begging way kids do as she'd feel him teetering on the verge of saying yes though he never did.

"You're always good, Amelia, always," he'd say and kiss the top of her head, inhaling the scent of her hair. "There's nothing bad about you, nothing." He'd then smooth her hair with his hand as he set her down. "Tell your mom I'll be back before dinner." And he always was.

It was sadder now as she thought back. Divided and bi-located for most of his adult life, Ted Sr. had inhabited two worlds that bore no connection. Somewhere, he'd become fragmented and maybe even lost. But as a girl, how could she have known?

They passed a stand of old-growth pines that were probably much smaller when her father had lived here in the late 1950s.

Just last week was her father's birthday. He would have turned eighty-six. How could he have a son and not tell her? Yet she'd done the same to Chris Ryan. Never told him how thirty-four years ago she'd had a son. Her stomach sank, with indictment, stunned as it hit her.

"Hey Bryce?"

"Hey yeah?" he answered as the GPS flag indicated they were approaching Bayfield.

"Haven't I done the same thing as my father? I mean Alex not knowing his father?"

He glanced at her.

"No."

"How not so?"

"Because Ryan was a dick who used you. Sounds like your dad loved this woman, I'm guessing, but it all got mixed up. We don't know."

"Yeah, but I never told Ryan, I never gave him the option of knowing Alex." Here she'd been feeling angry at her father but how easily she'd done it too.

"Hey—it was your best judgment at the time. He might have messed with Alex's head."

She'd always wondered since the day she'd parked by Chris Ryan's house, stumbling on the little domestic scene. Fear had made her stay away, fear that he might try and take Alex. Here he was a professor, with a house, a wife, a family and she had the Fish Market.

"And remember, you did tell Alex when he was twelve," Bryce reminded her. "Told him you'd look up the fucker if he'd wanted to meet him."

She laughed at how he said it. It was true. She'd said all of that and meant it though Alex had so far never taken her up on it or at least admitted that he had. Yet the sting of similarity ate at her the closer they came to Bayfield.

And while the dead can't answer questions, often the living share even less.

"Ah ha." Bryce pointed to her phone on the dashboard. "Now we're talking." There was a full signal.

Amelia phoned again. "Hi TJ, your stalker calling again." She looked at Bryce and smirked. "I'm almost to the property and wanted to know if I should wait for you there."

The GPS flag indicated they'd arrived in Bayfield. As they descended a steep ridge the harbor opened up, revealing a city embedded into the surrounding hills. The entire town looked bleached white with snow against the backdrop of gunmetal clouds.

"Looks like Camden, Maine."

Bryce rubbed his stomach and nodded. "It is a little déjà vu–ish."

The docks and the lakefront were winterized in that nautical way mariners secure a waterfront.

"There's Madeline Island." Her finger pointed from the GPS to the land mass across the bay. The only movement was a large boat she presumed to be a ferry steaming toward it. The ferry's hull crashed through what looked like icy chunks of rapidly freezing water, leaving an open trail in its wake.

They passed through a downtown area lined with Victorian-era homes. The GPS directed a right turn up a steep hill. The arrival "flag" was pinned at the top.

"Shit, it figures." Bryce mumbled a laugh.

As they turned, the Jeep's wheels began to spin.

"Come on, baby." She pumped her body forward as if to help the uphill climb.

As they reached the summit, both sat back and took a breath.

"This place has got some serious weather." Bryce braked at the first red metal fire sign that had matching numbers.

"That's it."

Bryce tried to roll down the window but it was frozen. He banged on it until it loosened and opened. "Honey, we're home," he called.

"Oh please."

In the driveway stood a two-foot snow wall created by the snowplow. A metal mailbox twisted like a corkscrew leaned over.

"Park on the street?" she suggested.

"Road's too narrow."

They looked at each other and shrugged.

"Let's take it like we own it, Am," Bryce said.

He downshifted, revved the engine, and traversed the frozen barrier.

They pulled partway in and stopped.

"Think I'll leave it ri-i-ght here." He turned off the engine. "Close enough to rock it out."

She felt Bryce studying her profile as she watched the gathering clouds.

"You know, Am." He paused. "If it turns as ugly as they're saying we might have to find a hotel."

She shot him a look.

"Especially if he doesn't call."

"He'll call." Her voice was soft with hope.

The dashboard temperature gage said eleven, Fahrenheit. It was twenty-eight when they'd left Duluth. There was no sign of a house, tire tracks, or any evidence of a structure; it looked like a parcel of vacant land.

"Let's walk it in." Bryce pushed open the car door. The hinge crunched. He stepped down. Snow reached the tops of his boots. "Shit, it's deeper than I thought."

Pushing open the door, she hopped down too. Snow tumbled into her boots as a gust of wind blew her ponytail straight up like an exclamation point.

"Damn, it's cold." She popped up her hood and reached into her pockets for mittens. "Shit." She'd left them on the kitchen table in the apartment. Pulling up her hands, she balled up her fingers in the sleeves for warmth.

Snow spilled over the tops of her boots, packing her ankles like beer cans in a cooler.

"Oh great," she said. In moments her feet would be cold. Snow would melt against the warmth of her body, canceling out the insulation value of wool.

Wet feet on the advancing edge of a storm was dangerous. Hypothermia was an odd thing. It came on in unexpected ways. She'd once seen a diver become disoriented and almost die in warm tropical waters.

"So where's this alleged house?" Bryce huffed up the steep incline. "I'll break trail, follow so you don't get as wet."

Her toes were already throbbing but she didn't want to say and risk having Bryce insist she go back to the Jeep.

A weird nervousness tickled in the bony recesses of her chest.

"Too bad we don't have snowshoes."

"Next time," he called back.

"Yeah, next time," she repeated in a quiet voice, stepping in his tracks. She liked the idea of a next time.

"Maybe over this hill?" she suggested, breathing heavy as they trudged in knee-high snow. She pulled on her bottom lip. "Hope it's the right place."

"The fire sign matches TJ's address."

"True."

She could hear Bryce breathing.

"Hey," she said. "Remember when we were in the Java Sea just off Jakarta and that captain entered the wrong coordinates and wouldn't admit it?" she asked.

"You mean the known meth and crackhead that the NSF had vetted and authorized as our charter for the dive project?" Bryce said.

"And the guy wouldn't admit we were going out to sea?"

"Yeah, and then the fucker locked himself in the bridge and Jason had to break the window so we could open the door and get in," Bryce continued the story, pausing to catch his breath.

Amelia paused too. Resting her hands on her thighs she bent

over to catch her breath. "God. I'd forgotten about Jason having to do that."

"And then remember Jen jumping on the guy and pounding the living snot out of him?" he said. It sent them both
laughing as they remembered the spectacle. "I'd never seen her
so pissed off."

Bryce continued the ascent. Amelia followed.

"Except at Brad."

"Yeah well." Bryce got serious. "Brad deserved it."

She couldn't see the top of the embankment, it just kept
going. Amelia felt uneasy and stopped.

"You know," she called up to him, resting for a moment. "I
can't shake the feeling someone lives there," Amelia said.

He'd stopped too and looked back at her.

"TJ said no one's lived there for years, right?"

"Yeah." But something felt off, or wrong. Maybe there were
squatters, or a homeless person living rough.

"Think they'll close the mall again tomorrow?" she asked as
they resumed the climb.

"Fat chance," he called over his shoulder.

"Tell me this wasn't a stupid idea?" she said, out of breath.

"I don't do stupid, Am," he called over his shoulder. But the
specter of his camo hat, Sea Life polo shirt collar poking out of
his gray wool rag sweater, and flannel pajama bottoms, the
whole thing struck her as funny and she started laughing.

Bryce stopped. She guessed he'd reached the summit by how
he stood taking in the vista.

"Here." Bryce took a few steps back, reaching to hoist her up.
His cheeks were bright pink from the cold.

"Look," he said quietly, his arm around her.

There was no sun, no overhead warmth. Charcoal clouds
tumbled into Chequamegon Bay advancing like the sandstorms
she'd seen in a *National Geographic* special on the Sahara Desert.
The view opened to Lake Superior. Heavily treed islands were
powdered white with snow.

"And that," he pointed to a tiny dot downhill, "is your house."

The land dropped off sharply and then leveled into a slight plateau on which stood a tiny mustard-colored one-story structure that had the same panoramic view of Lake Superior and surrounding islands.

The snowy field sloped down toward the lake, bracketed on either side by tree lines that marked where the forest began: pine and bleached birch, their leafless branches blurred into what looked to be a mishmash bouquet of bird feathers: sparrow, wild turkey, and natural-colored ostrich.

She paused to catch her breath.

"You okay?"

"More than okay." She was still smiling without realizing it.

The lake was unnaturally white with ice and a covering of snow. It was so dramatic and vivid against the dark sky that it resembled a stage set more than real weather.

It had a raw and unforgiving quality. The contrasts alone silenced them. An eerie stillness settled on the valley and she felt scared. Seagulls dove for cover—their bodies stark white against the dark sky as they passed through her field of vision like phantom floaters. No caws of crows, no last-minute rustling of foraging squirrels. Wildlife had the good sense to take shelter, not like the two of them wandering around half-cocked on some kind of nutty treasure hunt; the only exposed souls. She turned toward the pungent scent of pine.

There was a rumbling in the clouds.

Bryce looked out to the bay.

"Was that thunder or lake thunder?" Bryce asked.

"Don't know." The deep rumble was like she'd touched a live wire. Unnerved, she stood still; recalled the myth of the Greek Sirens who'd lure ancient mariners through their songs and beauty toward the rocky shoals and to their deaths. A shudder passed through her. She felt afraid again for no reason and tried to shake it off.

"Let's go." Amelia pulled up and snapped her hood under her chin and took the first downhill step toward the dumpy little mustard-colored house at the bottom.

They'd make it before the clouds were halfway across the bay.

Bryce stepped ahead to break trail.

"Dad," she whispered into the air as she lagged behind. What had it been like to live with a heart so divided?

Who was this woman he'd fallen in love with, the woman who, as TJ alleged, was his unbreakable love? A woman he couldn't give up yet had. One thing for sure was that nothing was indestructible.

26

It looked like a fifties' style raised ranch badly in need of repair.

A sooty cylindrical metal chimney rose from one section of the roof like a ship's mast, presumably venting a wood-burning stove. An ugly industrial-looking gray metal roof, one you might expect to find on a warehouse not a private residence, covered the entire house. The parts not covered with snow looked pitted and dented from having endured years of Lake Superior's temper tantrums. The mustard-colored aluminum siding along one side looked as if it had been pried up either by someone or something in search of what was beneath.

A snow-covered wooden deck surrounded the house, looking as if it had been nailed on as an afterthought. Three steps led up to what appeared to be the front door.

"Quarter says it's locked," Amelia called to where Bryce waited at the bottom step.

He snorted with disgust. "That's not even a bet, Am."

She laughed out loud. "Never know, country folk in Vermont don't lock their doors."

Bryce chortled. "Yeah, you wish, darlin'."

His deep voice made her chuckle again as she reached the steps.

A foot of accumulated snow lay undisturbed along the railing without so much as a bird's footprint. Amelia knocked it off in one piece with her sleeve and it fell without a sound. The railing underneath was splintered, reminding her of weather-beaten railings on the docks at Stony Brook. Every summer her Summers by the Sea participants would run down the dock, hands skimming the railing, snagging an array of splinters. Amelia would have to dig the slivers out with a needle.

"Ladies first," he said at the base of the front steps.

"Ain't exactly Tara, is it?"

"Well this ain't exactly Georgia now either, hon," he answered back with a mock drawl.

She thought of the Revolution House.

"Miss the Rev House."

"Yeah." He looked away and sighed. "Miss a lot of things."

The first step made a cracking noise so loud she flinched. "Think it'll hold?"

"Only one way to find out." Bryce jumped on the first step.

Amelia raced up the remaining three.

"Ta da!" She lifted her arms just as the deck popped like someone had shot off a gun. They both shirked.

"Temperature's dropping," Bryce reported, looking off at the tree line on either side of the property.

She felt it too. Her feet felt like wooden blocks.

"Think the deck'll hold?"

"No, but I'll say 'yes' if it makes you feel better," he said. Each footstep elicited a referred boom around the other side. "The fall won't kill us."

She stepped toward the plain vanilla-colored fiber-core door, no windows in which to peek, and no decorative raised panels. The bottom marred with generations' worth of dog scratches and scuff marks.

It was locked. Of course.

The doorknob's gold finish was worn off from tens of thousands of turns, only a key lock and no dead bolt.

"You could pop this baby open," she said.

Bryce faced her with his *give me a break* look.

"So?" she lifted her arms like, *do it*. "You think it's disrespect-
ful or something?"

"Not cool to break the door." He turned and headed toward
the other side of the house, following the deck. "Might be an
easier way in."

"Got your phone?" she called. He backed up and looked her
in the eye as he patted down his pockets as she did the same.

"It's on the driver's seat."

"Mine's on the dash."

"Guess we'll have to be like pioneers, Ammy."

She heard him on the other side of the house as the deck
shifted and popped under his weight.

She stepped lightly for fear of breaking through a board.
Across the field there was a half-collapsed outbuilding that
might have been a garage. Up under its eaves were dozens of
antlers nailed up, in the center a huge set that were moose.

Had her father nailed up those antlers?

"Hey," Bryce called from the other side. "Your dad a hunter?"

"No," she called back. "But then I didn't think he was a bigamist either."

Antlers all tacked up from the man who'd blanch at having
to drop a live lobster into a pot of boiling water. She'd remember her parents arguing over the baby lamb that Penelope's
brothers had bought from a farmer to slaughter in celebration
of Greek Easter. They'd cut its throat on one of their suburban
driveways in a bid to connect with peasant roots from the
motherland. Ted and Amelia had watched as they'd hosed off
the blood.

"Oh stop it." Penelope later raised her voice at Easter Dinner,
knowing why her husband had lost the stomach for the sliced
lamb she'd set on a platter. "Jesus was the Lamb of God that
got slaughtered."

"Yeah, but not in a driveway in Baldwin," Amelia said.

"Fresh mouth." Penelope's hand caught her in the face.

The lakeside of the house was all windows. The first two

were boarded up; in the third a shade was drawn around which Amelia tried to see.

An outdoor table and chairs were positioned on the far side of the deck overlooking the lake, each chair with a snow pillow in the shape of its seat. She imagined people sitting during the summer, looking out to where the waterline blurs into shades of an aqua-blue horizon. Amelia thought back to the picnic table out by the lab's pumping station on Narragansett Bay, the old part of the marine biology building covered with weathered shingles where they'd sit and gaze out onto such horizons. Sitting around with staff as they'd discuss foibles, plan research projects, and eat lunches they'd brought from home, wiping mouths on sleeves or the backs of their hands.

She paused, brushed snow off the railing, and leaned, taking in the frosty Apostle Islands. An eerie partial sun peeped though one side, making the dark storm clouds seem more so as they edged into Chequamegon Bay. Downtown the docks looked empty, the ferry battened down, even the fish tugboats looked frozen in for the season. She'd never seen a Superior fish tug in the water before, only in photos. They were legendary for their buoyancy in all kinds of seas. Many looked more like bathtub toys than serious fishing vessels. Known as some of the world's longest-working boats they were unique in marine design and construction, some had been in operation for generations—built of timbers harvested on land owned by family members.

She heard a noise. Turning her head, she held her breath, listening. Cocking her head to the side, she concentrated. It was faint—the sound of an animal softly mewing. Then it was joined by another. Looking around she tried to locate where it was coming from.

Amelia tilted her head, trying to decipher. Was it from inside the house? Glancing over to the ground below, she looked for animal tracks but saw nothing in the fresh snow.

Then it stopped. She waited, listening. Then she heard it

again. Bending over, she listened. The sound was coming from under her boots. She cleared away the snow with her foot and then dropped to her knees, digging with her fingers to clear the gaps between the boards.

"Hey, Bryce," she called out, momentarily balling her hands into fists, retracting them into her sleeves as they ached.

"Hey, yeah?"

"Can you come here?"

Laying her ear to the wood she listened. Mewing and soft grunting grew louder. Something was calling. She felt its distress. And while she wasn't familiar with topside mammals, she knew distress calls frequently triggered chemical reactions in humans.

"Hello?" she called through the boards, her lips pressed to the space.

Then there was quiet.

She tried to get a clear view. It smelled of moist hay and quiet—a den of sorts.

"What's up?" He appeared with hands on hips and then squatted as soon as he saw her.

"Something's down there," she said and glanced at him. "You hear it?"

He knelt and then lay his ear down on the gap, watching her eyes.

"Nope." Bryce sat up.

"Like crying," she said. "I just heard it, I swear."

"Mmm—baby raccoons?" he suggested. "A baby bear in hibernation? Newborn mammals are tough to ID, they look so much alike."

She thought it too high-pitched to be a bear, though what did she know about baby bears since she'd never heard one in her life? Providing that the size of the animal matched its sound, which wasn't always the case, she guessed it was small, perhaps with a protective mama poised to scratch out anyone's eyes.

"Any tracks on the other side?" she asked.

"None on the deck." He stood up, brushed off the front of his flannel pajama bottoms, and then stuck his hands in his coat pockets. "I'll go look in the field."

She waited.

"Nope. Nothing," he called.

Then they backtracked, climbed down the front steps, and split up, each circumnavigating the parameter of the deck to search for an opening.

Her fingers stung with cold. She partly unzipped her coat and tucked them into her armpits.

The space between the ground and the top of the deck was covered by a decorative wooden lattice. Amelia touched it. The wooden crisscross slats felt more like parchment. It would be easy to break through.

The snow seemed deeper on the lakeside. More icy talc filled her boots. Amelia leaned against a post, took off each boot, banged it empty, and then slipped it back on.

Then she spotted the opening.

"Found it," she called and rushed toward it.

Bryce met up lakeside.

She bent over and called, "Hello?"

Still nothing.

"I'm going in," she said.

"Let me."

"No. I'm smaller. It'll be easier."

"I'll follow."

"No. Stay out here in case the mom returns," she said.

"But what if she's inside?"

She turned and cracked a foolhardy grin which for some reason she felt certain.

Something had chewed and broken its way in by evidence of the irregular shape of the break. This was the only opening so she guessed the animal to be fairly intelligent. She'd heard former colleagues at the university griping about the stupidity of woodchucks that'd chewed into New Hampshire cabins but weren't smart enough to find the same hole and had to chew out through a second.

While there were no outside tracks, just inside there were pawprints frozen in the mud.

"That's one big dog," Bryce said and turned to her. He raised his eyebrows.

There was worry in his voice. They both knew dogs made her uncomfortable.

"Well." She made a stupid face to get him to smile but he didn't. "Here goes."

It was her stock line when kicking off a first dive on location right before biting into the regulator and falling backward off the starboard side of a ship.

Crouching down on all fours, she stuck her head in to listen. Rustling noises from somewhere, a critter moving around. It was dim but not dark, and very still. Bathed in a yellow glow from the mustard-colored siding the den was protected from the wind. She wasn't surprised that an animal would den up here.

"Hello?" She called again, crawling in slowly to announce her presence. If a wild animal lashed out, there was no protection. Pausing, she listened for a warning growl. The cries commenced, intensifying as Amelia approached. Her chest ached with a sweetness she'd only felt around newborn things.

The moist smell of hay was so strong she could taste it. It was light enough to make out objects. Several hay bales were stacked up, a garden rake and tools, a dusty lawn mower smothered with dried blades of grass. Some of the hay bales were still tightly strung into rectangles, others were broken apart and looked as though they'd been that way for a while. The animal cries came from the section closest to the lake, underneath the patio furniture.

"Anything yet?" Bryce called in.

"Getting closer."

"Yell if you need me."

As she approached the cries, Amelia braced and pulled down her hood over her face in the event of an attack. Reaching the farthest bale of hay, she noticed a pile of wadded-up clothes along with a crumpled-up red-and-green blanket that looked like a baby quilt.

Amelia pivoted alongside to see.

"Well, hi," she said. In the dimness, lying in hay from a bale that was broken open, were little animal forms huddled, writhing, and shivering, their enormous furry heads turned toward her, watching.

"Aw, I'm not gonna hurt you." She sat down and scooted closer, counted two moving bodies, a third appeared still. She touched it and recoiled. It was frozen.

The air smelled like sour milk and hay.

Her coat sleeve swished against the edge of the wadded clothes. She moved closer, they cried louder, either imploring or terrified, their faces oriented toward her as they stood on bent, wobbly legs that trembled.

"You're right, Bryce," she called. "I think they're puppies. So tiny."

Each was about double the size of her hand. The closer she got, the louder they cried and grunted. Both reared away but then approached, not sure of which. Their eyes were bright blue, not quite in focus. Their stubby legs pushed their disproportionately large bodies toward her as they head-butted and collided, reminding her of a deadlocked rugby team at the University of Rhode Island.

She touched the back of one pup and lifted it. It was cool to the touch and shivering. "Oh no," she said. Two white sticks like plastic picks at a buffet table stuck straight out from the side of the pup's head.

Amelia touched them. The pup yipped. Parting the fur, she could see a puncture wound, puss, and blood.

"Porcupine quills," she mumbled, not knowing why she knew. "I'm sorry," she said to the pup before gripping the end, wrapping the cuff of her parka around it to get a better grip. "Gotta do this." She yanked it out. The pup shrieked. She then pulled out the other.

Quickly she unzipped her coat partway, unbuttoned her sweater, and held the one close. As she tucked the pup against her skin, it felt cold. "Oh gosh." She picked up the second, pulled out a quill, and tucked the pup in with the other. Zipping up her coat Amelia cradled and leaned to share her warmth, rocking them she could feel their bones.

"Where's your mom?" she asked softly. They stopped crying and began grunting, almost in contentment, pressing their faces and biting her collarbone. She felt one sucking on her skin in its frantic struggle for existence. She reached in to touch the mouth of the other. It immediately rooted and began sucking her pinky.

"Aw, you're so hungry." She closed her eyes, feeling warm from the little mouth as needlelike milk-teeth tried to draw fluid out of the tip of her finger. One started a howl-like cry and the other soon joined in.

She heard Bryce grunting and thrashing his way toward her as he crawled around the hay bales.

"No signs of the mom?" she asked.

"Nothing," he said as he reached her. "Can I see 'em?"

She unfolded the top of her collar as he looked in. "They're shivering so bad." Their bodies were chilly next to her skin.

He reached in and felt one of them. "They're cold, alright." He looked up at her, worried. He pinched the skin, it didn't spring back. "Shit. Dehydrated too."

Bryce looked closer. "Eyes look like they've just opened. See how they're struggling to focus? Probably two or so weeks. Three tops." He peered in closer. "Bet their ears just opened too." He looked up in surprise. "Jeeze, these guys are newbies."

Amelia showed him the quills, the ends bloody.

"Someone's mixed it up with a porcupine."

Bryce bent over and parted the fur, looking at the wound.

"Might be infected. There's puss." The pup began furiously licking the side of his face and it made him chuckle. "Infections are not good for little ones."

"Hey there, kid," he said and looked at the other pup. "Yep, this one's festering too. They'll need antibiotics or it might get serious."

"Bet TJ's got some," she said and didn't like the way he looked at her. As if it was too much of a long shot.

"Yeah, Am, porkies are amazing. Have antibiotics in their skin so that if they fall out of trees and stab themselves with their own quills, they won't get infected. Go figure."

"Well that's convenient," she said, thinking too bad there wasn't such a slave for the human heart. She then glanced at the break in the lattice, anticipating the outline of a returning mother yet the fear of dogs felt distant, like someone else's story. Yet she knew how protective nursing marine mammals were. Prolactin, a hormone produced when nursing, enhanced acceptance and care for their young but could make them viciously protective. Once as a grad student intern while inadvertently stepping between a nursing harbor seal and its pup, the mother's growling and head thrusting was frightening. Amelia assumed it was the same with topside mammals.

"Let's sit here a minute," he suggested. "Maybe warm 'em a bit. Too early in the game for them to regulate their body temps—they're not like marine mammals. They rely on proximity to Mom's body temps and warmth from her milk to keep them from freezing."

Bryce faced her and scooted closer. Wrapping his legs around her, he pulled her close and hunched over, resting his head on her coat. She leaned on the front of his jacket near the side of his neck as he circled her with his arms.

"Bet they heard us," he said. "Probably smelled you."

She felt the warmth of his breath past her collar and on her neck.

"Bet the vibration of our footsteps triggered the crying."

"One of them rooted and is sucking my finger."

She felt Bryce raise his head to look around. "Poor kids. Something must have happened, looks like Mom's been gone for a while. Good thing nothing else showed up."

"What about the porcupine?"

"They're herbivores—eat twigs, leaves—I'm talking about foxes, coyotes looking for a meal."

Amelia clutched them tighter as she reached in and stroked their backs. Their fur felt slick like seal pups.

She bent over and breathed on them again, cradling them against her skin. It was bad. Tucking her chin on top of them she began the universal rock of comfort, feeling them shiver as she pressed her body to generate comfort and warmth. Their scent was nutty and gamey. She couldn't quite place it, it was so different.

"Hope their organs aren't shutting down," he said.

She knew they might be in the latter stages of hypothermia, more serious than being half-starved.

"Your coat smells like sausage patty," she said into the fabric.

"Yours like sea horse krill."

They were quiet for a few moments, hoping to generate more warmth.

"I know what Juney did," he said.

She looked up at him.

"I found out before we left Rhode Island," he said. "Jen knows someone in the grants office. Juney went against us for the grant."

Amelia tucked her nose into her coat, smelling the pups' scent. One was making soft grunting noises. She decided not to mention that she knew.

Bryce took a breath. "Jen went ballistic—called her everything but a white man. We didn't want to tell you."

"Why would Juney do that?" She looked up at him.

He sighed deeply before speaking. She felt his body shake. "To hurt you."

"Me? For . . ." she asked and then rested her face against Bryce's coat near his neck.

"For believing I was in love with you and couldn't love her."

The warm, sweet scent of chest hair at the neckline of his Sea Life shirt was a surprise. She felt his skin with her nose. And while the three of them had slept huddled together on boat docks in different places around the world, she'd never been close in this way.

"So . . ." She turned back to nestle in with the pups, confused by the moment with Bryce, inhaling their nutty smell to cancel out her feelings. She rested the tip of her nose against both skulls as she held them together.

Amelia felt him pause, considering whether to come out with it. "So . . . she knows a lot of people in power."

She never wanted to hear of Juney again.

They sat a while longer, listening as quiet snowflakes began to fall.

A few moments passed. She lifted her face toward him.

"Hey, Bryce?" She looked up at him.

"Hey what?"

Their eyes met.

"Yeah, I know." He looked away. "We're keeping them."

"Yeah, thanks."

She sighed and relaxed deeper into his coat for a few minutes longer.

"Think they'll make it?"

"Better head back to the Jeep," he said, withdrawing his embrace.

Amelia began to stir.

"I'll crank the heater," he said. "Better find an open pharmacy, grocery store, somewhere to get baby formula, bottles. At least give 'em a chance."

"Wish we knew where TJ lived," she said. "There's only a P.O. box."

"Maybe he's called."

She hoped to find a message in her phone back up at the Jeep.

"Being a wildlife biologist—bet he's got all the right shit," Bryce said.

One of the pups yelped as she moved. "Oh, sorry," she said, moving into position to begin crawling, holding them with one hand.

She looked over at the dead pup.

Bryce turned to look.

"It's dead," she confirmed.

He picked up a twig and reached to poke it. The body moved in one frozen piece.

"Dead for hours I'd guess."

He stopped to listen.

"Thought I heard something," he said. They both listened.

"How 'bout you crawl out first," he said. "I'll make one last sweep; make sure no one's left behind."

As she crawled toward the opening she heard him lumbering around, grunting as his large frame bumped into garden rakes and broken clay flowerpots. She trusted Bryce to not leave until satisfied.

Once outside, she stood up and opened her coat to check. The pups had stopped crying, though they were still quaking as she used her breath to warm them. One lifted its head to sniff her breath; the other was sucking on her chin as it tickled.

"You're giving me a hickey," she said and moved the pup.

She watched as their rib cages rose and fell with labored breathing. They looked bony. One was almost solid black except for white tufts on its chest and head; the other was solid charcoal. Their flipper front arms and back legs were out of proportion to their enormous heads.

As Bryce climbed out, he struggled to get through the hole that was small for even her. He stood, arched his back, and looked up at the sky.

"Better skedaddle," he said. "That's one mean-looking sky."

He began the trek back up in their initial tracks. Fluffy snowflakes had blurred the crisp edges of their earlier footprints; falling heavily where moments ago it had been lackadaisical.

Pewter snow clouds spilled into Chequamegon Bay, gobbling up each island as it advanced toward the lakeshore. The clouds undulated as they approached, almost roaring. It was as frightening as it was exhilarating and had it not been for the urgency of the pups, Amelia would have planted herself in that spot to watch it roll in, see what it would do. After Madeline Island became enveloped, clouds spilled into the bay down to the waterline before advancing to cover the docks, moving up the hilltop aiming right for them.

"Hey, Bryce?" she asked as they stepped up onto the ridge where the Jeep was parked.

"Hey, yeah?"

"Sure you didn't see any tracks?"

"None. Nada, Am. Nothing. No traces, no indications. Let's go."

She understood motherhood in a way he couldn't. And while he'd already scoured the landscape looking for the white-on-white tracks of a mother, Amelia felt unsettled. Picturing the mother hurrying to get in before the storm. What might she feel after returning with hard-earned food, hungry and tired, crushed and panic-stricken to discover they'd whisked away her pups? She was stealing someone's babies. That much she knew.

Her chest tightened as she opened the door and reached on the dashboard. No missed calls. Nothing.

The Jeep started right up, still warm from the drive.

Amelia paused before she climbed in, looking down at the house, scouring the landscape for signs of movement. Tears stung her eyes. "Forgive me," she said, feeling the mother dog's emotions. Her throat ached. The air smelled like snow. Knowing next to nothing about dogs, Amelia felt grief. Marine mammals never abandoned their young. Especially newborns. It was almost unheard of. She guessed it was the same with top-side ones. Something must have gone very wrong. Their tiny paws pushed against the skin of her breast—still cold.

"Let's go," he urged. "It's really coming down."

She guessed they hadn't eaten in hours—too long for as young and fragile as they were. She climbed in and shut the door.

Bryce flipped on the heater.

"It's still warm." Bryce held his hand up to the air vent.

He turned to look behind as he put the Jeep in reverse and then revved it over the wall of snow as they skidded into the road.

Bryce braked, and then turned the wheels downhill, feeling the air vents again with his hand.

The windshield was blanketed in seconds. He set the wipers on high.

Amelia looked out the windshield. The puppy drama had distracted them from the seriousness of the storm.

"God, this is slick."

She didn't like the sound of his voice or the feel of the Jeep sliding sideways down the steep hill.

Then a large-looking dog ran across the road. Bryce swerved to avoid hitting the animal.

"Oh shit." The Jeep's wheels locked. He steered toward the crusted snow for traction but it was too late.

"No," she yelled. The Jeep began to spin. It was that sick feeling of being at the mercy of nature and physics, spinning with a velocity that makes you fully live those final moments before impact.

The steering wheel spun like it was possessed. Bryce let go.

They spun in circles downhill until a tree broke their flight.

Silence for a moment.

"You okay?"

"Yeah." She took a quick inventory. "You?"

"Yeah."

She looked over at him; he seemed just as stunned. Amelia peeked in her coat.

"Them?"

"Think so," she said. Both pups looked up. "That was one big dog."

"Uhh . . . don't think it was a dog," Bryce said, rolling his shoulders to try and release the tension.

Her breath had fogged up the inside window. She wiped it off with her sleeve. "Think it was the mom?"

"Don't know," he said, wiping off the windshield with his hand as they both looked toward the trees.

The Jeep had landed in the opposite lane, facing downhill, driver's side wedged into a snowbank that butted up against a large tree trunk.

She unhooked the seat belt and pushed open her door; it made crunching sounds. Getting out, Amelia held the pups in her coat and began to assess the situation but then slipped and fell, banging her knee so hard she could have cried. Bryce climbed over the passenger seat to help but fell in the road too.

"Oh man," he said and crawled toward her, pulling her out of the road.

She grabbed the door frame and rose to her feet. The pups began licking her face. Then something caught her attention off to the side in the woods. Standing by the tree was the animal, half a face peering at them from behind a tree.

"Bryce," she whispered and motioned with her chin. Afraid to move, to make noise, afraid it would run off.

She could see the one eye, the fur ruff of his neck, tufts defined like a collar, the colors of gray, black, reddish brown, and ivory.

One golden-brown eye watched her. The eye shifted to Bryce once he saw the animal too. The wolf shifted his eyes from Amelia to Bryce as if trying to make up his mind about them. Both pups sniffed, watching from out of her coat. Neither moved. She held her breath. They stood for several moments until the wolf turned and ran off as if called. Her eyes memorized his profile, not wanting to forget the outline of his head.

The entire driver's side of Jeep was embedded in a wall of snow as if it had become part of it. The wheels were buried up to the top of the front end.

Bryce tried to rock it. It wouldn't budge.

"Well, shit," Bryce said as they both climbed back in. "Maybe get the heater working," he said. But the engine wouldn't turn over.

Her arm grasped both pups. At least she hadn't fallen on top of them. The outline of the animal's head was emblazoned in her mind. When she blinked she could see its head and eye as it watched her with curiosity. She churned with the idea that the animal might be their mother.

"Maybe we should go put them back," she said. "Maybe it was their mother looking for them."

"Listen to me." Bryce turned and slid his hands on either side of her face, holding it to get her attention almost nose to nose, his eyes set on hers. "There were no tracks; these guys are on the verge of death, I'm not letting you take them back." He let go.

She looked toward the woods and then closed her eyes, seeing the brush of its tail as it had run off.

"Let's focus on getting out of here," he said and tried to start the engine again.

At least they were off the road. Hopefully no one would come sliding down the hill and crash into them.

After a few more tries the engine slowly wound down with the inevitable groan of a dying battery. Bryce quit.

"This is useless; I'm just draining the battery." He rested his head on the steering wheel.

Amelia watched his form, draped against the wheel. He looked exhausted but not from lack of sleep. There was an air of defeat about him, like he would cry; she'd never seen him like this.

She looked at the dash. Her phone had two bars. As a scientist and mariner, she knew when to call mayday. They knew how to wait as the bilge pump worked, searching horizons for the Coast Guard or for the foreign equivalent, or else abandon ship into the Zodiacs and if all else fails, scuba up and swim for the closest land. They'd done it all before. This was one of those moments. Her toes ached, her knee throbbed.

"Fuck TJ." She dialed 911.

27

"Hi, Joyce." TJ put the Bayfield 911 dispatcher on speaker so that Charlotte could hear. "Helluva storm, eh?"

Charlotte looked over from where she sat reading. Their five dogs surrounded her chair while Barney the crow was roosting up on one of the ceiling beams, letting out an occasional "caw" as the situation warranted.

The two of them had just settled in to warm by the fire after having been out hours searching for a den of orphaned foxes reported by a cross-country skier but had found nothing. Though foxes mated from March on, they'd been skeptical of the sighting but had nonetheless investigated the report.

The worst of the storm was on its way. Estimates ranged from three to four feet and Charlotte had prepared a pot of whitefish stew that was now simmering. Her hands still smelled after slicing onions; for as many times as she'd washed them, she still caught a whiff after each page turn.

"Uh," Joyce the dispatcher went on, "got a vehicle stuck up by your mom's place, TJ, wedged in against that pine at the bottom of the hill."

He chuckled, thinking of the tree. "Crash landed there plenty of times myself." The two-hundred-year-old white pine had scarring on its trunk from the number of motorists who'd encountered it during similar road conditions.

"Reason I'm calling is that this individual might be a relative—"

His stomach tightened. *It couldn't be her.* He felt Charlotte turn in her chair.

"—one Amelia Drakos?"

Out of the corner of his eye he saw Charlotte stand up with an air of aggravation.

"Now that's not a name you hear every day," the dispatcher joked.

"Guess not." He'd regretted putting the phone on speaker. After Amelia's first message, he'd silenced his cell phone thinking that with the impending storm anyone with a lick of common sense would have turned back.

The dispatcher went on. "About to call for a wrecker, TJ, but everyone's swamped."

"I see." He bristled, gauging Charlotte's reaction.

"It's an hour wait, maybe more," the woman said. "Thought you could get there faster. Her car won't start, no heater, road's too icy to walk. Gettin' kinda dangerous out there, TJ, know what I mean?"

He heard Charlotte's footsteps by the coatrack in the foyer, rustling sounds of her parka and winter gear.

"Uh—probably so." He visualized how quickly the hill iced up.

"Says she's been calling you for the better part of the morning."

The rustle of Charlotte's winter parka stopped.

He winced.

"Landline's probably down," he said and heard Charlotte's intentional step into the kitchen to lift the receiver. She slammed it back in the holder.

"Plenty of outages," the dispatcher confirmed.

"Cell's been spotty too," he said. "Surprising you could reach me."

"Oh, save it," he heard Charlotte mumble in a tone that

rendered him indefensible. Sounds by the coatrack as she zipped her boots, bent over, rummaging to find mittens.

"Said something about finding pups at your ma's—"

Then he heard silence and looked, watching as Charlotte slowly straightened.

"There's a male party with her."

"We're leaving now, Joyce." He turned toward sounds of the inside garage door shutting.

As TJ climbed into the truck in the garage, Charlotte was already seated with a soft-sided cooler of supplies in her lap.

He asked, "Wonder if they're hers."

"I'm not talking to you," she said as they drove to his mother's place in silence.

"God, finally," Amelia said under her breath as TJ's number flashed on her screen.

"Hi." She tried to not sound irritated or like a kid talking to the high school principal.

"Dispatcher called," he said. "Sounds like you're in a bit of a jam there, Amelia." There was a certain irony in his tone as if happy and annoyed at the same time.

She didn't answer.

"You all okay?" he asked.

There was a hint of a chuckle and Amelia imagined him saying, *Yeah well, tough luck, kid.*

"So far."

"We're on our way."

She glanced at Bryce. His head had plopped back in relief on the headrest.

"Sure." *Asshole.*

"Joyce the dispatcher said you have dogs?"

"Why?"

"Just curious."

"Two. Pups. Found 'em under your mother's deck."

"Oh." TJ's voice dropped. The first note of sincerity she'd heard.

"Something wrong?" she asked.

He didn't speak for a moment, and then Amelia heard him murmuring.

"Be there in twenty minutes."

"How far—" He'd ended the call. "Jerk wad," she muttered and tossed the phone back on the dash. Bryce looked over in surprise.

"That's gotta be them," Bryce said as they watched head-lights through the snowy windshield from a vehicle that turned at the bottom of the street.

The truck slid uphill sideways, looking as if about to plow right into them until it veered over to park nose to nose near the Jeep and set on emergency flashers.

The two of them had just begun shivering. Their breath frosting up the inside windows like lace doilies and Amelia kept scraping them clear. Thin flakes of ice curled off like coconut shavings.

"It's creepy," she'd kept saying as she reached to scrape.

"Just leave it," Bryce said.

"No," she'd insisted, "it feels like being in a coffin if we can't see out the windows."

"First stages of delusional hypothermia," he muttered.

"Oh shut up," she said.

"Second stage—irritability."

She gave him the finger.

As soon as the emergency flashers started, she recognized the outline of TJ's frame as he walked toward them. Back in the truck Amelia spotted a woman sitting in the passenger seat up at full alert, watching.

Amelia rolled down her window. Ice crunched in the tracks.

TJ bent over, hands in his pockets, looking into her eyes, their noses a few inches apart.

"I left you messages," she said before he spoke and realized this was not the time.

TJ looked over at Bryce, reached in, and tossed something to him. "Here," he said.

Bryce caught them and nodded.

"Bryce Youngs," she introduced. "Friend and co-investigator."

"Glad you're both okay," he said. Bryce nodded. They had a rapport that she didn't share.

"Can I see the pups?"

Amelia unzipped her coat.

The braver of the two poked out its head and looked at TJ.

It made him smile in a sad way.

The other remained nestled on Amelia.

TJ sighed. It was laced with a finality that touched her.

"Yeah," TJ said. It was a sad admission.

"Are they wolf pups?"

"Wrong time of year."

"Should I have left them?" She turned and looked up toward the summit, aching with the urgency of return.

He didn't answer.

"We saw a—" she began to say but stopped, realizing he wasn't interested.

TJ turned to signal someone in his truck.

Then he opened the Jeep's passenger's side door and offered Amelia his arm.

"Hold on." She took his arm and stepped out, holding the pups in place with the other hand.

"Charlotte's in the truck. She's got food for them."

TJ steadied her as she teetered along the icy road. A gust of wind almost knocked her down; the scent of pine trees was strong, their needles clicked in striations of green as the wind rattled through their boughs.

"How come you're not falling?" she asked.

"Magic Indian feet," he said in his ironic tone.

"Bullshit," Amelia said. His chuckle made her soften.

The truck door opened. A tall, thin woman with glasses and closely cropped dark hair stepped out, pulling both sides of an unzipped parka together. Amelia felt the woman studying her in the same way as she'd just memorized the figure of the animal in the woods.

"Hi, Amelia," she said and reached for her hand. "I'm Charlotte, your sister-in-law."

Amelia's eyes widened. "Oh," she said and grasped the woman's hand, holding on to the pups under her coat with the other. "No one's ever said that to me before." She blinked back unexpected tears. "Thank you, thank you for saying it." Suddenly aware of how important that was, though surprised that it was. "I-I . . ."

"Well, it's true," Charlotte said in a matter-of-fact way. "That's what we are." The woman grasped Amelia's forearms and squeezed.

"Thank you." They exchanged glances and Amelia's throat ached.

"Well, come on in," Charlotte said, in a teasing way. "It's too goddamned cold out here."

Amelia climbed into the backseat of the truck's cab. Despite the lighthearted exchange there was something very somber about her and TJ.

As Amelia scooted over, Charlotte climbed in next to her.

"What's your friend's name?"

"Bryce." Amelia nodded and unzipped her coat. "I'm worried about these little guys."

"Can I see?" Charlotte reached toward her coat.

Amelia sensed something bad or that she'd done something that she wasn't supposed to.

She opened her coat. Charlotte reached for the braver of the two pups.

"Oh." The woman's voice dropped off. "Oh yeah," Charlotte said in a soft voice, her head lowering as she looked over the pup. "Oh yeah." Her voice quieted to a hush. "They're Lacey's."

Amelia looked at her. The pup began shrieking.

"Lacey's pups," the woman said as Amelia heard her unzip something on the floor and watched her take out two bottles, shaking them both in one hand.

"Who's Lacey?"

Charlotte handed one bottle over to Amelia.

The woman exhaled in an emotional way and lowered her head for an instant. Then she held the one pup under her belly, securing its jaw up as she touched its lips with the nipple from the bottle. The pup latched on and began sucking down the formula, the front paws paddling as if swimming. Immediately, the quiet one began shrieking.

Charlotte took a deep breath before she spoke.

"Lacey's their mom," she said and looked at Amelia with angry eyes.

Amelia's thoughts raced. "Their mom?" she asked as she positioned the black one as Charlotte had, and held the bottle in the same way. The pup also grabbed on.

Maybe that's why they'd both seemed so somber; maybe she'd taken the pups and Lacey was looking for them.

"Yesterday evening the road crew called me after they picked up a dead nursing female. It was Lacey. Somebody shot her," Charlotte said. "She'd been carrying a dead rabbit in her mouth. I went and got her after they called, her body's in my garage. TJ and I've been out looking for her den since the call, never thought to look at Gloria's."

"Somebody shot her?" The horror of the image stayed with Amelia. "Why? Why would somebody do that?"

Charlotte was quiet as if composing herself. "Wolf hunt's on, Amelia. Lacey's a wolf/husky cross who's more wolf than husky. Sad circumstances often come with having a wildlife biologist as a husband."

The woman sighed deeply and looked at Amelia for several moments.

"Was Lacey your dog?"

"Lacey was everybody's dog," Charlotte said, her voice curt, loaded with sorrow mixed with anger.

They sat, not speaking. The black pup lost suction and began to shriek.

"Sometimes you gotta keep trying," Charlotte said. "A rubber nipple's different than Mom, so every time the suction breaks, keep shoving it in. Sometimes takes 'em a while to get the hang of it."

Amelia gripped his belly again and lifted his head to arch up, pushing the nipple into his mouth until he latched on. His front legs too began paddling like he was dog-paddling.

"What is this?" Amelia asked.

"We call it paddling; it's how they use their feet to stimulate the mother's milk by kneading her nipples."

The dark pup's hind legs splayed out behind him on her thigh. He moved up his front paws to clutch the bottle. After gulping down a few swallows, he began grunting contentedly before the suction would break. Then he shrieked as his head rooted from side to side, trying to locate the nipple again before he latched on to finish off the rest of the formula. His tail moved from side to side like a furry earthworm. The pearly nails of his front paws gripped the fabric of her jeans with such pressure she could feel it. Clinging to her for fear of losing what little he had.

Neither spoke as the pups finished the formula, listening to their squeaking noises of contentment.

"Do we give them more?" Amelia asked.

"In a while," Charlotte said. "Not good to give too much at first. They've gone without since Lacy was shot."

Amelia nodded, stroking the back of the black pup as he laid belly-down on her thigh.

Charlotte turned over the squirming gray pup. It immediately began squealing, fighting, and shrieking as she looked under-neath.

"A girl," Charlotte said. "Like your mama."

Amelia took out the dark one and looked underneath. "This one's a male."

"Black like Jethro," Charlotte said.

They sat watching the pups. "So you've done this before," Charlotte said. "I can tell."

"Not with dogs," Amelia answered her. "Abandoned baby walruses, several seals, otters, orphaned baby dolphins but no dogs." She sighed. "I'm usually sort of afraid."

"Of dogs?" Charlotte let out an ironic chuckle. "You feed ani-mals who can roll over and crush you to death but you're afraid of dogs?" Charlotte looked at her in surprise with an ironic smile.

"Yeah, well." Amelia smiled shyly. "Maybe no more."

"Well, better summon up some courage," Charlotte chortled. "We've got five at home, and two are siblings to these two."

They sat watching as the pups fell asleep. Charlotte handed the grunting female back to Amelia.

"Tuck them back into your coat where you had them, next to your skin," Charlotte said. "Always keep them together."

Once in her coat they molded together, wriggling up to the same spot on her chest in the crook of her armpit. She zipped up her coat and rocked them, patting them as they made soft grunting noises through the fabric.

"You mentioned a wolf hunt?" Amelia was confused.

Charlotte continued. "Yes. Last year wolves were delisted as being protected under the Endangered Species Act. Now you can purchase a permit to go kill a wolf, trap, use dogs to tear them apart."

Amelia looked around and shook her head furiously; re-membering photos of early twentieth-century bounty hunters from an undergraduate wildlife biology class as they'd proudly displayed racks with rows and rows of dead wolf carcasses hanging upside down. The goal had been to eradicate both native people as well as wolves from North America. She'd remembered learning how deep the European hatred and fear of wolves was. It had followed them onto the North American continent. The goal had been eradication with heavy bounties placed per head and wolves were hunted to the point of extinction throughout the northern tier states. The parallel belief that both wolves and Native Americans had no place in North America, with a battle cry from General Philip Sheridan who'd stated that "The only good Indian is a dead one." Same had been with wolves, Little Red Riding Hood and all.

"She was a wild girl, never could keep a collar on her, but everybody up here knew her. Lacey's the town dog. On the docks, the streets, the rez. Sweet, friendly, not one mean bone toward anyone." Charlotte pulled one side of her unzipped parka closer.

"Had to be goddamned out-of-towner trophy hunters with their fancy hunting dogs wanting to say they'd bagged a wolf." The woman's voice shook with anger. "Probably the only time the bastards get hard."

Amelia's eyes opened wide. "I'm so sorry." She touched Charlotte's shoulder.

"Gloria, TJ's mother, always left out food for Lacey when she lived there," she explained. "Everyone did. And for Jethro too. Lacey's had one or two litters under that porch over the years. All the pups get adopted."

"Why didn't Lacey get adopted?"

Charlotte was quiet.

"We all tried to adopt her, we have some of her grown pups, wanted to claim her but she'd never let us," she said. "Apparently only a bullet could. Lacey belonged to the wild."

"I'm so sorry." Amelia didn't know what to say.

"She was out finding food, the road crew said. Someone probably shot her in the woods, seeing the rabbit dangling from her mouth, thinking they'd bagged a *real* wolf." Charlotte's eyebrows raised with the word *real*. "Sounds like she dragged herself, bleeding and mortally wounded to the road, trying to cross, get back to her den with the rabbit when a car came."

"Oh my God." The image was too much. Amelia covered her eyes. All the hair on her body stood electric, sensation flooded her, feeling the animal's angst, dragging herself bleeding across the road, back to her pups, blinded to her own safety by the instinct to return.

"I'm so sorry." Amelia choked up, raising her hand to her mouth. "I'm so, so sorry." Seeing the dog's struggle play out in her mind's eye, she couldn't stop the imagery from repeating over and over, the will to get food back to her pups. Amelia sat quiet, absorbing the emotions.

"Bet Jethro was with her."

"And he is . . ." Amelia looked over.

The woman sighed deeply before answering. "Their dad."

Charlotte looked at the bulge under Amelia's coat. "That black one is the image of him."

Amelia thought of his little jaws, his unfocused eyes that fought to make sense of the new shapes and smells.

"Hunters probably saw her red collar after they'd shot Lacey and took off, the bastards," Charlotte said.

"And Jethro?" Amelia asked quietly.

She sighed and shook her head. "Hasn't been seen." She looked up at Amelia. "They run together. They're mates."

"There were no tracks around the house, nothing. Bryce looked, we both did," Amelia said.

"Might have gotten him too," the woman said. "He's bigger, even more wolflike except for the collar."

Amelia looked up. "A big dog just crossed the road. It ran into the woods; in fact we swerved to avoid hitting it, which threw us into the skid. Bryce thinks it might have been a wolf."

Charlotte looked closely at her. Amelia saw her eyes narrow and didn't know what it meant. The irises were so dark Amelia couldn't see her pupils.

"Describe it."

"Sort of gray and white—"

"Nope." Charlotte cut her off and looked out the window. "Jethro's a black wolf, same size, about a hundred pounds. Amber eyes. That sounds like one of the pack members who live up on the ridge by Gloria's house."

Amelia felt the breath of the pups as they began to warm.

"What'll happen to Jethro?"

Charlotte looked at her.

"Dunno," she said. "Might turn up, might not. Might keep going back to the last spot he saw Lacey, wherever that was. They do that. Over and over again, they keep returning, hoping their mate'll be there," Charlotte said and looked out through the windshield to where Bryce and TJ were digging with shovels, working to free the Jeep. "For now, Jethro might be spooked, hiding in the woods."

Amelia turned to her. "So what about the Endangered Species Act?"

"What about it?" Charlotte ground out the question, her voice brittle as she shot Amelia a side glance.

"I thought wolves were protected."

Charlotte looked at her in a way that no one ever had, as if measuring her against the weight of all things.

"Yeah." The woman turned. "They were until that changed. It's called cronyism."

And it was as if she and Charlotte felt the heaviness of the rabbit in Lacey's mouth as the animal rushed back to her babies, before the sharp pierce of her flesh, that no matter how painful, she held on to her kill, knowing that she needed it, knowing she'd been gone too long from the den but dragged herself along the path and onto the county road she'd crossed hundreds of times before, bleeding out as the sounds, sights of traffic were getting fuzzy, too fuzzy for her to make sense of the approaching vehicle.

Then Charlotte looked away. The moment was too strong for Amelia and she almost couldn't breathe.

"Sounds like you and I have lots to talk about," the woman said while looking out the window, seemingly lost in her own thoughts.

Amelia sat thinking. One of the pups began twitching under her coat. Soon the other followed as if giving chase until Bryce's voice startled them all as he tapped on the window. She depressed the button to roll it down.

"TJs getting out jumper cables." His voice sounded bright. "Killed the battery alright." He snorted a chuckle as he looked over the side of TJ's truck. "Now this is what I call a real man's truck," Bryce said, his voice lusty with admiration.

Amelia couldn't focus on his words. It was the type of disorientation that comes from being startled from a daytime nap by a ringing phone.

Bryce stopped. "Hey, Am?" He touched her cheek. "Amelia." She looked at him.

"Are you okay?" He made the okay sign that divers make underwater. She thought his blue eyes looked even more watery, like the sea in the odd light of the storm.

"I-I don't know."

"Bryce." He turned toward his name. TJ was calling him back.

"Be right back," he said and then turned back once before joining TJ.

Snow was falling so heavily she could no longer see to the end of the truck's hood and listened to sounds of TJ and Bryce discussing strategies for freeing the Jeep. Their voices seemed amplified by the quietness of the hillside.

"I'll give you a jump, then tow you out as you give it gas." She heard TJ's voice trailing off with the business of extraction. Sounds of tow chains, winches, and motors whining, opening and closing of the truck's back gate. More snow shoveling and digging and scraping, TJ and Bryce called to each other.

Charlotte looked at her and smiled. "These two are gonna get big." Charlotte let out a sigh. "Lacey was almost ninety pounds; Jethro probably closer to a hundred, if not over. Never weighed either of them, it's just a guesstimate. He had that narrow-chested, long-legged conformation of a black wolf, those golden eyes of his. Lacey's were blue."

Charlotte sat up and reached for the cooler.

"Time for another feeding," she said.

The two women worked without speaking. Charlotte shook both bottles and Amelia handed over the gray pup in exchange for a bottle. This time she clutched the black pup with her forearm as she held the bottle, hoping he'd feel safe, hoping he'd keep the nipple in his mouth.

"Gosh, you look so much like TJ," Charlotte said with amazement, watching Amelia as she fed the pup.

"Think so?" Amelia said. "I never think of myself as looking like anyone. Even my son doesn't look like me." He'd resembled Christopher Ryan from birth.

"Eyes," Charlotte said. "Shape of your face."

Suction broke and the gray pup started howling with such conviction that it made them both laugh.

"Oh, sorry," Charlotte said with a soft voice. "I'm not paying you enough attention," she said in a funny voice.

"It's good you know how to do this," Charlotte said. "Some folks make the mistake of feeding 'em on their backs like a human infant and the darn things aspirate and choke to death."

The black pup sucked on the bottle so hard the second time that it felt as if it would go flying down his throat like a missile if Amelia loosened her grip.

The male had a look of desperation as he gulped down the food. Amelia stroked his velvet cheek with her finger. She bent over and leaned on the top of his head.

"He feels warmer."

"They're getting there." Charlotte nodded. "They have strong sucking reflexes." She looked at Amelia. "Always a good sign."

Amelia looked up at her, remembering how cold they'd felt less than an hour ago.

"Doubt they'd have lasted another thirty minutes," Charlotte said, holding Amelia's gaze for a few moments.

The tiny footpads that had felt like ice against her skin were now warm, the transfer of body heat had saved them.

"Funny," Amelia said, watching her pup drink. "I'm reminded of a time out in the Indian Ocean. The captain had a couple of sons. When I'd asked about their ages, two were the same age. I asked if they were twins, and he explained that the one young man, though not a biological relative, was now his son too because he'd saved him from drowning years before. In that culture you save someone, you are responsible for them."

Charlotte smiled with closed lips. "You'll need to feed them every two to three hours round the clock for the next two to three weeks," she instructed. "Can't miss a feeding when they're this young, this thin."

"How do you know when they're full?"

"They'll spit out the nipple . . ." Charlotte paused and then laughed just as her puppy did. "Just like that."

Charlotte sighed and pushed back her bangs with her free hand.

They sat in the stillness.

Amelia had no conception of dog size.

"So I take it one hundred pounds is big for a dog," Amelia said.

"Uhh—" Charlotte looked over her glasses at her. "You never had a dog I take it."

"Nope. My mother believed they carried disease," Amelia said and then chuckled. "My father wanted me to have one but Penelope wore the pants in that family."

"Huh." Charlotte looked at Amelia as if thinking of something she wouldn't share.

In the marine world, categories included sea horses and microorganisms that were so miniscule that their weight measured in grams, and then the larger marine mammals and fish that tipped the scales at anything from five hundred pounds to the weight of a small car. Tiger sharks easily weighed in at five hundred to a thousand pounds. Seals, sea lions, walruses were easily hundreds of pounds—newborns about fifteen pounds at birth before bulking up faster than the staff could get their wriggling bodies into a net to be weighed.

"Like I said, we've got the five dogs at home along with a few other house pets," Charlotte said. "An otter with only three legs so she couldn't be released and a beaver who's blind, but he's a sweetie. We usually have others but this has been a good year and we've been able to release most of them back to the wild."

The driver's side door opened and TJ climbed in.

"Okay, here goes," he said over his shoulder. The smell of cold and ozone had followed him in. He put the truck in gear and maneuvered it into position right in front of the Jeep. The wipers cleared the windshield.

"Think you got it?" Charlotte asked.

He looked at her in the rearview mirror, which had also fogged up. He wiped it with his land. "We'll see," he said and then turned around to look over the seat, his cheeks scarlet.

"They ate," Charlotte reported.

"Good." He nodded. "Got your engine started," he said and glanced back at Amelia as if to check if she was still there. "Now we'll see if it'll budge." His phone rang and he answered. "Ready, Bryce?" he said into his phone and put it on speaker.

"Alrightee." She smirked at Bryce's blasé response. She could picture him, camo hat, pajama bottoms, and all.

Amelia watched as the wipers cleared the windshield.

The Jeep budged and then moved out of its pocket.

"Good old Rhode Island Jeep," Amelia said, proud of it.

TJ climbed out, inspecting the outside of the Jeep as he unhooked the chains and winch.

"Follow me. Be careful, Bryce, it's really slick," she heard him warning. "Even worse in town; I'll be watching for ya."

"Sounds good." She heard Bryce.

TJ climbed back in.

"Here we go," he said. The truck began creeping along on the snowy road.

"Where you stayin'?" Charlotte asked.

"Ahh—nowhere." Amelia shrugged. "Was supposed to be a day trip, you know, a Sunday drive but on Monday since today's our day off."

Charlotte pushed glasses up on her nose. "Doozie of a day to take a drive, but lucky for them you did."

"Yeah, lucky for them we did," Amelia repeated in a soft voice, thinking about how so much depends on the actions or inactions of others. Had she not awakened, recruited Bryce, the pups would be dead. If she'd gone alone, she would have quit at Duluth. Even if she'd made it to Bayfield she'd probably have driven past the plowed-in driveway, and said "screw it" until spring.

"Sure hope you two are off tomorrow," Charlotte said in a teasing way that lightened the moment.

"Guess we are now."

28

The three of them rode in silence, hypnotized by the heavy snowflakes. Amelia dozed off, the pups like little heating pads tucked into her coat until the turn into the driveway woke her.

TJ parked and then got out, motioning where Bryce should park. The snow sounded squeaky under TJ's rubber soles as he walked toward the Jeep. The pups squirmed in protest when Amelia stepped down from the truck, like worms moving around beneath her coat. She could feel toenails, the hardness of skulls and paws kneading her shoulder. She swore they felt heavier even after only two feedings. The snow was almost up to her knees and the cold made her shudder.

Their squealing signaled they were either unhappy at being jostled about or else had awakened to discover they were hungry.

Charlotte looked over. "Someone's hungry again."

Though Amelia's feet had warmed, they hadn't dried. Once the cold air hit, she was chilled and began to deeply shiver. Fluffy snow tumbled over the tops of her boots.

"Let's get you both into dry clothes," Charlotte said, as if having read her thoughts.

Charlotte looked over at Bryce, who was trudging through the snow. "You two must be starving."

"Bryce is always starving," Amelia joked and turned to look at him.

"Fair enough," he said as he caught up with them.

TJ and Charlotte's house was a cedar-sided two-story with white Christmas lights lining the inside windows. It was positioned on a ridge overlooking Lake Superior.

Hard to believe it was early afternoon as the storm had darkened the sky. Snow weighed down the branches of surrounding trees, in other places the trees looked wrapped in quilt batting.

"As many feedings as we can get into these guys today, the better," Charlotte explained. "Increases their chances of survival."

TJ opened the front door and stomped off his boots before stepping into the foyer. The area was neatly organized with outdoor gear hanging on pegs, hooks. Low shelves were lined with boots and shoes.

As TJ opened the inside door to the house it smelled of cinnamon tea, pine tree, and leather.

Amelia heard a crow.

"Is that a crow?" she asked as TJ chuckled at the way she asked.

"Barney," he said.

All five dogs spilled out into the foyer, sniffing around Amelia, their noses pointing up to where the pups were huddled under her coat.

"They just want to sniff you," TJ said. "They're gentle."

Amelia noticed, as he walked ahead, there was a bald spot in the same shape as her father's framed by long strands of gray hair secured at the nape of his neck.

The dogs surrounded her and she felt panic coming on as Charlotte touched her shoulder.

"Now breathe, relax, and let your hand down, let them sniff. They're just curious."

Amelia did and a few rubbed their faces against her thigh. She held out her hand for them to sniff and then reached to scratch their necks.

"They're so sweet," she remarked, surprised by the sudden comfort she felt.

"Yep, they are," the woman said. "Roll around with my sister's grandbabies on the floor, sleep in the beds with them too."

Charlotte diverted them toward a darkened room. The sound of a clothes dryer door opened and shut.

"Bryce?" The woman handed Bryce a pair of sweats. "Bathroom's there." She pointed. "TJ's should fit okay." Then she handed Amelia a pair and chuckled. "You'll have to roll these up."

"She's small but tough," Bryce said through the bathroom door as he changed.

"Do you have a scale to weigh the pups at home?"

"No, but we have one at work." Amelia nodded.

"Good. So you know about weighing them every day."

Amelia nodded. "It's the same with orphaned marine mammals."

Bryce came out, wearing black sweatpants.

"Here." Amelia handed him the pups. "Take your children."

They shrieked in protest. All five dogs came barreling back to sniff at what the fuss was about.

"Oh, I'm not so awful," he whispered as all five noses looked up at Bryce.

"Yeah, he is," she said and went to change. Pulling off her wet pants and socks she was immediately warmer. Slipping into the sweats, she rolled them up around the waist and tied them off with the string.

Stepping back out, she reached for the pups.

"I think they like you better," Bryce said.

"Of course they do." She pressed her elbow into him as he turned. "Bet ya a dinner they always will."

"You already owe me too many dinners," he said.

Charlotte stopped and turned, her face surprised.

"My God, you do the betting thing too?"

"She started it," Bryce said.

Amelia shrugged. "My father always bet me a nickel, a quarter . . ."

Charlotte snorted and chuckled. "TJ's always done that too. From when we first started dating. Almost broke up with him a couple of times because it was so damn annoying, but like everything else, after a while it was funny."

Amelia looked at her and sighed.

The pups sniffed as they looked around. The male then rested his head on Amelia's shoulder.

"Hi, little one," Bryce said. He leaned toward her, moving his finger over the silky fur of the male's dark head. She could feel Bryce's breath against her skin. He smelled of the same fabric softener as her pants.

"So is TJ's office out there?" Amelia asked, her chin gesturing to the front door. Earlier she'd seen the GLIFWC sign half covered with snow, the organizational signature on his e-mails.

"Yes," Charlotte said. "When he's not in Bad River at the main office, he's here."

Amelia heard the front door open and close again. TJ walked in with a small medicine bottle, a scale, a molded plastic animal crate, plus a heating pad dangling from his arm.

They followed Charlotte into the great room where a Christmas tree filled the front of the house. The tree reached up two stories, touching the cathedral ceiling and covering much of the wall of glass windows that opened to frozen Lake Superior.

The tree was so tall that the top had bent against the two-story paneled ceiling. A railing spanned a second-floor walkway around most of the great room leading to the bedrooms.

"Wow." Amelia looked up to the top of the tree.

TJ bent down and crawled under the tree to plug in the Christmas lights. The room glowed.

"Rockefeller Center sized," Bryce said. They were hushed and began exploring the branches like little kids as they circled the tree. Ornaments hung from every branch, tinsel shimmered with the colors of the tree lights as strands swayed in unison from air currents.

"How do you get it all decorated?" Amelia asked.

"Our sons, my sisters grandkids, and kids from the community start from the bottom and go as high as they can reach. Then we use stepladders, and me and my sister go upstairs and do the top," Charlotte explained.

Amelia thought of their Minneapolis apartment with no Christmas anything yet. Alex was due in four days, they'd have to find a tree and do something festive. Maybe Jen had already.

The Revolution House would have been all "Yankeed" up, as Alex used to say. Christmas tree and decorations, bayberry candles, pinecone wreaths, fir garlands draped across the fireplace mantel, a strand of old sleigh bells hanging from the front-door knocker that Amelia had discovered in the attic. This was the first Christmas in decades she wouldn't be in the Revolution House, though Alex would be with her. She buried her nose in the two pups resting in the crook of her neck and closed her eyes.

"Look at her." Charlotte stepped up to study the female pup, turning her head as she did so. "It's a whole new universe, little one."

TJ bent over to look.

They stood watching the two as they looked around like moles coming up from their burrows after a long winter.

"Is this tree from your land?" Bryce asked.

"Yes," TJ said. His eyes darted to his wife. "Charlotte hates that I cut one." She turned her face away.

"It's a waste of nature," Charlotte said.

"I love a real tree," TJ said.

His wife crossed her arms and pawed the floor with her foot.

"It's true the kids and my sister's grandkids love it when they come home." Charlotte uncrossed her arms. She looked up the length of the tree. "A fake one would be just as beautiful," she said in a way that spoke of old disagreements.

"I'd miss the scent," TJ protested.

"Scented candles, darling, scented candles," Charlotte said.

"It's not the same," TJ said.

"I feel sad for the tree," the woman said. "Here this glorious thing has struggled for twenty-five years, competing for sunlight to thrive and become the magnificent thing it is, and there goes TJ with his chainsaw, props it up so I can watch it slowly die over the course of weeks for the benefit of everyone's enjoyment."

"She's still angry." TJ winked and pointed to her with his thumb. "Too much of a softie," he said. "But that's why I like her." He reached over and hugged her as she smiled but pulled away.

"Why don't you all go sit by the fire," Charlotte said. "I'll get the next feeding ready, put in powdered antibiotics for those puncture wounds. TJ, help her," she said and held out the puppy bottles for him. "I'll put out some snacks and fix us lunch."

TJ set down the bottles on the coffee table and then dragged over two chairs and an ottoman toward the hearth. He opened the fireplace doors and tossed on another log. Grabbing a black poker he stoked it up. Red sparks and cinders filled the firebox like a cloud of angry wasps.

Charlotte became a flurry of activity in the open kitchen.

TJ set up the bottom half of a molded animal carrier near where Amelia was sitting and tucked a soft blanket over the heating pad.

"You can set them down after they're done," he said, shaking the bottles and handing one to Amelia.

"Thanks," Amelia said. But so far holding the pups was as much a comfort to her as it was to them.

TJ stepped over to take the female, his clothes smelling of fabric softener, and then sat down on the sofa.

Amelia felt him studying her. It felt like an awkward first date where she didn't know what to say yet felt the burden of conversation was on her. She couldn't muster the guts to ask why he hadn't taken her calls.

He seemed at ease with the mounting silence. And then it dawned on her: it was like being with her father.

TJ set the female down on the blanket after she'd polished off the bottle. Amelia struggled with the male as he kept losing suction. Then after he finished she set him down and the two began ambling along in the crate. Looking at the lit tree, their heads bobbed before rolling against one another, and in moments surrendering fast asleep.

Alongside the table was a wooden buffet decorated with a pine garland and red candles, the wall above a collection of framed photos.

An entire time line of images spanned the early twentieth century, arranged in groupings of families and children. Some people were posed by photographers, several weddings and events, others holding up fish on fish tugboats, canoes with people waving, some black-and-whites, and fading color snapshots, others very old and yellowed.

Amelia walked over to the photos of her father as a young man. Images of him she'd never seen. A few arm in arm with a young woman she presumed to be Gloria.

"Over there," Charlotte motioned from behind, "are my relatives wearing traditional Ojibwe clothing." She pointed to photos of her relatives in full regalia. "These are clustered by clan—Bear, Wolf, Marten."

Amelia studied the faces of her father and the woman, both in Navy uniforms looking nestled together like they fit—their bodies as relaxed as their smiles as if finally home. Beneath was another of the same woman in what looked like a wedding suit, her father in military dress, she with a bouquet, him looking stalwart and very Greek, like photos of her grandfather on Ellis Island.

Amelia stopped. A photo of her as a baby. She had the identical one back at the Revolution House in a box with all her parents' photos. Then, photos of her at about seven with a stuffed whale, a dolphin, and then one of her posing with her first bike that she'd just learned to ride. How proud her father had been. Holding on to the bike seat she'd remembered saying, "Don't let go, promise?" and then looked back to see him standing by the curb, smiling at how she'd been already riding like that for almost a block without her knowing it.

They'd always take his film to double photo day at the drugstore. She remembered asking, "How come we always get doubles?" and her father would launch into the Doublemint gum commercial jingle: "Because it's two, two, two mints in one," and she'd join in, too distracted by his silliness to ask again.

Tears filled Amelia's eyes. She was on this wall, part of a family she'd never known. She didn't know what to say.

Amelia began breathing more deliberately to manage the emotion.

"What it must be like to have a place where you belong," Amelia said, thinking half out loud.

Charlotte turned slowly. "Don't you have one?"

She said nothing. Home was where the heart is until it's broken. Home is where the children are until they grow up and leave, home is where the dogs are until they grow old and die.

To belong to a place, to a set of people was an experience, a feeling of protection she'd not had. She'd known it sparingly and conditionally for periods of time but was at the mercy of circumstance. The D'Agostinos were for a while, but they were not her family. Bryce and Jen were her family. The lab had existed at the pleasure of the NSF until funding was withdrawn. It was an endless merry-go-round of uncertainty, the familiar trappings of the Place of No Comfort. And while happy for families like this, encountering them often reinforced all that she didn't have. Feeling more at home underwater than on land, perhaps it was a flaw in her DNA.

And when Amelia would point out how lucky her friends and colleagues were with such close families, they'd dismiss it.

The people from Rhode Island she'd known had extended families of cousins, aunts, and uncles, people whose family had been there for generations and so rooted that they'd pass up job opportunities even a few counties away if it meant having to move.

The ache in her chest was a primal pain with no resolution. Like baby orcas separated from the pod, a dolphin longing for its mate that had gotten caught up in tuna trolling nets, and the grief that she'd so closely observed when a sea horse loses its mate. She'd witnessed these creatures in perennial grief, their Place of No Comfort, and it would shoot through her like touching a live wire on an aquarium light fixture, an ache for a life that so far she'd not been able to assemble and was beginning to doubt if she ever would.

Maybe her father had felt the same. Maybe he thought he could adopt his wife's roots, rip off her heritage, and assume her sense of belonging. Always being the perennial outsider, only it hadn't worked. Belonging nowhere, she pictured her father traveling between New York and Wisconsin until his life was claimed by his ancestral home. Go figure.

Standing in front of the photo wall was everything that she'd never have. At first she'd blamed the death of her parents, the affair with Alex's father. All she'd had was Alex. For years she'd fought off the terror of something happening to him until something finally did. He grew up. Finished his education, got a job, and moved to Vancouver. And now his serious girlfriend was looking more and more like the cement that would anchor him on the West Coast.

She needed to sit. She picked up the puppies and sat down on the leather ottoman.

"How long has your family been here?" She turned to Charlotte.

"Who knows?" The woman laughed and pushed aside her bangs. She set down a tray of cheese, crackers, and smoked walleye on the coffee table. Handing out plates and forks, she said, "A little something until the whitefish stew heats up."

"So how long?" Amelia asked.

"There are stories and there is documentation," Charlotte said as she sat. "More than a thousand years at least. Long before the treaties."

They both sat looking at the photo wall.

"Can you tell me who these people are?" Amelia asked.

"They're in groupings of clans," Charlotte began. "Those tiny frames are daguerreotypes. That one's of Chief Buffalo."

Amelia leaned down and rested her cheek against the pup's charcoal head, inhaling its nutty smell. She would never be away from these animals. She knew it more than had decided it.

"Chief Buffalo canoed all the waterways through the Great Lakes in a twenty-four-foot birch bark canoe from Madeline Island to Washington, D.C. From Superior through the lakes into the rivers to meet with President Fillmore to ask why the treaty rights of the Anishanabe had been terminated after the Sandy Lake Tragedy of 1850 where hundreds of people starved and froze to death. The chief got them to reinstate the conditions of the treaty."

Looking into the fire, Amelia imagined canoeing all that way and then looked up at the wall of photos.

Bryce plopped down next to her on the ottoman, his hip bumped hers. He took off his cap and slipped off his sweater, tossing them onto the floor. The collar of his Sea Life polo shirt was half tucked in.

Amelia chuckled and pulled out the collar to straighten it.

"She's always trying to improve me," he said.

"He's like an unmade bed."

He turned to look at her, his eyes widening. "When you're perfect . . ."

"Yeah right."

Both women laughed in unison.

"Don't mean to be nosy," the woman said and tipped up the bottle as the pup drank. "But are you two a couple?"

"A coupla what?" Amelia asked. They all laughed but then Amelia felt an uncomfortable silence.

"Let me hold them," Charlotte said and reached for both pups. "Take a plate and eat, Amelia."

She took food and then leaned back in the sofa, her shoulder against Bryce as she listened to the crunching sound of his jaws devouring crackers. She wanted to lean her head on him. He was the constant of her life, yet she feared one day he'd fall in love and leave. And she'd understood that someday she'd get eased out, though not intentionally. That day would come and for his sake she hoped it would.

"Look at that little guy," he said. They both watched as the male pup twitched and then settled into bliss, like a slab of breathing meat in Charlotte's lap. Amelia rested against Bryce as they watched.

"Should we name them Lacey and Jethro?" she suggested.

"I like it," he said. "In homage to their parents."

"That's very traditional of you," Charlotte said.

"I'm a traditional kinda guy."

In a weird way it was true.

"But remember," TJ said from where he'd been leaning on the kitchen counter. "We don't know that Jethro isn't alive."

"Okay," Bryce said. "Junior then." Watching the sleeping puppies, feeling the excitement and fear of taking on two new creatures, she felt the same closeness with Bryce as she had under Gloria's deck.

"Jen's gonna go nuts," Bryce said.

"Should we tell her or ambush?"

They nodded together saying, "Ambush."

Charlotte bent over and set the pups down. "Stew's ready."

TJ and Charlotte stepped into the kitchen. Sounds of pots being set down on the stove, plates on the long wooden table, silverware, Charlotte and TJ chatting as the phone rang.

It felt overwhelming. Amelia wished to be home in the Revolution House on her couch, by the fire, tucked beneath the down throw, home with Alex when he was little, when everything felt solid and unchanging, not hollow and loose.

And now she was free-falling with no one to catch her, to call her own, no safe place that couldn't be ripped out from beneath except for the ocean floor.

She longed for the tickle of the limitless sea to lift her hair and be lost in the saltwater from which we're all made, back to our primordial home.

She looked around at the domestic scene, as rootless as the orphaned puppies that she'd stumbled upon. How their cries had prompted her to dig through a foot of snow on the deck like a lunatic and then hold them like her father had held on to her as if she was his anchor, perhaps now they were hers. Instead of ticking down all fifteen thousand reasons why she shouldn't take on two pups, she'd not thought of one.

It was almost too painful to soak up the goodwill of TJ and his wife. Maybe because it would only be a dream the minute she'd climb into her Jeep and shut the door on the drive back to Minneapolis. Amelia pulled inward. Her ribs felt as delicate as a discarded blue crab's shell left behind on a beach.

"I-I'll be right back." She backed away toward the foyer, the coats, boots and the front door.

The three of them turned as if she'd asked a question.

"Left something in the Jeep," Amelia half-mumbled as she slipped out the interior door.

Slipping into wet boots and wrestling into her coat Amelia then grabbed keys from where Bryce had set them on the bench.

Opening the front door, she stepped out and held the edges of her coat together. The wind chill stung her hands.

Snow blew in striations of white, looking more like fabric. Traipsing through the snow that was now up to her knees, she kicked through it and hurried to the Jeep.

She pulled the door handle. The driver's side was frozen. She leveraged her weight and then shoulder-butted the door to break the ice. After a second try it opened.

Climbing into the driver's seat she pulled the door shut. *Oh thank God.* Quiet. She breathed the ever-present rubbery smell of dive equipment and rested her forehead on the steering wheel, a substitute for the stillness of being underwater.

Just as the confusion of tears was about to release, the passenger door crusted open.

She startled.

Bryce climbed in.

"Am."

She rested her head down again.

"You okay?"

"No."

She felt his attention.

"Something's happening, Bryce." She turned and leaned on him.

"What?" He circled her in his arms.

"Seeing that wolf in the woods today, finding the pups under Gloria's house." She looked up and then turned on the map light to better see him in the dimness of the storm.

Bryce looked tired. "The way it looked at you too."

He lowered his head and nodded.

"Bryce." She touched the arm of his sleeve. "What's happening?" She shivered from the cold.

He hesitated; she sank into the puffiness of his coat.

"I keep seeing the outline of the wolf's head in my mind," she said.

The snowy, heavy-laden branches of fir trees, the way the wolf had hopped through snowdrifts and then scampered onto the animal path. She'd felt the power of the animal's breath in her chest, its excitement as it knocked snow off branches as it brushed past as if playing before darting deeper into the woods.

"Something's changed me or changed in me," she said. "Like the first time we saw a deepwater reef. Remember?"

"Yeah." He nodded. "You don't think it's real, like you've been transported to some alien wonderland." The way he said it made her laugh.

"How sunlight disperses the jewel colors, fluorescing like nothing else I'd ever seen in the topside world." Its vividness was right before her. "Never thought anything could touch me like that again."

She looked up at him.

They sat in the quietness of thought.

The cold was making her nose drip. "Like I've fallen in love with a whole other world—with creatures, rhythms, and a language of its own that I don't speak—one I was never aware of until now."

In the quietness of the woods it had found her. Looking into the wolf's face the rusty gates of her heart had creaked open, with curiosity being the oil to ease its hinges.

She tugged on the collar of his jacket.

"We saw the face of wild again, Am," Bryce said.

She looked at him, they both smiled.

"Am I nuts?"

"Of course you are."

She laughed darkly. "Was hoping you'd say that."

He brushed aside her hair.

She paused. "It claimed me, Bryce, as corny as that sounds, know what I mean?"

She heard the swish of his coat collar as he nodded.

"Like the first sea horse," he said.

"Yeah, but now it's the woods, the snow, Lacey being killed." She sat up and gestured out the windows. "Only you'd understand; only you would know because you always do." She rested back onto his coat, folding her hands into his pockets for warmth.

Amelia's eyes darted, realizing the Jeep was her only home. Minneapolis wasn't home, there was nothing to go back to—their airport apartment, the NSF grants—bits and pieces of somebody else's life they'd been trying to tape together.

"I don't want to leave," she said into the fabric of his coat. "But how stupid—with a half brother who hates me."

"Shh," he said and kissed the top of her head, resting his face against it.

"I don't know what this means," she said.

She felt Bryce sigh before speaking. "You don't have to."

"So you don't think I'm nuts."

"He didn't answer."

She breathed in a ragged way and then pushed back to look in his eyes.

"Something's different." She looked at him. "Is it different for you?"

He nodded but didn't speak.

"Well." He lifted her chin. "I'm in there with you." He then bent over and kissed her fully on the lips, as shy as an eighth-grade boy at his first dance.

She blinked and looked back, stunned.

"Did you just kiss me?" She blinked several more times.

He nodded.

She looked more closely.

"Did you mean it?"

He looked at her. "What do *you* think?"

"That's not an answer."

Then his eyes looked funny, out of focus, almost like when he'd smoked a joint, only she knew he hadn't.

Amelia looked away. "Think maybe we love each other?" She sat back in the driver's seat as he kept nodding. "Like love, love each other?"

"Yeah." He smiled and leaned over to kiss her again. "I do."

This time she leaned over and kissed him back, tasting his lips as her fingers felt through his hair, kissing his face, nibbling his cheeks as he laughed. She slid her arms around his neck and smelled the place on his chest that she had while under Gloria's deck with the pups tucked into her coat.

"I've wanted this for s-o-o long," he said and pressed her to his chest. "I wanna be with you."

It felt familiar. Safe and sheltered.

They kissed again. All of the years within inches at the lab bench and swimming together in oceans now felt like the love dances of sea horses, circling and folding into each other as they clasped hands.

Bryce was the one who always said yes. She breathed his familiar scent, giving over to what she'd at times suspected might be there, what she'd never seen coming and yet always had—aside from Alex he'd been her ballast; he'd kept her steady when the pull of the undertow felt stronger than her will. "You'll have to tell me to go away and even then I won't."

The porch light flipped on.

"Busted," he said.

She looked at the outline of his profile, always loving the shape of his nose.

"I've always loved your nose," she said.

"My nose."

"Yeah," she agreed with herself. "I like how it sits on your face."

"You *are* weird."

"Yeah," she admitted. "God, what I'd give for a bottle of wine," she said and sighed. "I could sit here all night."

"Yeah, except for the subarctic temps and the fact that they're gonna think something's happened."

She pulled the front of his coat closer and kissed him, nestling next to the side of his neck, kissing it as he chuckled. "Something has happened."

She watched him smile.

"Look." She pointed to the windows.

They'd all been fogged up.

29

They'd just fed the pups and set them down on top of the heating pad wrapped in a blanket in the crate by the side of the bed in the guest room.

Amelia shut the bedroom door as she sat looking around at framed photographs of owls, wolves, and eagles. She'd showered and slipped back into Charlotte's sweatpants. Sinking into the post-shower delirium brought on by the warm water, she startled at the knock on the door.

"Well good night," Charlotte called through the guest room door.

Amelia jumped up, opening the door.

"Thanks for everything, Charlotte."

The woman walked off with an expression as if knowing something that Amelia hadn't explained.

Amelia closed the door and sat on the edge of the bed.

The hall shower turned off. After a few moments Bryce emerged wearing TJ's sweatpants as he toweled off his hair.

"God, that felt good," he said, smoothing back his hair.

She watched as he climbed into bed, bare chested.

"They asleep?" He leaned over and looked into the half-open crate.

"For now."

She didn't move from the corner of the bed.

"Hey," he called.

She didn't look as he moved closer.

"Come here." He touched her shoulder.

"Maybe we should wait." She turned to look at him.

His face asked why.

"You know." Her eyes traveled around the walls, the dresser with candles, the rough-hewn night tables with lamps. "Kinda weird to have it be in my *brother's* house."

"Yeah, probably so," Bryce said and rolled back onto the pillows.

She watched him for a moment.

"Okay, so come here then." He gestured for her to cuddle.

"You okay with that?"

He made a face as if he'd be crazy otherwise. "No pressure."

She relaxed. "Thanks. I mean just look at me." She snorted and pointed at Charlotte's rolled-up sweatpants, dotted with white spots of dried formula where a pup had dripped; she'd not washed her hair in days, making an executive decision to skip the hair since it would've taken hours for it to dry.

"You're beautiful," he said.

"Ri-ight," she said with sarcasm, remembering how carefully she'd planned her first night with Myles—new silk bedclothes, high thread-count sheets that she'd washed and even went out to Walgreens to buy an iron, pressing them on the kitchen counter. Bought perfume, even had her nails and toes done at a salon near campus that she'd eavesdropped on students raving about while standing on line in the cafeteria. Her thumbnail had chipped on the drive home.

Bryce lifted the covers on one side, holding them up for her.

She scurried up and climbed in next to him, snuggling up to his neck.

"There ya go," he said and circled her with his arms.

"You're so sweet." She reached to turn off the lamp and then kicked Charlotte's sweatpants off the side of the bed.

· · ·

They hadn't slept between feedings every two hours and then making love; they'd dozed in and out of a state of twilight sleep. They lay looking at one another in the dim snow-glow from the windows, studying each other's faces as if seeing things that were new. Lying close they watched each other as if neither believed their good fortune and yet knowing that it had been there all along. They were used to the lack of sleep on project dives. Amelia had dozed folded against his chest with the pups on the pillows just above their heads.

The next morning Bryce had cleared the walkways with the snowblower, watching as TJ cleared out the driveway with several passes of the snowplow mounted on his truck.

Afterward he whispered to Amelia, "I'm getting a truck like that."

"Right. Try parking it on the street."

"I could quit Sea Life and start a business plowing parking lots and shit."

"Think that might have to be my job," she said with a sigh.

The sun was as bright as it gets for the day that far north, casting long shadows on everything, especially the trees. But even still, the surrounding groves of birch trees bleached out to the point of invisibility against the fresh snow, reducing all sense of dimensionality into a blindingly white canvas.

As they were preparing to drive down to Minneapolis, TJ invited them into his office. He'd already sent Amelia links on wolves and wolf dogs, and what to expect in the coming months from the pups in terms of behavior and biology.

Panic began to seep through the cracks in Amelia's will as she envisioned the pups at work and in their apartment. And while Bryce had already come up with a plan to cover the feedings at work, she wasn't so sure. She was already in trouble with the managers and was at a loss as to how they'd do their jobs, keep up with feedings, and keep the pups quiet.

Charlotte looked skeptical too as Amelia described her plan, and then she remembered Jen having reported that one of the tenants had just gotten threatened with eviction for having hamsters.

"I'll keep them in our office in the crate for now while we're at work."

"Think your boss'll mind?" Charlotte asked. It was the first time Amelia heard doubt in the woman's voice.

Amelia chortled with sarcasm.

"Well . . . technically, I'm the boss though I'm not," Amelia said, wondering if harboring wolf dogs might be the final eccentricity that landed her an invitation to leave.

Charlotte and TJ listened.

Amelia felt their skepticism, but also began to wonder if they'd wanted her to leave the pups with them. They hadn't said as much, but she felt their mounting doubts about her and Bryce being able to handle it. Anger rose up, a feeling of being threatened or competing with them and she had to calm herself for a moment. Such raw emotions were baffling. Being up there had stirred up so many things, as if their intensity matched the primal, raw beauty of the lake, the ravines, the forests.

"They're gonna get big real fast. Real big." Charlotte kept on in a way that signaled continued skepticism.

"And they're gonna crap and piss on everything," TJ qualified.

So what's your point? she'd wanted to say. She knew this, Bryce did too. They'd managed all sort of marine rescues and situations in the wild.

"Plus they howl," Charlotte said. "Really loud. Even this little. Wolf howls can travel miles. I could hear Lacey's howl, knew her voice—sometimes could hear her echoing off the surrounding hills." The woman looked toward the windows. "Signaling Jethro or somebody."

"Yeah." Amelia waved her hand, thinking of whale clicks and songs.

"God," TJ said as he crossed his arms and stood back, look-ing at her. "You said that just like your father."

Compliment or insult, she wondered. She didn't like the feel of the conversation and felt ganged up on. She slipped her hand through Bryce's arm.

She paused to look at TJ. "He was your father too," she fired back.

TJ looked away. She was going for funny but it didn't come out that way. Watching for a frown or smile she saw neither.

"I was hoping we'd have more time to talk about him—" *about what happened,* she'd wanted to say but chickened out.

TJ had turned back to his desk, collecting papers and arrang-ing them into a brown accordion file.

She'd seen his face as he'd turned away, wondering if she'd ever know what had happened with their father, why he'd left, how TJ felt growing up, and wanting to find a way to have some sort of relationship if not friendship.

Then by his elbow she noticed a shell. She reached past him and picked it up, turning it over. A Tyrian purple snail shell.

"Where'd you get this?"

TJ looked up at her. They stared each other down.

"Probably same place as you."

She set the shell down and turned away.

"But he—"

Amelia couldn't finish the sentence and instead squatted by the blanket, elbow on her knee, chin in hand to watch the pups. The shell made her feel as shaky as the pups—their back legs cow-hocked and bent at the knees as they ambled along, strug-gling to walk, explore, their heads up, sniffing as they looked around with their Mr. Magoo eyes as if having just landed on Mars for the fifteenth time since the day before.

"Maybe sometime we could talk, TJ," she said just loud enough for him to hear as he handed her a file with papers.

Amelia watched as Bryce listened to both Charlotte and TJ giving him the lowdown on raising Lacey and Junior. She was so confused, so overwhelmed, she hugged her knees and watched as Junior squatted and peed, wanting to look at the shell, but not allowing her eyes to wander.

She set down the file and stood, slipping her arm again through Bryce's. He squeezed it back as a lover, as men had in the past. Whatever happened, Bryce would be there. If it went bad, he'd be there. If it went good, he'd be there too.

"Just handed off information to Amelia," TJ told Bryce.

She wondered why he avoided speaking directly to her, as if she was some irresponsible teenager who couldn't be trusted.

Amelia bent and lifted the file from where she'd set it down, holding it up as evidence, trying to catch TJ's eye so he would look at her.

"Being that both their parents were high content wolf /husky hybrids, there's a high probability these will be too," TJ explained.

"So how do you tell wolves from regular dogs?" Bryce asked.

"I'll show you." TJ picked up Junior as if he was a specimen. The pup cried out, splaying his front legs. TJ looked at Bryce. "First of all—wrong time of year for wolf litters. Wolves are always born mid to the end of March through May," he said. "Same with foxes."

"How come?" Bryce asked.

"That's the mating cycle," he explained. "Maximizes the chances for survival. Weather, availability of food, water."

Amelia and Bryce nodded.

"This young," he continued, "we go by markings, conformation, and color of nails, eyes, and footpads. All wolves are born with blue eyes. They change to amber, green. Their eyes are heavily lined with black pigment and very slanted, almond shaped—it maximizes communication. They talk with their eyes."

Bryce and Amelia looked at each other. "It's the same with marine mammals. Dolphins, whales," Bryce said.

TJ turned Junior over. The pup shrieked. "For one, wolf pups are solid in color at birth, either charcoal, dark brown or black like this little guy," TJ said. "But if you look . . ." He touched Junior's chest. "He's got a white star on his chest."

Junior quieted as TJ turned him right side up.

"Then we look at nails." TJ held the pup's paw. "He's got black, but there's a few white, ivory ones on each paw. Dogs have lighter colored nails except for Arctic wolves."

He then went on to explain how the pads of wolf pups will stay dark, almost black.

"Wolves' tails don't curl like you see in domestic dogs," he explained. "They're either straight out, up in a form of dominance, or down at rest or tucked under in fear or submission. Tails have no white tips, only black or indistinguishable."

"You mentioned conformation," Bryce asked.

"Pure wolves," TJ explained, "much like this guy, have narrow chests, their legs are longer, close together, almost knock-kneed in appearance—it enables them to burst into speed. Very narrow shoulders and hind ends—very different from dogs, even this young."

He held up Junior.

"See his legs? Chest?" TJ asked. "They're young." He gestured to the sleeping gray female. "But right there you can see wolf conformation. Yet both their tails are tipped with white—that's husky."

He finished explaining and looked at them both.

"I've read somewhere that they have special scent glands," Amelia said.

"Yep. What's called a precaudal gland near the top of their tails." TJ held out Junior's tail. "It's marked by stiff guard hairs. See?" TJ began parting the fur on Junior's tail with his fingers. "He's got the marking but—I'll put my money on it not being a functional gland. Many old northern breeds have the caudal mark. Wolves also have glands up on their cheeks, behind their ears, between their toes, which is why they will rub their faces against you. People think they're being affectionate, and they are, but it's also to mark you. Dogs'll do the same thing. Left-over instincts."

Amelia crouched down and picked up Lacey to examine her tail. "She's got the mark too, but"—she parted the guard hairs—"no gland."

"Her pads?" TJ asked.

Amelia turned the pup over. "Pink, some black."

"With pure wolves they're dark gray and black," he said. "As they get older, you'll be able to tell more behaviorally. Some are more wolflike, like Jethro. I've forwarded those links to you; feel free to call us anytime."

"Thanks," Bryce said.

The pups began to cry. Charlotte quickly mixed formula at the office sink, shaking both bottles and she handed one to Amelia. Everyone watched as the pups latched on, drawing down an increasing amount of formula as the bottles were empty in a matter of under a minute.

"Gosh, they're so thin." Charlotte turned to TJ, shaking her head in worry.

"They'll fatten up," TJ said. "Though I'm a little more worried about Junior right now," he said. "He's thinner. But just keep to the feeding schedule. They cry, stuff a bottle in their mouths until they transition to kibble. It'll be another two or so weeks."

After the feeding, the pups were placed down on a mat on the office floor. Junior seemed more energetic, scooting around until Lacey found a burst of energy to ram him.

"Ma hadn't lived there for five years," TJ explained. "Bad arthritis, hard for her to get around."

Amelia turned to him, hoping he'd say more about Gloria, more about her life, who she was, but he didn't.

"No one's gone out there to leave food," Charlotte said.

They sat for a while.

"Bet she was running with Jethro though," Charlotte said. "The two were inseparable."

They watched the pups wiggling and rolling on a blanket in the middle of the floor with Junior lifting his head for moments at a time.

"These are more like house wolves," Charlotte said. "It's going to be a lot of work." She looked from Amelia to Bryce, checking one last time whether they were up for it. "You'll have your hands full."

"We know that," Amelia said, feeling like she was countering something that was not being said. They'd been on board with them taking the pups and now it seemed to have changed.

"It'll take a bit of recalibrating." Bryce winked at Charlotte. "But we've been in the animal biz a long time."

Marine science happened 24/7. Up all night in research vessels, running timed experiments that had to be tweaked every hour for days. She and Bryce were no strangers to round-the-clock work. If anything, the brief stint with unemployment and Sea Life had provided a short respite from the real work of science.

"I fed and cared for two orphan baby seals as an undergraduate one summer," Amelia said. "Lived with them in the aquarium."

"A baby seal. Bet it was cute," Charlotte repeated and shook her head, imagining what that was like.

"Cute but they stink," Amelia added. "I'm a marine biologist." She touched her chest.

"We know," Charlotte said.

"So's Bryce." Amelia looked to him. "Been at this for twenty-five years."

"TJ and I explored your Web site—University of Rhode Island."

Amelia looked down at the pup.

"Sorry about the grant funding," Charlotte said in response to Amelia's gesture. "Happens to TJ and GLIFWC all the time."

TJ had moved to his desk, seemingly working at the computer.

"Yeah, well." Amelia moved to sit down on the floor next to the pups. "We're working to get funding for next fall, restart our lab, and hopefully move back East."

"We stayed up one night reading about your work, the places you've been," Charlotte said. "Our sons Gavin and Skye—both are wildlife biologists like TJ."

"Alex, my son, did the same." Amelia pulled her phone out of her back pocket and began showing photos. "He's now working in Vancouver as a marine biologist."

"Animals must be in the blood somewhere," Charlotte said, scrolling through photos to show Amelia.

Amelia raised her eyebrows. Nothing about her father had ever indicated he'd been an animal lover.

"Take the crate," Charlotte suggested. "We have tons of them. TJ dug this one out of the shed. You'll want to get bigger ones as they grow older. And I'll send you off with enough Esbilac milk replacement formula to keep them for weeks until they're on kibble. It's powdered. Just add water like we've been doing. Make sure you shake well otherwise it'll clog the nipple."

Amelia felt Charlotte was saying good-bye forever.

Amelia's stomach lurched at the thought of leaving, of driving back.

"Hey." Charlotte slapped her thighs and stood. "You guys wanna go back to the house, make s'mores before you hit the road? I'll put on a pot of coffee."

"You got me," Bryce said as he stood and rubbed his stomach. "I haven't made s'mores since getting shipped off to summer camp in Maine."

"Got one taker," Charlotte said as if taking the first bid at an auction. "Anyone else?" The woman looked from Amelia to TJ before the hammer came down.

The two of them were quiet. Both lost in thought, lost in things not said, lost in maybe not knowing how to start and wondering if it was worth it to even begin.

"Fire's probably just about right now. Bryce?"

. . .

After the walk back to the house, they sat by the fire assembling s'mores.

"Can you tell me more about the wolf hunt?" Amelia asked, wondering how long he'd kept the Tyrian purple snail shell on his desk, seeing it in her mind's eye and guessing maybe her father had picked up an extra one for him after she'd made such a big deal about how special they were.

They both looked at her.

"Wolf hunt's forbidden on reservation lands," TJ said. "Always will be."

"But you hunt deer."

"Wolves are sacred animals."

"But off reservation?" she asked.

"Still sacred. But we have no control over hunting off-reservation," TJ said.

"He tried," Charlotte said. "We all did."

Amelia watched as he withdrew and became sullen. She backed off.

"Since this past October in Wisconsin. DNR took 'em off the endangered/protected list," he said. "Now everyone wants to bag a wolf. Permits to kill two hundred and one of 'em."

Amelia didn't know what to say. Her mind was calculating what must be the number of wolves in the region.

The little Amelia knew about *Canis lupus*, they were known to be shy, reclusive animals that hid from humans.

"They're curious like dogs," TJ said. "But in hundreds of years there's been only one or two recorded incidents where a wolf attacked a human in North America and even then the circumstances were peculiar, if not suspect. They live in family groupings." TJ turned to Amelia, seeking her out for the first time. It made her think she might be more in his thoughts than he'd led her to believe. "Like whales and seals, they bother no one, except for the deer and other wildlife that're part of their diet."

"Why would someone want to kill a wolf?" Amelia asked in disbelief. "It would be like shooting a dolphin."

Charlotte looked at her. "The public explanation is that they attack livestock, depredation, but the recorded incidences are low, more animals die as a result of farmer neglect and bad practices than wolves."

"The state compensates them heavily for loss, and often it's not from depredation. Very few are killed by wolves," TJ said.

"They also claim wolves kill pet dogs," Charlotte began. "So few are. More dogs are hit by cars and killed on country roads in a week than are killed in a year by wolves. And these are the ones that are allowed to roam and when they enter wolf territory, they're perceived as a threat to the pack family. Hunting dogs are attacked, usually bear hunting dogs that intrude on wolf territory, and injured for the same reason but then the state compensates the owner for that in addition to canine deaths because of bear hunting practices and the use of what are called bear dogs. Now they're using dogs to hunt wolves who've been snared and trapped."

"What's a bear dog?" Amelia asked.

Charlotte shook her head in anger. "Then there's others who are just bloodthirsty, they're trophy hunters who want to go on an African safari just to kill in these hunting areas. The only time they feel a thrill or alive is when they're killing something—something's that done them no harm."

Charlotte stood and walked toward the kitchen. Amelia could tell she'd gotten upset.

"Coffee's ready," she said in a subdued voice.

"I could use a cup before we hit the road," Bryce said and stood holding Lacey.

Amelia lifted Junior and held him to her cheek as he grunted in protest and peed down the front of her sweater.

"I've been christened."

Charlotte tossed her a roll of paper towels.

"So, Amelia." TJ stood and walked to the kitchen counter in a way that suggested she follow. "A matter of business before you leave." He turned toward her and held up a pen. "These are property transfer documents for the house that will make us co-owners."

Amelia walked over. She shifted Junior to her other hand and bent over. He'd already signed. She did as well below his name everywhere that was indicated.

"Done." She straightened up and handed him back the pen but he'd turned away.

"In spring we can decide what to do with the place," he said.

He turned back and handed her a key ring with two keys. "House. Garage," he indicated. "No one's lived there in five years—no heat, water, electricity."

"No heat?" Amelia asked.

"We kept it on for a year but the place just wasn't safe for an elderly person."

"Could someone stay there?" Amelia asked.

He looked long and hard at her before answering. Like she was an intruder and had butted up against a boundary of which she was unaware.

"Not without utilities." The way he said it made her feel distanced, like an uninvited guest and that no matter how many photos hung on their dining room wall, she'd never be a member of his family.

He studied her more as a warning. As if she better not have designs on coming up to stay at his mother's house. It was a protectiveness she'd felt about her father at the Mall of America the day they'd met, but hadn't felt from him until now—his turf, his home court, and she would forever be the visiting team.

She'd wanted to respond, but it was only a feeling, no words.

Instead she looked away. Amelia felt Bryce's tension too as he stepped behind her.

"More coffee?" Charlotte asked.

"Sure." Amelia held out her mug.

TJ walked back by the fire and sat on the hearth bench.

"You're welcome up here anytime," Charlotte said and reached to hug her. "You all have plans for Christmas?" the woman asked in a soft voice.

"Alex, my son, will be here the day before Christmas Eve and then leaving the day after."

"Short visit. But why not come up? Our kids'll be here too."

Amelia glanced over at TJ.

"We'll see."

"Oh." Charlotte turned too. "Don't mind him."

30

Amelia didn't want to leave. Every time she glanced at the threadbare baby quilt Charlotte had used to line the bottom of the crate for the pups, she felt an ache.

They stopped twice during the four-hour drive at rest stops along the highway to feed Lacey and Junior. Everywhere snow was piled high and the bright clear-as-a-bell sky and sun were blinding. They set the tote Charlotte had given them filled with food down on the attached chairs in an information center/rest stop near the Kettle River in Minnesota, preparing for a feeding.

The only person in the information center was a man in park ranger dress who looked more like a high school student. He'd perked up, trying to look busy as soon as they walked in. Amelia could tell the young man had probably been on his phone.

"Welcome to Minnesota, folks," he said in an effort at a smile. "Where ya headed?"

"Oh," Bryce said. "Just back to the Twin Cities," he said and set the pups down on the glass counter as Amelia got formula ready, shaking each bottle like mad until the granules dissolved.

"Can I?" the young man asked as he lifted Lacey and then Junior as Bryce discussed road conditions. "Hey, little guys," the young man said. "How old?"

"Coupla weeks," Bryce said. So far the road had been icy in spots and the little traffic there was, was moving slow.

"Can I feed one?" the man asked.

"Sure." Amelia showed the young man how as he balanced Lacey on his lap.

"I swear to God they're bigger since yesterday," Amelia said and lifted Junior over her head like a human scale, gauging his weight.

Bryce agreed.

They watched as the pup sniffed the air and began to look around.

"You're right, he does look like Mr. Magoo," Bryce said to Amelia.

"Who's Mr. Magoo?" the young man asked.

"The cartoon?" Amelia said. "You know. Guy who wears thick glasses? Makes all these funny mix-up mistakes?"

The young man shrugged and shook his head.

"We're old, Am," Bryce said.

"Can't wait 'til their bodies get fatter than their heads like Charlotte said should happen." Amelia examined and gently pinched the body fat around Junior's ribs.

"Charlotte's really sweet," Bryce said, taking Junior to feed.

"And him?"

"Umm—complex. A lot going on there: wolf hunt, his mom died. You."

She looked at Bryce.

"Me, huh." She watched the two men as the pups began eating. Watching Bryce she felt a longing that was new. Familiar, new, and was scared for a moment, wondering if the bottom of her life had dropped out.

"Maybe I should just sign the place over to him," she muttered. "Except I'm afraid I'd never hear from them after that."

She'd said it in a way as to invite Bryce's disagreement, to defend what she wanted, to say that TJ would never do that, but he didn't. Having someone dislike her because she was born was a new experience. Dislike was something she was far more used to having earned.

It hurt her feelings. Amelia snorted a chuckle to hide them.

Sometimes you get a truth you don't want to hear, and Amelia wondered why she was hiding such feelings from Bryce from whom she'd never hid a thing.

"Be right back." She motioned and rushed off to the ladies' restroom.

"Shower's closed," the young man piped up after her.

"That's okay," she answered with a wave.

Inside Amelia paused in front of her reflection in the mirror. She watched her eyes tear.

"Shit." She hated crying. Hated the situation she was in. Hated that she didn't know what the hell she was doing anymore. Hated that she suddenly felt scared with Bryce, with the pups, wishing that things would go back to the way they were in Rhode Island, yet was grateful they never would.

"—just a fucking psycho," she muttered. And she'd been doing so much of it in the last few days. Her irises became even greener in the saline bath. She reared back in surprise, suddenly seeing TJ's expression in them.

"Shit." She shook her head as if there was no use in anything.

Yanking out one tan paper towel after the other, she ran the faucet until the water turned cold and then saturated the towel. Holding it up to her eyes, she sighed. It felt cool but refreshing. Damn it, Bryce would know she'd been upset. He always did. He'd probably known by the way she'd just walked off to find the bathrooms and now she was taking so long.

She then waved her hands toward her eyes and even turned on the hand dryer, bending over to dry her face .

"Okay." Last look in the mirror, wishing she had bangs to help obscure her eyes. Then she pulled several more fistfuls of paper towels from the dispenser and hurried back toward the information desk to clean up after the feeding.

Amelia bent over, laying down a layer of paper behind the information desk. She positioned her back toward Bryce so he wouldn't see her face.

"There," she said. "When she's done," Amelia instructed the young man, "just set her down on these to do her thing."

She then rested her elbow on the info desk and began recounting the story of how they'd come to find Lacey and Junior as both men set the pups down on the towels.

The pups began to play. Lacey placed her paws on Junior's back and raised herself to peek over his back and then dropped down, rolling over as he stood over her, pawing her.

"Now that's a power move," Bryce commented as they sniffed about in the bunches of paper towels.

"I'll clean this all up, I swear," she assured the young man.

"Hey—no problem." He shook his head. "Please—this is the most exciting thing that's happened all winter." He looked at her in such a way that Amelia believed him.

"And you're saving me from chemistry," he said and set his elbows on the counter, resting on them. He'd been leaning over the center of a thick college textbook. "Been cramming for next week's final." His phone was lying across the pages. "At least trying to."

They switched drivers. Amelia climbed behind the wheel. She felt Bryce studying her as she started to blubber.

"So you want to talk about it?" Bryce asked.

She looked at him. The way he looked back, she knew he meant the night before.

"Not now." Her chin quivered and she had that post-cry shudder.

"Then when?"

"It's just crazy shit." She waved her hand.

"Like what?" he asked. She felt his eyes on her.

"Like us."

"What about us?"

"Everything's different." She choked up.

He waited for her to go on.

"I love you too much as a person to lose you, Bryce."

She felt him turn to her.

"Why would you lose me?"

"What if we don't like each other?"

"We already like each other."

She glanced at him.

"Yeah but as lovers."

"It's been happening in me for a long time, Am." His eyes were serious, his voice quiet. "Guess I wasn't sure how you felt." It made her shy. She felt embarrassed to feel him as a man. Yet she liked it. There'd been many times when he'd hugged her in the past few months that it had felt so good she'd not wanted to let go. Hugs of consolation, of comfort, but she'd felt something else and had cut it off.

"Maybe we should get to know each other better or something," she stuttered.

He laughed as if just having been told a good joke and looked around outside.

"Like how?" He snorted and made a face. "Go out on a date?" He lifted his hands. "I could drive around the block and then come upstairs to pick you up?"

She started to snicker.

"Come on, Amelia, I've smelled your farts."

He said the last sentence in such a formal way that she was laughing by the time he'd finished speaking.

They'd already slept next to each other on dive projects for years, gone to plays, movies; they'd never been apart for more than twenty-four hours, forty-eight at the most. It would be a whole recalibration, moments they'd share but with an added dimension. It was as exciting as it was terrifying.

"I don't want to fuck it up. I fuck everything up, you know that." She started to hiccup; it felt so little-girlish. "You're everything to me." Her voice came out in breathy, snot-filled gasps.

They were both quiet for a while until Lacey began to grunt.

"And what in God's name are we gonna tell Jen?"

He snickered. "She's practically living with Doby anyway, besides Jen probably already knows. She always knows these things."

A silent moment passed.

"You know, Am?" He reached to touch the side of her neck. She turned toward the feel of his hand, momentarily not recognizing the touch. "Sometimes you just gotta hold your nose and leap. Take a chance that maybe you'll be happy."

His words made her cry.

Bryce hit the emergency flashers and reached to take the wheel. Slowly steering from the passenger side, he pulled over onto the snowy shoulder that had been cleared by the plow.

His arms were around her before she had the chance to lean toward him. Their bulky down coats crushed together like two Pillsbury dough people trying to make up after a fight. He kissed her again and she grabbed his coat, kissing him back. The taste of his mouth was good.

31

There was no parking on the entire street. Bryce double-parked, flipped on the emergency flashers, and began to unload the dog crate and supplies as Amelia carried Lacey and Junior up to the apartment. Both pups were tucked in Amelia's coat, their heads peeping out.

Music was playing behind the apartment door. Amelia knocked.

"Special delivery," Bryce said in a fake voice.

"Right, Bryce," Jen groused through the door and then opened it, sounding annoyed with her phone tucked in the crook of her neck, in the middle of a conversation until she spotted Junior.

"Puppies?" She screamed once, and then again when she saw Lacey. "Call ya back," she said and tossed the phone on the carpet.

Amelia and Bryce laughed.

Amelia held up Lacey.

Jen started screaming with excitement, which elicited crying and howling as she reached for Lacey.

"Shh, oh my God, oh my God, little sweetie," Jen kept saying.

"This is Lacey," Amelia said as she handed the pup over. The dog began trembling, her head pulled in as close to her body as possible during the transfer.

"Sorry I scared you." Jen held Lacey, kissing her on the top of the head as she drew her close. "Hi, baby. Don't be scared," she said in a quiet voice. "I'm just a nutcase." She looked at Amelia with a serious face. "My God, they're babies."

Amelia nodded. "We're bottle feeding."

Jen began rocking as she tucked Lacey into every warm nook she could find near her neck.

"Whose are these?" Jen asked.

Amelia looked at Bryce. "Ours."

"Holy shit." Jen looked from Bryce to Amelia.

"It's a long, strange story," she began to explain.

"Not *that* long," Jen said. "Monday, no dogs. Tuesday, two of 'em. So what's up with that?"

"True."

"Hey—" Jen stopped and narrowed her eyes. "Now wait a minute." She pulled back, looking more closely at Bryce and Amelia and squinted. Her eyes registered something as Amelia looked away.

"Ahem," Bryce interrupted. "Where do you want the crate?"

"Coffee table's fine." Amelia pointed. Her voice came out formal, like directing one of the staff at Sea Life.

"I'll go find a parking spot." Bryce headed for the door.

Neither woman spoke until Bryce left and the door was shut.

"Huh." Jen inhaled in surprise, covering her mouth with her free hand as if to muffle a scream. She then grabbed Amelia by the elbow and dragged her sideways, inching past Bryce's aquarium and down the hallway into the bedroom. Jen shut the door even though they were alone. She took Junior from Amelia too, tucking him under her chin next to his sister.

Her face was frozen into a smile as her mouth moved like a ventriloquist's, her voice barely audible.

"You guys fucked," she said, her mouth fixed into a smile of surprise. "Don't tell me you didn't."

Amelia looked away.

"You did," Jen said. "I can see it." There was a seriousness about it as if Jen's mind was ticking down a litany of consequences.

Amelia said nothing but couldn't help but smirk.

"Well, shit." Jen hugged her and started jumping up and down. "It's about time."

Jen blinked several times, indicating she was ready to hear it. "So tell me everything."

"I don't know . . ."

"Oh come on, quit the bullshit, you've loved each other for years," Jen said.

Amelia looked away. "Not like this."

"Well, now you do—you're lovers. I felt it moving this way back in Rhode Island," Jen said. "A few people even asked me about it."

"Really." Amelia smiled and looked away. She began to think back, trying to decide whether it was true. "That far back, huh."

"Further ago than that even."

"So how could you tell just now?"

"Oh come on, Amelia, simple pair-bonding behavior," Jen said as if she were some old crone. "The way your bodies orient to one another, how he moved next to you, you leaned toward him."

Amelia frowned with skepticism. "I leaned?"

Jen sighed with happy exasperation. Amelia had never felt embarrassed in front of Jen, but she could do nothing but grin.

"You little hussy, you," Jen said and grabbed her arm in a congratulatory shake. "I always knew it would happen. Probably about eighteen years too late, but hey—better late . . ."

Amelia looked at the floor.

"At least he's got a queen-size bed in that hovel of a room," Jen said dismissively. "Shit, you gotta do something with that room, Am." Jen caught her eye and held it. "And I'm even happier for me because now I get the room to myself when I'm pissed at Doby."

. . .

Walking back into the living room, Amelia took out the quilt, arranged it in the bottom of the crate, and unpacked the formula.

"It's time for them to eat," she said.

Jen held them, rocking slowly from side to side as she studied them both as Amelia measured the formula in the bottles.

"Think their eyes'll stay blue?" Jen asked.

"Charlotte said probably not."

"Who's Charlotte?"

How could anyone explain Charlotte? Amelia turned from the sink to watch Jen, fingers under the faucet, waiting for the water to warm as she thought about it.

"Charlotte's my . . ." Amelia paused. "Sister-in-law. I want to know her more."

"What about TJ?"

Amelia looked at her, disappointed yet not at all deterred.

"Lost cause," she said, yet she felt driven to know him in the same way she'd been compelled to find evidence of sea horses on a reef in Nova Scotia waters. Divers had told her she was wasting her time and that there was no life on that dead reef but her gut had said otherwise. And soon after she'd spotted the first sea horse, she'd smiled inside.

She'd make TJ see her. And for as many no's as he'd lob at her, she'd volley back with a yes until he relented—a war of attrition. And while she had no idea what kind of stuff he was made of, she sure as hell knew the kind that she was.

32

They were on a collision course with Sea Life in the days following their trip to Bayfield.

It was two days before Alex's arrival and Amelia and Bryce had begun to smuggle Lacey and Junior in and out of the apartment building and into the mall and Sea Life under their coats. Charlotte had estimated they'd gain an average of two to three pounds per week and Amelia swore each day they were bigger and more alert. They were beginning to look like stuffed animals with a pulse.

The plan to make it work in the apartment (management had a no-pets policy) and at Sea Life (that also had a no-pets policy, as did the mall—except for companion animals) was doomed from the get-go.

While Amelia had underestimated the difficulty, it was usually Bryce, the sensible one, who would "save her from herself." Yet he'd fallen down on the job, generously chalking it off to "we'll figure it all out after Christmas." Lacey and Junior also contributed to defeating the plan by growing bigger and louder every day.

Upon Alex's arrival for his four-day visit, he was thrilled with the pups and with developments between Amelia and Bryce.

The evening of his arrival, Alex and Bryce had dashed across the street to buy a Christmas tree from a vendor in a gas station parking lot. Amelia decorated it with strings of popcorn she'd had to keep popping because Doby, Bryce, and Alex were devouring her "material" faster than she and Jen could string.

Late that first night, Alex had listened with rapt attention as Amelia recounted new revelations of the grandfather he'd never known and the man's secret life, along with information about his newfound uncle. His face had softened with intrigue and curiosity as if listening to a bedtime story about being lost in some sort of magical woods for the first time.

Alex had slept in Amelia's old room that night, Doby and Jen had crashed interlaced on the couch, too tired and inebriated to get up and go back to his place, and Amelia bunked with Bryce. Alex had insisted on sleeping with the pups, one under each arm, holding them like stuffed toys until they'd begin to squeal, ready for a feeding.

Amelia stood watching from the doorway as light from Bryce's aquarium bathed the scene in a soft aqua color. Her chest pulsed in a wistful way, yet it was offset by the satisfaction of seeing her son make a life for himself; he was now thinking about getting engaged.

Alex had offered to babysit for the remaining two workdays before Christmas and Bryce and Amelia were grateful. After the first day he met Amelia at the door, shaking his head, looking bewildered, holding a puppy under each arm.

"You look beat up," Amelia said as she shut the apartment door.

"Seriously, Mom. I don't know how you and Bryce are gonna handle this."

"I missed you all," she'd crooned, hoisting up Junior and kissing him all over his face as he squeaked. "So nice to come back and see you all together like this." She grabbed Alex, amused by his irritation as she kissed the side of his head and he pulled away.

"Mom." He sounded concerned. "Listen. I mean I had to practically hold them every minute they weren't eating, sleeping, playing, or crapping, or else they start crying."

"So you were held hostage."

"Essentially," he said, looking at her with worry. "It's sort of a full-time job to keep them quiet."

Amelia sloughed it off, though a deep core of worry began to form.

Lacey had one green eye and one blue with a white mask and facial markings, and a body that was wolf-gray. Junior had two light-colored amber eyes and stayed all black except for the one white star on his chest.

Later that afternoon, Amelia took Alex to a scuba store for his Christmas present, surprising him with a new regulator, face mask, and fins for the Andaman dive next summer. She also purchased a few other things for Bryce and Jen that they hadn't expected for Christmas.

In shops, the sales staff would immediately reach for a pup to cuddle, a holiday stress release for everyone who got a chance to hold Junior or Lacey. Amelia figured it was good socialization as TJ had emphasized the importance of exposing high wolf content huskies to as many people and situations early on.

On Christmas Day the mall was closed and it felt as if the whole world could finally take a breath.

Alex and Jen had taken Lacey and Junior outside to teach them how to walk on a leash. The pups would waddle along for a few steps and then collapse, rolling around on the snowy sidewalk to bite the leash as if it were a plaything before starting to shiver.

The girlfriend of the building manager, who resided on the fifth floor, spotted them as she exited the lobby.

"How cute," she said, eyeing Jen and Alex. "Whose dogs?"

Alex sized up the situation. "Mine. I'm visiting for Christmas."

"There's a no-animal policy in the building," the woman said, making sustained eye contact as she tried to figure out if he was lying. They'd allowed only fish as pets, but hadn't seen the magnitude of Bryce's aquarium.

"Sorry," Alex said. "I'm leaving tomorrow," he covered.

"So what are you guys gonna do?" Alex asked later that evening at dinner after having gotten busted.

Amelia felt his gaze and shared his doubts. "Figured after Christmas we'll come up with a plan," she said. "Find a pet-friendly apartment."

"Or doggie daycare," Bryce offered and looked at Jen who shook her head.

"Too young for doggie daycare," Jen said.

"We've got several grant applications in," Amelia said. "I'm thinking we can float at the mall for the next five months or so." She looked at Bryce who was quiet.

"Yeah, Mom, but even if you can . . ." Alex looked over at the pups. "What about this summer on the Andaman dive?" He looked from Bryce to Amelia. "We're gonna be gone for two months. What'll you do with them then?"

Good question.

Bryce looked at Amelia, who sat chewing her lip. "We'll figure something out," she said and felt Alex studying her.

"I mean," Alex continued. "It's not like you two to just go off half-cocked and do something crazy like adopt two dogs," he said, nodding his head in a serious way. "You always think through every contingency many times over."

Bryce and Amelia sat quietly. They were starting to feel like teenagers getting scolded.

"True," Bryce said as he reached for the opener and another bottle of beer.

"But you know something?" Alex began to nod. "I like it. Gotta say I love those pups—pathetic pains in the ass but they're you, both of you. I mean Sea Life's cool and all, but maybe it's not the right place to hang out even for now."

"Maybe, maybe not," Amelia muttered and looked to Bryce. But it was not the week to make rash moves. Yet it was Christmas, which by definition was all about rash moves, ill-conceived purchases, and belief in a fat man in a red suit who flew on a sleigh pulled by reindeer from the North Pole to deliver presents down every chimney of those who cling to make-believe. Besides, who would be heartless enough to evict or fire them during the holiday season?

"And jeeze," Alex said at the table after shopping with the pups tucked in his coat, "if I didn't love and have Susan in my life, I could have met at least a dozen women today by carrying around Lacey and Junior."

"Hate to burst your bubble, Adonis," Jen said. "But it's not about you—these things are chick and dude magnets," she said. She picked up Lacey, who'd been lying across her thigh after a feeding, and smothered the pup's face with kisses.

But such sentiments didn't carry over at work. It was the day after Christmas and Amelia had just dropped Alex off at the airport. Seeing him off always caused her to spin off into sadness for a few days afterward.

The mall was packed with shoppers, more so than before Christmas as her coworkers had alleged it would be. And while the pups had slept for the better part of that morning, around eleven Amelia heard their cries all the way from the specimen room. The staff stopped to listen, looking around, trying to decipher what it was as Amelia slipped out of the room.

Junior and Lacey quieted the instant they heard her key in the lock.

"Shh." She scooped them up and set them up on her desk next to the computer and the jar with the Tyrian purple snail shells. She'd discovered that being high off the ground silenced them.

"You have to be quiet," she whispered, turning on the faucet at the lab bench in the office to let the water run warm before mixing formula. Junior began to whimper while she readied the bottles.

"Shh." Amelia turned to them but spotted the glass jar with the Tyrian purple snail shells falling over the edge of her desk, helplessly watching as it crashed to the floor. Glass shattered, the shells flew about. They hadn't been out of that jar, except for Alex playing with them as a little boy until he'd lost interest.

"Oh shit." She stood there, hand over her mouth. She looked from the surprised pups to the glass and then scooped both up and set them down into the crate and shut the door.

Lacey and Junior watched through the metal grate of the door in silence. For the moment the new sounds had distracted them away from their bellies.

In the back hallway off her office, she stepped out and grabbed a broom, sweeping up the shards of glass and then kneeling down to feel for anything that might slice into their paws. They were still on the course of antibiotics from TJ for the porcupine quills.

Amelia sat down to examine the broken glass in the dustpan. The jar had been the only item remaining from her parents' house in New York that had a neck wide enough for each shell to pass through.

Broken glass, it's only broken glass. She sighed. *True.* Nevertheless she felt weird about dumping it into the garbage, like dumping Penelope in there, her home, her childhood. "Get a grip," she muttered before allowing the contents to slide off into the industrial-sized rubber garbage can. "I guess that's that."

She gathered up the five shells. Sliding on her stomach to retrieve the one that had gone flying under her desk, she sat back on the floor, turning each one over in a contemplative way, examining each for breakage, thinking about TJ, about the shell on his desk, wondering how long he'd kept it there.

She looked over at the pups, who were still silently watching.

"It's only glass," she said to them. Their ears twitched at the sound of her voice.

Standing up, she resumed preparing the bottles, shaking them to dissolve the formula and then opened the door of the crate.

Amelia sat back down as Lacey and Junior climbed into her lap and began to cry.

"Shh." They stopped. She'd become adept at wrestling both into submission, one under each arm, for a simultaneous feeding, especially if Bryce was busy. Feeding both silenced the shrieks of the one waiting. They'd quickly learned to move into position to eat. Lacey in one arm, Junior snuggling up in the other, they began to suck the formula down faster and faster. Amelia looked up to see the sharp spines of the shells as they sat loose on top of her desk.

Initially Amelia had wanted to fully disclose, pull the staff into her confidence, and explain that keeping the pups there was only temporary and that they were buying time, but Bryce put the kibosh on it. A few staffers still harbored resentment at not having gotten the jobs that Amelia and he were awarded, and he believed they would "turn us in."

So instead they'd left them in the crate in the office, tuning in the Pandora music channel on the computer in hopes it would soothe them between feedings, but so far it wasn't working.

As they grew bigger, her lap was smaller. Running back and forth was interfering with Amelia and Bryce's ability to care for the marine animals since it was impossible to police the office and be underwater at the same time. She realized that Alex was right. This was not sustainable.

Later one day as Amelia and a few staffers were headed to the freshwater tank to follow up on a report of a lethargic sturgeon, she heard the pups beginning to cry. Bryce was diving in the marine tank with a water-quality specialist.

"Be right back." She sprinted to her office as they looked on.

After the last feeding before leaving for the day, Amelia closed her office door and turned, startled by Meagan standing there, arms crossed.

"Does management know what you're doing?" Meagan refolded her arms and gave Amelia a sideways glance.

Amelia swallowed before answering: admit, deny, or assign some horrendous task that Meagan hated? But it wasn't fair to the intern, wasn't fair to the marine animals under her care, or to the staff. She was in the wrong and she knew it, yet was only trying to buy some time, for what she wasn't sure. Had Meagan been doing something that interfered with her ability to perform her duties, Amelia would have called her out on it in a second. The whole thing felt bad.

"Perfect timing, Meagan—just the person I was looking for," Amelia said in a lighthearted way, praying the pups were dead asleep as she cleansed all thoughts of them to clear her face of tension. Her stomach was like a stone, sick with deception.

"Have you checked in with the prep kitchen yet?" Amelia asked. "They're short two staffers; both out with the flu—don't know if you got the e-mail I forwarded earlier. Let me know if they're short for the evening feedings. Okay? See ya, Meagan." She waved over her head.

She was trembling inside as she walked away, masking it as best she could. Her defensiveness was eating away at her confidence. She was the boss yet wasn't being one. It would have been easy to be angry at Meagan; the young woman had her, yet Amelia "had herself" by having fooled herself into thinking it might work.

And as she headed down to the off-exhibit area, she recognized that sinking feeling one gets when a situation is falling apart. She'd felt it months before the NSF decision.

So much for the online conflict resolution course that Grace in HR had made a requirement of her continued employment.

Amelia was woefully behind on completing the self-tests and had lost the resolve to care. It wasn't working. Nothing was.

In less than an hour Amelia returned to the office and lifted the two pups, their muzzles wet as she watched them chewing on each other's faces. Both looked at her. Their fur was wet and spiky. She smiled and sat down on the floor, burying her face into the fur on their heads, breathing in their nutty smell, their puppy breath, feeling sorry that she'd ever felt the slightest bit of resentment and buyer's remorse. "You're such goofs." They climbed up her body like it was a steep hill, laying on her as she balanced both in her arms. And she held them tight, suddenly afraid of everything.

The next day the pups discovered howling.

"Ooh—listen, Mommy, wolves!" a young girl had said in the Ocean Tunnel.

Amelia was observing the sturgeon they'd placed back on exhibition through the Plexiglas wall. She stopped dead to listen. Tuning out the endless audio loop of crashing waves and seagulls, dripping water in gentle waterfalls, songs of the humpback whale, and bird calls in the rainforests of the world, she didn't recall a howl.

"Oh, God, no." Amelia was mortified.

"Isn't it beautiful, sweetie," the girl's mother had said. "How seamless nature is."

Amelia hurried off, clipboard in hand and pen in mouth, bolting back to the office. Once out of the exhibition area, a few staffers stood at the office door, listening. She and Bryce almost collided in the hall as they scrambled to unlock the door.

The next day she was called up to HR. In anticipation she'd typed up a letter of resignation and kept it folded in her pocket.

The letter felt like a dive weight. She'd never been so aware of a piece of paper before.

"What the hell are we doing, Bryce?" she'd asked the night before the meeting with HR. "I'm exhausted; I feel like a fifteen-year-old sneaking in a boyfriend at night at my parents' house through the bedroom window."

"So what do you want to do?" Bryce asked.

She didn't know, yet she did.

"If you want to quit, Am, stay home with them, do it," Bryce had said.

She'd considered it until thoughts of the Revolution House seeped through to corrode her will.

The same three managers sat staring across the conference table, the same crew who'd been at her initial interview back in October when offering her the job. The same three were at her subsequent reprimand. They regarded her as the problem child, as if not believing their eyes, that here she was again, sitting in front of them for something so clearly an infraction of the policy of both Sea Life and the MOA. She almost couldn't believe it either and fought the urge to laugh. No one spoke for a few moments as if they didn't even know where to start.

She fingered the fold in the pocketed letter before sitting down at the conference table, sharply divided about resigning and hoping they'd just fire her. She would have fired herself if she could. Why hadn't she and Bryce generated better options?

She sat and placed her hands on the desk, as if on a Ouija board. Under her fingernails there was grime from not having had time to wash after she'd been changing lab equipment. She felt them waiting for a confession.

"Yes. I've kept two orphaned wolf-hybrids in my office this past week."

Her stomach burned with anger and fear. "I will make other arrangements."

Resigning was the right thing to do but the Revolution House weighed on her like a boat anchor, dragging her down into the depths rather than being the source of joy it once was. Nothing about this job had been right from the beginning. What was she waiting for?

A late phone call on Christmas night from her neighbors back in Providence made her keep the letter in her pocket.

"Sorry to call like this, Amelia," they'd explained. After two snowfalls the renters hadn't shoveled the sidewalk and an official from the city had knocked on the neighbor's door to check whether the Revolution House had been abandoned. Reluctantly, the neighbors had handed over the key and upon entering, discovered that the renters had moved out without giving notice and left the house so cold that a pipe had burst under the sink, saturating the kitchen's wood floor down into the basement.

"Maybe I need to fly back there," she'd said to Bryce. She was heartsick thinking of the Revolution House, the floor, the damage, how she would finance repairs.

Bryce had pitched in. "I'll talk to my brother; it's one of his hobbies after law—renovating historic homes. He'll roll it into our expenses. We have several income properties, Amelia; we won't even feel it."

"It's my house, Bryce." She looked at him. It seemed everything was slipping away.

"Yes, but you're here," he'd said in the same exaggerated voice he used in the Ocean Tunnel to explain to ten-year-olds about the unlimited supply of zooplankton in the world's oceans. "You don't have that kind of cash to dump into it; we do, it's a business expense. Our family coat of arms—It's better than it was. So what's the big deal?" he said, dismissively. But it was.

"That's not the point," she'd said.

Bryce sighed. "You don't have to be the queen of everything, Amelia. Let others help, be part of your life."

She'd felt chastened. On top of everything, it burned even

worse than HR, worse than she could do to herself. And it hurt most of all because Bryce was right but she didn't know how to do it.

"Okay," she'd conceded. "I'll pay what I can," she'd said, having no idea what the cost of such a repair might be. Sometimes she felt irritated that Bryce had no idea how most people lived, teetering on the edge of fear.

She still had enough banked from the Sea Life job to cover two more months of house payments, but if she resigned she'd be penniless in no time with the Revolution House slated for foreclosure.

"Promise you'll tell him to bill me?" she demanded.

Bryce had begun nodding before she'd finished the sentence, leaving her the impression he wasn't listening.

After the meeting with HR, Bryce and Jen came up with a plan to leave the pups at home and stagger their shifts even further so that someone would always be with Lacey and Junior until they could find another apartment. But even still there'd be gaps of an hour or so in coverage considering travel time.

Amelia's stomach was a knot the entire first day of the new arrangement. She waited for her shift to end before dashing to her Jeep in the ramp, thinking that driving was faster than the bus. But then it took ten minutes to find a spot on the street. As she hurried around the corner she heard howling and broke into a sprint, bolting through three inches of fresh powder up the stairs only to find a notice already taped to the door—either get rid of the dogs or they had forty-eight hours to vacate.

The pups had howled the entire time after Jen had left. Neighbors complained. Someone even called the fire department.

Later that evening after their shifts had ended, Jen and Bryce sat reading the notice from the apartment manager.

"Oh shit," Jen had said.

Amelia sighed. She rested her face in her hands. Both pups walked over, trying to jump up into her lap.

"I'm sorry," Amelia said. "I can't do this anymore."

She pulled out her phone and dialed.

Jen and Bryce looked at each other.

"Hi, Charlotte, Amelia here."

"Hey, Amelia, how's life with pups?"

"Uh, not so good right now." Amelia's chin began to quiver. "It's not working out."

"Oh?"

33

Amelia pulled up to Gloria's house and sat. This time she'd driven up to the door, as Charlotte had arranged to have the place plowed where ordinarily it would be spring before the road was clear.

The Jeep idled as she sat chewing her bottom lip. It still felt like someone was peeking through the blinds. Doubt squeezed her insides like tightening fascia. What had seemed like a good idea was now unsettling.

She'd walked into the HR office and given her resignation.

"Thank you for this opportunity," Amelia had said. "It just wasn't a good fit."

Out of goodwill she'd offered to stay on, though prayed they didn't ask. And while they were gracious about it Amelia guessed she wouldn't be asking for a reference anytime soon. Amelia had talked up Jen as acting director and she was promoted into the job. She and Doby would keep the apartment until they moved to Duluth in late spring. The aquarium would also stay with Jen until they figured out what came next.

Bryce had also resigned but had agreed to finish out the week and then drive up to Bayfield and Amelia.

A few handshakes later, she'd handed over the security card, signed the necessary papers, and was a former employee.

It was three in the afternoon by the time she'd made it to Bayfield, hauling enough groceries to feed at least ten people for a week. The snowy hills glowed pink with the colors of the late afternoon sun.

Lacey and Junior were quiet for the whole ride. Amelia turned to check. Both were transfixed, surveying the landscape out the back window through the wire crate.

"Good doggies," she said. Junior glanced at her and then back to whatever had caught his attention.

She called Charlotte to let her know they'd arrived and to thank her for making arrangements to have the road plowed and utilities turned on.

"You're welcome," the woman said. "Taj Mahal it ain't." Charlotte chuckled. "But at least you'll have utilities. Fridge and stove work, I checked 'em, miracle of miracles after all this time."

"Thanks for everything."

"Inside's still musty," the woman warned. "Lower your expectations and you'll be fine," she made Amelia laugh. "Needs a good airing so you might wanna open the windows this afternoon. Storm front's not moving in 'til later tonight."

Amelia thought back to some of the older wooden ships on which she'd slept belowdecks for weeks, breaking into perpetual bouts of sneezing from eighty years' worth of moldy allergen buildup consisting of rotten wood, bilge water, and diesel.

"Can I at least reimburse you for getting the place plowed?"

"On the house," Charlotte chuckled in a way that spoke of a motive. "And once you get that woodstove going those little guys'll be panting."

"At least let me pay for the wood."

"Old man Whitedeer won't take a cent, was a close friend of Gloria's."

"Old man Whitedeer," Amelia repeated. "How can I at least thank him?"

Charlotte was quiet for a few moments. "He likes those blueberry coffee cakes they make on Saturdays at the bakery in

Bayfield. Bring him one of those. Bet ya he'll eat the whole thing right in front of you, doesn't eat anything else."

Amelia liked him already. "Deal—so where do I find him?"

"Why don't you get settled in and we'll talk tomorrow," Charlotte said. "But I'm warning you, the old man'll talk your ear off."

"Is it okay with TJ that I'm here?" Amelia asked. She wished Bryce had come with her but knew it was only right for him to transition duties to some of the other staffers.

Charlotte snorted an irritated laugh that Amelia guessed was aimed at her husband.

"It's your house too, Amelia," Charlotte said in a stern but encouraging way. "Besides, who do you think plowed the place out?" She said with mischief. "The two of you need to talk, he needs to. Maybe go for a walk in the woods sometime. TJ's talks better when he's outside—inside he sort of clams up."

Amelia doubted TJ'd go anywhere with her except at gunpoint.

"Charlotte, I don't mean to be nosy," she began as she sat looking at the house, the lake. "But why didn't Gloria rewrite her will? Why leave this to me too?"

Why would a woman allow half of her house to go to the child of the man who'd betrayed her?

"Don't know."

And while she'd paid the property taxes weeks ago, it felt like there was some sort of lingering debt out there waiting to catch up with her.

"Still got your key, right?" Charlotte asked.

Amelia looked at the house key dangling from her key chain. "Uhh, yeah."

"Call if you need something, have questions," Charlotte said. "Left you some clean sheets, towels, and blankets."

"You're a doll."

"Why don't you come on by tomorrow for dinner?"

"Thanks. I'd love that."

"And bring those two little rascals."

"Of course."

Everything had been hastily crammed into the backseat of her Jeep. Later that weekend Bryce was moving the rest of her things up in his truck.

All of the uncertainty about living in Gloria's house paled in light of what she was going to do for money. On a long shot she'd thought to ask TJ about a few positions for fish biologists for GLIFWC and had also seen two openings in University of Minnesota Duluth's biology department for the following fall semester that was an hour's drive away. It would be closer to Jen when she moved that spring to be with Doby. They also had five grants pending with notification dates of May and another three she was writing for the following fall.

"Well, here goes." Amelia climbed out of the Jeep and stretched.

The place looked smaller and dumpier than she'd recalled, more like a hunting shack than a residence. A mound of freshly cut wood had been left alongside the front steps, looking as if someone had pulled up, opened the back gate of a truck, and shoved it all out with a foot before driving away.

Sounds of puppy cries made her turn. They watched in unison as soon as she looked, as if she'd forgotten about them.

"Okay, okay." She opened the Jeep's gate and the door of the crate and grabbed the two leashes. Lifting them out, she set them down. Lacey rolled in the snow. Junior managed to get the leash wrapped around his head.

The second move in six months. There seemed no end to the paring down of personal possessions that had precipitated a shift in the meaning of things. Now included were places and real estate.

Standing at the bottom of the stairs she noticed animal tracks leading down around the house as well as up to the door. Although not shoveled, snow on the steps was scant since it was on the protected side of the house.

Lacey and Junior sniffed the first animal track and then both sat down. Along the sides of the house snowdrifts reached the windows. Amelia then lifted them both, carrying them as she followed the tracks downhill toward the lakeside and the opening in the lattice.

She set the pups down at the opening. Each lay down to rest, licking snow off each other's faces. Stepping closer, Amelia bent over. The tracks were that of a large dog.

She looked out to the woods.

"Jethro." She scanned the area.

Amelia knelt and looked in. Everything looked the same.

Lacey and Junior glanced inside and then back at each other. Their faces were pensive as they sniffed. Information passed between them. Amelia didn't know the language.

The hair on Amelia's body prickled. Hard to believe it had been only a little over a week—a discovery that had set off a series of cascading changes that didn't feel over yet.

Looking out to the edge of the woods she imagined what it would be like once Bryce arrived. Thinking back to that same night when he'd put it all on the line with a kiss. She smiled thinking of it. How tremblingly brave of him.

Lacey poked her head through the break in the lattice and looked around.

"Remember this place?" Amelia squatted.

Junior backed coyly away, sat down, and looked back at Amelia for reassurance, his ears flat against his head, his tail making a tiny fan shape in the snow. His sister wanted to proceed.

"You're the gutsy one, Lacey, aren't you?"

Amelia then lifted up both pups; balancing one on each hip as she hiked halfway back up and then set them both down.

"You guys are getting heavy," she said. "We'll come back later."

Loud sniffs on the ground as they puttered around, knocking against each other for a bit as Amelia tried to get them to walk but then figured they were still too young. Lacey jumped on top of Junior and then rolled over, sniffing in loud puffs until Amelia picked them both up and hiked back up to the base of the front steps.

"Hmm." Amelia set them down and pulled her keys out of her pocket, holding the one TJ had given her.

Stepping onto the first step, she stopped.

The woods caught her attention and she turned. The pups turned too. Their ears up in alert as the three of them watched. An uneasy feeling of eyes. Scanning the leafless trees there were no shadowed forms against the stark background contours of snowy ground. Her throat tightened. Something was there. Yet as puzzling as it was, for the first time in years she felt free.

"Dad."

She closed her eyes and thought back to that moment with Charlotte in TJ's truck. Seeing Lacey in her mind's eye and feeling the dog's will to return.

Amelia trounced down what little snow there was on the steps and scooted the rest away with her boot. Junior made a game of it, biting the tip of her boot and shaking it as if to kill it.

"Stop it." She couldn't help but laugh and pulled her foot away though Junior took it more as an invitation to play. She carried the pups up to the front door.

Setting them down she slid in the key and turned it, feeling the inside button pop.

Taking a breath, she turned the doorknob, and pushed open the door.

The inside air smelled as musty as Charlotte had said, and also as she'd suggested, nothing that a few hours of open windows couldn't improve.

The pups poked in their noses and stepped inside.

Amelia stood still until they reached the end of the leash.

Inside was dim. Thin ivory-colored blinds and fabric shades

covered the windows, in some places hanging down past the ledges to touch the floor.

She assumed it changed since her father had lived there. She looked around, imagining. That was so many years ago.

Amelia shut the front door and let go of the dog leashes. The pups stepped a few feet and then sat. Lacey stood as Junior followed, their loosely jointed bodies waddled and sniffed as they crisscrossed each other's path as the leashes wove into a kind of braid.

Floor tiles crackled beneath her boots. The long dried-out glue had reached the end of its shelf life. She flipped on a light switch and watched it illuminate.

"Thanks, Charlotte." The woman deserved a medal. Especially for living with TJ. Either a medal or else she needed to have her head examined, Amelia thought as she looked around. Maybe he was different with her. Nobody knows what life is like in private.

She felt for the blinds' drawstring and pulled. The window glass was hazy. Late-afternoon sunlight streamed in. The window shades no longer had that spring to them so she unhooked them, rolled them up, and set them in a corner.

It was as cold inside as out. Squatting before the woodstove in the living room, she opened the front grate, stuck in her head, and looked up, wondering if the chimney was clear. A box of matches sat on the mantel. She opened it and struck one. It fired and she let it burn out.

"Guess we'll find out."

She stood and walked down the short hallway and peeked into the two tiny bedrooms, then back to the kitchen.

The sink and cabinets were clustered along the wall like a ship's galley. A small wooden table was snug up against the lakeside windows, tucked beneath were three mismatched chairs. Amelia stood looking around, something about the interior felt boatlike.

A separate living room had been created by portioning it off with a tall blue-and-green-plaid sofa with wingback sides she'd once heard referred to as a divan, and two stuffed chairs facing the woodstove. Draped along the divan's spine was a crochet throw made of colorful connecting squares. The yarn looked faded along the sofa back, but as Amelia touched it, she could see it was only dust. She brushed her fingers off on her thigh.

Flanking the divan were mismatched side tables. Underneath one was a shelf piled with *National Geographic* magazines, their telltale yellow spines and size being a dead giveaway. A pair of matching table lamps on each table had golden-color round glass globes for bases, blending in with the kitchen color scheme. The walls were painted a sky blue.

Walking toward the kitchen sink she turned on the tap. The pipes knocked loudly, startling her with their vehemence. Nothing but air sputtered until a spurt of water made it out. Charlotte had mentioned that the well-pump might be broken, the pipes frozen, or both. Amelia turned it on again. After a few more moments of protest, a steady stream of water began.

The refrigerator was a harvest-gold color that she'd remembered seeing in people's houses when she was a kid. She opened the door, the interior lightbulb lit. Someone had placed an open box of baking soda inside. *God bless Charlotte.*

She shut the door.

The matching stove had a push-button control panel.

She pressed one and waited.

Sitting on the back ledge of the stove was a wire spice rack with glass jars containing tiny amounts of green material. Amelia lifted each cylindrical jar and turned it over, the contents tumbling as she examined it as carefully as a marine specimen. Oregano, thyme maybe, it had been ages since she'd cooked a proper meal. She placed each jar back in order— *Gloria's kitchen.*

The burner had turned red-hot. Amelia held her hands over, warming them.

She stepped over to the kitchen table and pulled out one of the chairs. One had a yellow seat cushion, the other two wood. All three had been pushed in as if Gloria might have done to tidy up the day she moved out, wanting everything shipshape, knowing that she might never return. What might it be like to live knowing that.

Amelia pushed the chair back in.

A tall empty bookshelf flanked the wall near the woodstove.

The pups were too quiet.

"Lacey. Junior." She clapped her hands.

There was no response. Amelia walked into the back room. They were tumbling onto each other and playing.

"Good doggies." She sat on the floor as they tottled over. Rubbing their tiny ears, she picked them up, one in each arm and bent over, inhaling the scent of their fur. "What'd you find in there?"

Junior began to wriggle. Amelia set him back down as he dropped into a play-bow, his front paws down, hind end up in the air, barking at Lacey.

Amelia set Lacey down too and then turned back to the kitchen, opened the bottom cabinets, and squatted down, holding onto the doors for balance.

"Oh, Gloria," she said softly, surveying the sizes of steel pots, lids, and pans all arranged by size, a pressure cooker, frying pans—the bits and pieces, odds and ends that had made up the woman's life.

Amelia bowed her head. Sighing deeply, she closed the cabinet doors and then stood, pulling out two drawers that she guessed from their weight held silverware and utensils. Cheese graters, spatulas, an array of wooden spoons, a garlic press, meat pounder, and other items were lined up next to a stack of clean pot holders. She picked up a metal spatula and looked closely, well-used but spotless. Gloria had been an ER nurse. The utensils were as clean as hospital instruments.

"Oh my God." She noticed the same patterned vinyl contact

paper in the drawers as Penelope's. She remembered her mother, measuring and cutting the paper to fit, cursing in Greek.

Amelia shut the drawers and looked out at the lake. She wished Bryce was there. She'd underestimated taking residence in another woman's home, especially this woman's.

"Why, Dad?" she asked the musty air. Why had he left this family? She'd asked TJ a few times, though she had not been given a straight answer or at least one that made sense, only cryptic, snarky little comments.

Loud sniffing came from the bedrooms; Amelia smiled at more sounds of growling and play-fighting.

It was a short walk down the hallway. Looking in one bedroom and then to the other, the pups were chewing on a sock, tugging it away from each other. Their ears flopped, faces wet as they tripped over each other until Junior stopped to shake off. His ears made a flapping sound as he began the game over again.

Amelia stepped into what she presumed was Gloria's bedroom. A double-size mattress stripped of all bedding filled the room, with a pile of Charlotte's clean sheets and towels set on a corner.

She pushed open the vinyl accordion door of the closet. It was empty except for a stack of towels, a few wire hangers, and a white train case placed on the top shelf. She hadn't seen a train case since Penelope's, which had been part of a luggage set they'd purchased for their trip to Greece. She remembered the blue color of their luggage.

Amelia stretched to reach the case but couldn't.

"Shit." In the corner was a wooden chair. Amelia dragged it over and climbed up, pulling down the train case and setting it onto the bed.

Flipping open the latches, she cracked open the lid. The scent of women's face powder, something she'd not smelled since being a girl when Penelope would powder her face on Sunday mornings before church. There was nothing inside except for a few bobby pins. How disappointing, but why? What was she looking for?

Amelia shut and latched the case, climbed back up, and slid it back where it had been on the shelf.

What right had she to even be in the house? Maybe that's why the will hadn't been changed after her father's death; to see what Penelope had done. Maybe that was Gloria's revenge. Amelia shook out the thought. Being in this house was doing something to her.

She noticed a night table on one side of the bed with a small fussy-looking lampshade, ruched organdy that was discolored with a heavy coating of dust. Across from the bed was a wooden dresser with an attached mirror. She looked at her face, surprised by how it looked as if belonging to an older woman. Two windows with blinds, she pulled the drawstring and looked outside.

Placing the chair back in the exact spot, she headed across to the smaller bedroom.

On one wall a poster of a man in full Indian regalia with an eagle superimposed over his face hung at an angle by one flat metal thumbtack. Two small bookshelves were empty except for a set of field guides to North American birds, weather, trees, and wildflowers. She pulled out the weather guide; the top pages had a thick coating of dust.

Then she spotted the blue desk.

Amelia stopped. She'd had the exact one, only hers was pink. She'd spent the better part of her childhood there. She'd had a Cinderella desk lamp. TJ's had a plain gooseneck desk lamp, the cord unplugged and set on top.

Pulling out the desk chair, Amelia sat, feeling the familiar contours of the seat and looked out the window just above. So much living had happened in this parallel universe. Why had they keep it hidden? What had been so shameful?

Snow-covered frozen Lake Superior turned blindingly white in seconds as sun rays poked through the thick cloud cover.

Amelia squinted and rested her elbows on the desk, leaning over. What had TJ thought about all those years while doing his homework as she was doing hers? He'd known all about her, but she hadn't known about him. He'd had photos of her, but she hadn't any of him. A calendar on the wall was dated June 1972. She stood and walked over, trying to decipher his scribbles in some of the squares, the top printed with a Washburn, Wisconsin, hardware store's insignia.

Lifting the top sheet, she paged back to January, but nothing was written down except for strategically placed *D*s.

She turned back to watch the lake a few moments and then sat back down at TJ's desk. Maybe he'd been counting down the months before his father would come back to visit, perhaps hating her for keeping him away. She would have hated her too. Or else just a brokenhearted boy imagining someone else was enjoying the sheltering care of a father who'd given it so freely to another during the short span of his life. She stood indicted and thought of Alex. She'd done the same thing to him, only he hadn't known a father to miss, to long for. And while Alex would ask from time to time and she'd make the offer to search for the man, he'd back off as quickly as he'd brought it up. As if her willingness had been enough rather than any sort of father quest.

The pups raced back and dive-bombed her as they squealed in excitement at discovering her in TJ's bedroom. Jumping up, each vied to get up into her lap first, their nails made rustling noises against the fabric of her jeans as they tried to gain traction.

Lacey then stopped.

"Oh no!" Amelia said. A stream of pee flooded TJ's boyhood rug. "Great." Amelia shook her head, wondering how to clean it up, thinking she'd better set up a system for a latrine.

Amelia moved onto the bed and rolled over. The room was cold. She'd better bring in wood, start a fire. Maybe air the place out another day. She lifted each pup up onto the bed as they dropped down beside her.

She breathed in Junior's fur, thinking that she should get up, unload groceries too but instead she drifted off.

She didn't know why she was so afraid that night. Tucked into her sleeping bag on the couch, the lights were on. The wood-stove had warmed the house.

And while the weather had turned rough like Charlotte had said, Amelia had been out on the ocean in far worse in all manner of rickety watercraft.

Just after dark the wind had picked up, howling like a grief-stricken animal.

The lights flickered a few times before blinking on and off. The off intervals became longer than the on. She toyed with the idea of running out to grab the flashlight from the glove compartment before settling in for the night, but wasn't sure the effort would be rewarded. She couldn't remember the last time she'd changed the batteries.

The house shuddered as winds burst against it like micro-explosions as Amelia imagined isobars on marine radar. The house squeaked and creaked like the sounds of a ship rolling in high seas and the roof sounded as if parts of it were loose and might lift off and blow away.

Settling on the couch in her sleeping bag, Amelia had ruled out sleeping in either bed, thinking it might be an invitation to unwelcome dreams.

Amelia picked up her cell phone to call Bryce. There was no service. Then she spotted a wall phone. Wriggling out of her sleeping bag, she lifted it but it was dead.

Hell, she'd have called Charlotte and even TJ if it weren't for his sharp corners that still poked.

"Damn," she said and looked at the window. She'd closed the blinds after dark, though they swayed in the drafts. Maybe go find a hotel or something but good luck with two dogs on a

Tuesday night at eleven thirty in the middle of a moonless, black winter night in a town of 480 people.

Snow pelted the windows and sounded more like sand, blowing in straight-line winds. Hail began falling, hitting the metal roof as if it had become a percussion instrument.

Then everything stopped. Nature had switched off. It all went silent.

Amelia sat up.

Neither pup seemed fazed, both were asleep, one along each of her arms. Maybe because they were home and she wasn't.

Or perhaps their mother's scent was the calming agent. So many things she didn't know.

Just as she lay back down to doze, a tapping sound on the window made her sit up. It sounded like a branch or a stick. She hadn't recalled any shrubs or trees touching the house.

Amelia listened and then turned toward the window.

Junior sat up and looked. Amelia waited for the tapping to stop. It did. She lay back down and turned onto her side.

Then it started again.

"Oh shit." She sat up.

Standing, she set Junior down and tried to imagine what it might be. The rhythm was steady like Morse code, not a branch. She crept toward the window.

The sound came from the bottom right-hand corner.

Crouching down, she winced as she lifted the blind.

On the outside ledge was a small bird, maybe a chickadee or a pine grosbeak looking at her, imploring. She looked into the shiny blackness of its eyes—unheard of for a bird to be out at almost midnight in such a storm and not sheltered or roosting in the arms of a tree.

The oddity was frightening, otherworldly, and personal in a way she couldn't deny.

She let the blind drop and stepped back.

The bird continued tapping its code.

It'll go way. She climbed back onto the couch and into her sleeping bag, pulling it up to her chin. Junior looked at her.

"What?" she said as he looked back to the window.

The image of the bird was a weight on her conscience, like she didn't have enough.

Then it stopped.

"Oh, thank God." She relaxed. Maybe it flew off.

But then it started again.

"Shit." Amelia got up. One hand on her forehead, the tapping persisted. She pressed her stomach and paced as if waiting for someone or something to die.

"Fuck, fuck, fuck." The tapping was on and off, her insides tensed with urgency. She squeezed her heart shut. What could she do, she couldn't just open the window and let the bird fly in. Yet why not?

The tapping stopped. Maybe it was gone.

Creeping over to the window, she pulled up the blind's corner.

The little bird looked at her.

"Shit, that's it." She pulled the blind up and fiddled with the window latches. "How do I open—" She turned the latches and pulled but it didn't budge. She felt like breaking the glass but that would've been hysterical.

The bird tapped again.

"Alright, alright, alright, hold your horses," she said.

Gripping the bottom handle she yanked. It budged up enough, the bird flew in.

Its wing brushed her cheek.

Amelia then shut out the storm.

The bird made one pass around the room and landed on the crocheted blanket on the back of the sofa.

The pups didn't seem to care.

"So?" she said to the bird as if it would answer.

The bird puffed up its feathers, round like a ball, and was instantly asleep.

. . .

About an hour later there was a loud scrape at the front door.

Amelia startled awake.

She sat up.

Both pups had climbed down and were sniffing at the bottom of the door, tails wagging. Lacey then barked and pawed back.

"Bryce?" She jumped up and scurried over to the door. "Oh, please be you."

No answer. Then the lights flickered on and off a few times, powering out long enough for the refrigerator to shut off.

"Shit." She looked around. The whiteness of the snow cast a blue glow that lit the room.

Everything was quiet again. Damn, she should have gone to get that flashlight.

"Bet ya got candles somewhere, Gloria." She tried to imagine where such an organized person would keep them. Just as she was opening and shutting kitchen drawers the lights went on again.

Another scrape at the door.

She turned to look. Junior began whimpering and sat down while Lacey scratched back.

Just then a gust of wind hit the front of the house like an explosion, startling her.

"I can't take this." Her voice was shaky, she felt unstable, like a frightened girl. Her skin prickled as the hair stood up.

"Hello?" she called through the door and knocked from the inside. Her chest quivered. "Bryce?"

She flipped on two light switches and an outdoor light flipped on. Looking out the window, there was no view of the top steps.

Junior sniffed at the bottom of the doorjamb and then looked up at her.

Another scrape. This one more insistent.

Amelia picked up both pups and set them into the wire crate in the kitchen and latched the door.

"Stay there for now."

She looked back at the roosting bird who was unconcerned.

Amelia walked up to the door and crouched down, listening. Something was there; she heard movement.

Standing up, she turned the doorknob and opened the door a few inches. Her eyes were met with the yellow eyes of a black wolf-looking dog wearing a red collar.

"Jethro?"

His face softened at hearing his name—his ears twitched. He looked curious, as if to ask, *Who are you?* He then looked inside with such yearning that Amelia opened the door wider for him to come in.

He lowered his head and looked at her.

"Come on." She stepped out of his way. His size was frightening as he passed by. His head was almost to her waist. Panic set in. She froze. Shallow breathing as she looked to locate her boots, her coat if she needed to make a run for it. Afraid to shut the door, afraid to be trapped with such a large animal in an enclosed space, but then she remembered Charlotte telling her how gentle he and Lacey were.

"Please don't kill me," she said and gradually lowered her arms. Her hands were curled up into her armpits like bird feet. She took a breath, watched Jethro walk into the house, and then gently closed the door.

The dog made one pass around the living room. He stopped at the wire cage and lowered his head. Lacey sniffed Jethro's teeth and then backed away. Junior rolled over, showing his belly. Jethro sniffed the puppy's undercarriage through the metal grated door and then turned away.

The dog walked up to the woodstove, stepped away and circled once, settling down onto the oval rug by the front door. He curled up and covered his nose with his tail.

Amelia walked backward to the couch, not wanting to turn

her back or make any sudden moves. She climbed into the sleeping bag, keeping an eye on Jethro as she saw the shine of his eye watching her back through the fur of his tail.

Amelia was wide awake, listening to Jethro's breathing. Half terrified, half amazed, she was no longer sleepy.

Each time Lacey or Junior shifted in the crate, she spotted the gleam of Jethro's eyes in the light of the fire. He lifted his head a few times to look at her and that was it.

Amelia didn't remember falling asleep yet awoke to the sound of Jethro's paw scrape inside the door the next morning. He turned to look at her after each scratch.

"Jethro," she acknowledged.

She loved it when his eyes softened and his dark bushy tail swished once.

She reached to touch his head but he shied away.

"Okay," she said and then squatted, holding out her hand. He was taller at that angle. "Don't gotta touch you."

He sniffed her palm, her fingers. She felt his wet nose. Then he looked straight at her. Panic tingled in her throat but she washed it clean. Yellow eyes, black face, she kept her hand out, held her ground.

All at once Jethro nuzzled his cheek against her hand, almost knocking her over.

"Hi, beautiful boy." Her voice was like syrup. The fur of his cheek was smooth and cool to the touch. She dug in her fingers.

Then he turned and pawed the door again, looking back at her.

She opened the door. "Here you go."

He dashed off as if he'd just spotted breakfast.

The bird was perched in the same spot where it had fallen asleep the night before.

After feeding Lacey and Junior, Amelia slipped on coat, boots, snapped on leashes, and took the pups out. The sun was out. The snow was so bright she had to shield her eyes.

After the pups had relieved themselves, she noticed the Jeep. It was heaped with about a foot of snow. She dug out more logs and carried them in to feed the fire.

The bird moved to the kitchen counter and stood looking at her.

"Hungry?" she asked.

Pulling out a loaf of bread, she crumbled it into fine crumbs, scattering it along the countertop.

"Thirsty too?" She then took one of Gloria's saucers and filled it with water.

The bird looked at her after a peck at one of the crumbs. It seemed so tame or maybe just unafraid.

She filled and placed a pot on the stove, waiting for the water to boil. Thank God she'd bought instant coffee.

The bird then flew back to the same window ledge and tapped again with its beak.

"You want out too?"

Amelia stepped to open the window. The bird flew off so quickly it seemed to vanish as she lost sight of it in seconds.

34

Amelia shoveled out the Jeep before calling Charlotte for directions to Whitedeer's place. She then hurried downtown to the Bayfield bakery on Rittenhouse Ave., nabbing one of the last blueberry coffee cakes. Staying at Gloria's house would have been impossible had it not been for Whitedeer's firewood.

Amelia drove as fast as was safe so that the cake would still be warm by the time she arrived. She heard sniffing from the back cage. With her right hand she kept preventing the bakery box that was taped shut from flying off the seat with each turn.

"Survived the storm, did ya?" Charlotte had laughed earlier while giving Amelia directions. "Was wondering how you'd made out."

"Well, I couldn't have called you if I tried. No phone reception," Amelia began.

"Not surprised."

"But I did have a couple of visitors late last night."

"Oh?"

She told her about Jethro's visit.

Charlotte was quiet for a few moments before speaking. "Oh thank goodness, that was Jethro, alright. " Amelia heard relief as the woman called, "TJ." She listened as Charlotte relayed the information.

Then she told Charlotte about the bird.

"A bird, eh?" Charlotte sounded skeptical. "What kind?"

"Greenish-yellow," Amelia said. "Tiny."

"Huh."

She could tell Charlotte was thinking about it.

"Sure it's okay to show up to Whitedeer's place without calling?"

"He doesn't answer the phone."

"What do you mean, he doesn't answer the phone?"

"It's what I said."

"You're kidding."

"Does it sound like I'm kidding?"

Amelia made a noise as she frowned.

"If Cherise, one of his daughters is there, she'll answer, but he only uses it to call out."

"Interesting strategy," Amelia said. "So how will I know if he's home?"

"He's always home."

"He's always home," Amelia repeated, shaking her head.

Amelia counted five driveways before arriving at the sixth as Charlotte had said. The mailbox jutted out onto the road; it said WD, in black and white letters like Charlotte had said. Amelia braked. Peeking down the narrow wooded driveway lined with birch trees, it looked freshly plowed. The white-on-white of trees against snow made the driveway entrance almost invisible.

Turning in, she secured the bakery box, the warmth of the cake felt good on her hand.

A yellow Lab mix stood guard, watching her arrival. The dog didn't bark, didn't give chase. Once she parked, the animal hobbled toward her in an arthritic way, tail wagging, happy to greet, walking as if its stiff hips hurt.

Whitedeer's place opened into a clearing. There were three metal outbuildings with open garage doors. Each housed machinery along with stacks of lumber.

She glanced through an open doorway where a man was running a long board through a sawmill with the help of another holding the other end. Both looked up as she pulled in.

Two trucks were parked, both with mounted snowplows, near a tiny older white clapboard-sided home with green shutters, trim, and door. Smoke steamed from a tall metal chimney. Two mountainous woodpiles were stacked on either side of the house. One for use this winter, as Charlotte had explained, the other to dry out for next winter.

Amelia parked, left the engine running for the heater, and carefully lifted the cake box, balancing it as she thought to drop it off, leaving the pups to wait.

Snow crunched under her boots. The dog approached.

"Hello." Amelia bent over and held out her hand. She touched the fur under the dog's chin. He smelled her hand.

The sawmill stopped. One of the men brushed off his hands as he walked toward her.

"Help ya?"

"Whitedeer?" she asked, already assuming he was too young to fit the description.

He smirked and looked at the bakery box, pointing to the house before turning back.

A few horses stood by in heavy blankets watching from a gated entrance in the barn.

"Hi, guys," she said and walked past.

Their ears twitched at the sound of her voice. She met their eyes. One of their tails swished, the other horse turned and walked away.

She approached what appeared to be the front door and stepped up onto the porch. Amelia was just about to knock when a woman about her age beat her to it and opened the door.

"Cherise." The woman held out her hand and then introduced the man standing behind her. "And Peter, my husband."

Amelia introduced herself, and passed off the coffee cake.

"Hey, Dad?" the woman called inside. "Dad. Someone's here to see you; brought you your cake."

Whitedeer entered what appeared to be the kitchen from another room.

"Why, you're Ma'iingan Ninde's kid sister," he said, motioning with a clawlike stiff hand. "I recognized you. Come closer," the old man said.

Amelia took a few steps.

He searched her face as if looking for something familiar and latched onto a few features.

"Yep. You look like him."

She didn't answer.

"Your father too."

"Oh. You knew my father?"

"Sure did," he said. "Were best buddies. Went hunting, fishing, harvesting mannomin with him."

She looked puzzled as she handed him the boxed cake.

"Wild rice," he said. The old man motioned for her to follow into the interior of the house, holding the box. "Warmer in here," he said. "Thanks for the cake."

"Well, thanks for the wood." Amelia laughed. "I think I got the better deal out of this, especially after last night."

"You haven't tried the cake," Whitedeer said. "You might be singing a different tune in a few minutes," he said. "Cherise?" he called to his daughter.

His daughter followed in with plates and forks.

"Did you deliver all that wood by yourself?" Amelia asked.

"Got two grandsons visiting."

"Have a seat," Cherise said as they sat near the woodstove.

Amelia noticed his daughter brought only two plates.

"Will you join us?" Amelia asked.

"No, thanks," the woman said. "We just stopped by."

"Every morning she checks to see if I'm dead yet," Whitedeer said.

Amelia laughed. "Sorry." She covered her mouth with a hand.

"No such luck today." Cherise laughed. "Only the good die young. Dad'll live forever."

"Love you too, baby girl," Whitedeer snickered.

His daughter shook her head and made a face, saying in a sarcastic voice, "No, more lucky for us, Dad."

"Oh bullshit." He laughed. Cherise bent over to hug him as they both chuckled. "Get outta here. You got my grocery list?" He tried to sound gruff and demanding.

Cherise held up the rumpled envelope with his list over her shoulder as proof before slipping into her coat.

"Why the bologna, Dad, not the ham?" She paused, reading the list.

"I don't know." The old man shrugged and stretched, contemplating as his hands patted his stomach just once. "Change is in the air, I guess."

"Fair enough," his daughter said. "Call if you change your mind about the ham.

"There's coffee on the stove," Cherise said to Amelia. "Mugs in the cabinet."

"That's my son-in-law," Whitedeer said. "Peter Holmgren. Fish guy from the DNR."

"Hi." Peter reached to shake. "Yeah, TJ told me about you."
Amelia wondered.

"I'm down one assistant," he said. "Kasey's out on maternity leave. I'm a fish biologist for the DNR. If you're sittin' around bored sometime and wanna come out with me to get fish samples before the lake opens, give a holler."

She looked at him and nodded. "Really?"

"Yeah," he said. "Can't pay you much," Peter said.

"I'll take it," Amelia said as they all nodded.

"Sure beats the hell out of just sitting around doing nothing," he said. "Go out to the Apostle Islands on snowmobiles; give you a tour all the way to Outer Island. I could sure use the help.

And this way you can tell me all about your work. TJ couldn't say enough about it."

She looked at him, a bit surprised that TJ would even mention her, much less be excited about anything she'd do except for maybe going away.

"I'd like that," Amelia said.

"I'll get your number from TJ," he said. "Set nets weeks ago; they need to come out soon. Some probably froze into the lake but we'll get 'em out."

"Does the whole lake freeze?" she asked

"Some years," Peter explained. "But it's been a warm one, one of the warmest on record but parts of it have, near the harbors, the islands—where we need to go. But even those parts'll be breaking up early so we need to get out there in the next week or two before they become too unstable to collect our samples. Otherwise they'll be lost."

"That sounds amazing."

"It is. Especially if you've never been out there." Peter's face changed into a blissful smile. "I've been out there hundreds of times, never gets old, still shocked by the beauty. You never get used to it."

She thought of the ocean, of coral reefs, the blue of the water. She lived for the feeling of something never growing old.

"I'm in," Amelia said. She raised her hand to high-five him.

"Cool." Peter hand-slapped her back. "I'll give a holler when they're ready to be pulled," he said.

"Thanks," Amelia said and felt excited about such an adventure.

The couple headed out. "Great to meet you, Amelia," she heard them both saying.

"Would you like coffee?" Amelia asked Whitedeer as she stood to get a cup.

"Not for me," he said. "Any more and they tell me I'll turn into a mass murderer. Have a seat."

"I have two pups to bring in if I'm gonna stay."

He held up both hands, motioning for her to bring them.

She dashed out, turned off the engine, and tucked a pup under each arm.

Amelia chuckled as she set each down in the kitchen. She riffled through his cabinets, chose a mug, and poured from the glass coffeepot, grabbing a few paper towels as napkins. She walked back into the room near the fire and sat on a wooden chair.

"Them look like Lacey and Jethro's pups."

"They are."

He'd already broken the tape and lifted the top. "Would you look at that—still warm too. And you got blueberry." He looked up with a smile of amazement.

"Wish I could take credit for it, but it was Charlotte."

He sawed off a third of the cake with a steak knife and began to eat, picking up a whole section, using his hand as a plate. "Why dirty a dish?"

She chuckled in agreement, watching as Whitedeer ate with zest.

He watched the pups as he chewed and they studied him back through unfocused eyes.

"They don't know to beg yet."

"I'm sure I'll ruin them in time."

He chuckled. "I like you," he said and pointed at her as he washed down the cake with clear liquid out of a coffee cup.

"She's a good girl, my Cherise. And that Peter's a great guy for putting up with all of us," he said. "Gave your dad all kinds of shit."

"Were you two close?"

"Pretty much," the old man said. He reached for the knife. "Ah, look at that. Have a piece or I'll eat it all."

Amelia smiled. "All yours."

"How'd you know about my cake?"

"Just following Charlotte's directions."

"That woman's a gem," he said under his breath. "Now TJ."

He shook his head. "He can be a piece of work. Good man, though. Give you the shirt offa his back."

Amelia sat back, letting the cake digest.

"Just have a taste," Whitedeer said.

"You broke my arm." She cut a thin slice. "Holy crap, this *is* good," she said as she chewed. "Maple frosting."

"Maple's the key," he said with a pointer finger, reminding her of a professor she'd had in graduate school. "Told ya I got the better deal here."

"Was hoping you could tell me more about my dad."

"Stole the woman I loved."

Amelia reared back. Stunned by the candid comment.

"Really?" She held the paper towel up to her lips. "I'm sorry."

"Ain't your fault," he said, wiping blueberry off his lips with his thumb. "Gloria and I were sweeties—loved her since we was kids. Went off to Duluth, became a nurse. Figured she'd come back and we'd get married, but instead joined the Navy. Shocked the hell out of everyone. Our women didn't do things like that back then," he said and suddenly looked antsy. "Don't be telling Cherise I said that or she'll kill me. It's different now."

Amelia nodded, watching him. He paused and sat back for a few moments, as if letting the cake settle and collecting his thoughts.

"Funny." His eyebrows rose as he chuckled in a pensive way. "Here I had this bad feeling about her going off to the Navy like she'd get killed or something. She was a flight nurse, danger-ous job—them choppers crashed all the time back then, not like those Coast Guard ones they got now," he explained, watching for Amelia to nod. "But something bad did happen."

Amelia turned her head.

"She came home with your father," he said and held up the box to offer Amelia the last slice.

She motioned for him to go ahead.

"That must have hurt."

Whitedeer looked at her. "I got all bitter, angry, like TJ." Whitedeer gestured in the direction of TJ and Charlotte's house. "Crushed my feelings about everything. Even long after I married somebody else. Was an okay life with Maddy. Had many years where I'd go feeling that if I'da killed her on my wedding night I'd be out by now, but by and by it was good life. Had good kids which made up for all of it, but Gloria and I were always close up until she died."

Amelia watched as his eyes teared up.

"I'm so sorry," she said.

"She was the kind of woman you'd never think would die." He wiped his eyes with his thumb. "It's like she always was, would always be."

"Sounds like my father ruined it for a lot of people."

Whitedeer looked at her and didn't say anything for a while.

"You know." He smiled. "Your father was a good man. He just couldn't live up to all he'd promised," Whitedeer said. "Some can, some can't. Some do, some don't. You never know it going in; you just hope you can be true to what you say you will."

He looked at her. She felt him searching for understanding.

"It likened to kill me to see Gloria done like that."

Both looked at the empty cake box. Whitedeer picked up his fork and began to scrape some of the maple icing and blueberry from the sides.

"I've tried to talk to TJ a bit," Amelia said.

"Oh yeah?" Whitedeer laughed in a knowing way. "How far'd that get ya?"

"Uhh." She smiled shyly and looked away, opening her eyes wide in amusement to share in the joke. "Not very."

"TJ don't talk," the old man said and sat back on the sofa, picking blueberry skins from his teeth. "I was like that when I was young too, after Gloria married Ted. Drinking too much, fighting, and getting into all kindsa shit. TJ don't do that, but he's always off by himself in the woods somewhere, tracking this or that critter so he don't have to talk to no one."

She pictured him.

"Mosta us get to a point where we forget why we're angry, why we're hurt," he said. "All them bottled-up secrets." He motioned with his hands. "You get too tired to hold on to 'em anymore, but not your brother. Festers in him still."

Amelia looked at him.

"What secrets?"

"About your dad leaving to New York for six months to work. About Gloria being stubborn, refusing to go with him even after he begged. About him having an affair and the other woman who demanded that you never know about TJ or Gloria, and about your dad giving over, giving in, giving up, betraying his wife, his boy, and all that was sacred."

Amelia was stunned.

"But why?"

Whitedeer shrugged. They were quiet for a while. "Amelia," he began. "Sometimes people get wore out. None of us is perfect."

Amelia thought of the car accident on Crete.

"Did Gloria have a pet bird?"

He looked at her, puzzled.

"A pet bird?"

"Yeah."

"Never heard of one and we were tight, I'd've known about that. No one's lived there for six years, though."

She told him about the bird, the way it tapped on the window, looked her in the eye like it knew her, and then roosted on the blanket on top of the divan.

Whitedeer looked down at the empty bakery box, shaking his head. He licked the fork clean and then tossed it into the bakery box, nodding as he smiled.

"That was her." His eyes softened as he studied her face. "There's a lot you don't know about us, our culture, our lives."

Amelia closed her eyes and bent over. She so clearly saw the bird's face in her mind's eye.

"I wasn't afraid."

"Of course not," he said. "That was Gloria. An undefended heart. That's why we all loved her, that's why she hurt so bad."

Both sat thinking, lost in the flames of the stove as a sap pocket in one of the logs opened up and began sputtering and popping. Both pups startled awake from where they'd dozed off in her lap.

"Spirits come to us in many forms," he said. "To teach or show us something."

"What was she trying to teach?"

The old man looked into her eyes. "You tell me."

"It's about the house, isn't it?"

Whitedeer shrugged with a funny expression, not giving her a hint. But his eyes said that she'd guessed.

"Why she never changed the will," Amelia said. "Why she left half the house to me."

He smiled at her and pointed at her. "I knew you were a smartie."

She shook her head with slow realization.

"Because she loved her son," he said. "Because TJ was so bitter about you, and became worse after your father died. Never wanted to meet you, wouldn't even mention your name. 'She who took my father away,' or some other nonsense like that. Maybe it was through her death she believed he would make his peace."

Amelia looked into the fire.

"She tried," Whitedeer said, "but could never get through that thick skull of his." He rapped his knuckles on the wooden coffee table in three quick successions. "Figured by making him face you, he'd face himself. "

Amelia looked away, thinking about it. Maybe so. And maybe it was her place to reach out to TJ, get him to talk, tell her what happened, to help relieve him of such bitterness as Charlotte had said. And while she wasn't one to reach out to broken souls, TJ was different. Tonight she'd try. She'd been invited for dinner around five. The temperature was mild. Maybe she'd try to convince him to go for a walk.

"So why's TJ such a tight ass?" She looked directly at White-deer.

The old man shrugged. "Maybe because he's just a tight ass."

35

Amelia told Charlotte she'd bring a salad. She'd gone all out with feta cheese, Greek olives, and any vegetable she could rustle up with the slightest bit of color in the downtown IGA grocery store.

It was late afternoon as she headed out to their place, having just talked with Bryce, telling him about meeting Whitedeer, Peter Holmgren, and the possibility of finding work through the Department of Natural Resources and Lake Superior. For the first time she felt excited as she drove along the lake toward Red Cliff. Looking out at the frozen lake, she couldn't wait to get out there, hoping Peter was serious about inviting her along for the fish count.

"Gosh, you sound so much better, Am," Bryce had said. "Can't wait to be there."

"Three more days." Her voice lilted with the words as she twisted a strand of hair.

"I know," he said. "It feels like more like a—"

"—month." Completing each other's sentences and thoughts was taking on new meaning.

"Yeah," he said. "Wanna meet Peter and especially White-deer. Guy sounds like a hoot."

Out in the bay the ferry was ice-breaking its way across to Madeline Island. Maybe when Bryce arrived they'd drive over on the ice road or else hike the few miles on the frozen surface. Upright Christmas trees were frozen into the surface, denoting the safe place for cars to follow although it was "travel at your own risk" for those who wanted to forgo the ferry ride.

Even though it was early January Amelia noted more little bits of lingering daylight each evening, each one adding up to longer days. A subtle shift in seasons that she'd smelled that morning, freshness to the air that had people chattering on the line at the IGA.

The pups were riding in the wire crate in the back of her Jeep. This would be their first trip back to Charlotte's since that first night with Bryce.

"So how you doing out there?" Charlotte asked as they passed the spaghetti and meatballs. The pups were barricaded in the kitchen once the dinner was ready.

"So far so good—day two, I'm still alive," Amelia joked and turned to TJ as she passed the bowl of sauce. "I discovered that we had the same kid's desk and chair."

He didn't answer as he spooned sauce onto his plate.

"TJ?" Charlotte said.

He looked up. "Oh."

Charlotte signaled with her eyes for Amelia to keep talking.

"How is it we got the same desk?" she asked.

"How do you think?" He looked at her and then set down the bowl, his face without expression. "Is this what you really want to talk about?"

It stymied her. She didn't know what to say. Her feelings smarted. Maybe it wasn't possible to clear a path to this man and maybe there was no right thing to say. But why was she even worrying about what to say—like a bad boyfriend.

Charlotte motioned with her chin to keep going. Amelia didn't want to.

"Well, I thought it might be a starting point," she said. "Was wondering why I never knew about you."

He set down the basket with garlic bread and watched her with a stillness that was as calm as it was frightening.

"The vinyl contact paper in your mother's kitchen drawers, also the same as ours," she said, knowing he didn't give a shit about it and probably didn't know what contact paper was.

"How come you never came to New York to visit?" she asked again.

He stood and walked out, leaving his plate.

Amelia waited until he was out of earshot.

"Guess I messed that up." She folded her hands in her lap and then moved to tuck each under a thigh for warmth. "Don't know how to talk to him."

Charlotte said nothing. "Few do."

"Think I pushed too hard?"

"Keep pushing." Charlotte stood up, motioning her to follow through the house to the door that led out to his office.

He was sitting at his desk chair looking out into the woods.

"Hi." Amelia crept in and snatched the Tyrian purple snail shell from his desk before sitting in the opposite chair. She felt tethered with an invisible cord as annoying as it was strong.

Closing her hand around the shell she squeezed its spiky points. A bird's song made her turn toward the window where TJ was watching, listening to the hopeful sound of spring.

"You know," she began, turning the shell over to examine it. "My life hasn't exactly been a walk in the park either."

He didn't respond.

"I get this sense that you think everything's come up roses for me."

He looked at her with a smile she couldn't read.

"He mailed it to me from Greece," TJ said.

She nodded and raised her eyebrows, surprised he'd offered up a piece of information like that.

TJ looked out to the woods. "Let me tell you about the day he left."

Without realizing it Amelia pulled up her chair.

"I was eight," he began. "They'd fought for months; was too young to know why."

He turned toward her and then back to the edge of the trees, scanning the clearing as he watched for animals. Two crows chased each other as snow toppled from powdery branches like smoke the instant their feet touched.

"He'd wanted us to move to New York, but my mother refused, saying that he'd promised in Germany to make this home," he said. "They had for years, until I was eight. Then something changed, not sure what.

"I remember him on the phone about his old job in New York, my mother angry, and then him leaving later that March, not long after trying to persuade my mother to come along."

TJ stood and stepped closer to the glass as he watched a deer tiptoe out from the edge of the woods toward a salt lick that Charlotte had just set out.

"The day he left . . ." He folded his arms, setting them on top of his belly. "My mother hadn't wanted me to see him off." TJ began to recount how Gloria had barred the front door to keep him inside.

"But I'd pushed her aside." He remembered the force with which he'd done so, recalling how Gloria had almost fallen, how slight she'd felt and how sorry he was but even sorrier for missing his father.

"I'd flung open the door, ran uphill to the road." He paused, seeing it all again. "I remember the urgency, it spurred me to run." TJ sighed deeply and rubbed his face, his whiskers made scratching noises. "Maybe I knew we'd never be together again as a family," he said, watching as the deer began to feed on the cube of nutrients. "I remember my coat sliding off and not caring, not wanting to waste the seconds it would take to shrug it back on, seconds that might cause me to miss my chance."

"Your chance?" Amelia asked.

"My chance to call him back, to tell him I wanted him to stay, as if that would change his mind."

How well he remembered his feet gripping the soggy March ground; his legs fighting gravity as he strained to reach the summit just in time to see the taillights of his father's truck drive off.

"I hollered 'til I was out of breath, saw stars, and could barely get out a sound."

His chest remembered.

"Once I reached the road, something kicked in." He paused, remembering how his heart banged against his ribs, about to burst. "I bolted after him, yelling to stop so that I could hug him or get into the truck and go with him." He turned to Amelia. "Not caring which."

The desperation of the moment quieted him. He remembered wanting to touch the giantness of the man's heart to make him turn around.

"But he didn't hear." He turned to her.

She looked into his eyes for the first time, imagining him as a little boy, the photos up on their wall in the dining room of him and their father. Photos of them harvesting rice, or manoomin as Charlotte had called it, in a canoe on Lake Superior, another of them fishing and holding up a salmon. Amelia wanted to touch TJ but didn't dare breathe lest he change his mind, stop talking, or walk off.

"Funny," he chortled. "For years I blamed noise from the fish tugs revving their old engines down in the harbor, tuning up for spring. Thought that it was their fault he hadn't heard."

TJ turned back to watch the deer. "Hated their eagerness to get out on the lake that was still so far from being open, believed they'd drowned me out so that I'd lost the chance to remind him of us, to remind him that he couldn't leave."

His boyhood cries had grown louder as his father's truck accelerated and kicked up red dust. A deep shivering had caused the boy to give chase, feeling his skin flash ahead to catch the truck, to seize it, anything to stop his father.

TJ then laughed to himself in a quiet way. "After a few years I realized that it wasn't the fish tugs."

He stopped talking and regarded another deer that'd joined.

"Hard to believe when you're a kid that life can change in a second—that all the years you drift off to sleep in your father's lap, smelling his cigarettes or the feel of his strength when he'd hoist me out of a riverbed that was always easier to climb down into than up and out of—that in the end, it had all weighed nothing on his heart."

TJ breathed as he recalled. To never hear the constancy of the man's breathing or the heavy sound of his father's workboots coming up the front steps after a long day was a fate from which he wondered if he'd ever recover. Parts he'd share with no one, not even Charlotte. And it was only in the woods, in the presence of wolves who never questioned their bonds or broke their promises that Ma'iingan Ninde was home. And that too, he'd never tell a soul.

TJ glanced at the pile of snow on the deck. A reminder he'd forgotten to shovel it off that morning. Yet how clearly he remembered the ache of believing he'd not been enough for his father to stay and then the sting of discovering that there'd been another child who was.

"So much I didn't know," TJ dismissed and sat back in his desk chair. His throat constricted with tears he refused to allow. Recalling how he'd leaned over on his thighs, struggling to catch his breath as Gloria caught up, holding his jacket. They'd waited for what felt like hours until his mother had said, "He's gone."

He'd felt Gloria crouch beside him, watching for signs of red road dust indicating that someone was driving back. He'd wanted to stay until his father remembered and the pull of their love was stronger than his love of the ocean or of the printing presses and the newspapers he used to print.

"Come on, Ma'iingan Ninde." He remembered the gentle way that Gloria had draped his jacket over his shoulders just as the chill that comes from having broken a sweat in such cold sets in. How he'd resisted slipping his arms into the sleeves as if it would be an admission.

Once he did, together they'd stood and walked back to the house.

"Let's go finish dinner," TJ said as he stood and held out his hand.

Amelia looked at his outstretched palm and then up at him, confused. Was his hand for her? To help her up? Should she touch it? Her stomach tickled.

"The shell," he said. His fingers wiggled.

"Oh." She placed it on his palm and stood, feeling foolish and embarrassed for thinking otherwise, glad she hadn't touched his hand.

"Charlotte's probably waiting on us," he said and walked away.

She paused, lost in the toss of emotion, back on the hill with that little boy, with Gloria, a few moments before Amelia realized that TJ had already headed back out the office door and toward the house without waiting.

36

It was impossible to go home after that. Amelia pulled over onto the shoulder of Blueberry Road, playing with her bottom lip as she sat thinking, the Jeep idling. The whole thing made no sense, yet she'd only known her father as a child knows a parent.

Amelia put the Jeep into gear and veered off onto County Road K, heading toward Whitedeer's place to see if the old man was still up.

Pulling over onto the shoulder opposite his driveway, Amelia leaned over the passenger's seat, peering down through birch trees and saw the hint of a dim interior light. She took it as permission to approach. Twice in one day. She had no coffee cake this time.

Turning into his driveway, she parked near the barn and sat; waiting for a greeting from the yellow Lab mix, but no dog. Maybe he was tucked away for the night inside with Whitedeer. Amelia sat, knowing that her presence was known.

The outdoor light switched on. She watched as the screen door opened and Whitedeer stepped out, walking to the edge of the stoop, looking at her car.

She rolled down the window.

"Hi, it's me again, Amelia."

"Oh, Amelia, come on right in." He waved for her to follow as he turned to go back in.

She called, "Mind if I bring in the puppies again?"

Whitedeer then waved more emphatically to follow, as if too cold for discussion. She wondered if he'd heard.

"Sorry to barge in on you like this," she said, stepping up to the door with a pup balanced on each hip. Lacey and Junior looked around in wonder as she stepped inside, each sniffing.

The old man turned to face her. "Something musta happened," he said and reached for Junior. "Bet it's that TJ," he said in a scolding voice and held Junior against the side of his neck.

"How'd you know?" she said in a sarcastic way.

He winked at her, enjoying the sarcasm as she followed farther into the house. Whitedeer began a conversation with Junior. "Second time today, buddy." He touched the pup's head. "And you look just like your papa."

Whitedeer motioned for the stove. "Help yourself to coffee," he said. "Or that shit herbal tea Cherise says I should drink for my bowels. You can take the whole goddamned box home if you want, she'll only bring more."

"Thanks but I'm fine," Amelia said. "Can I get you something?"

"Already got."

He walked into the living room and then turned to look at Lacey.

"Them guys hungry?" he asked as the yellow Lab mix began sniffling and pushing against Lacey.

"They just ate." Amelia held Lacey closer.

"Aw, that's Trixie, he's okay, would nurse them if he could. Former owner gave him a girl's name, thought he was a female. No cure for common stupidity. I kept the name, figuring he don't know he's got a girl's name."

Amelia smiled and nodded.

"TJ just told me about the day our dad left."

"Oooo," he commented and then carefully positioned himself in front of his chair, and then released his body to plop back.

"Wouldn't think it's such a goddamned effort to sit, but when you're eighty-six and you've worked a good long day it's hard work."

He then listened as Amelia recounted the events of the evening before speaking.

"You know, Amelia, sometimes people get stuck."

She blinked hard. Same words from Diane at the Biomes three months ago in Rhode Island.

"They can't shake something off when it's time," the older man said. "TJ's tried, Gloria did too. But they both got stuck. Your dad and her were stuck, neither would budge. Not good—somebody's gotta give. Sometimes one gives more than the other, one's the lion, the other the lamb," he said, playing with his lip as he thought. "I'm not too sure that's good either, too much bending makes a person break."

Junior began dozing in his lap. Her father always bent to Penelope; Amelia couldn't remember it being any other way.

Whitedeer looked at her and sighed. "Maybe when people marry from such different worlds, Amelia, one of 'em's always suffering."

Both were quiet.

"Do you know why my dad left?" she asked.

"Oooo. Been a while but I got a coupla theories." He brushed thin strands of white hair back with one hand. "At the time everyone around here had an opinion. Gloria's brother, Frank, everyone on the rez, people in town who knew both of 'em. Sometimes married folks have their differences, we'd figured they'd iron 'em out." He paused, recollecting. "That's what we thought when your dad left for New York."

Whitedeer took a sip of something in the same ceramic coffee mug and set it down. Lacey looked up as he did.

He wiped his lips on his sleeve. "Mind you, nobody expected your dad to leave for good, don't think he did either." He raised his eyebrows. "Figured he'd be gone a month or two, rake in some cash, but then late one night Gloria got a strange phone call.

Shook her to the bone. Your dad begging for her to take TJ, get on a plane, and come right away. I remember Gloria telling me he sounded frightened enough to make her change her mind."

"Frightened?" Amelia asked, having a hard time imagining that.

Whitedeer slowly nodded as if seeing young Gloria before him. "She told me she'd only seen Ted like that one other time, when TJ was six and between you and me, I don't think your dad ever got over it."

Amelia held Lacey up to her chest as she listened.

"It started with a call from a stranded fishing vessel whose engine quit out in the waters close to Outer Island, the farthest Apostle."

"I've seen a map."

"Think it says a lot about the kinda man your dad was," he said to Amelia and then was quiet. He had that look of being not sure how much to tell. "But that experience changed him, I believe for good."

He was quiet for a while, looking at the pups, thinking. Amelia sat up, leaning her chin into her palm to encourage him to go on.

"He'd told Gloria and me about it the instant he was back on shore." Whitedeer looked at her before going on. "Think maybe you oughta know this about your dad."

"Okay," she said to encourage him.

"He worked as a marine engine mechanic. Young family, they needed money, Ted jumped all over the call. Venturing out so early in April like that is a huge risk," Whitedeer said. "There's still icebergs floating the size of minivans. They'll tear into your hull and sink you before you can say, 'Boo.' "

"So why go out?"

He smiled at Amelia and sighed as if emptying unwanted memories from his lungs.

"Winter's long up here. Leaves everyone itching to get out on the lake, especially those that make their living from her.

That captain was no different. But when ya push too far out, bad luck often follows. Combination of hard times and a kind of cabin fever sets in when ya been snow- and ice-bound so long. It makes a person lose all sense of risk."

Except for swimming out past the lifeguard zones, her father had eaten the same thing every day, watched the same news station, worked the same job, and lived a life of such monotony that Amelia often wondered why it was he never lay down on the railroad tracks near the commuter station by their house just for a taste of different.

Whitedeer looked at her. "You mind throwing on another log?"

"Sure." She hadn't noticed the room getting chilly, and added Lacey to his lap as she sorted through a woodpile until finding a log that looked dry.

"Good girl," he said. "Just throw 'er on, it'll catch straight-away."

Amelia then brushed bits of wood off her hands and went to pick up Lacey.

"She's fine." He guided Amelia away with his elbow, enjoying the feel of the two pups piled together.

"The captain and crew was adrift in Superior," he continued. "Largest body of fresh water in the world that, pardon my language, you don't want to fuck with." The old man gave her a look. "The crew'd been pushing off ice floes with a boat hook before your daddy showed up. Ted had heard down at the Rumline that this captain always paid cash."

Amelia looked up in surprise. "Same tavern?" She'd driven by it just the other day.

"Damn straight," Whitedeer said. "Known 'em for a coupla generations. Their kids run it now, one of 'em's okay, the other a piece of shit if you want my honest opinion. Took three hours for your dad to reach Outer. Their anchor'd been dragged by the wind and current."

"That happens," Amelia said.

Whitedeer paused to look at her. "There's two times you don't want to be out on Superior." The man held up his hand to count. "November, December," his thumb went up, "and early spring when the ice is opening," his index finger went next. "Good chance you'll be dead either way."

"I'll remember that," Amelia joked.

"So their hull springs a leak under the engine block the instant your dad gets out his tools. Sprayed in the face with ice water, it takes his breath—he's thinking of his young wife and child then hears the son-of-a-bitch captain mumble, 'Christ, not again.'"

Whitedeer coughed. Amelia moved to take the puppies but he waved her away.

"Then what?" she asked.

"She's taking on water faster than the bilge pump can empty, electrical fails and so does the bilge."

"Knew it."

Whitedeer looked at her in surprise. "Smartie pants."

"No really. Just been there," she said.

"Couldn't reach the leak. Men are hand pumping."

"No one can under the engine block." Amelia imagined the chaos.

"Your dad tells me the boat starts to talk, metal noises as it lists portside."

Amelia blinked and held her eyes shut for an instant. "I've heard that sound myself."

"Mayday call went out." Whitedeer sighed as he watched the logs catch on. "Time was not their friend. They fought like tigers as the portside slipped under."

Amelia lowered her head.

"Your dad's boat was too small to take 'em all without losing seaworthiness so the captain and the first mate stayed."

Amelia sat back in the chair; she could see it so clearly.

"'Come on,' your dad yells to the captain, the men are all shouting too. He reaches for the captain and first mate but neither reaches back. 'Grab my hand, Charlie, damn it, Charlie, Bud,' but both stood steadfast."

"How far was the Coast Guard?"

He smiled at her before speaking. "Might as well have been a million miles, Amelia. Things were different back then. No one had choppers or them power boats they got now, or even those survival suits."

She nodded. "True."

"They'd kept shouting, 'Hold on, Coast Guard's coming,' but your dad knew better. They all knew better. Hard waitin' around for men to drown."

"I can't even imagine." She closed her eyes, remembering the feeling of doom that went with every ship she'd board before heading out to sea.

"Chattering teeth were the last sound, he told Gloria and me. The captain and first mate slipped under. Then the groan that bending metal makes when a ship is sinking," Whitedeer said. "Haunts a person for a lifetime."

He looked at her.

"Did your dad."

It was a kind of marine death rattle she'd heard of where a ship speaks for the last time.

He looked up at her. "Ever hear it?"

Amelia sighed deeply and recrossed her legs. "Thankfully no."

"Ted was haunted by the captain's eyes—they'd looked up at him as the man slipped under. Clear, icy water—his blue eye color so vivid like he's becoming the water—your dad knowing that he was the last thing that man would ever see."

They sat quiet for a few moments before he talked. "We believe when people die like that, sometimes they take spirits of the living with them. For company, for comfort, and we protect against that. Your dad didn't know."

"What do you mean?"

"The man's eyes stayed with your dad. Puzzlement then peace as the captain drifted down. Your dad said it looked as if the captain's feet were reaching for the bottom. Gloria'd wake him, whimpering in his sleep. Waterlogged souls reaching out to him, trying to speak but Ted couldn't hear 'cause his ears would roar with water."

She was too shaken to speak.

"Did a bunch of sweat ceremonies, trying to free Ted, to have him call his spirit back but don't think they worked. Sometimes spirits hang on 'cause the living need them more."

"You think my father needed this man?"

Whitedeer shrugged.

"That his spirit is still down there with the man like he's got a claim on him?"

He looked at her with an odd smile. "What do you think?"

"I guess I don't think." She didn't know what to say, didn't know what she thought. "With all due respect, I'm a scientist."

"Yes I know." Whitedeer set the pups on the chair as he stood to stoke the logs and turned his back, absorbing the warmth. "But some things are true whether you believe in them or not. Doesn't make a hill 'a beans."

Silence had surrounded them for a few moments before Amelia spoke.

"So how does this relate to the New York phone call and Gloria's decision to go?" she asked.

The old man set down the poker and turned to her.

"Because she'd heard the same fright in his voice, like the day he'd stepped back on shore." The old man sat back down, picking up the pups and rearranging them in his lap. "Like he was in danger but wouldn't say."

"Danger," she repeated and sat up, watching as the pups slept in Whitedeer's chair. "So what stopped her, why didn't Gloria go?"

Whitedeer sat down on the raised hearth and rested elbows

on his knees as he looked at her. The same odd smile spread through his face.

"You don't know?" he asked.

"Know what?" Amelia shook her head, looking puzzled.

"You don't, do you?" He nodded, looking amazed. "Why, he'd just met your mama and she was already anjiko with you."

37

Three days later Amelia listened to Bryce's truck tires rolling down the snow-packed driveway.

She was out on the steps the minute she'd heard sounds, to welcome him. Piercing blue sky, clear, the temperature had plummeted the night before.

The day before she'd spent scouring Gloria's house. Her back hurt from mopping the wooden floors and washing down the walls and ceilings like she'd done so many times on research vessels that were musty, and then left the windows wide open to air the place out until it was so cold she couldn't stand it.

Amelia stepped down and walked to greet him as he pulled alongside and parked. Wrapped in her sweater, her stomach jumped.

"Hi," she called to him. It sounded like someone else's voice and she felt embarrassed. Momentary awkwardness made her smile as she stumbled over casual conversation, "How was the drive?" until she reached him. He grasped her waist and she rested her lips on the side of his neck.

"Not fast enough." He looked at her and kissed the tip of her nose.

She stepped on the tops of his sneakers and he began walking both of them toward the front steps. He stopped. Both their eyes were tearing from the cold.

"So, eh," he joked. "You gonna invite me inside?"

"Uh-h-h, yeah."

"Cold out here." Bryce scanned the snowy hills in a way that made her laugh.

She felt his eyes on her and couldn't meet them. She felt shy and didn't know why. He stepped closer. He touched and lifted her chin. It was almost too painful to look into them. Instead she ducked down and threaded her arms around his torso under his parka, feeling the warmth of his form. They stood rocking for a few moments.

She felt him turn and guide her up the front steps. Opening the front door, he held it for her to. Lacey and Junior walked up to edge of the barricade that she'd constructed to cordon them off in the kitchen.

"They're huge!" he said. "Twice the size even than last week," Bryce exclaimed, his arms out as he lifted the barrier and collapsed onto the floor, squeezing his eyes shut as the pups stepped across his chest as if he were a boat dock. Succumbing to a face wash, he squeezed his eyes shut as Junior peed on his collar.

"Now you've been officially welcomed," Amelia said. Bryce opened one eye and looked at her. He shut it as Lacey's tongue approached. Amelia grabbed a wad of paper towels and knelt down, blotting.

"Come here." He reached out his arm toward her and lowered her down onto the floor.

She curled up and rested her head on his chest.

"God, I missed you," he said, pulling her closer. Her lips brushed the side of his neck and she smiled, the skin smelled good. Junior then began licking her lips.

"Uch." She pulled away, rolling onto her side as she wiped her mouth. "Junior!?"

Bryce then rolled onto his side and looked into Amelia's eyes. She had to look away. It was daylight with no place in which to recede. So far they'd made love at night. She'd never looked into him with all the nuances of a lover in this way.

He took her chin and turned her face toward him.

"Place looks nice."

"Thanks," she said. "You didn't see it before."

"Didn't have to."

A tear escaped from her eyes without even crying, then another.

His arm surrounded her and he pulled her close.

Just then Lacey nosed Amelia in the butt.

"Jeeze." She jerked back.

" 'Everybody's trying to get into the act,' " he quoted the comedian Jimmy Durante.

Just then the pup jumped over the two of them and started jabbing Bryce in the rear too.

Junior then wedged his face between the two of them, alternating between licking Amelia's nostrils then Bryce's before Amelia moved him.

"Yuk, enough," she said, just as Lacey poked Bryce again, making him jump.

Amelia started laughing and couldn't stop to the degree that tears wetted her face. She rolled away still laughing.

"So you think that's funny, do you?" he said and rolled her onto her back. On his knees he crouched over her, supporting his weight on his elbows as he lowered himself down.

He kissed her once softly and then they searched out each other's mouths like familiar objects that they'd lost somewhere along the way but had just now found.

He circled his arms around her as he stood and lifted her.

"Bedroom's back there," she said.

"I'll find it." He winked.

38

A few weeks after Bryce's arrival Charlotte invited them over for brunch on Saturday, the first week in February.

As they pulled up to the house Amelia noticed that TJ's truck was gone.

"Bet ya a beer at the Rumline he's drummed up some lame excuse not to be around."

Bryce shot her a look.

As they parked and walked toward the house, Amelia noticed that a few cars and trucks sped by on the reservation road. Small, portable flashing lights had been placed on their roofs as if deputized.

"Hi." Charlotte met them at the front door, hurrying as she slipped into her coat, seemingly on her way out. "Got an emergency right now. Just left you a message."

"What's going on?" Amelia asked.

"Poachers on rez lands." She lowered her head. "Viola says there's a wolf caught in a snare not far from here."

"Still alive?" Amelia asked.

Charlotte looked at her and sighed as if not wanting to know the answer either way. "I'm on my way." She rushed toward the side door to TJ's office.

"Can we help?" Amelia asked.

"Just have to grab IV bags of fluids, blood," she said. "You can help carry stuff to my truck."

Bryce opened the side door as Charlotte walked down the shoveled path to the office.

"Maybe you two can join the volunteers and help locate the other traps and snares," she said. "TJ will show you how to search out traps under the deep snow."

"Where is this?" Amelia asked.

"Oh, down around the point, not far," Charlotte said as she unlocked TJ's office door. "Near Sand Bay. There's a wide surface area—some open fields, other dense woods," she said and began pulling open cabinets and drawers, opening refrigerators and pulling bags of blood as she piled them into two carrying cases.

"Can I help find something?"

She turned and smiled at Amelia.

"Thanks but I know what I'm looking for," Charlotte said. "Maybe later."

Bryce crossed his arms and sighed.

"Very deep snow in the woods," Charlotte said as she gathered the vet supplies. "Very remote area too. Who knows how many traps they set or when they were set."

Charlotte piled the carriers in Bryce's arms. She locked the door and then headed to her van.

"Follow me," the woman said over her shoulder. "Now you get to see what your brother does."

Charlotte then turned to face them. She took a deep breath, waiting before speaking. "It may not be pretty."

"We're used to not pretty," Bryce said. Amelia stood by his side.

They heard wolf howls just as they parked behind a line of vehicles pulled up alongside the road. Sounds of howling, yelping, and panic grew louder as they approached on a path tromped down by many boots. Charlotte led the way.

Amelia spotted TJ giving quick instructions to a group as to how to search for traps and snares under the deep snow using a pole. He demonstrated and then cautioned.

"Triggering one can shatter your foot," he warned. "So go slowly, step gingerly, first poling down into small areas at a time."

"What about the people who did this?" one of the men yelled.

TJ looked at the man for a few seconds. His eyes narrowed. "Don't worry about them."

Everyone was quiet for a few moments.

"The goal is to get to the wolf quickly and without injury," he said and paused once he spotted Amelia. "And clear out the traps."

He motioned for the volunteers to begin their search.

People turned.

TJ walked toward Amelia after the group dispersed and asked in a quiet voice, "What are you doing here?"

"Charlotte told us," Amelia said.

TJ looked at her. "We've got this covered."

"But I want to help," Amelia said, turning toward the sounds of howling.

"Stay out of this, Amelia," he said. "This is not your area. It's dangerous work. You're leaving soon anyway so back off."

He hurried off, carrying tools as his staff walked alongside him.

She looked at him. *You're leaving soon?* What a thing to say. Her face burned with humiliation. A few staffers turned away, some pretended to check their phones, one demonstrated the pole technique of locating traps to those just arriving, others sauntered away to avoid listening.

Amelia rushed up to him. "What's with you?"

"All these people live here, it's our struggle, our home. We've been here hundreds of years. You're just taken in by some liberal bullshit thing."

"What the fuck is your problem?" She shoved him.

Bryce stepped up.

"I came up here to find you, get to know you," she said. "I'm not trying to be some pain in the ass little sister and you're really pissing me off."

"Well, good." He turned his back and walked away.

"You're a fucking asshole," she yelled. She reached down, made a snowball, and threw it, hitting him square in the back. He didn't flinch.

"No wonder my father left," she hollered. "You're a jerk and you got what you deserve, asshole."

At that TJ turned around and came walking at her.

Charlotte quickly separated the two, striding toward her husband and pulling him aside. He pushed away her arm.

"I don't have time for this shit," TJ said. "That wolf is sitting in a minefield, every second counts."

Just then there was a yelp of pain and a long mournful howl.

Amelia turned and took off running toward the cry. She lifted her knees and hopped through the snow, her heart pounding as the cry drew her as if it had been Alex calling for her.

"Amelia," TJ yelled. "Stop. We don't know where the traps are."

"Amelia," Bryce yelled.

But she ran like a shot across the field, her legs aching with fatigue as she kept lifting them forward, undaunted by the threat of anything as she ran toward the woods and the sound of the cries.

"What the hell is she doing?" TJ yelled to Bryce as they both followed in her steps, using the pole to poke through the snow on all sides to spring traps.

"She's doing what she always does," Bryce said with an air of resignation, out of breath as they charged in her footsteps, their pace slowing in the deep snow the farther they went.

"That's fucking crazy."

"That's your sister."

. . .

She didn't know what she'd do when she found the wolf, but that wasn't important. What was important was that she had to witness, had to comfort, had to sit with, had to offer whatever humble assistance she could.

Through the trees she heard the clank of a heavy chain. As she approached, the gray wolf was caught by the face around the neck. It was lying down on its side, its body emaciated and Amelia could see the outline of its pelvis through the dense fur. Its tail moved so she knew it was alive.

Amelia squatted and went down on her knees. Her chest was heaving from running in the deep snow.

The wolf barely opened its eyes, two shiny slits.

"Oh my God, my God," she said. "I'm so sorry." She quickly looked at the apparatus, not having a clue as to how to release it.

She looked up.

A black wolf stood watching—the long knock-kneed stance, thick coal-black ruff of his winter coat. Amelia hadn't noticed him until his yellow eyes met hers. They were the color of Junior and Jethro's.

The snow had been tamped down. It was soaked with blood and the smell of rotting meat.

The black wolf then walked back to lie down next to his mate. With his head on her flank, he nuzzled her. She closed her eyes at his touch.

Amelia turned and called as loud as she could, "TJ," not thinking they'd just follow her tracks. "I found them. They're here."

"We're almost there," he called back.

"They're coming," she said to the wolves. "They'll help. I promise they will."

Alongside his mate were offerings of deer meat, only her face and jaw were clamped shut in the trap. The black wolf didn't understand but nevertheless kept bringing fresh food, setting it near her face. The only thing he could do was watch her slowly starve. She emitted high-pitched whimpers with her jaws firmly clamped shut by the snare. She lay ready for death to take her.

TJ, Bryce, and his wildlife staff caught up. The black wolf stood, moving to block access to his mate. His guard hairs rose in a defensive posture until picking up TJ's scent.

"It's okay, buddy," TJ said and crouched down. "That's B-34, the alpha male. Looks like B-33, his mate, is snared." He reached out his hand. The black wolf didn't move. "It's okay," he said in the kindest voice, so kind Amelia didn't recognize it.

The wolf paced, and wouldn't let the men near.

"Go on." TJ stepped toward him to chase him away. He clapped his hands and moved menacingly toward him. The wolf darted into the trees and stood watching.

"Jimmy," TJ called to his coworker.

The chain was instantly cut.

"We know this pair," TJ said. The biologists gathered around. "If her neck's broken, releasing the snare will kill her."

TJ slid his hands under the wolf's head to brace her neck.

One of his assistants cut through the snare and released the steel claw. The animal was free. The wolf lay there as TJ and the other biologists examined her.

Amelia took off her jacket. She spread it down under the wolf's head.

Charlotte caught up to them with the fluids.

Carefully they lifted the animal's body, supporting her head and face and lay her down on Amelia's coat. She'd done that with a coat once before with an orphan baby seal after its mother had gotten eaten by a walrus on the Labrador coast.

"Jaw's broken," TJ said as he examined the animal. "Maybe other bones in her face."

He looked at the other biologists.

"Neck seems okay, though," TJ said, watching as the gray wolf moved her legs. "Severely dehydrated—that plus the shock of moving her might kill her before we even reach the van."

Charlotte began to inject fluids under the skin in the wolf's hip. "This'll get her started," she said to Amelia. "Gotta combat the dehydration, prevent shock if we can."

"How long's she been here?" Bryce asked.

TJ shrugged. "A few days, maybe a week." He pulled out his phone and tossed it over to Darrell, his assistant. "Get Evan on the phone. See if his plane's available."

The animal whimpered in high-pitched sounds when they moved her. Her mate stood near and gave off a pitiful cry. Every hair stood up on Amelia's body. She understood family. She understood love.

Amelia was overcome with distress.

TJ looked around. It was a long hike to the road.

"Here." Bryce helped lift the wolf by grasping Amelia's coat to raise the animal to lay it down on a canvas stretcher.

TJ and his associate then lifted the stretcher by the poles slipped through on each side, hiking with the hundred-pound animal back toward the road.

"Evan says he'll be at the airfield in twenty minutes," Darrell called over.

"Excellent," TJ said. "Call the Twin Cities Vet Hospital; let 'em know we're coming.

"With wild animals," TJ said to Bryce, "unfortunately the transport alone kills so many of them. Die from shock, fear."

Amelia looked as blood wetted the lips of the female's mouth.

"Okay," TJ said. "We're heading toward Charlotte's van."

"What about him?" Amelia asked. The male looked like a relative of Junior. The wolf looked at her through the trees.

"He'll keep coming back, looking for her," TJ said as they hiked.

TJ slipped one arm out from his coat, then the other, and tossed it at Amelia with his free arm.

"If this girl makes a full recovery we'll release her here, in this very spot," TJ said. "He'll wait. He'll find her. If she doesn't make it, he might come back and keep looking. Or he might stop eating and choose to die on this very spot."

The rest of the crew searched the area with sticks, poking the ground every few feet. A few steel claw traps went off, one after the other. This was an area that had a healthy wolf pack that had been chased off the national forest into reservation areas that were remote, loaded with edible wildlife and few humans.

"Hey, TJ?" one of the volunteers called.

He briefly turned, carrying the female as they approached the van.

"Uh—think we've got a deceased wolf here. Caught in a snare under the snow."

39

It had been forty-eight hours since B-33, or the wolf they'd nicknamed Smiley, had undergone surgery. The name stuck because of how the wolf endured every poke and prod of the hospital staff with patience and goodwill as if understanding that they were trying to help.

The wolf had already been flown to the vet hospital in Minneapolis when TJ got a call from Roy, owner of the Rumline Tavern in downtown Bayfield.

"Got some info for ya, buddy." He and Roy had gone to high school together, back then Roy's father had run the place. The two had remained friends ever since, despite rumors of him moving drugs into some of the smaller towns.

"Some guy came in shootin' off his mouth about setting traps in Red Cliff, 'sticking it to the Indians' and all that shit."

"Really."

"Thought you'd want to know."

"You know the guy?" TJ asked.

"Unfortunately I do," he said and proceeded to give TJ all the details of what he'd heard. "From Hurley. Son of a guy I can't stand. Guy's a veteran and all but still a piece of shit."

"You talking about who I think you're talking about?"

"Yeah," Roy said. "That's the one."

"Says they're sneaking in tonight to check the snares," Roy

said. "Said they set 'em last week before we got them three feet that fell."

"Thanks, Roy," TJ said. "I owe you big time."

"Nah, buddy, you don't owe me nothing. Hate these wolf hunters, give humans a bad name. Let me know if you need help."

"Will do."

It took two phone calls to mobilize the enforcement arm of Red Cliff's tribal police, the conservation wardens, plus GLIFWC's team who were cross-deputized with the state of Wisconsin.

The entire area had been set up, thirty armed enforcement officers surrounding the entire territory, hidden in the woods. It had been a warm winter despite the abundance of snow. Wearing white windbreakers over their uniforms to blend into the woods, they staked out and waited.

The information from Roy indicated that the men would be out after dark on the extensive snowmobile trail system, figuring no one would think it unusual if they were to be out at night, tooling around in national forests and on reservation land.

Three hours had passed as all the men sat in silence, radioing each other on occasion if they heard engine sounds. The sky was staying lighter in the evenings and it was just after eight when they heard a group of snowmobiles heading their way.

"You hear that?" TJ said.

Several of the men checked in. "Copy."

"Let them come directly to the site, dismount, and then look around," said Terry, the chief enforcement officer at GLIFWC. "Don't want to move too soon. Let them look at the snare, handle it, talk. We've got the night-vision video camera going there to record their conversations and actions. And let them find their way to the deceased wolf under the snow. We need enough evidence on tape to nail these individuals. Let's let them go right to the traps—they know where they set 'em."

"Copy." Several of the officers checked in.

"So no one moves until I give the word," Terry said.

The engine noise was getting closer, men were laughing, making hooting noises that echoed through the trees.

TJ wondered if these were the same men Roy had mentioned. They certainly weren't sneaking up by any stretch of the imagination yet the area was so remote out in this part of the reservation.

Just then there was a hush as the three snowmobiles reached the snare. TJ held his breath. They parked and turned off their engines.

"What the fuck?" One of them picked up the chain that had been cut and showed it to the other two. Another picked up the snare and looked at it.

"I thought you said they couldn't get out."

"They can't," the other said and looked around. "Someone sprang it. Fuck."

They started up their snowmobiles and drove over to the other snare, the one with the buried wolf.

"Looks like we got something here," he said, pulling on the chain and feeling the frozen fur beneath. "Looks like someone's been here." He shined his flashlight on the dozens of footprints.

"Probably raccoons," the other one said. "They ain't bear tracks, that for sure." He laughed.

"Uhh—I don't think so, Chuck." The man's voice quivered. "This looks like people tracks."

Just then all of the headlights from the enforcement officers turned on at once, light flooding the area.

The third man ran to his snowmobile and jumped on. Revving the engine, he took off, chased by a number of enforcement officers.

The other two were handcuffed by the tribal police.

"You have the right to remain silent," they began and were summarily shoved up the trail toward the road where the tribal police cars were waiting.

"Don't say nothing, Chuck," the one yelled to the other.

"Good advice," TJ said. "Too bad we already got you on tape. Wanna see?" He held up an iPad. "Freshly downloaded. Thanks for making it easy." He hit the play button and the men's voices came streaming out.

Then TJ turned away, mounting his snowmobile as he powered off to aid in the chase for the third man.

40

Smiley's jaw had been surgically wired together by the wild-life veterinarian, removing a few bone fragments that might cause trouble for B-33 in the future. Luckily, it had been a clean break and not shattered. Given that the wolf had survived the plane ride despite dehydration and shock, the vet was confident of her recovery. But as to whether or not the jawbone would heal to the point of being strong enough for wild release to join her mate was unknown at that point. It would be Charlotte and TJ's call in the next month or two as they supervised her recovery to assess how well she'd be able to tear meat from a carcass in order to survive.

Charlotte and Amelia drove down to Minneapolis and stayed the first week of the wolf's surgery with Jen in the apartment. Bryce stayed behind with the pups and had picked up a part-time job with the Tribal Fish Hatchery helping to upgrade their filtration system. During the day the two women had practically camped out with Smiley, taking her on brief walks when the anesthesia had worn off. The wolf didn't seem to fight them as Charlotte was skilled with handling wild animals.

Jen was ecstatic to see them, though she and Amelia talked several times a day. She'd transformed the apartment into what

she called her little "Love Nest" with Doby, the only impedi-
ment being Bryce's mammoth aquarium. Amelia gave Charlotte a tour of the varieties of corals, and showed her the sea
horses. The woman was transfixed, watching the little micro-
cosm of marine world that had been an extension of their lives.

"I'm moving with Doby to Duluth this April," Jen said. "I already gave Sea Life my notice."

"What are you going to do there?"

"Don't know. Be with him," she said and smiled. "Work in
his new club."

"What about that UM-Duluth job we both saw in the *Marine
Biology Quarterly*?"

Jen looked at Amelia for a long time. "I was thinking more
for you or Bryce. Met the chair of the biology department
through Doby while in Duluth a few weekends ago. I gave her
your names and numbers, she was interested."

"Thanks, but why won't you apply?"

Jen smiled and hesitated for a moment.

Charlotte bent and whispered in Amelia's ear.

She then turned to Jen, almost in a whisper. "Are you pregnant?"

Jen nodded. Her eyes teared as Amelia grabbed her and the
two hugged.

"I'm going to have a baby, Ammy. I wanna be a mom like
you."

"You're going to be the best mom ever, Jen," she said into her
hair.

"Hope so," she said.

"I know so," Amelia said, wiping her eyes.

They both turned to Charlotte.

"How'd you know?" Amelia asked.

"Eh, let's just say a little birdie told me." Charlotte smiled.

"You're scary," Amelia teased her.

"TJ says that a lot."

Jen turned to Amelia. "They also run that Lake Superior water initiative, which you're a natural for. Seriously, Am, they're interested in both of you, give them a call."

"Thanks, I will," she said. "As long as it's not something funky like working out of a shopping mall," Amelia said as they both chuckled.

"Hey—don't knock it—I met Doby." She raised her eyebrows, smiling as broadly as Amelia had ever seen.

"True." Amelia nodded, looking at Charlotte. "It was all worth it then."

"And how's Bryce, the jerk who never returns my calls?" Jen asked.

Amelia smiled.

"Enough said." Jen laughed and pushed her away as if not wanting to hear any more details. "What about this monster?" She pointed to the aquarium.

Amelia sighed and shrugged. "Oh, one way or another we'll come get it before you guys move."

She and Charlotte spent most of the week with Smiley in the vet school's critical care unit. They slipped her small bits of dried fish and venison broken up into tiny pieces that Smiley could chew, and Charlotte made a special healing porridge into which the hospital staff crushed and mixed the wolf's meds. As soon as Charlotte placed the bowl in the area, Smiley's eyes lit up, her ears would lay back as she'd slurp it down. The following week the wolf was to be released into Charlotte and TJ's care for the rest of her rehabilitation, which was estimated to be a four to six weeks, maybe longer depending on her progress.

At one point Smiley managed to stand up, though the enclosure was too low for her to fully stretch.

"What a good girl," Amelia said, hand feeding her more bits of dried whitefish that she gobbled down. She loved the feel of the wolf's soft lips and tongue as Smiley picked up each piece.

It was Amelia's idea to take the used cloth bedding, very thin blankets, from the vet hospital on which Smiley had curled up and slept. She'd bagged up the bedding and brought it back to Red Cliff the week after Smiley's release as they transported the wolf back to Charlotte's for six weeks of rehab.

The evening of their return there was still light enough out to see. It was pinkish. Amelia had driven out to the field where Smiley had been trapped.

It hadn't snowed since then and the ridges of tire treads from where people had parked the previous week were still visible in the last bits of sunlight before darkness began to fill the sky. It was mid-February and felt different from even December. Everyone kept saying it was going to be an early spring.

Amelia pulled over and parked, gathering her thoughts for a few moments before climbing out of the Jeep. She thought of Smiley and of B-34, the black wolf, and how so many things in her life had changed since Rhode Island. How odd it was that rather than feeling strange, it felt commonplace, like she'd always known these woods.

Amelia pushed open the Jeep's door with her foot and stepped down, carrying the clear plastic bag as she looked around for the path into the woods. It was immediately obvious and Amelia began hiking through the birch and white pines, across to the clearing, to where the snow was still marked by many footprints and poles seeking out traps.

TJ and his coworkers had dug a large hole to remove the deceased wolf's body. The area was scattered with flecks of brown material. Amelia walked closer and leaned over. Touching the flakes, she lifted a few to smell. Tobacco. Looking up in the dim light she spotted tiny blue and yellow pouches and ribbons tied throughout the trees to the east where the wolf had died.

She then walked toward the area where Smiley had been snared. The reddish pallor of residual blood from the black wolf's offerings of meat glowed scarlet with the setting sun.

Amelia set down the bedding from the vet hospital, spreading it on the very spot. She then crumpled up the plastic bag and tucked it under her arm, slipping her hands into her pockets as the evening chill set in.

Scanning through the leafless woods she longed to see B-34 and the rest of the shadowy figures and for the feel of being watched. But the woods were silent, no one was watching.

The next morning Amelia came back and parked where she had the previous evening. The sun was blinding as it cracked the horizon. The bare hardwood branches were frosted in that kind of way that happens as winter loosens its grip and the night's dew gets caught in such transitions. It was like white fur, left over before having caught the sun.

Amelia hopped down from the Jeep and pulled up her scarf to cover her nose and mouth as she hiked through the woods along the path to the open field. It was a damp cold as she zipped up her coat.

She thought of Smiley, thought of Bryce as she hiked toward the spot. Wondering if any of the grants they'd sent out so far would pan out—thinking to check out the UM-Duluth biology positions, wondering if she'd ever get to work in marine biology in some capacity again and if it even mattered anymore.

The reddish snow where Smiley had been caught looked dark in the morning sun.

Amelia stopped. The blankets were gone.

"Huh," she gasped in surprise, her hand covering her mouth. She hadn't known what to expect, figuring it was an experiment.

Walking around, she looked for evidence that maybe the

cloth blankets had gotten blown somewhere by the strong winds of the previous night. The little mustard house had shuddered in the wind.

The bedding was so light that perhaps the wind had lifted and deposited it into the surrounding branches. Amelia hiked looking for evidence but saw nothing.

Then she spotted a narrow wolf trail. It was off to the side, leading into the woods—a narrow track, a single track, as TJ had explained the gait of a wolf vs. dog.

There were other marks alongside the tracks, like something had been dragged through, creating a smooth indented imprint of a piece of fabric, perhaps being carried by a creature in his mouth.

She was tempted to follow the trail, see where it went but something held her back.

Then she looked through the lower branches, and saw two eyes watching. Standing in the trail was the black wolf that she presumed was Smiley's mate.

Amelia smiled.

"Hi again." She squatted in the trail and held out both hands as she'd done to Jethro, palms up. She made a few kissing sounds. "Are you B-34?" she asked, knowing it was a scientific name and not one the animal would respond to, but she was certain it was the same wolf. She felt more recognition from him than an introduction.

The animal's ears moved up to form a point and he looked from side to side as if embarrassed.

"Well, hi," she called in a soft voice. "Did you take the blanket with Smiley's scent? We named her that. I hope it *was* you," she said. The wolf's head turned from side to side in such a way that she took it as affection. She'd seen Junior do the same thing after eating.

"Are you all okay?" she asked. He backed up a few steps and then turned around. She watched the top of his head as he trotted down the path, presumably back to the den.

Amelia smiled, imagining the black wolf dragging the flannel cloth back to the den where the pack lived to assure them all.

And at that moment there was nothing that Amelia had ever hoped for more.

41

It was the end of February and Smiley had been in Charlotte and TJ's care for almost two weeks. The wolf had begun to show an interest in chewing venison carcasses, bones, ripping meat, chewing on branches—everything that a healthy wolf's jaw should sustain.

Both agreed the wolf was making good progress and if it continued, she could be released as soon as a month to six weeks after her last vet check and jaw X-ray.

TJ was up having coffee as he stood looking out the bay window in the kitchen, surveying the perimeter of the fenced-in wildlife rehab area. He looked closer. B-34 was standing outside the fence, touching noses with Smiley through the open squares in the fencing.

"Hey Charlotte?" he called before hearing water from the shower.

"I'm in the shower," she called back, sounding annoyed at being disturbed.

"Well I'll be damned," he murmured and then crept out onto the deck through the kitchen door. Both animals looked up at him. He stepped back inside and then hurried downstairs to the first floor, opening the back sliding glass door as he stepped out in his socks on the packed snow into the rehab pen.

"Hey guy." He stepped up to the fence and held out his hand, setting down his coffee cup.

B-34 took a step back but as Smiley rubbed against TJ's thigh the black wolf stepped closer and dabbed his cold nose against TJ's open hand through the fence.

"Wanna come in?" he asked.

Smiley stood still.

TJ then grasped Smiley's temporary collar as he walked over to unlatch the gate, letting the door swing wide open.

B-34 skulked down low and began to pace, feeling stressed as he looked to Smiley for reassurance.

"Come on," TJ encouraged.

The wolf then tiptoed toward the open gate. B-34 paced a few more times before making a run for it, darting through the opening as if it was too narrow for his rangy body. He then began to nuzzle his mate, sniffing her as he rubbed his head on hers.

The couple was too busy with their greetings and vocalizations to notice as TJ stepped to close and latch the gate.

He raked out more hay as bedding and dragged in another half-butchered carcass of deer from the back door of his office/garage that the road crew had dropped off the night before—fresh meat for the mates to share together.

Walking back upstairs, he peeled off wet socks and poured another cup of coffee since he'd forgotten the other one down in the pen and didn't want to disturb the couple.

Standing at the bay window, he watched as B-34 carefully sniffed Smiley's incision wounds as well as the smell of her mouth.

"Whew, that felt good," Charlotte said, laughing with impatience as she appeared in sweatpants and wet hair. "Heard you calling."

He looked at her with an impish smile and then turned and pointed.

"What?"

TJ crooked his index finger for her to join him and pointed out the bay window.

She let out a delighted scream.

He moved to stand behind her, surrounding her with his arms, leaning his chin on her shoulder as they stood watching as the two wolves began playing chase games inside the enclosure.

"Well I'll be." She slipped her arms through his and leaned back against his chest as they began to sway. "I love it how families seem to have a way of finding each other."

The swaying stopped. He let go. "Wish that was true, Char."

There was such sadness in his voice that Charlotte turned to face him.

"Oh but it is, TJ," she said.

"Not always."

"Try harder," she said. "Life goes on. Stop acting like some thirteen-year-old kid."

TJ left the room, walking off as if she'd spoiled the moment.

42

It was the first week of March by the time Whitedeer's son-in-law, Peter, had finally called to invite her to help collect fish samples out on Lake Superior. She'd given up hope, figuring he'd forgotten or else had recruited another member of the staff to do the work.

Bryce had wanted to come along but Peter had only two complete gear sets. His nets had been set out in the ice weeks ago, as far out as Outer Island, which was the farthest point from the shore. Peter had mentioned that this was their last window of opportunity to get out on snowmobiles before the melt to retrieve the nets, which would mean losing the winter samples that were critical for assessing the lake's health.

She was set to meet Peter down by the Coast Guard dock later that morning and for the past few weeks she and Bryce had been helping the tribal Fish Hatchery in Red Cliff update their filtration system.

Both had begun to feel the restlessness that's ingrained in the DNA of people born with the call of science that needles you early in the morning or late at night when ideas begin to flood you with the burning drive to know. "What ifs" swirl through your dreams in the middle of a deep sleep, awakening and compelling you to get up and try them out. It was a physical, intellectual, and what Amelia had come to believe was a hardwired calling. They'd both applied for the two positions at UM-Duluth in the biological science department and were waiting to hear. The positions seemed promising, as promising as any of the grants they'd submitted and were waiting to hear about.

Amelia had taken Lacey and Junior out for an early-morning walk up the steep hill to the crooked mailbox on the ridge to retrieve yesterday's mail. She figured the hike through deep snow would tire them out but she was wrong.

As she pulled out a few forwarded scuba catalogs, on top was a letter from her mortgage company.

"Great, what now?" she muttered. She'd been current and had just mailed off a payment that by her calculations should have arrived well in advance of the due date. There was enough money in her checking account to cover it. Ever since leaving Rhode Island, every piece of correspondence from the bank elicited a rush of adrenaline that took hours to wear off. Even their junk mail credit-card promotions threw her into the cycle.

She held up the letter to the morning sun, trying to see through to the type. It was thin and personally addressed, unlike the standard stock window envelope that bore a threatening message.

"Come on, you guys, House!" She gave the command to the pups and they turned and ran toward the house. Lacey ran ahead, Junior in the opposite direction. She'd call the bank and explain how the payment had been sent.

She stopped midway down the hill and ripped open the envelope.

"Hey Bryce," she called, entering to the smell of frying eggs and toast as Bryce fixed breakfast. She shut the front door.

He looked up. "Hey yeah?"

She didn't answer.

"You hungry?" he asked and motioned with his elbow to grab two plates.

She stopped in the middle of the room and held up the copy of her original mortgage note from many years ago stamped CANCELED.

Her stillness made him turn.

She stepped close enough for him to see.

"It's a payoff notice."

It made no sense.

"Did you pay off my house?"

He turned and looked at her, then back at the frying pan, averting his eyes.

"Yes."

Holding the papers in her hand she kept blinking, not knowing what to say. She stood stunned. She let both leashes go and the pups ran over to the water bowl and began to drinking like this would be the last fresh water they'd ever be presented with in life.

"Why? Why would you do this, why would you not talk with me first—it's not like springing for an oil change on the Jeep or something."

"Maybe because I can," he said. "Maybe because I love you and don't want to see you worried all the time about something that I have and you don't. Something I can fix. Maybe because we're a couple and I want to share what I have." He turned to look at her. "My life, my resources."

"I love you too but this has nothing to do with that. We didn't discuss this—a person doesn't just go off and pay someone's fucking mortgage like this." She began to raise her voice.

He looked at her.

"You're right. Sorry. Okay? I'm hungry, are you?" He grabbed two plates and then divided the omelet, arranged slices of toast, and walked to the table under the window and set down both plates. "Coffee?"

She hadn't moved. She could tell he was uncomfortable, even annoyed, but didn't want to pretend it didn't bother her. "Stop minimizing this, it's patronizing, at worst insulting."

He stopped.

"I didn't mean for it to be insulting," he said. "Maybe I wanted to surprise you, to make you feel taken care of. Nobody has ever taken care of you, Am, you never let them." He stood and moved toward her.

"Bullshit." She looked at the original note stamped in red: CANCELED. "Maybe because no one's ever given a shit."

"Sorry," he backed off. "That was a bit harsh."

"We have to discuss things like this, Bryce, the Rev House has been a big part of my life."

"I know," he said. "I was there. Remember? When you signed the note." He turned to catch her eyes. "I lent you money for the closing costs. You paid me back. My brother was your lawyer for the closing."

She knew he wasn't being patronizing, he never was. It was a sore spot with her. Aside from the D'Agostinos, no one had taken care of her. In so many ways she'd felt like she'd raised herself, which was why she and Jen had always had such a kinship.

"You can't just come in and bulldoze right over me." She was getting angry.

"I'm not bulldozing—it's called help, Amelia." He began to raise his voice.

"Sharing a life together."

They were both quiet, as if each was in their corner, thinking. He sat down in front of a plate, noticing that he hadn't grabbed silverware or coffee cups. He leaned his face in his hand, his eyes watching her.

"I know." She felt herself about to concede but knew she shouldn't roll over too quickly. "We need to talk about stuff like this, not unilaterally act."

"True."

She sat down at the other plate.

"We never talked about what this would mean," she said.

"What would it mean?"

Neither spoke, both lost in thoughts.

Bryce broke the silence. "It doesn't mean anything other than you no longer have a mortgage that you have to worry about," he said. "The Rev House is in your name. Consider it an engagement present since you don't want a ring. Yes, it was a unilateral decision that I made in the moment that made sense and I apologize if I offended you in any way."

His apology was terse. She'd hurt him. She could feel it. Maybe she should have been more gracious rather than miffed, but there was a fine line between generosity and being bulldozed. She hated second-guessing a reaction.

"I know you did it out of love, I am grateful," she said. "But this has nothing to do with love."

She caught his irritation by how he moved but wasn't sure if it was aimed at her or at himself. She wanted to stop belaboring the point though she couldn't stop bringing it up.

"Just because you have more doesn't mean you can do things like this."

He pulled her chair closer to kiss her as an apology but she leaned away.

She laughed as he made exaggerated lips and kissing sounds toward her. "Stop making me laugh," she play batted him away. "You can't do this without talking about it first."

"I get it, agreed, you're pissed," he said. "I promise I won't pay off another house of yours again."

"Oh shut up." It made her laugh though she didn't want to. "Doesn't mean I don't appreciate what you did, but I'm still a person, Bryce."

"Oh, so this was treating you as a nonperson," he said.

"I didn't say that."

"You just did." He looked at the food. "I'm eating." He stood to retrieve utensils for both of them from the dish drain.

Amelia made herself eat though she was too agitated to be hungry. Thinking it would be too long of a day to start on an empty stomach, she washed the eggs and toast down with coffee.

After breakfast, Amelia gathered the cold weather survival gear that Peter had dropped off the day before, too riled to discuss it any more with Bryce.

"I'm sorry," he offered as he helped her to the Jeep with her gear.

"Thank you," she said and pulled his collar closer. She could tell he wanted to kiss her, make it all better, but she was still annoyed.

She needed to be on the lake—if not actually in the water—and hurried to meet Peter down at the Coast Guard dock in time.

Amelia beeped as she drove off and waved.

"Amelia Drakos's phone," Bryce answered early that afternoon after coming home from the Fish Hatchery. She'd left her phone on the kitchen counter before going out on the lake.

"Hi, I'm the dean of the School of Marine and Atmospheric sciences at the University of Rhode Island and I'm trying to reach Amelia Drakos."

Bryce listened for a moment and then looked at the display. "Phil?"

"Bryce? Holy shit, is that you?"

"Shit yeah."

"Where the hell are you two?"

"Up on Lake Superior."

"Tracked you down as far as Minneapolis," the dean continued. "Frieda retired to California with her husband so it took forever to find the two of you. Called Sea Life this week, said you'd both left months ago. Talked to Jen and she gave me Amelia's cell and a quick lowdown."

"Yeah, well, things happen. Jen stayed."

"Been trying to get ahold of Amelia but you'll do."

Bryce pictured her out on the ice.

"Uh—she's out on Lake Superior in the Apostle Islands help-ing a DNR Fish biologist with a winter fish survey before the lake melts."

"Sounds horrible."

"More like Siberia, but that's what we do," Bryce said as his friend laughed darkly. "They're bringing in gill net samples of fish to test viability and health of the whitefish and trout pop-ulation and the monitoring of invasive species—sea lampreys."

"Jesus, enough already."

"Well, you know Amelia," Bryce said. "I can have her call you tomorrow, think they might be winter camping out there for the night."

"Uch," Phil said. "Sounds positively awful, but this concerns you too."

He had Bryce's attention.

"What the hell are you two doing up there anyway?" Phil asked.

"Long story. Not much, yet everything," Bryce said as he stroked Junior's ears as the pup panted by the woodstove.

"The reason why I'm calling is that after you closed the lab, we've been working like crazy to find a way to offer the two of you permanent positions as principal investigators," he said. "And we have. Permanent positions, Bryce, no more soft money. Come back, restart your lab, fully funded. Health care, retirement, the whole shebang. "

Bryce was quiet.

"You wouldn't be shitting me, Phil." The two of them had been in high school together.

"Nope, no shit here, Bry. Everyone felt terrible about what happened and though the university is scrounging for funds, like everyplace else, I managed to add this to the agenda for discussion with the Board of Regents before winter break," his high school chum explained. "The administration wanted to drag it out until fall of next calendar year, but we were able to push it through. They just approved the addition of the two P.I.s based on your extraordinary contribution over the past two decades and a budget was just approved this week for you to reestablish the lab."

Bryce had to sit down at the kitchen table. He looked out to the frozen lake, resting his mouth in his hand.

"Permanent," Bryce confirmed.

"You betcha," Phil said and laughed. "Isn't that what they say up there?"

Bryce was too stunned to speak.

"Stipends won't start until September," he said. "Though monies will be available in August to begin the lab setup."

Bryce kept blinking; it was hard to take it in.

"In fact we couldn't figure out where the three of you went so quickly," the dean said. "By the time I got a strategy together, you'd run off. Nonetheless I pushed it through, along with your colleagues in the marine biology department."

Bryce couldn't speak. He sat there, stroking Junior's ears, trying to get calm. He had to get ahold of Amelia.

It had been a bright, sunny March morning when they'd left Bayfield harbor with temperatures hovering in the low twenties. Peter wasn't much for conversation as they'd set out on snowmobiles towing rubber sleds and Amelia was grateful, except when they'd stop to empty the sample nets into buckets. Then he had a nonstop arsenal of funny stories about Whitedeer that not only put Amelia at ease but also had her doubled over with laughter, picturing his father-in-law's antics.

As they headed farther north into Superior's deeper channels between the Apostle Islands, she thought of Smiley's reunion with her mate, of GLIFWC's sting operation as they'd caught the poachers, and then of Bryce. She felt deep happiness and peacefulness that she never wanted to end. It was as if she was settling into a new life. Something other people were graced with and here it had been sitting beside her on the lab bench for more than twenty years and in a place she'd never been. Amelia was glad she'd stood her ground about the Revolution House, and while she understood it was well-intentioned she believed she'd made her point. She wanted to tell him how much she appreciated it. She felt a sudden urgency to do so, a desperate sense of wanting to speak to Bryce now, yet her phone was back at the house. She didn't dare ask Peter to use the satellite phone for such a call.

A month earlier, Peter Holmgren and his assistant had drilled through five, six feet of solid ice until they hit water where the fish swam freely. They'd set twenty-five gill nets, marking each with a tall blaze-orange flag, and Peter hoped to retrieve the last of them before the ice degraded.

Samples taken during winter were the most important. They contained information about native and nonnative species as well as water samples from the lake as it lay undisturbed for months by fishermen and pleasure boats alike. The gear in the rubber sleds contained augers that were powerful enough to dig through ice pack that was thick enough to support supply trucks.

The rubber sleds were loaded with enough gear and provisions for days should they get stranded in one of Superior's sudden storms. The lake was known to let loose with unpredictable fury without warning and wreak all kinds of havoc before disappearing just as quickly.

"I'm hoping to recover most of the specimens," Peter explained as they passed Basswood and Oak Islands, the closest islands to shore. "A few nets might be hopelessly frozen in, but sometimes you can chip 'em out."

They'd collected the first samples offshore at Basswood. Fir trees covered most of the island with two-story icicles frozen like pillars into the sides of red granite shorelines.

Peter's orange markers were set along the ice corridors between the islands including Manitou and Stockton, past Ironwood and Cat to Outer Island, which was the farthest and most unprotected of the Apostles.

Amelia scanned the white surface through binoculars, searching for markers.

"They're hard to see," Peter said. "Sometimes the tips get iced over but I've got the coordinates marked."

The trip had taken the better part of the day. It was late afternoon and they'd retrieved twelve samples, some more deeply embedded into the ice than others. Peter's plan had been to locate six more, gather samples, and then make the last of the thirty-mile trip to Outer Island before calling it quits for the night. They'd camp and then make it back the next day through more channels to retrieve the rest.

But before they could do so, the sky had begun to change. Something didn't feel right. Amelia stood looking around.

They'd paused at one of the flags as Peter turned up the VHF radio.

"They're saying weather's clear," he reported. "Some evidence of ice degradation to the west by Bark Point," he said. "But I'm sure the last few nights of frigid temps took care of that." Once the ice broke up, the samples would be lost.

"Damn," Peter had said after they were farther into the islands near Manitou. He'd pulled out several sea lampreys from the nets. They were a devastatingly invasive species, eel-like with mouths like suction cups with sharp teeth that would clamp on and kill everything in their wake. "I hadn't expected to find these up this far."

As Peter pulled them from the net, they fought and twisted until Amelia helped coil them into the plastic bucket labeled INVASIVE. The density of the lamprey range would be monitored up to Outer Island. He recorded the number at each stop. Whitefish, which thrived in the icy cold waters, were doing fine, but walleye density was low in certain spots.

He winced as he rubbed his left shoulder. "Think I pulled something getting them out. Old rotator cuff injury."

"I'll get the next one," Amelia offered.

This was the farthest she'd been out on Superior. She was curious about the sharp wind shifts in the channels between islands. Some were more of a friendly breeze; other gusts burst with such force as to shove her snowmobile off course making it impossible to steer and she skid long after pressing her foot on the brake. The farther they ventured, the stronger winds picked up, screaming through their gear and making all sorts of high-pitched noises.

The sky had changed. Darkening clouds moved in like smoke from a forest fire.

"Wind's shifting," Peter called over the sound of the engines. Amelia turned her face and felt it. They hit a pocket of icy air that made her eyes tear.

Peter gave the hand gesture to stop.

"Just wanna check." He paused to monitor the VHF radio for weather advisories. The Coast Guard continually monitored it for distress calls. He tossed her the satellite phone. "Mind calling the office? Get the weather from them too?"

Amelia dialed the number on the front of the phone to get updates.

"Front's moving in," Peter said. He pointed with his one hand, still gloved in an expedition mitten, to the sky.

"Your office says it's passing south."

Yet there was a dark cloud shelf creeping over the tree line of Otter Island, moving toward them. From memory after briefly looking at Peter's map, Amelia began calculating how far to the nearest island.

"Weather moves fast here," he said, rubbing his shoulder.

"I'll pull up the next sample," Amelia said.

He smiled. "Thanks. Sucks getting older."

"How far's the closest island?" she asked. Something didn't

feel right. The color of the sky, strange wind patterns that blew then suddenly died.

"About fifteen miles as the crow flies," he said. "We're okay. It's going south."

His assurance didn't sit well. She'd been out on waters that changed in moments. The thing she loved about the sea is that it would kill you and not care. Never personal, though at times it felt like it was after you.

And while they'd taken enough provisions for a few nights just in case, from land Amelia had witnessed Superior's storms come in a fury only to disperse like it was nothing. There was no way of knowing how this one would go. She lacked experience in this part of the world and deferred to Peter's expertise.

They were near Manitou Island, halfway through pulling samples, when the ice quaked. It was a deep rumble. She felt her 550-pound snowmobile shudder. Felt the vibration echo through the channel like a type of sonar. The wind was dead calm.

Peter looked at Amelia and then up at the sky.

Amelia said, "I don't like this." She was uneasy.

"Wind's picking up," he said. "Mostly to the west. Ice is beginning to shift. No biggie. Just lake thunder, Amelia, nothing to worry about."

His voice was calm though he didn't look it. She didn't like the mixed messages.

"I've always believed it's easier to stay out of trouble than to get out of it," she offered.

"Heavy ice plates just west of here. Thirty-two inches thick, some of 'em, that's all, Amelia." He sounded more somber than nonchalant. "Compressing northeast."

"How about I radio in on channel sixteen, ask to update conditions," she suggested, not wanting to buck his authority yet not wanting to be endangered either.

"Already checked. We're good."

Something still felt off.

"Think we should make for South Twin?" she suggested. "Get out of this until things settle?"

Peter looked toward the west. The sky was already dark, moving directly toward them, cutting off any chance of making a run through the channel to shelter on Stockton.

"Might have to," Peter said. "If the wind picks up any more, might degrade the ice."

Amelia monitored the Coast Guard's channel 16 on the VHF as he talked.

"Think we'd better shoot more northeast, say for Outer," he said and climbed back onto his snowmobile. "It's farther but it'll get us out of whatever's gaining. I'll radio once we make it that far."

They wove in and out of the smaller islands, dodging them like a pinball machine, at times going against the wind, at times having it at their backs, all to avoid the unprotected ice that often sports straight-line winds powerful enough to blow everything away like toys.

Another deep rumble beneath the ice made her slow and turn to Peter. It seemed to quake throughout the channel.

"Told ya," he said to reassure. "Just lake thunder."

She noticed small cracks and then heaves along the seams, lifting up into four-inch ridges.

"Nothing to—" Peter stopped talking midsentence. His face tensed. He looked at her.

Amelia's stomach lurched. "What?" she asked.

"That sound."

"What sound?"

"Like seismic ice plates. One large chunk is pushing up from underneath, pushing east. Gales from the west are causing the shift."

They were eight miles north of Cat Island. Peter cut his engine to listen. He then turned his ear. You could hear the winds whooshing, over the tops of the islands, invading the protected areas as they rushed the channels, blowing in strange circling patterns from every direction.

"What does this mean?" She imagined the map of the Apostles in her mind and could only guess they were in trouble.

He powered up his snowmobile. "Either we try to make it to Outer or risk being on open ice pack with no protection," he called over the engine and the roar of the wind.

Amelia wasn't familiar with the ways of ice.

"Whichever you think is best," she said.

He paused. She didn't like the pause.

He looked up at her, his eyes round with worry.

"Not sure."

Her stomach shrank.

"Let's try for Outer," he said. "If we can't make it, we'll call it in."

"Why not call it in now if you're worried?"

"I'm not worried."

He grabbed his left shoulder again to massage it and then revved his snowmobile, heading northeast toward Outer.

They'd nearly made it a half mile when the sky dipped down to touch the surface, obscuring everything.

Clouds were a dark navy blue. With one gust, the wind blew both their snowmobiles, making it impossible to steer.

The bungee on Amelia's rubber sled snapped. Gear blew from where it had been cinched, knocking off the white plastic specimen pails as they rolled, strewing out the contents of live fish wriggling and flopping on the ice.

Peter slowed to a stop.

"Peter," she called to him through the howling wind. "Peter," she yelled.

He was slumped over the front of the snowmobile. She wondered if a piece of gear had hit him in the head, knocking him out.

Amelia set the brake on her snowmobile, and took off

running. She heard the zipping sound of wind blowing her snowmobile across the ice.

"Peter." She reached him. "Are you okay?" She touched his head and then propped him up, cradling him. He opened his eyes and looked up with sad, frightened eyes. "My arm's cramped. I think I'm having . . ."

"Where's the radio?"

"Back of . . ." His voice trailed off. He winced. ". . . my sled."

Amelia helped him off the snowmobile and laid him flat on the ice. She scooted the rubber sled around and dragged him onto it, covering him as best she could with a sleeping bag. His hat blew off.

For a moment a tinkling sound like ice cubes in a tumbler began hitting the surface as she realized it was freezing rain. Amelia slipped and fell. She tried to gain a foothold but couldn't. The wind was blowing sideways, stinging her face. She then lay flat, using her hands to pull herself toward Peter.

She managed to grab the rubber sled and pull it toward her.

"It's gonna be okay, you're gonna be okay," she kept saying as she lay down beside him, digging through the gear, feeling for the VHF radio.

Just as she located the radio and pulled it out to call the Coast Guard, an eighty-mile-an-hour gust knocked it out of her hand and then blew her out of the sled, both sliding on the ice, the radio sliding faster until something resembling a hockey puck slid past and both disappeared.

There were flares in the sleds. A few had blown past her, scattering across the ice. She trapped one with her foot but then lost it as it blew off with the rest.

"Fuck," she yelled and tried to get back to Peter, to find more flares, but the wind was blowing her farther away.

Then everything stopped.

"Peter," she called, using her fingernails to claw toward the sled, wriggling like an earthworm, using the fabric of her clothes for traction to reach to him.

Just before the storm picked up again, she reached him and crawled onto the rubber sled.

His face was gray. His eyes were open and looking up into the rain.

"Tell. Cherise." His voice was weak. "Kids."

"No, you're gonna tell them," she insisted, trying to find a pulse on his neck. Then his eyes stopped seeing. He didn't blink as the freezing rain commenced. She turned him over, covered him, and began sobbing. "Oh my God, oh my God."

Then she stopped. She looked around. Everything in her knew she was about to die. A strange coherence settled as all extraneous emotion evaporated except for thoughts of how to steady and not get blown away.

Gale-force winds picked up again, screaming so loud it hurt her ears. She reached for Peter's snowmobile and grabbed on to part of the engine. She held on as it slid across the ice with no resistance until it smashed against a pressure ridge. The abruptness almost threw her but she gripped tighter. The ice shifted, she felt another crack. It groaned as it widened like continents being pushed by terrestrial urges. Half the machine dipped sideways into the crevasse. Amelia could feel it crunching as the ice plates moved.

Everything in her was telling her to let go, let the wind take her but she was so terrified until suddenly she didn't care. Nothing mattered. She closed her eyes and let go like it was nothing, sliding and spinning with nothing to stop her, like the ocean undertow. She shielded her face, covered her eyes.

Then the wind stopped. She looked around, amazed she was alive.

Then the sound of marbles hitting ice came from every direction. She curled up into a ball, being blown sideways, all their provisions scattered and blowing across the ice, pelting her like demonic toys to punish her. A thermos flew and hit her in the back, the augers slid past like they were weightless, Peter's log books blew by and bashed her cheek. Everything was out of context on the ice and in the air, sliding without direction, without meaning as debris kept scattering about in the dictates of the wind.

Then it died again.

So still she could hear the ringing of her own ears.

But she didn't trust it. In the quiet a deep, low-frequency rumble echoed through the depths, spreading for miles.

"Dad?" she called, looking around.

As the wind let up on one of the pressure ridges she noticed a blinking red light, an incoming call. It was the satellite phone.

"Oh thank you." She tried to get up, bashed her knee, and slid, clawing her way to grab it. Just within reach, the wind blew, sending her sliding farther away until she no longer saw the light.

"Fuck," she yelled. The wind stopped. She moved in earthworm posture toward the phone. She reached to grab it. Her fingers were so frozen she hit the redial with her nose.

"Hello, we need help," she yelled over the wind into the phone before anyone answered. "Please."

"Amelia?"

"Oh, Bryce. Oh, God, Peter's had a heart attack, the wind is gale force, and the ice is breaking up. Call the Coast Guard, Bryce."

"Copy," Bryce said. "I'll stay on the phone—"

But as soon as he said it a gust blew the transmitter out of her hands, tumbling along, smashing it into pieces against the rocklike pressure ridges.

She screamed and tucked into a ball as the wind blew her, crashing headfirst into a ridge of ice and was immediately knocked out.

Wind like an eggbeater woke her. She covered her head with one of her hands. What now?

"Ma'am?"

How could the wind be talking? She wouldn't listen, wouldn't be its friend.

"Amelia."

Too late. It knows her name.

"Amelia Drakos?"

She turned to look. Her head throbbed. Everything spun.

A Coast Guard swimmer in a red uniform was suspended from the air. He lowered toward her.

She reached for his arms.

"Peter . . . he had . . ."

"We know."

She tried to stand but her foot slipped and turned underneath her.

"Don't try," the young man said. "It's glare ice."

She nodded.

"I'm going to slip this harness around you," he instructed. "Under your shoulders and then tighten it. I've got you. Try to relax as we're lifted. You're safe. You're okay."

The whirling sound began to change as her body lifted, leaning against the diver.

"That's right," he said. "Just lean against me."

"I'm gonna throw up."

"That's okay," he said as the two of them spun up like the double helix of DNA, up toward the safety of the door.

The ambulance waited at the marina as the helicopter set down in the empty parking lot.

The Coast Guard transferred Amelia onto a gurney as paramedics took over, rushing her toward the ambulance. Bryce leaned over.

"Ammy."

She started to cry at his voice and grasped his hand. She tried to speak, to tell him about Peter, but couldn't. Bryce climbed up into the ambulance, following her in.

"How is she?" TJ asked, standing outside beside the door.

"Banged up but stable," the paramedic said. "They'll check her out more when we get to Ashland General."

"Can I ride along?" TJ asked.

The paramedic turned to TJ. "Are you family?"

Bryce reached to give TJ a hand up.

"Yep," TJ said, as Bryce hoisted him up. "She's my sister."

43

Two weeks later Bryce and Amelia flew to Rhode Island to discuss the offer of permanent positions with the university.

They were sitting in the dean's office.

"This is one of those rare happy moments when things go right," said Phil, the dean of the marine biology department.

Pages from both their employment contracts lay arranged on the conference table before them. Amelia and Bryce had read and checked off each stipulation in the margins as the dean sat, smiling. A few from the Board of Regents who'd fought to fund the positions sat ready with a bottle of champagne and glasses.

"All we need are your signatures." Phil handed both Amelia and Bryce a pen.

"Ladies first," Bryce said.

She bent over to sign but then retracted the pen. She sat, thinking.

"Um." She pushed out her chair. "Mind if I take a minute here, Phil?" Amelia asked.

The dean looked surprised. "Why . . . sure, Amelia. Questions? Is something not clear?"

"Um, no, not really," she said. "It's all perfectly clear. I just need a moment to think." She looked at Bryce and stood up.

"Take as long as you need," Phil said.

She tipped her head toward the door, for Bryce to meet her out in the hall.

. . .

Standing outside the office Amelia recalled the last time she'd walked down that hallway after turning in her security badges, cards, keys, thinking she'd never be there again.

"So, eh . . . what's up, Chuck?" Bryce asked, folding his arms as he leaned against the wall next to the water fountain.

She looked at him. "Why am I not more excited about this?"

"Why am I not more excited about this either?"

"Six months ago I would have crawled on hands and knees all the way back from Minneapolis for an offer like this."

"But . . ." He raised his eyebrows.

"But it makes me feel claustrophobic or like I'm moving backward."

"Claustrophobic," he repeated, smiling in an amused way.

"Yeah," she said. "Confined, like you say when you're wearing flip-flops in winter."

He sniffed, amused, and then shifted his weight onto the other leg.

"It's like this whole other life germinated out there right under our noses," she said and folded her arms.

Amelia leaned over to take a drink from the hall water fountain, wiping her chin on her hand before she spoke.

"I think I want to take the UM-Duluth offer."

"You do?"

"Yeah." She turned to look at him. "What do you think?"

"You go first."

"I'm thinking we could teach," she said. "Reopen a lab for our research, make a contribution to the Fresh Water Initiative for Lake Superior," she said. "Hire Jen and have her little kid run around like Alex used to." She giggled.

He nodded slightly as he listened.

"After all, Bryce, how could I never again hear Jethro's scratch at the door to be let in for the night?" Out of nowhere, remembering the first night choked her up.

"How could I live here knowing the wolf hunt's still on? Thinking of Smiley, B-34, what happened to Lacey and the others. How much work there is to be done to get wolves relisted, to fight the sway and power of special interest monies that could affect all endangered species and even those that are not. I have to help in whatever way I can."

"Come here." Bryce reached and pulled her close.

"And that Charlotte and TJ are out there and I'm not. That Whitedeer and Cherise are there too and I'm not close enough to even put a Christmas wreath on Peter's grave." Again she felt the sorrow of his passing.

"That Jen and Doby are going to have their baby in Duluth and I won't be there to see it grow up, be the godmother, the auntie who spoils it rotten and then goes home."

As Bryce kissed the top of her head she felt the warmth of his breath, Amelia leaned back and studied him, watching for a long while as if giving him the chance to disagree.

"That every day I won't see that big, bad, beautiful lake that tried to fucking kill me. And that like the ocean, it showed me the limitless of chance if you only stand still long enough for it to find you." She closed her eyes. *Dad.*

Bryce pulled her close again and leaned his head on top of hers. "Well, I for one will stand still next to you."

"You will, will you?" She chuckled.

"Of course, Am, for better or worse, you're stuck with me. Either here or out there. But betcha I can stand still longer than you," he said.

They turned and walked arm in arm down the hall back toward the dean's office.

"Betcha a whitefish dinner and unlimited Spotted Cows that you can't," she bet.

He frowned and offered his pinkie to bet. "That's not even a bet, Am."

"You're so arrogant—always think you can do what I can do better."

"Maybe it's because I can." There was a lilt to his voice.

"You're delusional," she said and stopped.

Amelia turned toward him.

"Come here." She crooked her index finger and he moved closer.

And with that she pulled him close, giving him the finger before she stood on her toes and reached up to kiss him.